THE FLAMES OF RESISTANCE

WOMEN SPIES IN WWII

KIT SERGEANT

THOMPSON BELLE PRESS

This book is dedicated to all of the women who lived during the Second World War and whose talents and sacrifices are known or unknown, but especially to the real-life women upon whom these characters are based

And to Mom and Dad, thank you for helping me become the strong woman that I am today

GLOSSARY OF TERMS

Abwehr: German Military Intelligence

Appell: German word for roll call at concentration camps

Appellplatz: the location, usually a clearing, where Appell took place

Boches: a derogatory term for Germans

FANY: First Aid Nursing Yeomanry; members of the all-female charity often worked for the SOE

Feldwebel: a German military rank, approximately equivalent to a sergeant

F Section of the SOE: the French Section of the British Special Operations Executive

Gestapo: Nazi Secret Police

Halifax: a bomber, mostly used for dropping supplies and parachuting agents

Hudson: a Lockheed light bomber, used for reconnaissance and agent pick-ups

Huns: another derogatory term for Germans

Lysander: another bomber, also used for reconnaissance and agent pick-ups

MI6: British Secret Intelligence Service

RAF: The United Kingdom's Royal Air Force

SD: *Sicherheitdienst-* the Nazi's intelligence agency

SS: *Schutzstaffel-* a Nazi paramilitary organization

Wehrmacht: the German armed forces

Whitley: another bomber, also used for reconnaissance and agent pick-up

PROLOGUE

*V*era Atkins did not rise when the man was brought into the interrogation room, nor did she offer him a seat. She'd never laid eyes on him before, but supposed they knew each other well—without her knowledge, she'd been communicating with him, the enemy, for the past two years via messages over the wireless.

He was taller than she'd imagined, with a shock of white hair and penetrating brown eyes. His intelligence file, which she had memorized before the meeting, said the man, Dr. Josef Goetz, had been a schoolteacher before the Gestapo had recruited him, in part because of his flair for language.

Miss Atkins lit a cigarette and then put the pack back into her purse.

"Can you spare one for me?" Goetz asked as he took the seat across from her.

She blew a ring of smoke into his face. Normally she wouldn't dare be so rude, but there was something about this man that aggravated her. Probably because he had been directly responsible for the disappearance of many of her best agents. "First tell me how it began."

"With Bishop," Goetz replied.

Miss Atkins nodded. Bishop was the code name of Marcus Bloom, the wireless operator for the Prunus network. He'd been one of the earliest ones captured, though the SOE wasn't informed of his arrest until many months after the first peculiar message from Butcher came in. She'd been in the signals room that day. Even then it had occurred to her that it could have been someone else operating his radio, but her boss, Major Buckmaster, dismissed that possibility, in much the same way he did when more odd messages came through from other agents afterward.

Miss Atkins handed Goetz a cigarette. "And the Dutch?"

He clicked the lighter and examined the flame. "We had control of their radios since 1941. From then on, every agent the SOE sent into the Low Countries landed right into our hands." He put the cigarette into his mouth and lit it. "We called it Funkspiel."

The radio game. Miss Atkins had been made aware of this information, but only after the war.

"We received more detailed knowledge on how your codes worked, including crystals and frequencies, when we captured those Canadians." He shook his head. "Really, those accents were terrible. You made it easy for our men to impersonate them."

It had been Miss Atkins' job to vet all agents before they left for France. She wholeheartedly agreed with Goetz about the Canadians' accents, but Buckmaster had once again overruled her when she'd voiced her concerns.

She folded her hands in her lap. "The rendezvous at the Rue de Rome address. Was it you who arranged that?"

"Yes. We set up surveillance there for days, waiting for one of your men to turn up. Eventually one did."

The hand holding her cigarette trembled, causing ash to drop onto the table. She discreetly wiped it away. "And the security checks… how did you become aware of them?"

He stabbed his cigarette into an ashtray. "I think you know the answer to that."

He was right, though she would never admit it to anyone. She shut her eyes, not wanting to see the smug look on his face anymore.

One of her greatest regrets was that she hadn't tried harder to convince Buck that the radios of some of his favorite operators had been compromised. As a result, they'd dispatched arms and agents into France under the suspicion that it had been the Germans who'd requested them. Many of those agents and operators had never returned…

Miss Atkins got to her feet, the chair scraping along the concrete floor like fingernails on a chalkboard. "I think we are done here." She nodded at the guard standing next to the door, who let her out. Too late, she realized she'd left her lighter. Through the little window, she saw that Goetz had lit it again. He caught her staring and blew out the flame.

She decided to let him have the lighter: it would be the last prize he'd get from the SOE. She turned and walked away from the room, the heels of her smart, sensible shoes click-clacking down the hallway.

CHAPTER 1

YVONNE

*Y*vonne gripped the railing of the *Seadog* and leaned over as her stomach heaved again.

A male voice from somewhere behind her shouted to be heard above the pouring rain. "Not the best weather, is it?"

"No." She pulled herself upright and discreetly wiped her mouth. "I told Buckmaster that I have a fragile stomach, but he thought I was too old to parachute into France and insisted I go by boat."

"You?" Paul Frager stopped near enough so he could be heard, but not too close in case she vomited again. "You don't look a day over… thirty-five?"

He was lying, but she shot him a weak grin anyway before brushing a lock of white hair out of her face. No matter how many times she colored her hair, that one stubborn streak refused to take up any dye.

Paul lifted his arm and pointed to a giant land mass across the gray, angry sea. "We're entering the Strait of Gibraltar. That's North Africa there."

Yvonne swallowed hard. "Where the Allied troops are finally making a show against Hitler."

He held up crossed fingers. "Let's hope they continue to do so. Are you done there?" He nodded at the railing.

Yvonne put her hand on her stomach, which seemed calmer, though the same couldn't be said for the waves. "For now, at least."

"Can I escort you downstairs?"

"Yes." Yvonne never resisted the arm of a handsome man. Not to mention her queasiness had made her legs unsteady.

Since she was the only woman on board, the captain had given up his usual accommodations for her. But as they approached her cabin, Paul gave a low whistle. Yvonne looked down to see a puddle at her feet.

He opened the door to find the water was ankle deep in the small room. "Flooded," he confirmed. "You'll have to move into our room."

All she wanted to do was lie on a bed and collapse. She gave a heavy sigh as Paul led her into the tiny, musty room he shared with Nick Bodington, who was currently sprawled out on the bottom of a bunk bed, reading. Paul moved his bag from the other bunk to the one above Bodington and gestured to Yvonne. "Her cabin flooded. She'll be sleeping here tonight."

Bodington gave her an oily grin. "Welcome."

"Thanks," she said as she settled onto the now-vacated bed. She was still wet, but didn't have the strength to change, especially not in front of the two men.

"Frager," Bodington's deep voice cut through the silence that followed. "We should talk."

"Here?" Paul glanced around the room uncertainly.

"You want to go on deck in this weather?" Bodington demanded.

"No, of course not."

"We're all F Section here anyway," Bodington sat up and waved toward the lone chair. "Tell me all about Carte. How many people do you have working for you?"

"Probably around 50," Paul answered in a low tone as he sat down. "We recruited many of the same people who helped Autogiro after Lucas was arrested. Some of them are the lucky ones who escaped detection in the witch hunt that resulted in Interallié's collapse."

Yvonne knew Paul Frager was the second-in-command of Carte, the French Resistance network that had formed after the original, known as Interallié, was infiltrated by Germans. Carte's leader, André Girard, had sent Paul to London to meet the SOE leaders—who were training agents like Yvonne in order to start their own, sanctioned networks—and ask for supplies. Bodington's mission in France was to investigate Carte and report back to F Section's head, Major Buckmaster, if it was worthy of the sizable quantity of arms and ammunition Girard had requested.

Yvonne fell asleep to the sound of her companions debating the finer points of the Carte network.

The weather improved the next day as the felucca rounded the Cape de Cata, near Almeria, Spain. The sea at last became tranquil, sparkling as green as an emerald under a cloudless sky.

Finally clear of her seasickness, Yvonne went on deck to soak in the glorious sun. The main cabin was still flooded and she wanted to give Bodington and Paul their space. The captain, Jan Buchowski, was on deck, fiddling with a rope. She nodded at him before taking her place at the railing, this time with a somewhat healthier stomach.

As they approached Menorca, Yvonne noted a patch of driftwood floating in the water. "Is that from a ship?" she asked Buchowski, pointing.

"I hope not," he replied. "There are Italian submarines all around these waters." Both of them leaned over to peer overboard, Yvonne with trepidation, wondering if her mission would be over before it had a chance to get started.

Suddenly a white spout appeared, like steam rising from the water, so close to the boat that Yvonne was soaked.

"There's your culprit." Buchowski gestured toward several dark forms surfacing. "Whales."

Yvonne dried her wet face with a towel, relieved that it wasn't an enemy U-boat rising to the surface. She watched as the pod played about in the waves, oblivious to both the felucca and any sinister submarines that might be lurking underneath. "It's as if they don't know there's a war going on," she pondered aloud.

At night, the moon shone so brightly that one could read a newspaper on the deck. Yvonne worried they would be spotted by German patrols as they neared the shoreline. Soon they were close enough to see the lights from Cannes and smell the heady scent of jasmine.

Buchowski used binoculars to sight his guides for where to land: two large villas painted white. Paul, who had left for England from that same spot, explained to Yvonne that one villa belonged to Prince Aly Khan and his wife, Rita Hayworth, while the former Prince of Wales had once owned the other. "He met Mrs. Wallis Simpson there," Paul added.

But both were now clearly abandoned, Yvonne concluded as the *Seadog* approached the rocky shore. A dinghy was dispatched, and the right passwords must have been exchanged, for the dinghy soon returned and Buchowski ordered his passengers to disembark.

Yvonne's heart began to pound, sure that they were being watched. As if reading her mind, Bodington looked up. "Full moons are great for landing Lysanders in abandoned fields, but maybe not for getting boats ashore in Occupied France."

Despite his ominous admission, they made it to shore almost without incident, save for Paul ripping his pants and Bodington dropping his suitcase into the surf.

They were greeted on the rocky shore by members of a local Resistance group, a branch of Carte who called themselves *L'Equipe Renaudie.* They informed the newly-landed agents that they'd arrive at their initial destination via the sewer systems of Cannes.

"Just the way I've always wanted to travel," Bodington commented without enthusiasm.

Concealed from the moonlight, the tunnels were shockingly dark. Even with the help of Paul's flashlight, Yvonne could barely see in front of her, but she could smell the fetid scent of decaying organic matter. She could also hear the sound of dripping water as her feet once again became soaked.

They ended up at the Villa de l'-Aube, near the main road. This time Yvonne was given her own room. She promptly shed her wet shoes and socks, relieved to be on dry, flat ground. She was now officially the first F Section woman to be transported into Occupied France. Her last thought before she fell asleep was that, now that she'd arrived, it was finally time to get down to business.

The next morning, Yvonne parted from the men. Her orders were to report to Tours while Frager and Bodington stayed in Cannes, presumably to rendezvous with André Girard. For the first time since they'd left London, Yvonne was officially alone.

She walked to the Cannes railroad station and bought a ticket to Lyon, using the forged papers that Miss Atkins, Buckmaster's assistant, had obtained for her.

"Jacqueline Viallat?" the stationmaster asked, peering at Yvonne.

"That's me," she replied in the most confident tone she could muster.

The stationmaster stamped her paper and shoved it back at her. "Next."

Though the SOE had drilled Jacqueline Viallat's backstory into Yvonne's brain until she could recite it in her sleep, she decided to elaborate it even further during the lengthy train ride. *Jacqueline is a refugee from Brest and fled to Tours to escape the bombing.* Yvonne hadn't been in France since she'd left with her daughter Connie fifteen years ago, but she was certainly no stranger to bombing. Her London house had nearly been destroyed in the Blitz. Thankfully she and her many tenants had survived, mostly unscathed, but

Connie's poor little cat had been so badly burned it had to be put to sleep.

After that, Yvonne had become more determined to help the Allied cause. She'd been left the building by her estranged husband, and once it was gone, so was her source of income. She took a job as a waitress at the Ebury Court Hotel and told anyone within earshot how disappointed she was in her fellow Parisians for succumbing to the German invasion so easily. She could not believe that Marshal Pétain, the Great War hero who'd led the French troops to victory at the battle of Verdun, had agreed to an armistice and let the Nazis enter France. One late night, she had expounded on her burning desire to help rescue her native country to a guest named Ernest.

"I have nothing to lose," Yvonne told him. "My daughter has made a good marriage, with a husband who takes care of her. Outside of that, I have no other relatives." That was not strictly true, but Ernest must have been impressed by something she'd said, for, a few weeks after the conversation, she received a letter from a Captain Selwyn Jepson inviting her to interview for a position with the War Office. She found out later that Ernest was employed by the F Section of the Special Operatives Executive, the same agency for which she now worked.

Yvonne glanced out the train window, deciding that her alter-ego had also lost a cat in the Brest bombings, but instead of being a political refugee, Jacqueline Viallat was really fleeing from her over-bearing husband. And she would be an artist, a poet like T.S. Eliot, a man whom Yvonne had met once through one of her London tenants.

When the train arrived at the Gare de Lyon-Saint-Paul station, Yvonne booked a nearby hotel using money that had been thought-fully provided by Miss Atkins.

Once again Yvonne slept soundly, so soundly in fact that the next morning she forgot one of the SOE's cardinal rules: after waking, wait at least half an hour for your mind to clear before interacting with anyone.

As soon as she got out of bed, she called the front desk to ask about breakfast.

"I don't understand," the person on the other end said in French. "Can you please repeat your request?"

With horror, Yvonne realized she'd just spoken in English. "*Excusez-moi, je suis désolé.*" She racked her brain for an excuse. Since British citizens were rarer in France than German soldiers these days, she replied in French, "I'm learning German and forgot myself for a moment."

"*De rien.*"

After ordering toast, Yvonne hung up the phone, cursing herself for her mistake.

For the next leg of her journey, Yvonne would have to cross the demarcation line. She knew it was well guarded, and that she would be subject to searches every few kilometers. Though she had the forged identity papers, she did not have the proper pass that would allow her to enter the Occupied Zone.

She walked toward the train station, remembering the numerous guards from yesterday who had been scrutinizing the papers of people boarding the trains. Instead of entering the line to buy a ticket, she decided to take a stroll along the back side of the station to see if she could figure out a way to bypass the German checkpoint.

As she walked, a train slowed to pass the station. From far away, it appeared to be a cattle train. But as it came closer, Yvonne noted that, instead of cows, the cars were filled with men and women crowding around windows and doors hanging slightly ajar. She caught the gaze of one woman, whose eyes held a haunted look. As the train picked up speed, the woman grasped the small child she was holding tighter to her, but not before Yvonne glimpsed the large yellow star pinned to her chest.

A lump formed in the back of Yvonne's throat as she watched

the train head east toward Germany. She was so transfixed by the thought of this human cargo being carted off to certain death that she didn't hear anyone approach.

"*Es-tu Juif?*" a man in a striped hat asked, startling her.

Yvonne's mind flashed to the woman's yellow star. She shook her head.

The man rubbed the back of his neck as he looked at her travel-worn dress. "Come," he told her, waving his arm. He led her to a tiny alcove in the coal tender and pointed. "You can ride here and no one will bother you."

"*Merci beaucoup,*" Yvonne replied. Despite her denial, he clearly thought she was a Jew trying to escape the round-up. She crossed her fingers at her side, hoping there might indeed be some escapees from that horrible train.

She gave a heavy sigh as she folded herself in among the coal in the tender. It was cramped and foul-smelling, but at least now she had a way to get across the demarcation line.

CHAPTER 2

ANDRÉE

The roar of the airplane engines on either side of her did nothing to soothe Andrée's nerves, but at least they were loud enough to cover up the thump of her heart, which seemed ready to hammer itself right out of her chest. She glanced up at a window, though the blackout curtains prevented her from catching any glimpse of the French countryside rushing by outside.

Before they'd left England, Miss Atkins had suggested she get some sleep, a seemingly impossible task at the moment, but Andrée adjusted her sleeping bag and shut her eyes anyway. They flew open moments later as the plane rocked in its course. She glanced at her companion. Adele was snoring contentedly.

The dispatcher appeared beside Andrée. He had to shout to be heard above the noise. "Care for a snack?"

She blinked. "A snack?"

"All part of the RAF service."

"Thank you."

The Royal Air Force-provided SPAM sandwich also did little to calm her. Andrée made a little pile out of the crusts and tucked them into the napkin.

"You're lucky to have a reception committee waiting for you," the dispatcher commented as he picked up the napkin. "Sometimes we do blind drops, but you have to be really familiar with the countryside."

"I'm pretty acquainted myself—I only left France a few months ago. I was on the Pat O'Leary line, helping downed Allied pilots escape," she told him with more than a hint of pride.

"Well, I'll be." He leaned over to peer at her through the darkness. "Is that why you're working with the SOE? You look so young, especially compared to her," he nodded toward Adele's gray hair.

Andrée shrugged.

He broke eye contact and then disappeared behind the curtain separating them from the pilot. "We're getting close," he said when he returned. He stooped to shake Adele's shoulder.

"Wha—?" Adele asked, sitting up. "Is it time?"

He handed her a helmet. "Just about."

Adele fastened the chinstrap before looking expectantly at Andrée. "Do you want to go first or can I?"

They'd been told they would be the first women to parachute into Occupied France, and now Andrée couldn't help thinking it would be even more of a distinction to be the very first to land. "I'll flip you for it. Heads, I go first."

A few minutes later, Andrée, who'd won the coin toss, got into position, scooting forward on the floor of the Whitley bomber until her legs dangled out of the hatch. As soon as the indicator light turned from red to green, she dropped through.

She plummeted toward the French countryside until the static line unfurled the parachute and then everything slowed, including her heartbeat. The white expanse of the parachute seemed so obvious against the dark sky and she shut her eyes, imagining a Nazi aiming his rifle at her. When nothing happened, she opened her eyes again, barely discerning the sturdy form of Adele a few meters away.

As she drifted down, Andrée reflected on the past few months— how she'd fled France with Maurice only to willingly go back into enemy territory. *Would Maurice be alright?* She'd made Miss Atkins and Buckmaster promise to look after him but, considering Maurice had been a prisoner of the Free French, Buck had told her that guaranteeing his safety could become a political nightmare.

"Aren't we all fighting for the same cause?" Andrée had asked.

"In the strictest sense," Miss Atkins replied. "But their methods are a little different than those of F Section."

Andrée had gotten her own taste of how the Free French worked. Both she and Maurice had been invited to join them by General Charles de Gaulle himself, the esteemed leader of French soldiers exiled to England. They'd made separate appointments to interview at 10 Duke Street, the headquarters of the Free French.

In Andrée's opinion, the interviewer had asked too many questions. She'd learned a long time ago to keep her mouth shut: the less you said, the safer you and all of your comrades would be. The Free French had struck a chord of anger in Andrée, those men who'd never set foot in Occupied France and yet thought they could control the course of the war from the comfort of their Duke Street office. As far as she knew, the Pat O'Leary, or PAO line, was mostly intact, and her comrades—ordinary citizens risking their lives to save Allied pilots from the Nazis—were still at it. Who knew what General de Gaulle would do with the information they insisted she provide?

Her lips had grown tighter at the barrage of questions from the interviewer: *What routes did you use? Where were the locations of the safe-houses? How did you get money and supplies?* and finally, *How did you get out of France?*

After a few minutes of silence on Andrée's part, the interviewer had crossed his arms and demanded, "How do you expect us to hire you if you cannot provide us with every detail of how the PAO line worked?"

She stood and gathered her things before retorting, "I think a more appropriate question would be why you would hire someone inclined to give away such details."

The interview with Captain Selwyn Jepson of Britain's Special Operations Executive had gone much better. A few days later,

Andrée found herself training to be an on-the-ground agent with F Section.

Maurice had fared far worse, but there was no time to ruminate over that. The dark earth was quickly expanding beneath her, so she pushed the thought of her lover's battered and bruised body out of her mind in order to concentrate on her landing.

She hit the ground just as she'd been taught, with her chin down and her legs slightly bent. The parachute settled softly around her as a dark form approached her. Sensing there were more bodies hiding in the bushes, Andrée put her hand on the pistol tucked into her belt.

The voice cutting through the night was deep. "Are you Denise or Adele?"

"Denise," Andrée replied, relaxing her grip on the gun. Denise was the code name Buck had provided to use in the field. "And that's Adele," she said as her companion landed with a thud and a barrage of French curses. "Are you Gaspard?"

"No." The man stuck out his hand. "Pierre Culioli. You wouldn't have wanted Gaspard to show up anyway," he continued bitterly as more parachutes touched down, speckling the terrain with their inanimate cargo: guns and ammunition, bomb-making equipment, and the women's suitcases.

"Why not?" Andrée asked.

Pierre shook his head. "We can talk later. For now we need to hide all of this."

She removed her coveralls as Pierre and his men buried the evidence. Although the parachute's silk fabric could have netted them a lot of money on the black market, it was important to never let the Huns know that Britain was covertly dropping agents into France.

Pierre led them to a small shed and explained that, since it was well after curfew, they would spend the night there and he would give them further instructions in the morning.

This time when Andrée laid down, safe in France—at least for now—she fell asleep right away.

. . .

She awoke at dawn, eager to get on with her mission. Pierre had brought along a horse-drawn carriage. "Gasoline is reserved for the Wehrmacht," he stated as Adele and Andrée climbed in.

Andrée discovered in the morning light that Pierre was much older than he'd appeared the night before. His handlebar mustache did not do much to conceal the pockmarks on his face, but his brown eyes were warm.

When they arrived at a small house on the edge of the woods, an elderly couple came out to greet them. Pierre introduced them as Madame and Monsieur Bossard before turning to a small woman, slightly younger than the Bossards, but with even more gray hair than Adele. "And this is my contact, Yvonne. She will take it from here."

Andrée refrained from exclaiming in recognition and instead held out her hand stiffly. Yvonne returned the gesture, her hazel eyes twinkling. They'd been in the same training class at Beaulieu. The instructors there had referred to Yvonne as "The Little Old Lady," but they knew as well as Andrée that Yvonne could outrun almost all the males in their class.

Yvonne squeezed Andrée's hand in reassurance before introducing herself to Adele. She led the newcomers inside and poured three glasses of wine, even though it was not quite 10 am. "Welcome to France," she told them, taking a seat at the kitchen table.

Last night neither Adele nor Andrée had much to say, but now that the morning sun revealed there were no Nazis waiting for them, Adele was much more talkative. "I've never seen a real German in uniform before," she told them after a few sips. "Only the pictures they showed us in training. I left before the Occupation," she added in a softer voice, almost as an apology.

"You'll see plenty of Germans now," Yvonne replied.

"Yes," Andrée agreed. "They take all kinds of liberties with the French citizens. They used to come into the bakery I worked at on the Avenue Kléber to demand free food."

"Not the *Merci Jérôme?*" Adele's voice was incredulous.

Andrée was equally surprised. "Yes."

"I used to buy croissants there all the time," Adele said.

Andrée shot her a smile before finishing her wine. They were bordering on breaking F Section's number one rule: discuss nothing about your past lives, but she couldn't see what harm it could cause. She'd probably served Adele in the swanky café at least once.

Andrée kicked the valise at her feet, making sure it was still there. Inside were 250,000 francs, equivalent to what a fish merchant such as Monsieur Bossard might make in five years, a huge amount of money for a woman from a working-class background like herself. It was meant to be the starting funds for the Physician network, provided she made it to Paris without being stopped. "What happened to Gaspard?" she asked.

Yvonne frowned. "I'm not exactly sure: something went foul between him and Pierre." She took a bite of bread and chewed thoughtfully. "You have to watch these SOE men: sometimes their egos get so large it becomes impossible to work with them."

Andrée thought of the head of her circuit, the handsome and capable Francis Suttill, code-named 'Prosper.' He'd given her a copy of Rudyard Kipling's *If* when he came to the RAF base to see her off. "I know it's about a boy becoming a man," he'd said. "But the words are still meaningful." Andrée couldn't imagine someone like Prosper ever acting egotistically.

Yvonne stood and brushed breadcrumbs from her trousers. "You two will stay here a few days and get acquainted with being back in France before moving on to your missions. I suppose I should try to soothe things between Pierre and Gaspard."

"Is that your job because you are a woman?" Adele asked.

Yvonne gave her a wry smile. "That and the fact that, according to our cover story, Pierre and I are husband and wife." She put her hand on the doorknob. "Good luck and remember what we Resistance members say around here: *merde alors!*

"*Merde alors,*" Andrée and Adele echoed. Loosely translated, it meant 'well, shit.'

CHAPTER 3

NOOR

*N*oor pulled at the bottom of her uniform jacket as she stared up at the imposing structure at 8 Northumberland Avenue. She hadn't thought the letter she'd received commanding her presence at the War Office was something to be alarmed about, but now she gave an involuntary shudder.

She suppressed her trepidation as best she could and entered the lobby of what had once been the Victoria Hotel. Her voice was softer than usual when she asked for the man whose signature was on the letter. She cleared her throat and tried again. "I'm here to see Captain Jepson."

"Certainly," the concierge—or perhaps he was a secretary, Noor thought—led her to a doorway and then up a flight of stairs. "The elevator's broken," he said between gasps as he paused on a landing. By the time they'd reached a solid wooden door on the third floor, he was completely out of breath.

Noor was in considerably better shape than the secretary, thanks to the extensive training she'd recently undergone as a member of the Women's Auxiliary Air Force, but even so, she felt light-headed as she wondered what lay beyond the door.

The secretary rapped twice. After a gentlemanly voice called out a welcome, the secretary opened the door to reveal a kindly-looking man with graying hair hunched behind a small desk. He gestured for Noor to sit. She sat gingerly in the only spare chair, which appeared ready to fall apart at any moment, while the secretary saw himself out.

The gentleman picked up a manila file. "Noor Inayat Khan?"

She nodded. Her given name was really Noor-un-nisa, but, on the advice of her brother, she'd shortened it when she applied for a position with the WAAF. The clerk who registered Vilayat as a member of the Royal Navy had abandoned trying to spell his name and told him to just go by the more English-sounding 'Vic.'

"I'm Captain Selwyn Jepson," the man continued in French. "What kind of name is Noor, anyway?"

She assumed he was questioning her background, as most people did when they first met her. "My mother was British, a quarter each of Irish and English, and half Scottish. My father was Indian." Her father had also been the great grandson of Tipu Sultan, a ruler of Mysore, which technically made Noor a princess, but Captain Jepson didn't need to know that.

"You speak French very well," he stated, flexing his hands in front of him. Noor couldn't help noticing how clean they were.

"My father was a musician and we moved around a lot. I was born in Moscow, lived in England for a short while, and then relocated to France when I was six. I grew up outside of Paris and attended the Sorbonne." The wool of her uniform skirt was beginning to itch her knees but she refrained from scratching them.

He wrote something down before looking up again. "And you are an author?"

"Yes. I've written a few children's books." She hoped eventually to write something more sophisticated, but felt she couldn't yet because her life experience had been so limited. Perhaps this meeting with Captain Jepson would set her on a course to change that.

"I was a writer too, once." His voice took on a wistful note. "I wrote thrillers, if you can believe it."

The lone lightbulb above their heads flickered as something

occurred to Noor. "Espionage thrillers?" she asked, in a more confident tone.

He coughed, quickly covering his mouth with an immaculate hand. "What makes you say that?"

"Well," she reached into her bag. "I did get this out-of-the-blue letter, and here we are, in a clandestine office…"

He leaned forward. "And if I *was* in the espionage business, what accounts for your presence here today?"

Her heart lifted, thinking this might finally be the opportunity she'd been waiting for ever since she'd fled France. "I imagine you'd want to recruit me as an undercover agent. You are clearly in need of people who speak French. Not to mention I am excellent at the wireless."

"We don't put women wireless operators in the field," he said, more to himself than Noor.

"But people with skills like mine are hard to come by." She had no idea whether or not that was true, but it sounded good. "I am familiar with the territory and speak the language."

"You're right," he replied. "If we deem you suitable, you might ultimately find yourself working with other British officers in the underbelly of France, sabotaging the Germans."

She sat back, digesting his words. She hadn't actually expected him to confirm any of her speculations. After a moment, she replied, "I'll take whatever test you need me to."

He attempted a bland smile. "It's not that simple. Some of our agents have already gotten into trouble and found themselves in Gestapo interrogation rooms." The smile faded. "Do you know what happens there?"

"I can only imagine," Noor replied.

"No." He pointed at her. "The reality is worse than anything you can envision, even with your writer's mind." He dropped his hand and looked out the window adjacent to his desk. "You will not be given a field uniform, which means if you are captured, you will have no protection under the international laws of warfare." He met her eyes again. "If you do pass our tests, and we end up sending you to France, you might not come back."

His words were like a blast of cold Arctic air, but Noor squared her shoulders, refusing to show her fear.

"Even if you do come back, no one can ever know what you did," Captain Jepson continued. "The only recognition you'll have will be internal— the knowledge of your service to the Allies. You'll not receive any bonuses and your only salary will be what the WAAF is providing. We'll hold it here for you in case you return, and if not, we'll give it to your next of kin."

"Okay."

"Okay?" The captain set down his pen. "Most potential agents are a little more hesitant when I explain what working for us entails. Don't you want at least a few days to think about it?"

She shook her head. "I'm ready now."

"I'm always wary when people agree so quickly, as though they have some sort of alternative motive. But..." he put his hand under his chin and stared at her thoughtfully. "I do feel there's something authentic about you. Maybe it's because we're both writers." He reached into his desk and pulled out a stamp. With a quick movement, he pressed it to the front of the file before passing it to her. He'd marked APPROVED in red ink.

CHAPTER 4

FRANCINE

"$\mathcal{I}$'m afraid I'm just not cut out for this," Francine stated.

Major Buckmaster shuffled the papers in front of him. "It's true your instructors' reports haven't been the greatest."

Jack waved his hand. "We both know Major de Wesselow doesn't believe women should be in the field. Has any female actually received a glowing recommendation from him?"

"One." Buckmaster closed the file. "She's already in France, although we've recently sent in two more whose final reports were less than stellar. But you're right—Major de Wesselow and I don't see eye-to-eye on the advantages of women agents." He gave Francine a searching gaze. "Are you sure you want to work in the field?"

She shot a helpless look at Jack, who nodded. "Yes, of course," she told Buckmaster.

He turned to address her husband. "I don't know, Jack. You've only been married a few months. I understand that working undercover can be trying. Perhaps we can find Francine a job as a wireless operator here in England. Hell, she could even be your personal transmitter."

Jack shifted in his chair. "You can complete the training to the SOE's satisfaction, can't you, Francie?"

"I can do better," she replied. "I promise."

Buckmaster tapped his pen several times against the desk, clearly hesitant.

"I'm told the SOE is in desperate need of native French speakers," Jack said. "Francine was born there, and only recently arrived in London."

"Oui en effet," she agreed with a perfect French accent.

"I'll take it upon myself to help her," Jack continued.

Buckmaster let out a heavy sigh. "Very well then. But if she gets another poor report…"

"I know, I know." Francine held up her hands. "Wireless school will be next."

"You know this is for both of us, don't you, Francie?" Jack asked as they walked out into the sunshine.

"Yes. It's just that it's so hard, all this gun training and running and map reading." She stopped suddenly, noting that they weren't heading toward the main house of Wanborough Manor, where her room was. "Where are we going?"

"The obstacle course."

"Not now, Jack." Francine looked up at the sun. It was unusually warm for mid-October. "It's almost one o'clock. We usually do the obstacle course in the morning, before it gets too hot."

"C'mon, Francie. I'll help you."

She followed him reluctantly, kicking pebbles as she walked. After they'd reached their destination, Francine put her hands on her hips as she looked over the course. Trainees were given points for every obstacle surmounted correctly under the time limit of five minutes. The objective was to achieve 50 out of a possible 90 points. So far Francine's highest score was 40, and that was in much cooler weather. She wiped her sweaty hands on her trousers as Jack reached up to shed his sweater.

"What are you doing?" Francine asked.

"I'm going to do it with you."

She shook her head as he started stretching. The last thing she wanted was to have Jack leading the way; she didn't want him to notice how long everything took her. All the same, she couldn't help admiring his athletic form through his thin t-shirt. She still couldn't believe she was married to such a handsome man. She'd fled to England only six months ago with Sergeant William Reynolds, a member of the Royal Signals Corps. Reynolds had claimed to be a POW who'd escaped from the Nazis and they'd forged a marriage certificate. Under further investigation, it was revealed that her new husband already had a wife, and the inspector at Portsmouth declared the marriage void. He seemed ready to also void her presence in England but took pity on the tearful Francine. "Please," she'd begged, pulling on the inspector's sleeve.

"Isn't there anyone else you can call on?" he asked.

She replied with the first name that popped into her head. "Jack Agazarian." She'd met him briefly when he was a student in France. They'd had a casual friendship, but Francine always suspected Jack had carried a torch for her.

The inspector looked up his address and dutifully arranged a car to bring her to Jack's apartment in London. Jack had been surprised to see her, and then pleased. They'd had a short courtship, a quick ceremony, and a nonexistent honeymoon, for there was nowhere to vacation in war-torn Europe.

"Ready?" Jack's voice startled her out of her reverie.

She stretched her arms over her head briefly before dropping them by her side again. "Yes."

He glanced at his watch. "In ten, nine, eight…" As he continued counting down, Francine took a deep breath. "Go!"

She followed Jack as he ran toward the first obstacle: a 15-meter-high tree, covered in narrow planks, which he scaled easily. Once up to the top, he began to run across the rickety bridge. Francine wasn't too far behind him, yet. She might have been small, but she was agile—climbing trees and running weren't the hardest parts, though she did struggle a bit with sliding down the rope.

Once on the ground again, Jack mounted a thin wire stretched a half meter above a mud puddle. He navigated it with his feet while gripping another wire above his head. Francine had to flex her toes in order to reach the upper wire. She kept her eyes on her feet and the mud beneath her as she maneuvered across.

Next was a crawl through the dirt under barbed wire, which Francine particularly hated because her hair always got caught.

"Two minutes left," Jack hollered over his shoulder as he reached the final and hardest obstacle: a three-meter-high wooden wall. He scaled it effortlessly and then called out his time while he watched Francine's progress.

She paused at the wall, gasping, as Jack stated from the sidelines that she had one minute and thirty seconds left.

She put her hands on her knees, still trying to catch her breath. "I can't do this one."

"Francie, the wall is 25 points. You have to."

To demonstrate, she lifted her arms as high as they would go, but they barely reached halfway up.

"Look," Jack placed his hands on the diagonal support brace on the side of the wall. "Use this for leverage and stay to the inside."

She eyed it with distaste and was about to refuse, but Jack's eyebrows rose as he implored her to give it a shot.

She jumped, grabbing the brace at the highest point she could.

"That's it, Francie. Now swing your legs. Good."

Her feet didn't connect with the top of the wall and she released her grip.

Jack was relentless. "Try again."

"I can't do it, Jack. I'm too short."

"No, I've seen people smaller than you scale this thing. You just have to think that you can do it, like that little engine train from children's books." He set his strong hands on her shoulders. "Do it for me."

She took another deep breath. This time when she swung her body, her leg made it over.

"Now pull yourself up!"

I can do this, Francine thought as she hauled her body upright. Soon she was sitting on the top of the wall. "Do I have to jump?"

"No, you can use the brace on the other side to climb down."

She hit the ground with satisfaction. "Time?"

Jack looked at his watch and grinned. "A little bit longer than five minutes, but next time you'll be quicker, now that you know how to do it."

"Thanks to you."

"Isn't that what husbands are for?" he asked, coming closer. His t-shirt was soaked through and sweat dripped down his face, but Francine had never been more attracted to him.

"I'm proud of you, Francie," Jack told her before their lips met for a long kiss.

CHAPTER 5

YVONNE

*Y*vonne left the newcomers to become acquainted—or in the case of Andrée, reacquainted with France—to head back to her room in Tours. As she climbed onto her bicycle, she reflected on the two new recruits. She herself had been the first female sent to the field, and Buckmaster must have decided she'd done a good enough job to send over two more women. Yvonne also felt quite confident that they would do fine in their new roles: Adele would head to Poitiers to start a safehouse for newly dropped agents in that part of the country, and hopefully Andrée's circuit leader, someone named Prosper, would be more accommodating than Yvonne's own leader.

Thinking about her Gaspard made her pedal faster. When she had arrived in Tours, he had acted as though her coming was a surprise to him, though Yvonne knew his wireless operator, Marcel Clech, had been in touch with Buckmaster and had been given information on her arrival time. After Gaspard had basically ignored her, Yvonne had to locate a safehouse on her own, something that was not altogether easy in an unfamiliar country occupied by the enemy.

She had been lucky enough to find a vacant room, complete

with its own exterior door and bathroom, in a house owned by a Monsieur Caye. After introducing herself as Jacqueline Viallat, Yvonne provided the overly curious potential landlord with the backstory she'd come up with for her alias in its entirety, down to the tyrannical husband.

That last embellishment may have been a mistake, for Caye's eyebrows rose as he gazed at her, in a manner that some might have called 'ogling.'

Yvonne decided then that Jacqueline should also be a bit eccentric. "Do you hear that?" She held her hand up to her ear for good measure.

"Hear what?" Caye asked.

Yvonne tilted her head one way for a few seconds, and then swiveled it in the other direction. "Never mind. It must be the ghosties again." She put her hand to her mouth, as if she'd said something she shouldn't have.

"Ghosties?"

"That's what I call them. Occasionally I can see them, but usually just hear them. I believe they are the ghosts of children who have passed." She clicked her tongue at a nearby rosebush.

Caye's bulging eyeballs seemed ready to burst from his skull. "I'm sure I don't know what you're talking about."

"I'm sure you don't." She shrieked the next line in the highest octave she could manage. "I hear you, girls! You don't have to hide. This man seems nice and I'm sure this room will be perfectly suitable as well." She shot Caye a wide smile. "When can I move my stuff in?"

He rubbed at his chin as he stared at the rosebush. "I guess… whenever you'd like?"

Once she'd gotten settled, she'd gone again to Gaspard's headquarters. He was out, but Marcel, the wireless operator, gave her a lowdown of her new circuit. He invited her to sit across from him at the little table before stating, "I've been working for the SOE since the start of the Resistance. I was Armand Borni's wireless operator until he was betrayed by The Cat. They brought me to London for training before sending me back to France to be the operator for Autogiro."

"Except Lucas had already been arrested," Yvonne concluded, remembering what Paul Frager had said.

"Exactly. So they told me to travel to Tours to work with the Monkeypuzzle circuit, of which Gaspard is the head."

"Some head," an unfamiliar voice stated. Both Yvonne and Marcel looked up, startled, at the newcomer. Though he couldn't have been much taller than Yvonne, with his raised chin and stick-straight posture, he carried himself with a commanding presence. He had a handlebar mustache, and, with his slight form and heavy eyebrows, was the spitting image of Charlie Chaplin. He must have caught her staring, for he ran a finger over his mustache. "It's hideous, isn't it? Just like the hair on the Fur-herr."

"The what?" Yvonne asked.

The man sat down next to Marcel. "The Fur-herr. Because his lip is furry, and he's German so he's an 'herr.'" When he got no reaction from either Yvonne or Marcel, he added, "Adolph Hitler." He spread out his hands, which were surprisingly large considering his small frame. "Never mind."

Marcel leaned forward. "Yvonne, I'd like to introduce you to Pierre Culioli, one of our local recruits."

Pierre held out his hand to Yvonne. "You're the courier."

Though his tone implied it wasn't a question, Yvonne answered anyway, "Supposed to be."

"Let me guess. Gaspard hasn't given you anything to do."

"No."

Pierre exchanged a look with Marcel. "I suppose the first thing you should learn is that our purported leader is completely incompetent." Pierre obviously minced no words when it came to his own point of view. He was what Yvonne's mother would have called, *impétueux*, a word she usually reserved for her own daughter.

Yvonne looked around the messy room. "Where is Gaspard now?"

"Who knows?" Pierre replied.

She sighed. "Look, I've come here to work, not sit around waiting for a leader who doesn't seem to care that I'm here. Is there anything for me to do?"

Marcel gave an appreciative nod. "I'm sure Pierre can find you something, can't you?"

Pierre had mentioned the incoming agent drop, and that was how Yvonne had come to greet Adele and Andrée upon their arrival in France.

Once she reached Monsieur Caye's house, Yvonne dismounted her bicycle, hoping there would be a message from Marcel detailing her latest assignment.

Something was wrong. As she went to put the key in the lock, she realized her room's exterior door had been left slightly ajar. She pushed it open and then immediately went into the fighting stance she'd been taught at Beaulieu. Instead of an intruder, Yvonne sighted an unfamiliar, new-looking black suitcase sitting on the bed. She tentatively walked over and undid the latches.

Inside was a wireless transceiver complete with tuning crystals, a Colt revolver, and a notebook. Upon further investigation, she found that the notebook contained both radio frequencies and a poem code. She tossed the book back on the bed, cursing. Had anyone seen these incriminating articles, they would have jumped to the correct conclusion that she was a spy. She picked up the book and placed it back in the suitcase. For all she knew, her nosy landlord had already checked in on her and seen everything.

Yvonne threw a few essentials on top of the evidence: underwear, an extra pair of stockings, and another blouse, before securing the latches. Protocol dictated that she contact her circuit leader, but something told her Gaspard might have been behind the suitcase plant. At any rate, he'd not been very helpful thus far, so she headed for Pierre Culioli's apartment.

She got straight to the point when Pierre answered the door. "This was sitting on the bed in my room. In plain sight," she added for emphasis.

He took the suitcase from her and led the way into the living room. She leaned over to push her undergarments aside when he opened it. He cursed in French before asking, "Gaspard?"

"Do you really think it was him?"

Pierre sank into the couch. "I've met some rats in my time, but never one like this, with all the worst vices contained in one man."

"But why would he betray me like that?"

"I don't know. I will say that he told Marcel Clech—who later told me—that he thought his new 'secretary' was fluffy and the less he saw of her, the better."

"Me? Fluffy?"

Pierre shut the suitcase. "He's clearly wrong in both his opinion of you and of me. I've repeatedly requested that he send me to London for training, but he always refuses, saying I'm more useful here, though he's made it quite clear he thinks the opposite."

"What do we do now?"

Pierre stood up. "I think it might be time for us to find a new circuit."

CHAPTER 6

ANDRÉE

*A*ndrée strolled down the Parisian sidewalk in her usual manner: with a purpose but not too hurried. Though the streets were nearly void of cars, save for the ubiquitous black Citroëns of the Wehrmacht Army, bicyclists were everywhere and once she had to quickly step to one side to avoid a collision.

Outwardly she was as calm as ever, but her stomach felt jittery as she checked her watch. It was nearly noon. Her rendezvous instructions were to arrive at the café in the Rue Caumartin at exactly 12:00 p.m. and only stay till five minutes past. If either of them was late, they'd not be able to meet up for yet another day. There had already been three failed attempts and Andrée hoped today would not be the fourth.

She entered the café and quickly scanned the interior, her eyes landing on the dark-haired man who sat alone at a corner table. Andrée's face relaxed as she approached him, noting his unmistakably large ears. "Where can one get lighter fluid?" she asked, pausing next to him.

"You mean gasoline?" the man replied.

Andrée could almost smell Miss Atkins' perfume lingering on his suit, which was just the right combination of stylish and shabby, as though he'd been subject to Parisian rationing for two years and not training for covert operations in England. She knew Miss Atkins had checked over every centimeter of his outfit before he'd left, making sure there were no hints of foreign influence. Just as she'd done with Andrée. "You're finally here."

"Sorry I was late." Prosper winced as he stretched out his leg. "Had a bit of a rough arrival." Unlike her and Adele, Prosper had been instructed to land 'blind,' or without a reception committee to help him navigate the French countryside.

"Yes, I can see that. Wait here." Andrée went to the counter and ordered two ersatz coffees.

"You've obviously become well acquainted with your surroundings," he said when she returned.

"It's not been that long since I left."

"You'll have to tell me everything later." Prosper took a sip of coffee. His lips puckered from the bitter taste as he set the mug down.

"It's roasted chicory," Andrée told him. "No caffeine, though you look like you could use some."

"I could indeed. But first we have to figure out what to do with this." With his good leg, he nudged a beat-up leather suitcase covered in grass stains.

"What's in it?"

"Communications," he replied vaguely. Andrée realized he meant a wireless set.

"I thought it was my valise, but it's not," Prosper continued. "And I don't really want to be traipsing through the city with something so..." he looked around the room before lowering his voice, "incriminating."

"I know just where to take it." She nodded at his coffee. "Finished?"

"Yes." He pushed his still-full mug to the middle of the table and got heavily to his feet.

Andrée led a limping Prosper out of the café and back into the sunshine. He pretended not to notice the stiff, straight German officers mixing in with the still somewhat fashionable

Parisians, though he did clutch the suitcase tighter as a car passed.

"Where are we going?" Prosper asked in a low voice.

"To see the Tambour sisters," she replied. Part of her initial instructions from Buckmaster had been to make contact with them, a task that had proved to be more than fortuitous, for as soon as Andrée said the code words she'd been given—that she was "a friend of Charlie"—they'd showered her with food and wine and even found her lodging.

Now Andrée paused at 38 Avenue de Suffren, a pale-yellow building with black wrought iron railings decorating the upper floors. "They live on the fifth floor," she told Prosper, eyeing his leg doubtfully.

He managed to pant the words, "I can make it."

Germaine answered the door. She was the plainer of the two sisters —the younger one, Madeleine, had been an actress before the war —but also the more knowledgeable. Pre-war, Germaine had been a secretary to André Girard, the head of the Carte network in the Unoccupied Zone, and now ran a safehouse from the apartment she shared with Madeleine and their mother.

Germaine raised a thin eyebrow at Andrée as she ushered them inside. "Prosper?" she asked when she'd shut the door.

"In the flesh," he replied dryly as he sat down on the couch.

Andrée took a seat on the opposite end. "Germaine, it seems Prosper has arrived without his valise."

"What's that then?" She nodded at the suitcase before entering the little kitchen.

"A wireless set," Andrée said, loud enough for Germaine to hear her over the slamming of cupboard doors.

Germaine returned with three glasses and a bottle of brandy. "I have some sherry too," she told Andrée.

"Brandy is fine."

Germaine arranged herself in an armchair. "Do you have a W/T operator?"

Prosper frowned. "No, not yet. That's why I'm not sure who this transmitter was for."

Germaine took a long sip of her drink. "And here you are," she leaned forward, "in a foreign country, without any clean—what do you call them in England—knickers... and no way to get hold of Buck to send you some. With the rationing, it's not like you can just go down the street and buy them."

Prosper smiled in spite of himself. "That's right. Can you help?"

"Not directly with the underwear situation, but I can contact someone who can."

"Thank you."

Now it was Germaine's turn to frown at Prosper. "Your accent is not so great."

Andrée had been thinking something similar. While it was in no way English, it wasn't quite French either.

"No, I don't suppose it's as perfect as my partner's," he replied almost apologetically, nodding at Andrée. "My mother was French and I grew up in Lille, but I've spent most of my adult life in London."

"Partner?" Germaine waggled a bony finger. "She might as well be in charge: you're going to need her. You can't go around the country, speaking like that to every Boche you meet." She gestured to Andrée. "Let her do the talking for you."

"I could pose as your unduly chatty wife," Andrée suggested.

"No." Proper pulled at his collar, clearly uncomfortable. "I don't suppose my real wife would appreciate that. How about brother and sister?"

Andrée shot him an innocent grin. "Perfect."

CHAPTER 7

NOOR

"*M*ams!" Noor burst into her mother's London apartment. She stopped suddenly when she saw her sister sitting in the living room. She was wearing a brown uniform only slightly darker than her skin and her black hair had been cut into a smart pageboy. "Claire?"

"Noor!" Claire exclaimed, getting up to give her a long hug. "What are you doing here? I thought you were in training."

"I could say the same about you." Claire had been called up by the Auxiliary Territorial Service, the women's branch of the British Army, a few months ago.

"I'm on leave," Claire replied. "I came home to check on Mams."

"Where is she?" Noor asked.

"She had another one of her headaches and went to lie down."

Noor took a seat on the couch. After their father had died when Noor was 13, their mother had developed debilitating migraines. She was often bedridden and it had been Noor who cooked, cleaned, and looked after her three younger siblings.

"Have you heard from either of our brothers?" Claire asked.

"Vilayat is studying for a navigation exam. I haven't heard from Hidayat since we left Lyon."

"Nor have I." The worry was obvious in Claire's voice. "I hope they are handling the Occupation all right." Hidayat had a wife and two children and had chosen to stay in France while the rest of his family fled to England.

Both sisters looked up as their mother entered the room, a drab-colored sari and veil covering nearly every inch of her fair skin and graying blonde hair. Mams had been born Ora Ray Baker and raised in America, but had taken the name Amina Sharada Begum upon marrying their father. When Noor had once asked her why she preferred wearing the outfits of the Indian culture, her mother had replied that she "appreciated the seclusion they offer."

"Your uniform is different," were Mams' first words to Noor.

"I've joined the FANY."

"What's that?"

"The First Aid Nursing Yeomanry. I'm going into the Foreign Service." The FANY was a cover for what Noor would really be doing, but she knew that Mams would never approve of her eldest daughter's new line of work.

"You look different," Mams stated.

Noor adjusted her collar. "I do?"

"In a good way," Claire quickly filled in. "More confident, I think."

"What will you be doing with this new position?" Mams asked.

"Oh," Noor tried to play casual. "I think they are going to train me in parachuting."

"Will you be going overseas?" Claire asked. "To Africa?"

Mams put a hand to her forehead.

"You need tea." Noor got up from the couch.

"I'll get it," Claire told her. "You stay here."

"Yes, Claire can get it," Mams agreed. "I'd like to talk to you."

Noor watched her sister's slim form as she bustled around in the kitchen. In contrast to their mother, ever since she was little, Claire had always insisted on wearing pinafores and black Mary Janes, the same as her French classmates. She'd been born Khair-un-nisa, but had insisted from an early age that even her family call her the more Western 'Claire.'

Noor had tried to appease their mother by dressing in traditional *pattu pavadai* as a child but had quickly given it up when they moved to France. Her dark skin was different enough from the rest of her schoolmates—she didn't want to stick out any more.

Mams straightened the pillow next to her. "You know I don't approve of this war business. You, your brothers, your sister, all leaving. Vilayat might even find himself at the front."

"He is in the navy, Mams."

"What does that have to do with anything?"

"The front is in Africa. Vilayat is still in training."

Her mother waved her hand, indicating that part of the conversation was over. "Still..." she looked out the window, clearly gathering her thoughts. "I am glad you are getting some form of independence. Claire is right, you do look more confident, and that khaki is much more flattering than the navy of your old uniform." She paused again. After a moment, she reached for Noor's hand. "Sometimes I'm afraid I did wrong by you. You spent so much time taking care of me, your siblings... I fear you never had time to have a life of your own."

"No, Mams." Noor squeezed her mother's hand. "You needed me. Everyone needed me, after Baba died."

Claire returned with the tea tray and set it on the table before disappearing into the bedroom.

Mams eyes were red as she picked up her cup. "Noor-un-nisa, you go and find the world."

Up until that moment, Noor had wanted nothing more than to do so, but now she was suddenly filled with regret. "Mams, who will take care of you?"

"I will be fine on my own. I've done a good job so far."

Noor cast her eyes around the apartment, cluttered with Baba's various instruments, now covered in a layer of dust. Even in death, his presence dominated the room.

She stood and went over to the piano, pushing back the wood covering that protected the keys. Baba would have been sad that it had been so long since someone had played it. As it had been expected that Noor and Claire would have arranged marriages to rich Indian men, Baba had pushed music on them in lieu of academics. Both girls had learned the piano and another instrument—the harp for Noor and the violin for Claire—while intellectual pursuits were supposed to be left for their brothers.

Not wanting to end up as the society wife to some rich man, Noor had taken it upon herself to excel academically. She'd flourished in languages and literature and achieved a license in the Psychobiology of the Child from the Sorbonne. By the time she was twenty-five, she'd published her first book, *Twenty Jataka Tales*, a children's translation of traditional Buddhist fables. Most of the stories were about animals engaging in acts of noble sacrifice. Soon after that, the war had started, and Noor was motivated to perform her own noble deed. She wondered if she were about to be sacrificed for the greater good, like so many of the creatures she'd written about. *Was she ready to die for a country that wasn't technically hers?*

Deep in thought, she reached out her finger and gently pushed down on the piano's middle C key.

Her sister's voice brought Noor out of her reverie. "It's out of tune," Claire said, walking over to stand beside her.

"Like Mams' snoring." Both girls glanced at their mother, who had fallen asleep on the couch. "Do you think she'll be all right?" Noor asked.

"She'll do what she has to do, like all of us." Claire turned her gaze to Noor. "Will you? I know how badly you want to help the Allies, but you are probably the last person I can see going to war. You're the dreamiest of all the dreamers I've ever known."

"I'm not going to the front."

"Then where are you going?"

Noor dropped her eyes, knowing that the ever-practical Claire would be disapproving if she understood the dangerous endeavor her sister was about to embark on. "I can't tell you." She reached out to touch the sleeve of Claire's uniform. "But if they ask you to do something called 'liaison duties,' you must say no."

"What do you mean?"

Noor dropped her arm. "Because you've been brought up in France, they might want you for something else, what they might call translation work. But, little sister, promise me you will say no."

Claire gave her an indulgent smile. "Of course. I promise."

Noor went over and kissed her sleeping mother's cheek. "I have to go now."

Claire moved toward the door. "Let me walk you to the station."

Her request was innocent enough—it wasn't as if she could possibly discern Noor's destination, even if she saw what train she took. Mams' words repeated in her head: *Go and find the world.* "No, that's okay. I want to say goodbye here." Noor pecked Claire's cheek. "Be good, little sister."

"And you, big sister."

CHAPTER 8

FRANCINE

"*H*ere," Major de Wesselow handed Francine what looked like a lump of clay.

"What is it?" Francine's nose wrinkled at the almost overpowering smell of almonds.

"Nobel 808. It's an explosive."

As she sucked in her breath, Francine could faintly hear the other students around her whispering. She moved her extended, frozen palm as slowly as she could back toward the major.

"Don't fret," he told her. "It's not dangerous at room temperature, though you do have to worry about it if it gets too hot." To her relief, he finally took it back from her. "I'll show you the proper way to heat it up to make it pliable, so you can cut it in any shape you want. In a pinch, you could stick it under your armpit to warm it, but sometimes the skin absorbs some of its properties and gives a person headaches and stomach pains for up to 24 hours."

"Is that all?" Francine asked faintly.

"Well, and if any Boche smells those almonds on you, you'd better hope you positioned the 808 in the right spot." He set the explosive carefully on the desk before going to the chalkboard.

As de Wesselow started writing, the man sitting next to her,

42

France Antelme, gave her a sheepish smile. "That was a bit of a hairy scene."

"No kidding." Now that Jack had been sent off to an SOE finishing school in Scotland, Antelme was her closest friend here. She watched as he furiously copied what was written on the chalkboard. Even though it was almost winter, he had kept his ruddy, outdoorsy appearance. He was at least ten years older than Francine, but was always in the lead on runs and was clearly favored by their instructors.

Francine sat up and forced herself to focus on de Wesselow's lecture on explosives. He showed them how to make a 'sausage,' by wrapping the 808 or its cheaper alternative, gelignite, in wax paper and then inserting a fuse. He went on to introduce other incendiary devices, such as a 'clam' and 'firepot' and taught them the appropriate time to use each one, depending on if it was day or night, and the intended target.

"But try to avoid pylons—they look as if they would be good targets, but in all actuality, most towns have back-ups that can be up and running in less than a day." De Wesselow checked his watch and then set down his chalk. "I think that will be all for now. We'll put your knowledge to the test this afternoon. You are excused for lunch."

Antelme shut his notebook and stood up. "Fattening for the kill."

"What?" Francine asked as she fell in step beside him.

"Our poor soldiers are stuck with army rationing, and here we are, eating steak and eggs." He took a deep breath as they entered the dining hall. "But damn, it sure does smell good."

"What do you think de Wesselow meant when he said they'll put our knowledge to the test?"

"I think exactly that." Antelme grabbed a tray and got in line.

"They can't possibly expect us to actually use explosives."

"Why not? We're isolated enough."

It was true: Wanborough Manor, which was used as an SOE training house, was located on hundreds of acres of land near the Hog's Back. Francine accepted the proffered steak and then sat next to Antelme, eating her lunch in a nervous silence while the rest of her classmates, all men, chatted animatedly.

After lunch they were divided into two different teams; Francine was relieved to be on the same one as Antelme. They were directed to the nearby limestone quarry a little over a kilometer from the manor. Tired of being last, Francine forced herself to move quickly up the steep slope and got to the top before half of the others.

De Wesselow was waiting for them. "Now keep in mind, things will probably not go as smoothly in the field, but I will show you how it *should* be done." He held up what looked like a fountain pen. "This wonderful Polish invention was brought to our attention by Major-General Gubbins himself." Gubbins was the head of the SOE, and second in command only to Lord Selbourne, the Minister of Warfare.

De Wesselow showed them how the device, which he called a time-pencil, was divided into three parts. A tiny glass vial containing cupric chloride was located in front of a spring-loaded striker, which in turn was connected to a thin metal wire.

"When you crush the vial, either with pliers or by stepping on it, the cupric chloride will be released and will eventually disintegrate the wire. This," he showed them a colored strip near the top, "tells you how much cupric chloride there is, which translates to how long the delay will be. Red means thirty minutes, the blue ones are for twenty-four hours. Once the wire has been dislodged, the striker will then hit the percussion cap to detonate it. If the pencil was inserted properly into an explosive, then BOOM! Good-bye German railways or ammunition dumps!"

"He makes it sound so easy," Francine said to Antelme under her breath.

"I think it really is that easy," he said, equally quietly. "Genius," he said in a much louder voice.

"In theory," de Wesselow agreed. "But they can sometimes be a little tough to work with. It takes a certain, how do the French say it?

Je ne sais quoi." He handed Antelme the device. "Give it a try. I'm going to check on the other group."

After de Wesselow left, Antelme held the pen out to Francine. "Do you want to try it?"

She shook her head numbly, afraid to touch the thing.

Antelme sighed. "Francine, imagine how good it would look on your record if you were the one to successfully detonate it."

When she still didn't take it, he added softly, "I know Jack would want you to."

Their two other team members shifted impatiently. "Let's get this over with so we can get back," one of them, a man named Victor, said.

Francine had never particularly liked Victor, and now she realized why. She rolled her eyes before reaching for the time-pencil.

"Good," Antelme said. "Now step on it."

She carefully placed it on the ground before putting her boot over it and shifting her weight. They heard the faint but satisfying sound of breaking glass.

Antelme stooped down to check the inspection hole. "I can see right through it. That means the countdown has started."

The time-pencil Francine just detonated had a green indicator, which meant it had a ten-minute delay, enough time for them to rush to a safe distance away. She stuck the fuse into a wad of 808 and then attached it to the quarry wall.

"Let's get out of here," Antelme said once she had finished.

The team crunched through the quarry as fast as they could, the chalk dust flying around them. Antelme paused at about 50 meters, far enough away not to be hurt by any limestone shrapnel, but close enough to see what happened.

"How long has it been?" Victor demanded.

Antelme peeked at his watch. "About ten."

They watched for a few more minutes, but the explosive remained intact.

"Looks like we failed," Victor stated.

You mean I failed, Francine silently corrected him.

"Just wait," Antelme said. "The timer on them isn't perfect."

45

After a little while longer, even he had to admit nothing was going to happen. "I guess that's it."

"Should we go back and fix whatever is wrong with it?" Francine asked.

"No," Victor replied. "That's about the stupidest thing you can do. What if it all of a sudden decides to go off?"

"It was probably just a dud pencil," Antelme put a reassuring hand on Francine's shoulder. "Let's go back."

They were nearly all the way down when they heard a loud boom. The rock beneath them shook as a cloud of chalk dust formed, covering everything around them in a thin white powder.

Francine coughed and rubbed at her eyes with white hands before clambering to solid ground.

"You did it!" de Wesselow exclaimed from his vantage point a few meters away.

"Francine did it," Antelme corrected him.

De Wesselow gave an approving nod. "Not bad, Mrs. Agazarian. Not bad at all."

CHAPTER 9

YVONNE

*Y*vonne's legs were killing her. She stopped for a moment to catch her breath, glaring at the split skirt of her culottes. If only she had a pair of trousers—they would have made riding a bicycle so much easier.

In the days since discovering the suitcase in her room, she'd been cycling all over the Occupied countryside. Though she and Pierre hadn't officially broken with the Monkeypuzzle circuit, he had refused to take orders directly from Gaspard and only received them via the radio operator, Marcel Clech. Through Clech, the SOE at Baker Street had requested they find suitable hiding places for the arms and ammunition that were expected to arrive from England later that month, under the next full moon.

But this time she wasn't looking for places to stockpile ammunition. Yvonne readjusted the Colt pistol strapped to her thigh before pedaling on.

Finally she reached the barn belonging to one of Pierre's contacts. She wheeled the bicycle inside and carefully removed the suitcase tied to the back. She hauled this and her large purse to the nearest station and boarded a train bound for Paris.

She'd been given instructions to drop the case at a Paris safehouse. Luckily the contents were innocuous enough, so Yvonne wasn't overly worried when a German soldier stopped next to her seat and asked to look through her bags.

"It's for my husband," she told him when he held up a pair of men's underwear. "Can you believe he left for Paris without his own luggage?"

"What does he do?" the soldier asked in a cursory tone.

"He's a traveling salesman."

The soldier shut the case. "You'd think he'd be better about not leaving things behind then."

Yvonne felt her face heat up. Had her deliberately casual comment made the Boche suspicious?

But he merely handed her the case and then continued on to the person behind her.

When the train arrived in Paris, Yvonne walked out into the city of her youth, stopping a moment to check her watch. *Right on time.* That was perhaps the only advantage of having German troops in France: the train timetables had become much more efficient.

Before embarking on the mission for which she'd been sent to Paris, Yvonne had one small errand to do. She headed over to the Rue de Rivoli, keeping her head down rather than have to nod at the well-fed Boches in their grayish-green uniforms.

She paused before reaching the Angelina tea shop and arranged herself behind one of the wide, Greek-style columns where she could watch the comings and goings of the customers without being noticed herself.

Yvonne's heartbeat quickened when she saw a gray-haired woman approach. The woman, though nearing eighty, still sported the tiny waist she'd always been so proud of. Rumor had it that Madame Cerneau wore her customary, tightly-laced corset even throughout her numerous pregnancies, which might have been the reason she'd lost eight out of ten babies in miscarriages or right after birth. Yvonne had been the last born and the only one to survive to adulthood (her brother, Jean, had passed away at the age of 17 as the result of a riding accident at his English boarding school). Consequently, Yvonne grew up "rather spoiled," at least according to her grandmother.

Yvonne watched as her mother prodded a German soldier out of her way with the steel tip of a black umbrella before going inside Angelina's. A frequent haunt of the Parisian elite, the tea shop was owned by distant cousins of Madame Cerneau, the Rumpelmayers, and Yvonne and her mother had spent many hours there, indulging in its famed hot cocoa after shopping all day on the Champs-Élysées.

A waiter led Madame Cerneau to a table in the back. Though they hadn't seen each other in at least two decades, Yvonne had no intention of making contact with her now. The supremely nosy Madame Cerneau would be guaranteed to ask a million questions about what Yvonne was doing in Occupied Paris, all questions she could not answer without putting her mother in danger.

Madame Cerneau had never been much of a hugger—a trait she'd clearly passed on to her daughter—but for once in her life, Yvonne longed to be in her mother's embrace. Knowing that was impossible, she checked her watch once again before wiping away a stray tear. She swallowed hard before picking up the suitcase to continue on her way.

The cargo was meant for the new head of the Physician circuit, who'd apparently parachuted in without his valise. Yvonne's instructions—delivered from London via Clech—were to give it to a contact at 38 Avenue de Suffren, but when she arrived there, she was pleasantly surprised to see Andrée waiting outside the building.

"Denise!" Yvonne called loudly, using her friend's code name. She set the suitcase down to give her a hug. "How are things going?"

"Busy," Andrée replied. "Since Prosper landed, we've frequently been out and about…" she looked up and down the empty street before leaning closer, "recruiting." She stepped back and nodded toward a sinister-looking poster hanging on the side of the yellow building. "Have you seen those?"

Yvonne walked over to the poster to get a better look. It was written in French, though some of the grammar was not correct. It stated that any person aiding or hiding enemy parachutists would be subject to martial law: males would be executed and females sent to Germany. At the bottom was a statement offering a reward of 10,000 francs to anyone who supplied the German soldiers with information on Allied air drops or parachutists.

"Yikes," Yvonne commented when she returned to the curb.

"I know," Andrée said softly. "Hopefully it doesn't put a damper on any of our missions." In a louder voice, she asked if Yvonne would like to come in for tea.

"Why not?" Yvonne replied.

"Where's Prosper now?" Yvonne asked once they were safely ensconced in Andrée's apartment, a sparsely furnished set of rooms on the third floor of the building.

"Chartres. He had information that there were some sympathetic farmers there with large tracts of land and empty barns."

Yvonne knew vacant fields were good for air drops, and the barns would serve as hiding places until the weapons could be distributed. "How did you hear about these farmers?"

Andrée handed her a teacup. "Some men from a network down south called Carte. Have you heard of it?"

Yvonne nodded. "I have. I traveled to France with one of the heads."

"That's mostly what we've been doing: traveling to the countryside to convince these contacts to aid the Resistance. Most of the time I do the talking because Proper's accent isn't the greatest. But this time he thought it better for me to wait for you. He has a favor to ask."

"Of me?"

Andrée took a seat across from her. "We still don't have a radio operator. Prosper is hoping you can make arrangements for us to secure one, so we can contact Baker Street on a more regular basis."

"Sure." Yvonne set her cup down. "I can get the one from Monkeypuzzle, Marcel Clech, to send a message."

"Can you do it soon? Prosper wants to have his own W/T operator by the next moon period."

Because pilots didn't use lights, they used nights when the moon was brightest for flying across the Channel and navigating the fields of France in order to make drops. The next full moon was in less than a fortnight. Yvonne stood up and grabbed her purse. "I'm on my way."

CHAPTER 10

ANDRÉE

Two weeks later, Andrée found herself once again traveling to the Bossard's field, to the same place she and Adele had landed only a month ago, though, with all the work she'd been doing, it felt like a much longer time period had passed.

Although Pierre Culioli was also along, it was clear from the way Yvonne barked orders that this time she was in charge. The rest of the reception committee were men, and at first they seemed uncertain whether to obey the commands coming from the barely five-foot, gray-haired lady. "Are you just going to stand there or are you going to do what I asked?" Yvonne demanded of one man, putting her hands on the hips of her grass-stained culottes. "Get moving," she told another, using her flashlight to apply a forceful nudge.

Soon they were all in the customary, T-shaped position and the low humming of a Whitley could be heard.

"Now!" Yvonne hissed from somewhere to the right of Andrée.

Andrée blinked her torch four times—two long, two short— and watched as the others followed suit. The Whitley circled over them twice. If all went as planned, the needed arms and requested radio operator would be arriving any moment.

Indeed, Andrée soon could see a dozen black shapes dropping

from the sky, silently, like so many of the leaves that had fallen around her while she'd been waiting.

Someone hit the ground near her with a thump. A male voice swore in English.

"Only French from now on!" Andrée shouted at the dark form.

"*Excusez-moi,*" the voice replied before rattling off a few choice French curses.

Pierre went over to help the man shed his parachute and coveralls. Andrée followed, resisting the urge to shine the torch into the newcomer's eyes. From the dim light of Pierre's flashlight, Andrée grudgingly recognized the man was able-looking, with dark eyes and hair that blended into the night. "You must be Archambault."

He stuck out his hand. "Gilbert Norman."

She made a point not to shake it. "Is that your real name? If it is, I don't want to know it."

He shoved both hands into his pockets. "Gilbert is a lot easier to say than Archambault. Besides, I'm not using an alias while I'm here. *Denise,*" he added pointedly.

Andrée narrowed her eyes. Their new wireless operator, Archambault—or rather Gilbert—seemed quite full of himself. She'd met a million men like him before: smooth, arrogant, the kind that usually did well with women and knew it.

He pulled a brown envelope out from under his coat. "Can you tell me which one is Culioli?"

"That's him," Andrée nodded at Pierre, who'd gone over to introduce himself to the other new arrival. "The one who helped you out of your harness."

"Oh." He opened and closed his mouth as if to say something, but then hesitated, seemingly unsure all of a sudden.

"What's in the envelope?" Andrée prodded.

"Nothing," Gilbert said, tucking it back under his coat.

The group made their way to the Bossard's farmhouse. The elderly couple were just as welcoming as before, clearly unconcerned about the German warnings against people willing to help Allied parachutists, and joined in for a little wine before going to bed.

"Here's to the King of England," Yvonne declared, raising her glass of claret. "He pays for all this."

"Here, here," the other new man, whose name was Roger Landes, agreed. "Buck told me I'd be greeted by a 'reception committee,' but I didn't expect to be given such a warm welcome."

"Drink up, now, men," Yvonne told them. "We have a lot of work to do in the morning." She reached out to cheers with Landes and then Culioli.

Someone clinked their glass to Andrée's. Now that they were out of the darkness and in a room well-lit by candlelight, she could tell her initial instinct had been correct: Gilbert was indeed handsome, and tall with an athletic build. He also had a mustache, though unlike Pierre's, it was a well-groomed one, which balanced out his thick eyebrows nicely.

Gilbert took a gulp of wine. "Where's Gaspard?" he asked when he'd swallowed.

"I don't know Gaspard," Andrée replied. "Is that who the envelope is for?"

"Yes." He held his wineglass out to Yvonne, who was circulating the room with another bottle. She filled his glass to the rim before offering some to Andrée, who waved her on.

"Yvonne doesn't strike me as the type who would be in cahoots with the Boches," Gilbert commented once she was out of earshot.

Andrée's mouth dropped open. "Who told you that?"

"Major Buckmaster. He received a report that she and Culioli were traitors and 'must be taken care of.'"

"Buck can't possibly believe that, especially not about Yvonne." Not for the first time that evening, Andrée queried the envelope's contents.

Gilbert drained his glass and set it on a nearby table. "It's a cyanide pill, meant for Culioli."

"No." The word came out more vehemently than she'd intended. The intense anger she'd felt when she interacted with the Free French resurfaced. What right did this suave newcomer have to immediately try disrupting things? What he spoke of so nonchalantly was the intentional murder of one of her trusted coworkers. *For that matter, what right did Buckmaster have to try to control things from his desk in London?* He had no idea what really went on behind the curtain of German-occupied France. And neither did Gilbert.

"It is," Gilbert insisted, rather sheepishly, Andrée thought, as if he could sense how upset she'd become. "Gaspard requested it, but now I'm starting to think I should just get rid of it."

"I've never met Gaspard, but I can tell you for certain that neither Yvonne nor Pierre are, as you said, 'in cahoots with the Boches.'"

He turned to gaze at her. Andrée could now see his eyes were actually gray, sprinkled with nearly imperceptible flecks of brown. "Do you vouch for them?" he asked.

The rage suddenly dissipated. "I do. Wholeheartedly."

"Well, then come on." He grabbed her hand. "Help me find some other way to dispose of this pill."

CHAPTER 11

NOOR

*N*oor's destination was less than 50 kilometers outside the city, but the quiet countryside felt like another world compared to bustling London. The train conductor had announced their arrival in Surrey, but when Noor got off, there were no directional signs anywhere—not even a name on the station platform. Whether all this secrecy was because they were afraid of a lone operative finding the SOE's preliminary training grounds or a German invasion, she had no idea.

An olive-green military lorry was waiting for them and the driver directed Noor, along with two other women, to get into the canvas-covered back of the truck.

After an hour of driving, one of the other women sat up and crossed her arms. She had a cherub face and wild, curly hair, which made her seem young, but Noor guessed she was probably near the same age as herself, in her early 30s. She turned to Noor and whispered, "This isn't right."

"What's not right?" Noor asked.

There were no windows in the truck, but now that Noor was aware, it seemed as though the curly-haired woman was indeed correct: there was something definitely off. She felt them turn right, then another right, then right again.

"I think we're heading in circles," the woman said.

"More like squares," the third woman said with a grin. She was much older, with a stocky build. She stuck out a sturdy arm to the curly-haired woman. "Cecily."

"Yolande," she replied, shaking the proffered hand.

"I'm Nora Baker," Noor said, instantly creating a code name for herself. Baker was her mother's maiden name.

"Baker?" Cecily repeated, with a touch of disappointment in her voice.

"Yes, why?"

"Nothing." Cecily gave her a searching look. "I just thought your last name would be… something more colorful. You're so exotic-looking."

"Well, at any rate, it's good to meet you both," Yolande said. After a moment, she added, "Do you think they're trying to confuse us by driving around aimlessly?"

Noor and Cecily shrugged as the truck slowed for another turn.

Finally they reached their destination and Noor exited with shaky legs. "Where are we?"

"The Hog's Back," Yolande replied.

"As in the back of a pig?" Cecily asked in her odd accent. It was not quite English, but definitely not French.

"No, as in the hill. We must not be that far from Guildford station." Yolande nodded to herself before stating under her breath, "I knew we were driving in circles."

"This way," the driver told them, making no offer to help carry their bags.

They trekked through at least an acre of woodland before arriving at an enormous Tudor-style mansion with ivy covering that had turned brown in the late autumn and nearly blended in with the brick. To Noor, the house, with its gabled roofs and brick chimneys, seemed as though it had been taken from a fairy tale.

"Welcome to Wanborough Manor," the driver said. He gestured

for them to enter the main house before he disappeared around the back.

The doorbell was answered by a butler, who invited the three women into an oak-paneled parlor. The house appeared well-kept, though Noor could tell most of the furnishings weren't original. She reached out to touch one of the rectangles on the wall. It was much darker and less dusty than the surrounding sun-bleached wallpaper. The owners of the mansion obviously had removed their priceless art and furniture before the SOE moved in.

A tall, thin man with a black mustache strolled into the room. "Good evening, ladies. I am Major de Wesselow." He signaled to the maid behind him, who entered and set a tray of sandwiches on the table. "I suppose you all know that you are here because you have the potential to become SOE agents." He glanced at all three of them in turn. "That doesn't mean it's a guarantee. Wanborough Manor is the first of many steps in the selection process—if at any point you fail a physical or mental test, you could be transferred to another building. We can't send you home at this point—you already know too much about our operations—but we will put you in a remote location where you can do no damage until the war is over."

Noor took a deep breath. The last thing she wanted to do was fail at becoming an agent.

"I'm afraid it is only you three in the house tonight," de Wesselow continued. "Our most recent class has just left, and the rest of your group isn't due to arrive until tomorrow morning." He nodded toward the food. "You'll need your strength, for this evening I will be introducing the first of the physical tests: the obstacle course. I've found it behooves women recruits to get extra practice before the men get here."

"Is that so?" Yolande asked.

De Wesselow narrowed his eyes at her. Clearly he was not a man who enjoyed being challenged. "Six pm, sharp."

Cecily must have not assessed de Wesselow as quickly as Noor had. "It will be dark by then," she said.

"And?" de Wesselow demanded.

"And we'll be there," Noor told him.

Upon sighting the obstacle course—a series of ropes, barbed wire, and various hurdles and walls constructed from heavy wood—Noor frowned. She had never been fond of the physical portion of her WAAF training, given that cold weather usually exacerbated the thick calluses she'd developed after years of playing the harp. Not to mention she was naturally a bit clumsy.

Cecily too seemed dismayed, especially when de Wesselow began briefing them on the first task: climb a towering tree and then use the swing rope to cross a bridge.

"When I get to France, I will walk over a bridge like a normal person," Cecily stated. "What would the Boches think if I produced a piece of rope under my skirt and tried to navigate it that way?"

"Nonsense," was de Wesselow's reply. "You'll need to be prepared for anything, and my job is to help you get over your feminine disabilities."

"Feminine disabilities?" Yolande repeated. "Watch this." Without waiting for de Wesselow's whistle, she started running toward the tree.

Noor followed, though Cecily soon passed her. Noor trailed the other two up the tree. Despite her earlier objections, Cecily used the rope with ease.

Noor managed to keep the distance between her and the other girls steady until she fell off a log while running across it. She limped through the last of the obstacles, and of course finished last. Still, she thought she'd done as well as she could have in near darkness.

"Last but not least," she panted.

De Wesselow lifted his wrist to look at his watch, but Noor reckoned it was too dark for him to check her time. "Okay ladies, we'll call it for now. Go find your new accommodations on your own and get whatever rest you can."

.   .   .

Although Noor was exhausted, she found herself unable to sleep. She had been given her own bed, while Cecily and Yolande shared the other bunk bed. Noor listened to Cecily's soft snoring as she thought about what she was doing there. A part of her was excited, knowing the three women had been specifically chosen for the Special Operations Executive. She wondered what her father, a prominent Sufi mystic who always taught his disciples about love and forgiveness, would think of her new role, especially as de Wesselow had told them to report for weapons training in the morning.

Noor turned onto her side, remembering what Krishna had told Arjuna in the *Bhagavad Gita*, the Hindu spiritual treatise she'd first read as an adolescent and then reread several times after Hitler invaded France. The text opens with the possibility of a massive war looming and the warrior Arjuna questions whether it is right to fight, especially since he would be battling against some of his own family members. His counsel Krishna replies that there is no way to avoid *karma*, or action, since abstaining from war is also an action. If there is a chance to negotiate peace, then peace should be sought, but that cannot happen if one side insists on creating conflict. Krishna tells Arjuna that those who act selflessly for the right cause, and who strive to do their dharmic obligation, are fulfilling God's work.

Noor closed her eyes, deciding that she would be able to take up a sword as long as she was not motivated by hate, only by the intent to heed her civil duty.

The next morning Noor awoke to someone shaking her. "What is it?" she asked sleepily. Another of her father's beliefs was that children should never be startled out of sleep, so he used to sing her and her siblings sacred Sufi songs to wake them up gently.

"The other recruits are here," Cecily told her. "They're all eating breakfast."

Noor sat up. "So?"

"So let's get a move on," Yolande said. "We don't want to be late and have de Wesselow blame it on having to do our hair and makeup or something."

Indeed the dining room was filled with male voices. There were only two seats left, at the foot of the table. Noor told her companions to sit down. "I can eat standing up just fine."

Cecily and Yolande were unusually quiet. Noor couldn't tell if it was because it was so early in the morning or if they were as nervous as she was. At any rate, none of the women ate much breakfast.

After a post-breakfast two-mile run, the new recruits were led onto a vast field. On a table in front of them lay a display of small handguns, rifles, and various bullets.

Their mustachioed instructor saluted de Wesselow before turning to his pupils and asking, "Have any of you had any experience with firearms?"

Noor kept her arms at her side as most of the men raised theirs. Yolande put her hand high while Cecily sort of waved.

The instructor made a note before focusing his gaze on Noor. "Around here it's kill or be killed. My job is to teach you how to survive in a hostile environment." He picked up a revolver and extended it toward Noor. "This is the lightest one we have."

She accepted it, thinking it was still enormously heavy in her hand.

The rest of the recruits all selected their guns. Yolande made for the bulky Thompson gun just as one of the men grabbed it. "It's too much for you to handle anyway," he told her.

"That may be," the instructor said. He took the gun off his shoulder and gave it to Yolande. "This is a Sten gun—the preferred weapon of SOE agents in the field. It's easier to operate and much lighter than the Tommy."

They spent the morning learning the finer points of their newly acquired weapons. Each recruit was given their own private teacher and section of the field with moving wooden targets. The targets were human-shaped cut-outs painted a grayish-green, clearly representing German soldiers.

Noor was taught to shoot close-range from her hip and to always pull the trigger twice, in what the SOE called a "double-tap."

"Don't worry so much about aiming—it has to be instinctive," her instructor, a man named Maxwell, told her, shouting to be heard above the noise. "Never hesitate."

Noor just had time to wonder, *But what if I shoot the wrong person?* before Maxwell hollered, "Now!"

A target popped up a few meters in front of her. She pointed her gun and fired twice.

"Again," he called as yet another target appeared.

Six more cut-outs and twelve bullets later, Maxwell held up his hand before walking to the nearest target. He checked to make sure they were not in anyone else's shot before waving Noor over. Together they examined her handiwork. Most of the cut-outs had at least been hit, and several had holes in what would have been their heads, had they been real people.

"Not bad for your first time," Maxwell commented.

Noor looked down in wonder at the still-smoking gun in her hand. "I did it," she said aloud.

"You certainly did," Maxwell agreed. He kicked the base of the cut-out. "Maybe someday you will have the chance to do the same to real Nazis."

CHAPTER 12

YVONNE

*Y*vonne arrived at the Bossard's farmhouse in the late afternoon. Her instructions were to escort the newcomer Roger Landes to Bordeaux. It was safer for a man to travel with a woman rather than by himself, especially because of the latest law signed by Marshal Pétain, the supposed head of Vichy France, which demanded that able-bodied men between 18 and 50 and single women from 21-35 "be subject to do any work that the Government deems necessary." Every day, hordes of people, mostly Jews, were being deported to Germany by train, never to be heard from again.

"Buckmaster suggested I spend the night in your flat," Landes said—rather shyly in Yvonne's opinion—after greeting her.

She hadn't been back to her room in a month, not since she and Pierre had left so abruptly following the suitcase incident. "I'm not sure that's a good idea—my landlord is a little too nosey for my liking. But I know of a hotel in Tours where you'll be safe," she told Landes. "I'll meet you tomorrow morning at the St. Pierre des Corps railway station."

. . .

Rather than go back to her room, Yvonne slept on a blanket spread over a pile of hay in the farmhouse. When she set off the next day on her trusty bicycle, she was dismayed to note that it was a gray, foggy morning. She could barely see a meter in front of her, and focused all of her attention on the road. Consequently, she didn't hear the horse cart come up behind her. She had no choice but to swerve off the road, cursing loudly at the driver, though he didn't turn around. She cursed again as she lost her balance and fell sideways into a ditch.

The spill was hard enough that she could see stars. She blinked them away before getting unsteadily to her feet to take stock of the damage. Her culottes had a giant rip and her hands were scraped from the landing. Everything else, including her knees, was covered in dirt and grass stains. She knew she would attract too much attention in trying to board the train looking as she did and had no choice but to return to her little room for fresh clothes and a shower.

When she arrived at Monsieur Caye's house, she discovered her hands were shaking from a combination of shock after the accident and uneasiness at what she'd find. The suitcase Gaspard had planted would be enough to draw anyone's suspicion. Perhaps Monsieur Caye had contacted the Gestapo to set up surveillance.

Yvonne unlocked the door to her room and opened it slowly, hoping she wouldn't find a member of the secret police waiting for her.

What she saw instead made her mouth drop open… the room was spotless. Someone had been in there, not only to clean and dust, but to wind the clock on the mantle, which kept perfect time.

Without bothering to investigate further, Yvonne found her own suitcase at the bottom of the closet and stuffed it with the rest of her belongings. She left the grounds as quickly as possible, and then fled to the station, only to find she'd missed both Landes and the train to Bordeaux. She had no choice but to take a room in the hotel to which she'd directed Landes the previous evening.

As she unpacked some of her much-needed underclothes, she felt something odd in the bottom of her suitcase. With trepidation, she dumped the contents on the floor. Several envelopes fell out. She picked one of them up, noting it was addressed to "Jacqueline Viallat," the name she had given Monsieur Caye. Perhaps it was a summons to report to a German court as soon as possible.

She tore open the envelope and opened the letter inside, which read:

My dearest Jacqueline,

Do not fear, I have been taking care of your room in your absence. Your mantle clock, like my heart, will continue to tick away the seconds until we can be together again.

Yours always,

Michel

The rest of the letters were similar: it seemed Monsieur Caye, or rather Michel, had written a letter for every day she'd been gone. The latter ones become bolder, with him outright confessing his love for Jacqueline.

Yvonne ripped them all up and put the scraps into the metal trash can before lighting a match. It was, she decided as she watched the paper burn, most definitely time to relocate.

CHAPTER 13

ANDRÉE

Gilbert Norman had arrived with a valise full of clothes for Prosper, another wireless set, and several hundred francs from the SOE for the new Physician network.

"We don't need money, we need guns," Prosper commented dryly once they'd reconvened at Andrée's apartment. "And money does not get you arms in Occupied France."

Gilbert shot Andrée a helpless look. She pretended to ignore him and got up to get them drinks as Prosper continued, "They call the SOE 'Churchill's secret army,' but what we really need is our own secret army of Frenchmen that will help assist in the Allied invasion."

"Who do we have in Paris?" Gilbert asked.

Prosper shook his head. "Not many so far. Just the Tambour sisters and some of their contacts. They said a man named Marsac was going to deliver a list of possible recruits from the Carte circuit, but we haven't heard from him yet."

Gilbert frowned. "Buckmaster told me before I left that Marsac fell asleep on the train to Paris. When he woke up, the case carrying all those names of contacts was gone."

Andrée's hand shook as she set down two glasses of whiskey. "You don't suppose the Nazis…"

Prosper gave a heavy sigh. "Nothing's ever easy, is it?" He sat back in his chair and clasped his hands behind his head. "Germaine Tambour did tell me about a place in Montmartre, where the jazz players meet."

Andrée sank into a chair. "Jazz? What does jazz have to do with the Resistance?"

"You'd be surprised." Prosper dropped his hands. "Tomorrow night we dress in full zazou-hilt and make our way to R-26."

"Got it, boss." Once again Gilbert turned his gaze to Andrée, but just then someone knocked on the door. Prosper reached for the gun in his holster as Andrée held up her hand.

It was Yvonne. Andrée led her into the kitchen.

"I didn't know you had company," Yvonne said. "You're the man from the other night," she continued upon seeing Gilbert.

Andrée folded her arms across her chest. "Yes, and I do believe he has something to tell you about one of our mutual acquaintances."

Gilbert had the grace to color slightly as he told Yvonne about the cyanide pill meant for Pierre Culioli.

Yvonne reached for Gilbert's glass and drained it. "I don't understand why Buckmaster would believe Gaspard over Pierre."

"It was obviously a misunderstanding," Prosper told her. "Forget about it. You and Pierre will work for me now. I heard you did a fine job organizing the reception the other night. We hope to have a few more before the end of the year. In the meantime, I'd like you to start establishing a team south of Paris. The word is that Pierre's got some credible connections with the locals—we're going to need their help hiding the goods the SOE will be providing in preparation for an Allied invasion."

Yvonne gave him a mock salute. "Yes sir."

Prosper nodded at Gilbert. "We'd better get going."

Yvonne touched Gilbert's sleeve. "You're the wireless operator, correct?"

"I am."

"Can you send a message to Roger Landes with the Scientist Network?" She pressed a piece of paper into his hands. "Tell him I'm sorry I couldn't meet him the other day. I'm sure he'll understand."

"No problem," Gilbert replied. He nodded at Andrée. "I'll see you tomorrow."

Andrée stretched her lips into an almost-smile.

"They're both so handsome," Yvonne said as soon as the door shut.

Andrée shrugged. "I hadn't noticed. Besides, Prosper is married."

"And Gilbert?"

She lifted her shoulders again. "I didn't ask." She decided to change the subject. "Have you heard of R-26?"

"No. Why?"

"Prosper wants us to go undercover there as zazous."

Yvonne scrunched her face. "It's been a while since I was in Paris. What's a zazou?

"It has something to do with jazz." Andrée ran her fingers through her dark curls. "Will you dye my hair?"

Yvonne smiled. "If you do mine… it's probably time for me to revamp my own look as well."

Andrée went to grab her pocketbook. She scooped the money Gilbert had left on the table into it before grinning at Yvonne. "Let's go shopping."

Yvonne told Andrée about the letters from her landlord as they walked to the nearest pharmacy. In addition to buying the hair dye —blonde for Andrée and red for Yvonne—they purchased a variety of eyeshadows and dark lipstick. As they stepped back out onto the street, Yvonne nudged Andrée and nodded toward a young girl passing them. She had on a short, flared skirt with heavy wooden shoes and, though the day was bright and sunny, she carried an umbrella.

"A zazou," Andrée said under her breath.

"C'mon," Yvonne said after the girl had passed. She pulled Andrée back into the drugstore, where Andrée found the requisite black umbrella. She purchased a pair of large sunglasses as well.

"You look great," Gilbert told Andrée when he arrived at her apartment the next night.

"Thanks," she replied, fluffing her new blonde coiffure. It turned out Yvonne had a penchant for styling hair. It was too bad the same couldn't be said for Andrée, who, despite the appearance-altering training the SOE had given them, had a hard time trying to hide her friend's streaks of gray. Yvonne had left to meet with Culioli wearing a headscarf to cover the horrendous dye-job.

Gilbert was dressed in a baggy suit coat over tight-fitting dark trousers. "You look the part as well," Andrée said, doing her best to hide her appreciation for the way his pants hugged his muscular legs.

"Will you help me with my hair?" Gilbert pulled on a stray lock. "It won't stay down."

Andrée studied him critically. "I think you need more cream." She took a blob of Brylcreem and rubbed it into his scalp. To distract from her unexpected nervousness, she asked, "What do you know about this place we are going to?"

"It's a jazz salon owned by the Perriers in Montmartre. Jazz has become somewhat of a symbol of clandestine defiance to the Germans. Prosper seems to think we'll find some allies within the club."

Finished, she wiped the cream off of her hands. "And what do you think?"

Gilbert shrugged. "Prosper's in charge. I do whatever he tells me to."

"How did you manage that get-up?" she asked, pointing at his outfit.

He gave her a sly smile. "I have my ways." He indicated the jacket he'd set on the couch. "That one's for Prosper. Apparently these jazz fiends like their coats to be really loose-fitting. We all know how Prosper is with his clothing, but I figured he can wear one of my regular-sized coats and it will be baggy on him."

"Is the coat from Miss Atkins?"

His grin widened. "You know it."

Someone knocked on the door. Andrée opened it to see Prosper dressed in a thick tie and unpolished shoes. "Evening."

Andrée moved aside to let him in.

Gilbert handed him the suit coat "Here you go, boss."

"Do we need a cover story going in?" Andrée asked.

Prosper fiddled with the sleeves of his coat. "I don't think it will be a problem, but we'll keep to us being brother and sister."

Gilbert reached over to adjust Prosper's collar. "What about me?"

Andrée glanced at the taller man. From his cocky demeanor and polished mannerisms, it was clear Gilbert had been raised wealthy. He had that arrogant attitude she'd only seen in people who didn't have to work for a living. Although Prosper had been a lawyer before the war, Andrée knew his parents had been working-class, like her own. "I don't think you'd pass as our sibling."

Gilbert held up both hands. "Okay then. I'm just a friend." He nodded at Prosper, "His, not yours, clearly."

Prosper shook his head. "You two are going to have to learn to get along if we're going to become a triumvirate." As if sensing Andrée's forthcoming protest, he stated firmly, "We need a talented wireless operator like Gilbert. Maybe even two if we can extend the Physician network to the size I'm thinking."

"And the first step would be to see what these jazz hounds have to offer." Gilbert extended his elbow toward Andrée. "Ready?"

She reluctantly accepted his arm. "I suppose so."

26 Rue Norvins was a spacious apartment located next to a paved courtyard. The man who answered the door seemed to ooze contempt for all the Vichy decrees. In defiance of the fabric rationing, his suit coat hung nearly to his knees, and he wore his hair

long at a time when the government was asking men and women alike to cut their hair and donate it to be made into blankets for the troops. In addition, the man had a yellow star, much like the one the Jews were forced to wear, pinned to the breast of his giant coat, though his star had the word 'swing' printed on it.

"Welcome to the Hot Club." The man motioned them in and then shuffled toward the bar, keeping time to the beat of the guitar coming from the corner of the smoky room. There were only a few people seated, all of them apparently absorbed in the music. The women were dressed similarly to Andrée, in fabric-rationing-friendly, low-cut, tight blouses and short skirts. She was happy to note the presence of another black umbrella lying near a woman's chunky-heeled shoes.

"Care for a drink?" Their host walked behind the bar as the newcomers situated themselves on stools.

"I'll have a beer and grenadine," Prosper replied.

"Same," Andrée said quickly, though the combination sounded somewhat unsavory.

"I'll have a glass of your best French wine," Gilbert declared.

The man gave him a funny look before turning to make the drinks.

Prosper narrowed his eyes at Gilbert, who returned with an apologetic shrug. Once the drinks had been delivered, Gilbert turned to watch the guitar player. "That's Django Reinhardt."

Prosper followed Gilbert's gaze. "I think you're right."

"Who's Django Reinhardt?" Andrée asked.

"Only the best jazz guitarist in the world," Gilbert replied. "Think he'll give me his autograph?"

As Django put the guitar down for a break, Gilbert and Prosper headed over to talk to him.

"He's a Gypsy," the bartender told Andrée. "Or as he says, Roma."

She sipped the grenadine beer. "I thought the Nazis…"

"Are detaining Gypsies? They are. But not Django. At least not if we can help it," he added in an undertone.

She took another gulp of beer. It was definitely overly sweet, but drinking it was a welcome distraction from her anxiousness. "Do you think it's strange to be running a jazz club during the Occupation?"

He shrugged. "We musicians see it as our civic duty to maintain something of the heady days of Free Paris. It's our own form of rebellion against the Boches, but…" he leaned forward. "I think I can offer some assistance in the organization you work with as well."

Andrée set her drink down. "How did you know I'm with the Resistance?"

"Well," he scoffed. "I didn't really think you were here to listen to the music." He stuck out his hand. "Charles Delaunay, though most people call me Benny. Tonight is all about jazz, but if you and your…" he nodded toward Prosper and Gilbert, "associates would like to come back tomorrow, I can introduce you to some of my friends. You might find them useful in your missions."

Andrée looked around the club. It did seem like an almost perfect cover. *Almost.* "Don't you worry about the Boches barging in? They're everywhere nowadays."

He shrugged. "The Nazis don't allow their soldiers in here. Hitler seems to think that jazz runs in opposition to his Reich, which I tend to agree with. Still, Goebbels hasn't completely banned jazz —he even allows them to play it on Radio Paris. They think their propaganda will come off better if it's accompanied by good music."

"Don't you mean great music?" Gilbert asked as he returned to the bar.

"Gilbert Norman, I'd like you to meet Benny Delaunay." Andrée finished her drink. The bottom was all grenadine and she grimaced.

After Gilbert shook Delaunay's hand, he set his still-full wineglass in front of Andrée. "You'll probably find this more to your taste."

She shot him a grateful smile. "Delaunay has invited us back tomorrow for a more 'intimate' gathering."

"A private concert?" Gilbert asked hopefully.

"More like a meeting amongst friends. *French* friends," Delaunay added.

Gilbert nodded knowingly. "Those are always the best kind." He held his arm out to Andrée. "Let's go tell Prosper the good news."

CHAPTER 14

FRANCINE

After Wanborough Manor, Francine was sent to Beaulieu, in Hampshire's New Forest, to what was called an agent "finishing school." She hadn't heard from Jack in more than a month and half-hoped he might be one of her fellow trainees, to no avail.

The goal of the finishing school was to teach the agents what France Antelme referred to as "the secret stuff." Although the gray-bricked, Gothic-style Palace House couldn't have been more different from Wanborough Manor, the routine was much the same: after another hearty lunch, Francine found herself in yet another classroom.

The squat, muscular man who stood behind the desk, however, looked the polar opposite from the lanky, dark-haired de Wesselow. He had short, curly hair that might have once been blonde but was now nearly all gray. "Name's Johnny Ramensky. I am probably in the best position to teach you how to break into, or out of places since I'm one of the most skilled safe-blowers there ever was. They call me Gentle Johnny because there's no need for violence when you do the job right."

Francine raised her hand. When he nodded at her, she asked, "You're a burglar?"

"Indeed. From early childhood, my feet were planted in the crooked path and took firm root."

"How did you end up working for the SOE?" Antelme inquired.

Ramensky shrugged. "Felt kind of guilty robbing people during rationing. Not to mention me mum likes to see me in uniform."

This earned a chuckle from the majority of the class.

The first thing Ramensky taught them was how to forge a key using a mold made from a bar of soap. After that, he showed them how to pick a safe with the aid of a piano wire. Francine found that she was quite good at this task. There was something eminently satisfying when the wire hit the sweet spot in the lock and the safe opened.

She was not nearly as enthused by the next lesson: coding. It was taught by a diminutive man with unruly black hair who introduced himself as Leo Marks before stating, "As you are to potentially become field agents, it's essential you learn how to send and receive coded messages. I'm here today to teach you our new system via Worked-Out Keys, better known as WOKs." He produced a tiny strand of fabric. "The transposition keys have been typed out on silk. They can be sewn into the lining of a jacket or skirt, and stay undetected if a German should run their hands over your clothing during a random street search."

He passed each of them a strip of silk and instructed them to copy the numbers printed upon it onto a piece of lined paper. Francine's looked like this:

14	2	13	4	6	12	1	5	7	15	3	9	11	15	10	8

Marks picked up a hunk of chalk and wrote, 'Fix dropping ground for agent will land anywhere soonest,' on the chalkboard. "Write each letter of this message under a number."

Francine did as directed, so that her paper ended up like this:

14	2	13	4	6	12	1	5	7	15	3	9	11	15	10	8
F	I	X	D	R	O	P	P	I	N	G	G	R	O	U	N
D	F	O	R	A	G	E	N	T	W	I	L	L	L	A	N
D	A	N	Y	W	H	E	R	E	S	O	O	N	E	S	T

Marks set down the chalk. "Now all you have to do is copy the letters underneath in order of appearance, starting with 1." He walked down the aisle, monitoring the agents as they wrote.

The new message became:

PEE IFA GIO DRY PNR RAW ITE NNT GLO UAS RLN OGH XON FDD OLE

Francine peered at it, noting that a few of the three-lettered groups formed recognizable words such as 'dry' and 'raw,' but the rest of it seemed like perfect gibberish.

One man—Francine thought his name might have been Johnson—threw his pencil on his desk rather forcefully before asking, "What happened to the poem codes I learned in my initial training? They are much easier than these, wonky WOKs or whatever you call them."

Marks grimaced. "I understand that, but these are far superior in that they cut down on unintentional but crucial mistakes such as misspelling words from the poem, or numbering your key wrong. Tiny slip-ups like that can turn a regular transmission into what we term an 'indecipherable.'"

Another man waved his silk in the air. "Talk about an indecipherable."

"WOKs work under the same principle as the old system, only without the need to memorize a poem," Marks replied. "A wireless telegraphy operator will get 200 of them when they leave for France, and each one can be burned after use. Unlike poems, you'll never be able to reveal individual WOKs, no matter how much torture the Gestapo uses."

Both Johnson and the other man seemed unconvinced.

Marks tried again, "If you look at it another way, if the Germans home into your poem, they can then interpret every message you transmit."

Johnson shook his head vigorously. "That could never happen."

Francine was doodling on the paper and only half-listening, but when she glanced at Marks, something in the expression on his face made her ask, "Has that happened?"

"Not in the F Section," Marks replied. "At least not yet." He spread his hands. "My ultimate objective is to make your tasks easier, especially for you wireless operators. In this way, you can get your message out more quickly, before the Germans detect your signal." He stuck his hands in his pockets. "The latest rumor is that they can do it in as little as three minutes, which is why the average lifespan of a W/T operator in the field is only six months."

Francine's hand froze. "What's that?" This was the first time she'd heard such a thing. "My husband is going to be a field operator."

"That's another reason to learn WOKs then," Marks replied gently. "And now for security checks…"

As Marks continued his lecture, Antelme, who up till now had been unusually quiet, put his hand on Francine's shoulder. "Your husband's an extremely capable operator and can outsmart any German he encounters. Given the choice, I'd want him as my wireless man over anyone else."

Francine managed a tiny smile. "Thanks."

Once the lesson had concluded, Francine trudged slowly back to her lodging, a small cabin on the grounds of the enormous estate. Her head hurt from all the coding and she was now even more worried about Jack. He'd never told her how dangerous being a wireless operator could be. Marks' words repeated in her head as her feet crunched through the fallen leaves. *Six months, six months, six months.*

The last time she'd heard from Jack, he mentioned he might be leaving for France at any time. If that were true, she'd have to finish her training as soon as possible so she could join him.

A loud, gruff voice coming from a clump of bushes forced Francine to stop walking. "Agazarian."

"Yes?" She focused her gaze on a man standing just to the right of the bushes. It was one of her trainers, Nobby Clark.

"It's time for another field exercise."

She looked up at the darkening sky. "Not again." Francine had quickly grown to despise being out in the New Forest after dark. Clark often took them out to practice 'bear crawling' on the ground or to teach them the appropriate signals to hail incoming aircraft. Once, on a near moonless night, he had deserted them, forcing Francine and her fellow agents to find their way back in pitch blackness.

"I want you to go to the Careys Manor Hotel in Brockenhurst. There's a contact there I need information from."

Francine sighed. Brockenhurst was a little more than 10 kilometers away. But then again, if she wanted to be put into the field with Jack as soon as possible, she would need to prove to all her trainers, including Nobby Clark, that she was more than capable to succeed at any task. "When do I leave?"

"Now. But this time I'll allow you to take a bicycle," Clark said.

It was dark and probably past curfew by the time Francine arrived at Careys Manor. In her hurry, she'd forgotten her watch.

She paused to think before she rang the bell at the concierge's desk. The SOE had instructed her to never use her true name when possible, but she would not be given an official code name until after she 'graduated' from Beaulieu. And since Clark had told her to make contact with his man at this hotel, she reasoned, he'd probably given the concierge her real name.

When the uniformed man approached, she told him, "Francine Agazarian."

"Ah, yes, Mrs. Agazarian, we've been expecting you."

Francine hadn't worn her wedding ring since she'd begun training and wondered how the concierge knew she was a "Mrs."

He looked at a spot in the lobby past Francine's shoulder and cleared his throat loudly. She turned to see a man reading a newspaper. As if in slow motion, he folded the paper and Francine caught a glimpse of his face. It was more drawn than she remembered, with dark circles underneath both eyes, but it still closely resembled the visage she'd dreamt about every night for the past few months.

"Jack!" she exclaimed, running into her husband's arms. "I missed you so much," she sobbed into his chest as he stroked her hair.

He put his hand under her chin and tilted it before kissing her. She moved her hands to his arms, feeling unfamiliar muscles underneath his thin jacket. Time once again slowed until he broke from her embrace. "Let's go upstairs," he said, brandishing a key from his pocket. "I got us a room."

Jack started kissing her again as soon as the door to their room shut. "I've missed you too, Francie," he said as he guided her to the bed. His kisses went from tender to needy, and she eagerly returned the sentiment. She helped him remove his shirt, noting with relish that, due to all of his training, his already well-developed chest and arms had become herculean.

Sometimes when he kissed her like that, Francine couldn't help wonder why such an Adonis had chosen her to be his wife, but this time she was able to suppress her feelings of inadequacy. Jack was here now, and nothing else mattered. Not even the fact that he was about to leave her.

After they'd made love, Francine lifted her knees to her chest and held them there.

"What are you doing?" Jack asked.

Francine's reply was simple. "I want a baby." It had suddenly occurred to her that if she couldn't always have Jack with her, at least she could have a little piece of him. And if he knew she was pregnant with his child, he might decide to stay, after all.

"It's not a good time," he countered tersely.

She relaxed her legs. "Jack, is there ever really a good time to have a baby? Does it matter when two people love each other?"

"Francie, we're at war. And France needs us both."

For some reason, her mind flew to France Antelme, her closest friend from training. "Maybe France just needs you, not me."

"Sweetheart," he reached out to stroke her hair. "Are you having second thoughts about going over?"

"No." *I'm having second thoughts about you going over.* Why hadn't he told her how dangerous his job would be? Francine swallowed hard, trying to get rid of the lump in her throat. Even if he had told her, she knew she would have never been able to persuade him not to leave. And clearly her own refusal to go wouldn't convince him either. "I'm just going to miss you."

"It won't be too long."

"Less than six months?"

His eyebrows raised. "I don't know. Why?"

She shook her head. "No reason."

"Francie, you don't have to do this if you don't want to. I'm going to accomplish whatever they tell me to, and do my part to help defeat Hitler. When the war's over, and the Allies have won, then we can start a family."

She sat up. She wasn't afraid for herself, just for him. But she also knew she'd never be able to wait for him alone in England. She had been given the opportunity to be in the field with him, an opportunity she knew many women whose husbands had enlisted would have jumped at. "If you go, I go. I've come this far."

"I was hoping you would say that." Jack rubbed his face. "Let's table the baby discussion for now. I've got a big day tomorrow, and until then," he reached for her, "I'm going to enjoy every moment I can with my wife."

CHAPTER 15

YVONNE

*Y*vonne glanced at the black sky. There were approximately two weeks each month when there wasn't enough moon to land parachutes or supplies. Tonight was one of those evenings—the lack of moonlight made it ideal for sabotage. She and Pierre had left late that morning to travel by train to Montrichard and bicycled out to a railway tunnel in the waning daylight. Now the sun had set, it was time for action.

They heard a low whistle reverberate through the darkness. Pierre immediately returned the signal with a whistle of his own.

Yvonne could hear a man's boots crunching through the leaves. "Do you know where I can get lighter fluid?" he asked, using the expected code phrase.

"You must mean gasoline, of course," Pierre replied.

The man crept closer to the narrow beam of Yvonne's torch. He wore dark clothing and a cap that obscured his face. "There are sentries on either side of the tunnel."

"We are well aware," Pierre acknowledged. "But there's another opening." He motioned for the man to follow him up a slight embankment. Yvonne trailed after them, walking both her bicycle and Pierre's.

Pierre stopped suddenly and aimed his flashlight at an iron grating. "This is an air shaft that leads straight into the railroad underpass. We can plant an explosive inside, and it should blow the whole tunnel."

The man bent down to inspect the interior of the shaft, but the light from his torch did not penetrate far. "What if there is another grating blocking the way? We wouldn't be able to get the bomb deep enough to do any significant damage to the line."

Yvonne set the bikes down and stepped toward the men. "Lower me into the shaft and I'll plant the bomb."

She could feel the stranger sizing up her barely five-foot, forty-kilogram frame. "It might work."

"No," Pierre said. "It's too dangerous."

"Nonsense," Yvonne replied. "What else am I here for?" The railway represented a key target: the tracks in question eventually led to Berlin and were a supply line for Nazi troops and ammunition. If they successfully destroyed the tunnel, they could set the Boches back a few days, or even a week.

"Do you know how to detonate a time-pencil?" the man asked.

"Of course. I was specially trained by the SOE," she told him, with more than a hint of pride.

Pierre resignedly handed the device to Yvonne. It consisted of a small block of 808 explosive and a time-pencil detonator. The whole thing weighed less than half a kilogram. He also gave her a roll of sticky tape to fix the bomb to the wall of the air shaft.

It took them mere minutes to quadruple a length of parachute cord for extra support and lower her into the shaft. Luckily there wasn't another grating below. Hovering in mid-air, Yvonne held the time-pencil against the wall and used the end of her flashlight to break the copper tubing. She then tucked her flashlight under her armpit and lifted the time-pencil to her eye to see if she could see through it. Something shook the cord, nearly causing her to drop the bomb. *"Merde alors!"* she cursed as her flashlight fell instead. As there was no other light in the tunnel, she couldn't see if the time-pencil had been detonated or not.

"Are you finished yet?" Pierre hissed down the shaft. "We've got to pull you up now."

"Just a minute," Yvonne said, her voice echoing through the shaft. "These things take time if you want them done right."

Working in the dark, she managed to place the explosive on the wall with the tape. She crossed her fingers that the time-pencil had been detonated properly before tugging hard on the cord for Pierre to pull her back up.

Once she was back on solid ground, Yvonne glanced up to see a man wearing a beret and carrying a clipboard a few meters away, heading right toward them. "What's he doing here after curfew?" she whispered.

"I think he's a native, here to survey the tracks," Pierre replied.

The man seemingly hadn't spotted them yet, but there was no way they could pedal away on their bicycles without being seen.

Yvonne put her hand on the pistol tucked into the pocket of her culottes. "Should we kill him?"

"No. I have another idea." Pierre wrapped his arms around Yvonne. His mustache tickled her upper lip as his lips met hers.

"Well, what do we have here?" the Frenchman asked as he came upon them.

Pierre stopped kissing Yvonne and managed to look surprised. "Oh, I'm sorry. I didn't know anyone else was around." He gave Yvonne a sheepish look. "Guess we've been caught."

She turned to the man, hoping he wouldn't be able to smell the almond odor of the 808 on her hands. "We came here because we thought it would be a good hiding place. My husband is a very jealous man."

The Frenchman held up his hand. "Say no more. I understand affairs of the heart. But now I'm afraid you must be going—the Boches don't like anyone near their tracks, otherwise known as the arteries they use to bleed France dry of coal and food."

"Of course." Yvonne couldn't help but check her watch. They only had about 45 minutes left until the time-pencil ran out. "Carry on," she told the man before picking up her bicycle.

Pierre and Yvonne pedaled away from the embankment. They'd

lost track of their Resistance comrade, but Yvonne assumed he'd waited before the Frenchman was far enough away before exiting the bushes and making his escape.

Pierre braked as they reached a small grove of trees. "Let's wait here to see what happens."

Yvonne parked her bicycle without saying anything. Her heart was hammering and her face felt hot, but whether that was due to their close call with the Frenchman, anticipation of the explosion yet to come, or because of Pierre's kiss, she wasn't sure. *I'm too old to be a giddy schoolgirl,* she reminded herself. Besides, Pierre, with his short stature and ludicrous mustache, was not her type.

Yvonne checked her watch again. There should have been a few minutes left on the detonator, but the silent night was suddenly punctured by the thunderous burst of splintering metal and imploding brickwork. She shot Pierre a wide grin before maneuvering to get a better view. It was too dark to see anything, but the fact that her ears were still ringing from the blast must surely have been a good sign. "Leave it to the SOE to not have accurate timing on their fuses."

Though Pierre was standing next to her, his voice sounded as though he were meters away. "Let's get out of here before anyone finds us."

CHAPTER 16

NOOR

*N*oor stared at the paper, sweat forming under her arms. De Wesselow had only given them ten minutes to commit the plans of an entire building to memory. While her background in music had helped her to interpret Morse fairly well, it didn't do much for memorizing blueprints. When de Wesselow announced they only had five minutes left, Noor sucked in her breath, realizing she had just wasted half her time. She stared down at the blueprint, dots and dashes swimming before her eyes.

Bang!

Startled, she looked up, thinking a chair had been knocked over. Instead, two men had rushed into the room, one of them in hot pursuit of the other. The first man fled past the row of desks and out the other door as his stalker shouted something and aimed a pistol at the ceiling. As soon as she heard the second gunshot, Noor flew under her desk.

There were a few more shots and then the room was silent. She assumed by the second slamming of the door that both men were gone.

"Right," de Wesselow said loudly as the rest of the class tittered.

Noor peeked out from her refuge to see them all staring at her. She sheepishly resumed her seat as de Wesselow passed out new sheets of paper. "I hope you were paying attention because we are now going to put your observation abilities to the test."

He began firing off questions. "How many gunshots were there?"

Noor counted on her fingers. She figured there had been one before she dropped to the floor and then maybe two after that. *Or three.* Noor drew a line through the 3 and after another moment of hesitation, wrote '4.'

She was so busy concentrating on the first question that she missed what de Wesselow asked next.

"Question three: what did the second man shout?" he spouted off, then, "What were the men wearing?"

By the time de Wesselow told them to put their pencils down, Noor had seven blank lines on the paper from when she didn't catch the question, and she wasn't confident that she'd given the right answers to the ones she'd heard. Her face felt hot as she passed in her paper.

De Wesselow glanced at it and frowned. "All right, take a five-minute breather outside," he announced when he'd collected all of the papers.

Noor went out into the sunshine, a rarity for mid-December, and joined Cecily and Yolande, who were standing off to the side, away from the male recruits.

"How did you do?" Yolande asked.

"Not good," Noor replied. "I'm sure you saw me under the desk. I guess I panicked when I heard that first gunshot."

Yolande shrugged. "They probably figured we don't have to deal with the same stress in the classroom as we would in the field. They had to mimic the danger somehow."

"I think I did pretty well," Cecily said.

Noor managed a smile for her friend, noting that Cecily's accent sounded more authentically French than it had when they first met. But deep down, her friend's success only served to make Noor feel more like a failure.

. . .

When de Wesselow called them back in, he started by saying, "I'm sure you can guess that some of you did an adequate job on the test." Perhaps it was Noor's imagination, but it seemed he looked directly at her as he added, "And some of you did not get any questions right." He picked up a sheet of paper. "Cecily Lefort managed to get all ten correct." He put the sheet back down. "Can you give us a hint as to how you've developed such excellent observation skills, Miss Lefort?"

Cecily sat up straighter, her face pale. She thought for a minute before replying, "I see colors."

"What do you think *we* see, black and white?" the man sitting next to her asked.

"No," Cecily retorted. "I mean I think I see colors more vividly than most people. Sometimes they even appear as if they are coming off a person." She pointed at the man. "Like right now I see dark brown surrounding you, so dark it's almost black."

"That's ridiculous," the man spat back. "Colors are just reflected wavelengths that stimulate the photoreceptors in your eyes."

De Wesselow cleared his throat. "Thank you, Miss Lefort, for that amusing, uh, insight. Now, to move on..."

He posted a large-scale drawing of the earlier blueprint on the board, explaining the best entry points for the building, which he stated was the French headquarters of the Nazi secret police on Avenue Foch. Noor could tell from Cecily's slumped form that she was no longer listening.

"What's wrong?" Noor asked Cecily as they walked back to their bunk half an hour later.

Cecily sniffed. "That man, Nora. He made fun of me in front of the whole class."

Noor put her hand on Cecily's arm. "He was rude, but you don't have to let it affect you."

Cecily stopped walking and glanced at Noor. "I used to see

colors coming off you too, Nora. Yours was this reddish-violet that I'd never noticed on anyone before." Her eyes filled with tears. "But now it's gone. It's as though my whole world has gone gray."

Noor led her over to a nearby bench. "I know how you feel." She patted the space beside her and waited until Cecily sat down before she continued, "When I was little, I used to think I saw fairies. They lived in flower petals, and to me they were as concrete as the flowers themselves."

Cecily dabbed at her eyes with a handkerchief. "What happened to make you stop seeing them?"

Noor shrugged. "One time I asked a grown-up, my uncle in fact, about them. I assumed he saw them too—that everyone saw them—but when he laughed at me, I realized he thought I was imagining them. After that, they were gone, and the garden was full of vacant flowers. It was like losing many good friends all at once."

"Did the fairies ever come back?" Cecily asked.

Noor hesitated, wondering if she should lie. Cecily had always been better at every task at Wanborough, and it felt strange for Noor to now find herself in the role of mentor. "No," she said finally.

Cecily kicked at a rock. "It's funny how someone else's words can destroy your whole world."

Noor had often thought the same thing. "Perhaps it's because we're too worried about people judging us. So what if some people see fairies, or colors, or ghosts when others can't? Maybe we just need to accept that we are different and not care what everyone else thinks."

"I agree, though it sounds easier than it is," Cecily replied. "Someday I hope to live free from other people's expectations."

"Speaking of expectations," Yolande had appeared beside them. Clearly she was taking her stealth training to heart. "Nora, de Wesselow would like to see you in his office."

Noor felt her stomach drop. *This can't be good.* She reached out to touch Cecily's shoulder, trying to recall some of the hope that had dissipated at Yolande's summons. "Someday the colors and fairies will come back to us."

"What's this about fairies now?" Yolande took her spot on the bench as Noor headed back to the main building with a heavy heart.

It was now dusk and the first floor of the main house was almost all dark, save for a light coming from an open door off the parlor. De Wesselow sat behind a large, ornate desk and the lamplight made his face look ominous, which only added to Noor's nervousness.

De Wesselow gestured for her to sit down in the chair opposite before asking, "Do you know why I wanted to see you?"

She straightened her skirt. "Does it have something to do with my performance today?"

He nodded.

"Sir, I want to apologize…"

He held up his hand. "No need to apologize. Many people would have had such a reaction to the sound of a gun, though perhaps being easily startled is not the best trait for an SOE agent. But there's something I want to know." He picked up a pen. "Nora, let's say—hypothetically—you are in France, working for the Resistance, and you receive an order to sabotage a munitions factory."

She sighed inwardly. It was yet another one of de Wesselow's tests. "Is it after hours?"

He paused. "Does it matter?"

"Yes," Noor replied softly.

He scribbled something on the paper. "Okay, the factory is empty, but it is guarded by the Milice, the Vichy police. As you recall, some members of the Resistance consider the Milice more heinous than the Gestapo because they are native Frenchmen. Could you kill the policemen in order to gain access to the factory?"

There was only one thing she could say. "No."

He put his pen down. "That's what I thought."

Fearing she had said something wrong, Noor leaned forward. "Does this mean you won't let me continue the training?" Everyone at Wanborough knew they could release a potential agent who failed a task at any time. Many times Noor woke up to find one of her fellow recruits had 'disappeared.' Yolande had told them the rumor was they weren't sent home since they knew too much about the SOE's covert operations, but rather to a remote place, where their top-secret knowledge could do no harm, until the war was over.

De Wesselow looked thoughtful. "I'm told you have a natural knack for Morse."

She nodded. "I had some preliminary instruction with the WAAF."

"We don't have any female wireless operators in the field yet, but I can probably convince Buckmaster to allow you to do W/T training instead of becoming a courier."

She'd originally asked the same thing of Captain Jepson, figuring—rightly it would seem now—that she was more suited for transmissions than treachery. "Please sir, I'll do anything that you ask."

"I know." He ran his hand through his hair. "That's why I'm reluctant to let you go, even if you have the worst record at any of our tests." He held up his hand as Noor was about to protest. "Initially. But I've also seen you put your heart and soul into your exercises, both physical and mental. Your morning run has become a full minute faster since you first got here, and I have no doubt that the next time you are asked to make observations, you would do 100% better."

She moved her right hand under her skirt to cross her fingers. "I would, sir. I was just… thrown off by the scenario today, but I won't allow it to happen again."

He lit a cigar and took a puff. To Noor, it seemed to take forever before he said, "See that you don't. I'm going to give my recommendation for you to move forward in your training."

She relaxed her hand. "Thank you, sir."

He nodded as Noor rose to leave.

"And Nora?"

She turned back around. "Yes?"

He exhaled his smoke, filling the room with the stench of cigar. "Don't make me regret my decision."

Noor shook her head vigorously. "I won't sir. You have my word."

He ashed his cigar. "That's good enough for me, but let's hope it's good enough for Buckmaster."

CHAPTER 17

ANDRÉE

*S*ometimes, as she went about her daily routine of making the rounds of lock boxes throughout the city to pick up messages, Andrée found she forgot that she was one of the hunted. It was as though she, Prosper, and Gilbert were just all on a grand adventure together, with only a hint of the danger that lurked underneath.

She felt that same exhilaration the afternoon Prosper arranged to meet her and Gilbert in the alleyway outside the jazz club. Once again they were clad in their zazou gear and were about to enter the club via a hidden door when they heard a woman scream.

Gilbert's self-assured swagger was absent as he walked over to peek around the corner.

"What is it?" Prosper asked.

"It's the Secret Police. They are doing another round-up of Jews." Gilbert's voice dropped. "Looks like it's women and children this time, judging by the occupants of the black Maria."

"What's a black Maria?" Andrée asked.

She tried to get a better look, but Gilbert blocked her with his arm. "A Gestapo van," he replied.

Andrée's high spirits left her like a deflating balloon, as someone shouted, "Dirty Jew, be gone!" This was followed by a child scream-ing, "*Maman!*"

A gunshot sounded and the screaming stopped.

In the ensuing silence, Gilbert dropped his briefcase and cocked a fist.

Prosper's voice was quiet but firm. "Leave it."

"No, boss, I can't."

Prosper put a restraining hand on Gilbert's arm. "I know how you feel, but going out there will only get you killed. There are other ways to fight the Milice."

He guided Gilbert toward the door of the jazz club and Andrée trailed after them, her heart now heavy. Scenes like that brought her back to reality, demonstrating how much they were all risking their lives. At the same time such incidents also reminded her just how important their job was to the people of France.

Benny Delaunay greeted them once again. He seemed about to make one of his quips, but changed his mind when he saw their downtrodden expressions. Instead he waved for them to follow him up several flights of stairs. "You'll find this room perfectly suitable for your purposes." He paused at an innocuous-looking door. "No one even knows it is here."

He led them into a small room filled with at least twenty men, many of them wearing black or red berets and beige overcoats. One of them, a short man with a days-old beard, rose from his folding chair to approach Prosper. "Are you another one of de Gaulle's worthless henchmen?"

Prosper looked taken aback. "No, I am not with the Free French."

"You are not French at all." It was not a question.

"No," Prosper replied. "But I am here with a goal, which I think is the same as yours—the liberation of this country."

The bearded man looked doubtful. "We have been doing fine on our own." He nodded toward the rest of the men. "Members of our group have already killed several uniformed Fascists in Bordeaux and Nantes, even in the Paris Metro."

Andrée had been informed of these uprisings in her training. Most had been committed by the *Francs-Tireurs et Partisans,* or FTP. The Wehrmacht army had retaliated by murdering fifty French citizens as payback for every slain German soldier. From the comfort of his hideout in London, General de Gaulle had pleaded with the FTP, saying that killing one German was not worth the lives of so many innocent people. Still, the attacks had continued.

Andrée turned to Gilbert, who was standing next to her in the corner of the room. "They're communists," she said in a low voice. "Should we really be providing them with guns?"

"Does it matter?" Gilbert whispered back. "They want to fight. As far as I'm concerned, I'll give anyone a gun as long as they use it to kill Nazis."

"We don't need your training," the bearded man told Prosper. "What we need is supplies, specifically arms."

"If it is weapons you need, we can provide them." Prosper nodded at Gilbert and Andrée, who moved to join him. Gilbert set his briefcase on the table and undid the locks, revealing several steel components tucked inside.

The bearded man peered at the contents. "You planning on unclogging a toilet?"

"Toilet?" Andrée asked.

The man pointed at one of the metal pieces. "Looks like a plumbing pipe."

"These are Sten gun parts," Gilbert stated. "So easy to put together, even a woman can do it."

Andrée rolled her eyes as she picked up the barrel and began to assemble the gun. "It can shoot up to 500 rounds a minute," she said as she inserted the bolt, which became jammed. Gilbert reached out to try to help her, but she snatched it away and tried again. This time the bolt slid into the barrel with a satisfying click. She stuck the spring in and then attached the handle before passing it to the bearded man.

He gave a low whistle as he examined it. "It's pretty light."

"Yes. It will even work after being submerged in water," Andrée told him. "And it takes almost any stolen Wehrmacht ammunition, even from a Luger or Schmeisser submachine gun."

Gilbert folded his arms across his chest and gazed at her thoughtfully.

"Where can we get more of these guns?" a short, squat man asked. "Our numbers are growing steadily, especially after the *Service du travail obligatoire*. The last thing our comrades want to do is become German slaves and be forced to manufacture their war machines."

Andrée looked at Prosper, who shrugged. "We'll ask London for them."

The short man nodded. "You are new here, so I'm going to give you some advice. Be aware of the Milice. Their goal is to help the Germans to destroy the Resistance and they take no prisoners." He pointed to someone in the back of the group. "They shot his brother as he lay wounded in the hospital. They're trying to infiltrate our networks, so you should be mindful: the enemy walks among us."

A chill ran down Andrée's spine. One by one, she gazed at the men in the room, most of whom stared back with expressionless faces.

"We will be on the look-out." Prosper turned to address the room. "We will get you the supplies you need. In return we ask that you help us prepare for the day the Allies land in France."

"And when will that be?" someone asked.

Prosper held out his hands. "I have not been told an exact date, but it may come as soon as next spring."

"Let us hope so," the same man replied.

"Put your faith in Churchill."

"We'll put our faith in you. What is your name?" someone else asked.

"I am Prosper and my circuit is called Physician."

"Physician? Why not the Prosper Network?" the short man asked.

"Why not indeed?" Gilbert whispered under his breath.

Andrée nodded at the short man. "Go ahead and call it the Prosper Network from now on. And tell all your friends."

Prosper walked the short man to the door and grasped his hand. They spoke in hushed voices as Prosper followed him out.

As the rest of the men began to leave, Gilbert closed his suitcase before asking Andrée, "Can I take you to dinner?"

"Now?" She gave him a strange look. "You do realize this is Occupied France?"

"Yes, but I also know that the black market is thriving." He took a wad of bills from his pocket. "Anything is for sale. Well, except maybe butter and milk." He put the money back in his billfold.

She shook her head. "It's too dangerous. And how can you be seen out and about? If you were actually a French citizen, you'd be subject to the forced labor draft."

"Buck gave me papers that justify my exclusion." He stepped closer to her. "And I know the restaurant owner. He says the Boches don't normally come on Tuesdays because they're not allowed to serve alcohol."

She glanced around the now empty room. "What about Prosper?"

"He's doing some paperwork tonight and then leaving in the morning."

"Leaving? Where's he going? I'm supposed to accompany him at all times."

"You're not his keeper. He's going to meet up with Pierre Culioli tomorrow. You have to admit, Prosper's accent has improved since he's been in France. He doesn't need you to accompany him every-where." Gilbert grabbed her hand as she started to back away. "Prosper was the one who told me to take you out for a nice dinner, to reward you for all your hard work."

"Well, if Prosper suggested it…" Andrée said doubtfully.

"Why do you hate me?" Gilbert asked once they were seated at a corner table in the dim restaurant.

"I don't hate you. I just find you… a little irritating."

"Why?"

Andrée considered. It wasn't the quality of Gilbert's work—he was just as dedicated to his job as she. And he had always been respectful of her. It was just… "You remind me of the boys I went to primary school with." Most of them had been cruel, taunting her for having a working-class family and accusing her of trying to rise above her station. But she couldn't tell Gilbert that—the SOE had forbidden its agents to talk about their former lives.

A waiter delivered tall glasses filled with a dark liquid. Andrée assumed it was grape juice until she tasted it. It was red wine, thick and sticky-sweet, but wine just the same. The restaurant probably just wanted to hide the fact they were serving it by using water glasses. *Or the Boches had destroyed all of their stemware.*

To change the subject, she asked Gilbert about the papers Buck had given him to get out of service.

He took a big gulp of wine before replying, "They say I have syphilis." He grinned at Andrée's visible reaction. "But don't worry, it's in remission."

She had to assume he was joking. The waiter returned then with their meal: rabbit stew. Gilbert picked up a cooked carrot and made a big show of imitating Bugs Bunny. His eyebrows raised in surprise when Andrée giggled.

"Are you shocked that I can laugh?" she asked.

"No." His face reddened. "I'm just bowled over by how delightful a sound it is."

"What did you think it would sound like? A witch's cackle?"

"No. I don't think you are a witch at all. No matter how mean you've been to me."

Andrée set her spoon down. "I haven't been that mean to you."

"No," Gilbert agreed. "Just dismissive."

He looked so earnest that Andrée declared, "I won't be any more." She grinned. "Just as long as you keep your Bugs Bunny imitations to a minimum."

He reached out to shake her hand. "It's a deal."

It was nearing curfew by the time they left the restaurant. Gilbert walked her back to her new flat in the 10th Arrondissement.

He was clearly not impressed by the seedy neighborhood, brimming both with women of the night and men doing their best to avoid the labor draft by hiding out on the dark streets.

He glanced at the café on the first floor of her apartment building, clearly baffled. "You live right above the Bony-Lafont gang's hangout?"

"The who?"

"C'mon." He took her arm and led her away. "Bony is an ex-police officer wanted for extortion and Lafont was a gangster before the war. Now their racket is to work with the Gestapo to stalk Resistance members and to use painful coercion methods when they catch them. Not the sort you want to associate with."

Andrée squinted up at a street sign. The Nazis had changed them all to German, but, due to the blackout, it was too dark to read it anyway. "Where are we going?"

"You're going to have to stay in my apartment until we find you a better place." The corner of Gilbert's mouth turned up. "Don't worry, I won't try anything." He patted the note tucked into his coat pocket. "Wouldn't want to give you syphilis."

When they arrived at Gilbert's apartment, a tiny hole-in-the-wall that he kept unexpectedly tidy, he graciously offered Andrée the only bedroom and a clean shirt to sleep in.

However, after getting into bed, she found she couldn't sleep. The sheets smelled like Gilbert's cologne and every time she closed her eyes, she saw gangsters with Sten guns chasing small children wearing yellow stars on their coats. She threw the bedclothes back, realizing she was disappointed that Gilbert was sticking to his promise of not trying anything with her.

She took the comforter off the bed and crept into the living room. Gilbert was sprawled out on a blanket on the floor, snoring softly.

He woke up with a start as she curled up beside him. "I did give you the bed," he told her sleepily. "I know it's not much, this being war-time France and all, but it has to be better than the floor."

"I like it right here," Andrée replied. She nestled under his arm and closed her eyes. After a moment, she opened them again before nudging him. "You don't really have syphilis, do you?"

"No."

The last thought Andrée had before she fell into a peaceful oblivion was "good."

CHAPTER 18

YVONNE

*W*ith Prosper's permission, Pierre Culioli set up a subcircuit which he named *Adolphe* in honor of his mustache. Pierre had no need for the list of names from the Carte circuit that had been in Marsac's stolen briefcase. He'd spent most of his life in south-central France, and had plenty of friends, and friends of friends, willing to join Adolphe.

After the *Service du travail obligatoire* was passed, many young men had fled into the countryside to escape being deported to Germany and formed their own resistance groups called *maquis*. Pierre and, to a lesser extent Yvonne, set about recruiting these *maquisards* into Adolphe, with much success.

When Prosper met them at a café in Meung-sur-Loire, a small town about twenty kilometers west of Orléans to check on their progress, he was visibly impressed with how quickly Adolphe had expanded in such a short time.

"It was mostly Pierre's doing," Yvonne explained. "He has contacts everywhere."

Pierre waved his hand. "Not true. Yvonne has been a great help. She manages to charm any gendarme who stops us to ask questions."

She shot him a grateful smile.

"And where are you staying, when you find time to rest?" Prosper asked.

Pierre shrugged. "Wherever we can."

Yvonne made sure no one else was in earshot before adding, "Sometimes we sleep in the woods with the maquisards."

Prosper searched Pierre's face and then did the same with Yvonne's. From the way he frowned, Yvonne could guess what he was thinking: *you are both too old to be sleeping outside.* "It's getting colder out. Let me introduce you to a couple I met when I first landed— the Flamencourts. They let me stay with them while my leg healed. The patriarch, Edouard, is a poultry farmer and often smuggles people across the demarcation line in his wagon. I know he'd be willing to provide you a safe place to recoup."

"We are fine with the way it is," Pierre replied.

Prosper threw a few francs down on the table and then stood. "Nonetheless, I'd hate for Adolphe's good work to be halted because its leaders come down with pneumonia. The Flamencourts' farm is not far from here."

He led them on bicycles across the frost-covered fields to a well-kept farmhouse beside a small stream. "This is all the Flamencourts' property," Prosper told them as he dismounted. "They call it *Petit Aunay*." He pointed toward a neat row of sheds. "That's where they keep their incubators for the chicks."

Yvonne watched with amusement as a family of geese waddled over a bridge. "How idyllic."

"You'd never suspect the Flamencourts' involvement with the Resistance, would you?" Prosper asked.

Yvonne shook her head. The SOE had taught her that the ideal local recruit would be self-employed in the type of job that allowed them to move freely about the countryside without suspicion, such as postmen, doctors, and priests. And, apparently, poultry farmers.

An unfamiliar voice with a thick French accent called out. "François, you are back so soon?"

Yvonne turned to see a man wearing a dark beret over his graying hair approach .

"Yes, Monsieur Flamencourt." Prosper indicated Pierre and Yvonne. "I've brought some friends in need of a place to stay."

Monsieur Flamencourt's wrinkled eyes were kind as he shook their hands. "Of course. Friends of François are always welcome."

"We don't mean to impose," Pierre stated.

"It is no worry," Monsieur Flamencourt assured him. "We are well hidden here, but if anyone asks, you are associates of mine from…" he paused and looked at Yvonne.

"Brest," she replied. "We're refugees from the bombing." She took Pierre's hand. "We're married."

"Yes, of course." Monsieur Flamencourt seemed satisfied with Yvonne's cover story. "I will ask my wife to get your room ready."

"Thank you," Pierre told Prosper, dropping Yvonne's hand. "This should work out fine."

Prosper nodded. "I think so." He led them to a wooden bench by the stream. "And now I have a favor to ask of you two."

"Anything," Pierre replied.

"We are expecting a shipment tomorrow night. Do you know of any good DZs in the region?"

DZ meant drop zone, Yvonne mentally translated.

"I do," Pierre said. "I used to travel this area as a tax inspector. There's an abandoned air strip to the west of town."

"Great." Prosper made a note on a slip of paper. "I will tell Gilbert to wire the details to Buck." He pocketed the paper. "Can you arrange a team? We are expecting several packages and a few men."

"Yes, Yvonne and I will personally see to it."

"Thank you both." Prosper shook each of their hands before remounting his bicycle. "I will see you again soon."

Dinner at the Flamencourts' was only slightly awkward. Madame Flamencourt, a pretty woman with blonde hair, was much younger than her husband. She asked polite questions of Pierre and Yvonne but avoided probing too deeply. Monsieur Flamencourt's secretary, Mademoiselle Durand, also joined them. They were surrounded by servants, and Yvonne wasn't sure who knew what happened behind the scenes, so there was no talk of the Resistance.

Afterward, Madame Flamencourt showed them to their room before bidding them goodnight.

"I'll take the floor," Pierre said once they were alone.

"We can trade off if you'd like," Yvonne offered.

"No," Pierre laid a blanket down and then stretched out. "It's better for my back anyway."

The weather the next night, though cold, was clear and perfectly suitable for a drop. The moon hung low and luminous as Yvonne and Pierre bicycled to the DZ. There they met Théo Bertin, one of the newer members of the Adolphe subcircuit. Théo was an ideal addition to the reception party, because his home on the edge of town would serve as the safehouse for the new arrivals and, as he himself stated, he knew the surrounding woods like the 'back of his hand.'

"Because he's a poacher," Pierre whispered to Yvonne.

"I heard that," Théo said in a louder voice. He patted his ample belly. "How else am I supposed to keep a figure like this with all the rationing?"

"I'm not judging you." Pierre licked his finger and held it in the air. "The wind is blowing south." He indicated a clear spot, void of any shrubbery. "If the plane comes north, the parachutes will blow there."

Yvonne, Pierre, and Théo laid their torches in a straight line to help orient the plane. Pierre was in charge of flashing the Morse signal to the pilot to let him know the DZ was secure.

After everything was ready, they still had time—possibly hours—to wait. Yvonne passed around a thermos of chicory coffee.

"Do you have anything stronger?" Théo asked.

"I brought some cognac for the newcomers," she replied.

He indicated for her to hand it over. "Are you two estranged, or is being married just your cover story?"

"What?" Yvonne asked.

"You and Pierre. You're clearly not in love."

"No," she agreed. "It's our cover."

"Have you ever been married?"

"Yes. I have a daughter."

"Where is she?"

Yvonne nodded in the direction of the Channel. "Her father and I separated a few years ago." She was surprised at the bitterness in her voice. After all, it was she who'd had the affair, not Alex, but only after several years of him refusing to consent to a divorce.

"What about you?" Théo turned to Pierre.

"My wife is dead," Pierre replied.

Yvonne's eyes widened. "I'm sorry. I didn't know that."

Théo passed Pierre the bottle. He uncapped it and took a gulp. "I was in a prison camp in Poland when they told me. It was the Boches. They probably raped her before they killed her." He swallowed hard. "I was so distraught that one of the men in my squad asked them to release me."

"I didn't know they liberated prisoners because of medical issues," Yvonne said softly.

Pierre handed the cognac back to her. "I guess I looked pretty bad at that point." His next comment was inaudible due to the roar of an approaching plane. The three of them looked up as a Lysander came into view. Pierre raised his torch and flashed it. One long, one short, repeated three times, as deliberate as he could. If he didn't give the signal correctly, the pilot might get spooked and fly back to England without delivering his precious cargo.

The plane circled twice before retreating, leaving Yvonne's ears buzzing. "Did he leave without dropping anything?"

"No." Pierre indicated a white, ghostly fleck pulsating above them. "Here comes one." The trio crept closer to its approximate landing spot.

When Yvonne heard a thud and a curse in French, she called, "Welcome to Meung-sur-Loire."

The unmistakable sound of a gun cocking was the reply.

"Put that down," Pierre said gruffly. "We're friends."

Yvonne could just make out the form of a man, now with his arm relaxed. "Is one of you Prosper?" he asked.

"No." Pierre stepped forward. "But we're associates of his."

The other parachutist hit the ground nearby with an audible, "Oof!"

A large cylindrical object landed to the right of them and Yvonne could see another one a few meters away.

"Let's get going," Pierre went over to one of the cylinders and cut off the parachute ties. "We've got to get these canisters off the field as soon as possible."

"Shouldn't we bury our parachutes first?" the newest man asked. His accent was not English, but not French either.

Pierre shrugged. "It takes too long, and if you're not careful, the Germans will notice the newly dug mound."

"Not to mention silk is in high demand around here," Yvonne added. "We can get a good price for it on the black market."

Théo pulled out a long knife and began to cut the tell-tale white parachutes into small pieces and the other men followed suit. There were four cylindrical canisters in all. They were painted dark green and were about one and a half meters in length.

The two new men and Pierre each lugged a canister while Yvonne and Théo took the last one together. At one point he asked Yvonne if they could switch sides. "I wounded my hand in Verdun and it's never been the same since."

Yvonne complied, pondering how Théo had clearly been a soldier in the Great War, and now here he was, serving his country again, albeit in a more clandestine way.

They slowly made their way back to Théo's property to deposit their cargo. When he opened the door to his shed, Yvonne's nose wrinkled in protest at the overwhelming stench of decaying meat. Clearly Théo utilized the outbuilding to skin the rabbits and deer he poached.

Noting Yvonne's look of disgust, he told her she'd get used to the smell in a few minutes.

"What's in the canisters, anyway?" Pierre asked, still panting from carrying the heavy load.

One of the new men shrugged. Yvonne took note of his stocky figure and wide, handsome face. He would have been just her type in her younger days. *Like Alex. And Michel.* His bright blue eyes flashed in the light from her torch as he stuck out his hand and introduced himself as Henri Déricourt.

"Are you destined for the Prosper circuit?" Pierre asked.

"Sort of." Déricourt shifted his legs in the itchy hay. "My official title is 'Air Movements Officer.' I've been asked to coordinate all the drop zones and landings from now on."

"I thought it was up to each network head to organize them," Yvonne said. "Like how Prosper had us arrange your arrival."

Déricourt shrugged. "Most network heads don't know what designates a proper DZ because they aren't pilots. I am."

Feeling insulted, Yvonne demanded to know if he was SOE-trained.

"Not fully. The RAF has been complaining there have been too many failed missions—which translate into too much fuel being wasted—so Buck decided to send me over as soon as possible." His voice took on a challenging tone. "I don't suppose you're with the SOE."

Hers was equally challenging. "Actually, I am."

"Yvonne is better trained than most of our crew," Pierre informed him.

Déricourt raised his eyebrows. "That surprises me. All the women I saw tooling around Baker Street were all very pretty. And very young." He lifted his torch to cast light onto her face. "While you probably once had a nice bone structure, you definitely aren't the latter, so you don't fit the mold."

"Mold?" She resisted the urge to poke her finger into his broad chest. "I'll have you know I made the mold. I was the very first woman Buckmaster recruited. It's because of my success that these young ladies are all currently 'tooling around Baker Street.'"

The other newcomer, who had been silent until now, cleared his throat. He was tall, with brown eyes and an easy smile, which he bestowed on Yvonne. "Jack Agazarian." He shook her hand. "I'm Prosper's wireless operator."

Yvonne released his hand quickly, wondering if he was going to be as rude as his companion. "Prosper already has a wireless operator."

Jack shrugged. "I guess Buck thought he might need another one. The F-Section is hoping to increase the drops in the spring leading up to the Allied landing, and they'll want to be in constant communication."

Pierre grinned. "Not to mention I've heard Prosper's other W/T operator, Gilbert, has been distracted as of late." He nodded at Déricourt. "He's taken up relations with Prosper's courier—a former Baker Street 'pretty girl.'"

"Is that so?" Yvonne was surprised at first, but then she recalled the frisson between Andrée and Gilbert that day in Andrée's apartment. "Well, Andrée is much more than just a pretty girl. Gilbert's a lucky man."

"Gilbert?" Déricourt repeated. "My alias is supposed to be Gilbert."

"That's going to be confusing to many in the Prosper circuit," Yvonne said. "Gilbert's SOE code name is Archambault, but no one in France calls him that."

Déricourt waved his hand. "I already told them I intend to use my real name anyway. I'm too well-known in Paris to go by anything else."

Yvonne met Pierre's gaze before rolling her eyes. She could tell Déricourt was going to be difficult to work with, and she hoped the Adolphe network wouldn't need to use him very often.

She bent down to examine the canisters and decided to open the one labeled, 'Conforts' first. As she expected, it contained luxuries to be distributed among members of the Resistance: coffee, tea, soap, and cigarettes. All were unlabeled, of course. It wouldn't do any good for a Nazi to come upon a native Frenchmen smoking an English cigarette. Yvonne secretly pocketed some tea, intending to find a way to send it to her mother in Paris.

"Chocolate," Théo exclaimed, his grubby hands grabbing a few squares. "It's been too long since I've had chocolate." He bit a chunk off and started chewing with a wide, open mouth. "Oh!" he exclaimed a few moments later. He spat out a mouthful onto the hay. "Tastes like detergent."

"Sorry about that," Jack told him. "Looks like they packed it next to the soap. The chocolate must have absorbed some of the scented oils."

The other canisters contained gun parts and ingredients for explosives: Nobel 808, plastique, and various detonating devices. Luckily the SOE had been more careful in their packing of the hazardous materials than with the chocolate.

"We'll dump the empty canisters in the lake this evening," Pierre said once they had finished. "I'll let Prosper know about the guns and ammunition and he can decide what to do with them. For now, it's time for breakfast."

Théo led the line of exhausted, hungry rebels up toward the main house. It was past daybreak now, and in the dim light of morning, Yvonne could see an unfamiliar man approach the driveway. She froze. The man was dressed in the uniform of a postman, but that didn't mean he wasn't also a Gestapo informant.

"Hey, Victor," Théo called out. "I want you to come here and meet my new friend Gilbert. He's just arrived from England."

The man looked over at the little group, his eyebrows furrowed. Then he burst into laughter. "Such an imbecile you are, Théo. Always joking." He dumped the mail on the porch before heading back to his car. They all blew out a collective breath of relief as the postman drove away with a friendly wave.

"That was close," Jack commented from behind Yvonne.

She turned to shoot him a warning look. "You'd better get used to it. Such incidents happen a lot."

"Welcome to Occupied France," Pierre said dryly. He resumed walking. "Let's get some food."

CHAPTER 19

NOOR

*M*ajor de Wesselow ordered Noor to pack her bags while the others were on a five-mile run, which meant she didn't have the opportunity to say good-bye to Cecily or Yolande. It saddened her a little that her friends would probably assume she'd been yet another trainee failure.

She was moved to The Drokes, on the Beaulieu Estate in the New Forest, to continue her wireless training. The Drokes was a modern-looking house almost eclipsed by the towering evergreens that surrounded it. As soon as Noor arrived, the sight of the frost-covered trees caused an immense wave of pain to crash over her, almost making her drop to her knees in the snow with the realization that this would be the first Christmas she wouldn't be with her family. As Sufis, her family didn't technically celebrate the birth of Jesus, but they did indulge in the celebrations. When they lived in the mostly Catholic Suresnes, France, her father had often been invited to play at holiday parties and concerts and Noor and her siblings would revel in the festivities. One memorable year, they'd even gotten a Christmas tree. Noor loved Christmas so much—especially the brightly-colored decorations, the caroling, and the notion ot good will towards all—she had even written a short story about it once.

Before going inside, Noor said a small prayer, asking for her mother, Claire, Vilayat, and Hidayat and his family to be safe. She missed them all terribly, especially her mother, but tried to soothe the ache in her heart by reminding herself how important it was to be doing this work. *Someday, when the world is free again, we can all celebrate together.*

The interior of The Drokes was decorated in Art Deco, with polished wood furniture in geometric patterns. A uniformed butler showed Noor into the parlor, where quite a few people had gathered. She stood rather awkwardly, her feet sinking into the leopard-print rug, noting that all the women were young and pretty, while most of the men were handsome and in great physical shape.

A gray-haired woman approached Noor and held out her hand. "Welcome to The Drokes. I'm Adele, one of the instructors here."

"Is this a training academy?" Noor asked.

Adele smiled. "Yes. I'm sure you've noticed by now that the SOE has requisitioned quite the array of mansions. The Drokes is one of many such manors, all with their own tracts of land and well hidden. Perfect for our purposes." She handed Noor a glass of champagne. "It's pleasant to have female company for once. Did you know you are the first class of women to be trained as wireless operators?"

Noor shook her head.

"Well, you are. Thanks to the relative success of the female agents we have in France now, F Section has decided to train women as operators." She pointed at a dark-haired girl, who looked much younger than Noor. "That's Alice Wood, another of Buckmaster's favorites."

Noor took a tiny sip of champagne to cover her confusion. The way Adele spoke, it sounded as if Noor herself was a Buckmaster favorite. *But that couldn't be.* Noor had never even met the man, though she knew he was in charge of F Section.

Alice Wood sat alone on the couch, her spine straight and her gaze focused on nothing in particular. Like Noor, she seemed quiet and reserved, but there was a spunkiness in the way she didn't bother to socialize. Noor sensed that underneath the timid demeanor, Alice had a determination that equaled her own.

The training they underwent at The Drokes was just as intense as at Wanborough, though here it was more specialized. The classes focused on logistics, such as the technical features of their transmitting sets, how to use crystals to determine their frequencies, and how to put up aerials.

At the same time, they had to improve their Morse skills and practice coding. Noor was given a crash course on something called WOKs, but after an hour or so, she ended up more confused and Adele told her to stick with the poem codes she'd learned at Wanborough, which were infinitely easier. "Just be sure to write your own poem," Adele said. "If the Germans pick up your signal and your poem is something they know, they can decode every message you send after that."

Noor felt a coldness drip along her spine. "I'm a writer. I can definitely come up with an original poem."

Adele nodded. "Good."

The culminating exercise at The Drokes was to put everything they had learned together. Another of Noor's instructors, a man named Kim Philby, told Noor that her task would be to visit the nearby town of Brockenhurst to find a safehouse from which to transmit a message. To do this, she would have to make her own contacts using a plausible cover story and set up letter boxes.

"You will pretend that you are in enemy territory," Philby told her. "You have less than three days to find a fitting locale from which to encode and transmit a message, based on what you've been taught. If you go beyond your time limit, we will assume that you have been captured by the Boches. Keep in mind that the SOE will be watching to see if you make any mistakes," he added.

"Yes, sir," Noor replied.

She decided to be a writer charged with interviewing children on what they thought of air raids for a BBC article. This time she would use the alias Nora Kirkwood.

It was difficult to find a safehouse. The first boarding house owner she visited was a white-haired woman, who wore a permanent frown. "There's no room here," she stated before slamming the door in Noor's face.

"Especially for non-white women," Noor said to herself.

She finally found a room let by a Mrs. Harvey, who asked far too many questions for Noor's liking.

Her next task was to assemble her wireless and send a message to The Drokes. Her training dictated that she transmit somewhere other than her residence as there was always the chance that the German detectors could hone into her signal. It was best to rotate among several transmission hubs, but for her practice mission, she only needed one. For this she chose a flat owned by a Mrs. Sutton, who was in her late seventies and nearly deaf. The rental was on the upper floor of the building, with its own door and a large back window opening onto a private balcony. It was a perfect spot for transmitting: the rafters provided a place to hide the aerial equipment, and the balcony led to the roof for an easy escape route, should the need arise.

An electric pulse radiated through Noor's whole body as she unpacked the contents of her W/T suitcase. The case itself was designed to look as innocuous as possible. It was made of cheap brown leather and contained 20 meters of aerial wire, the transmitter and receiver, a Morse key, a headset, and various tools such as screwdrivers and extra battery packs, all individually packed within the felt lining. The tuning crystals had their own Bakelite containers to prevent them from rattling around.

Noor began to code her message, which she kept as simple as possible. *Circuit now secure and transmitting. Ready for operations.*

The next step was to set up the aerial. The wire itself was rather cumbersome and Noor had to stand on a chair to string it around the rafters before securing one end to the metal radiator. She then put her headset on, inserted the calibrated crystal into the transceiver, and tapped out the encoded message on her Morse key.

If this were the real thing, she would only have thirty minutes to transmit her message and then wait for a reply. More time than that, and the enemy could home in on her signal and locate her safe-house, putting both Noor and old Mrs. Sutton in grave danger.

Noor took a deep breath in an effort to remain calm. If she had made any mistakes in either her coding or her Morse, the SOE radio operator would not understand her message and would be unable to send a timely reply. If the message was rendered indecipherable, she would have failed her mission. Maybe this time they really would kick her out of training.

She refrained from checking her watch, reassuring herself that it had only been a few minutes. Instead, she inspected the tip of her pencil, to make sure it was sharpened, and adjusted the pad of lined paper in her lap.

Finally a beeping began to come through her headset. Her pencil moved rapidly, recording one letter at a time as her well-trained ear interpreted the Morse. When the beeps ended, Noor decoded the transmission.

Message received. Well done.

She allowed herself one tiny smile before she got up to take down the aerial. She repacked everything neatly into the case before leaving the apartment. She'd managed to accomplish everything in only two days.

The next morning, Noor paid Mrs. Harvey for the entire week of lodging before climbing onto her bicycle. The old lady's eyes widened at the cash, but for once she did not demand information —namely, why her new tenant should be leaving so soon after arriving.

Noor whistled as she headed back to The Drokes. Everything had gone according to plan, and she could only imagine how pleased Philby and Adele would be with her when she returned.

She slowed as she approached a crossroads. There was a stop

sign, but she could also see that no one else was on the road. She didn't want to be late getting back, so she ignored the signpost and pedaled right through the intersection without pausing.

A shrill whistle and a voice calling, "Halt!" interrupted Noor's thoughts.

Noor looked back to see a policeman emerge from a clump of bushes. She had no choice but to turn around.

"Didn't you notice the sign?" the policeman demanded.

"I did, but I didn't see anyone else, otherwise I would have stopped."

"What is your name?"

Noor could feel her face heat up. "Nora Baker." Too late she remembered that her alias for this mission had been changed. Clearly her nerves were getting the better of her.

The policeman flipped through a notebook. "I'm afraid you are going to have to come with me." He led her over to a nearby car that had also been concealed among the bushes and told her to dismantle her bicycle before putting it into the boot.

They'd shown her how to do this at Wanborough, but Noor's hands were shaking too much to get the wheel off and the policeman had to help her. After the bicycle was secured, she got in the back of the car and he drove her to the police station.

Instead of sending her to the front desk, he led her down to the basement of the station and had her sit in a hard wooden chair. A bright light was aimed at her face.

"What were you doing in Brockenhurst?" an unfamiliar voice demanded.

"I was working on a story about children…" she stammered as beads of sweat formed on her forehead.

"Stop!" the voice told her. "No more lies. Tell us what you were really doing."

"I told you, I was researching a story. I am a writer for the BBC."

"Lie!" The voice was closer this time, sounding as if the man were next to her, but she couldn't see because of the light. "What were you *really* up to in Brockenhurst?"

This time when Noor opened her mouth, someone slapped her across the face. *Hard.* She began to suspect that she wasn't dealing with the police. She tried to convince herself that it was just another training exercise, but part of her wondered if the Gestapo had managed to sneak into England.

"What is your name?" the voice demanded.

Her face stung, but she did her best to ignore the pain. "Nora."

"Nora what?"

Now she had a dilemma: she'd blundered when the policeman asked her name earlier. Should she stick with the name she'd given him, or the alias she was supposed to be traveling under?

Her pause incurred another slap. "Nora what?"

"Baker!"

This produced a grunt. Clearly she'd said the wrong thing. "And what have you been up to these past few days, Miss Baker?"

"I rented a room from Mrs. Harvey," she replied honestly.

"And also from a Mrs…" he paused and Noor heard footsteps retreating and then the sound of papers rustling. "Sutton. Are you always in the habit of renting two rooms simultaneously?"

"No."

"Then why the two rooms?"

Her mind raced. *Why indeed?* Her father had always taught her that the worst sin she could ever commit was to lie. But at the same time, if this were a training exercise, she knew the SOE would want her to make something up. If an agent was captured, they must try to not give anything to the Gestapo for at least 48 hours: enough time for the rest of the circuit to leave town. After that, Philby had told her, you could tell them whatever you needed to in order to save your own hide. "For my lover," she replied finally. "He is still married, and…"

"What is his name?" The footsteps were coming closer again and Noor braced herself for another slap.

"Ja—" she stumbled, searching for a good English name. "Jonathan."

"Not fast enough."

Noor blinked as the light was turned off. Now the room was in total darkness.

"Nora." This time the voice was familiar. "You can't hesitate like that." A small lamp was switched on and she saw her instructor from The Drokes, Kim Philby, sitting behind the desk.

A strange man occupied one of the chairs opposite the desk. He focused his cold, gray eyes on Noor. "I'm sorry about the slapping."

Philby waved his hand. "It's nothing compared to what the Gestapo would do."

The policeman gave her a searching look. "If this girl is an agent, then I'm Winston Churchill."

"That will be all, Clive." Philby watched the policeman walk out before turning to her with a sigh. "Nora, you…"

"I did badly," she finished for him. "I'm sorry, I just got so nervous."

"Do you think you won't get nervous if the real thing happens?" Philby demanded. "In the field, you will not only be putting your life at risk, but all of those in your circuit." He shook his head. "We can't have our agents slip up like that."

"I'm sorry," Noor repeated.

He put a hand to his forehead and rubbed it. "You have to be quicker in your replies. Much quicker. Silence will only get you more beatings."

"I didn't know what to say." *Kind of like now.*

Philby blew out his breath. "You were getting there—the affair would have been a decent cover. It's always good to confess to a minor crime to throw off the Gestapo. Their interrogation techniques are built on brutality, not necessarily on sound judgement or intelligence." He got to his feet. "If you are arrested by the Gestapo, don't immediately assume that you are doomed. You might still be able to outwit them." He handed Noor a wet rag for her face. "With practice, a lot more practice, you just might get there."

"Thank you, sir." *For not giving up on me,* Noor wanted to add, but she figured Philby knew what she meant.

"If only we weren't so hard up for wireless operators…" he said, more to himself than Noor.

She left before he could finish his thought. As she mounted her bike, the policeman's skeptical comment repeated in her head. *If this girl is an agent...*

Well, she was an agent, or at least on her way to becoming one, and she was now even more determined to prove all her doubters wrong.

CHAPTER 20

ANDRÉE

*A*ndrée's old flame, Maurice, the one she'd met on the PAO line, had been long forgotten. The younger, more attractive Gilbert Norman had taken his place, and he and Andrée became as much of a couple as they could while living as secret agents in Occupied France. He let her stay in his apartment whenever she wasn't traveling across the countryside with Prosper, but Gilbert had to contact London twice a day for his regular "skeds" and was often gone as well. A lot of his time was spent scouting out new locales to operate his wireless set in order to avoid the Gestapo homing into his signal.

After a particularly long week during which they had not seen one another at all, Gilbert burst into the bedroom. "I've found the perfect place to transmit, one the Boches will never be able to locate."

"Where is it?" Andrée asked sleepily.

"In Grignon, northwest of Versailles, at the École Nationale d'Agriculture."

She sat up. "The agricultural college?"

Gilbert nodded. "The director there, Dr. Vanderwynckt, was introduced to me through some Resistance contacts, and invited us all out there. Prosper too. We'll leave this afternoon. In the mean-time," he reached for her, "we have some catching up to do." He buried his face in her hair. "I've missed you."

Andrée wasn't usually the type to reveal her feelings to a man with whom she'd only recently started a relationship, but there was something vulnerable about Gilbert that struck a chord in her. "I've missed you too," she confessed before meeting his lips for a long, passionate kiss.

The main residence at École Nationale d'Agriculture was a Louis XIII style, orange-bricked castle with gabled roofs. It sat in the middle of the extensive college grounds like a monarch holding court.

The president of the college, Dr. Eugène Vanderwynckt, was a balding, short man with a well-trimmed mustache. After Gilbert introduced him to Andrée and Prosper, Vanderwynckt presented his wife and adult daughters and invited them all into the dining room for lunch.

A man was already seated near the foot of the table. He had heavy, dark eyebrows made even more pronounced by his receding hairline.

Vanderwynckt nodded at him as the others took their seats. "I'd like you to meet Professor Serge Balachowsky, the head of the Grignon Sector. His specialty is entomology."

Andrée took a sidelong glance at Gilbert, wondering if he knew what *entomology* was. He was nodding in recognition. "So you must be an expert with invading pests, like locusts. Or Nazis."

Balachowsky smiled widely. "I'm not sure about expert, but I'm definitely familiar with both types of pests."

Andrée joined in as everyone at the table laughed.

Balachowsky continued, "If there is one thing I've learned in my years of study, it's that every insect, no matter how unwanted, has a place in the ecosystem. Another creature may depend on it for food, or it keeps other populations under control." His smile disappeared and his voice grew serious. "That's one reason I despise Hitler's notion of a superior race; in biology, there is no such thing. Evolution is based on chance mutations that can—though it's very rare—provide a species with a survival advantage. Every creature you see is a product of millions of years of evolution, and no living thing should have the right to cause another's extermination just because they desire to."

Vanderwynckt slammed his fist down on the table, causing a maid to jump.

"Papa?" one of his daughters asked.

He waited until the maid had left the room before stating, "Balachowsky's right—Hitler is a terrible example of what our species is capable of. I just wish I could fight the Boches now like I did at Verdun. I don't like this sneaking around."

"The reprisals for openly interfering with the occupiers are just too great," Prosper replied from his place at the foot of the table. "Let the communists attack them directly. Our job is to give them the weapons they need to do so."

"Where do you get these weapons?" Balachowsky inquired. "If the Boches caught you carrying a gun, you'd be sent to one of their German work camps."

"London sends them to us in air drops," Gilbert answered. "That's what we need your assistance with: attending these drops, and then storing the supplies here at the college until we can collect them."

Balachowsky nodded. "You can count me in."

"And me too," Vanderwynckt added. "I'll do anything I can to help the Allies."

Gilbert rubbed his hands together. "They are probably planning their European landing as we speak."

"Hear, hear," Prosper held up his wine glass and the others met his in an enthusiastic toast.

After lunch, they took a tour of the extensive grounds and Vanderwynckt's wife showed them their lodgings: empty dorm rooms in a wing of the main mansion.

"There are only two rooms," Andrée noted.

Prosper put his bag on one of the beds. "Gilbert and I can share."

"Actually, boss," Gilbert ran a hand through his hair. "If it's okay with you, I think Andrée and I are going to room together."

"Oh?" Prosper raised his eyebrows as he glanced at Andrée. She gave him a sheepish smile. His face returned to its customary neutral expression. He started to reply, "Well…" but didn't seem to know how to finish his sentence. After a moment, he retrieved his bag from the bed. "You two can have this room and I'll take the next one."

"What do you think?" Gilbert asked after Prosper had left.

"About Prosper?"

"No. He's fine with our relationship."

Andrée started to unzip her bag and then paused as a thought occurred to her. "Do you think Buckmaster would be as well?"

"Does it matter? Chances are he'll never find out."

"You're right." Andrée doubted that Buck would be pleased to hear of any budding romance among his F Section agents, but Gilbert was indeed correct. The only one who knew about them was Prosper and he would never say anything.

Gilbert tried again with his inquiry. "What do you think of the grounds?"

"They're amazing," Andrée admitted as she shoved her underwear and an extra pair of trousers in a drawer. "And so are Dr. Vanderwynckt and Professor Balachowsky."

He walked over to embrace her. "This is the perfect spot for me to transmit. The Gestapo will never pick up the signal. We're safe here."

She had to stand on her tiptoes in order to wrap her arms around his neck. "You did good."

"I know." Gilbert started undoing the buttons of her blouse.

He led her over to the tiny bottom bunk bed. "Shh," Andrée said as Gilbert's long legs hit the baseboard with a thud. "Everyone's going to know what we are up to."

"They already do," Gilbert said, kissing her on the lips.

Andrée soon forgot all about Buckmaster, Prosper, and the rest of them, concentrating only on Gilbert's strong arms, his tender lips, and how good he made her feel.

After they made love, Gilbert got up to wash his hands in the little sink next to the cupboard before changing into clean clothes. His posh mannerisms still sometimes surprised Andrée. At any rate, they made it clear that he came from a completely different world than she did. She didn't know much about the person Gilbert had been before he joined the SOE, but she imagined he hadn't had to quit school at fourteen, like she did, to bring in an income for a widowed mother.

"What will we do after the war?" Andrée asked, pulling the bedspread up over her bare breasts.

"What do you mean?"

She wanted to inquire if he still planned on being with her once he returned to his old life, but didn't know how. Instead, she said, "You are comfortable in places like this, with educated people."

"And you're not?" He shrugged on a suit coat. "I can't imagine you not being comfortable anywhere."

"You mean uncomfortable." She was silent for a moment, then tried again. "Do you think your family would approve of me?"

He gazed at her. "Of course they would. You make me happy. That's really what they would care about. My father might be a little… demanding, but he would come to his senses." His next word did little to ease her anxiety. "Eventually."

She pushed her jitters to the back of her mind. "Where are you going now?"

"I have to meet my evening sked, and then greet the new contacts who are expected to arrive later."

"Oh," Andrée sank back down into the pillow.

"Do you want to come?"

She sat up again. "Sure."

. . .

They walked across the grounds to a small greenhouse where Gilbert had already set up an aerial. He immediately got to work while Andrée explored the greenhouse. She took her time sniffing the roses, dreaming that they might someday be used in Parisian perfumes when the Germans had left and the rationing was over. After she was done, she returned to Gilbert's side and leaned over his shoulder. "What are you writing?"

He moved his hand so that she could read the uncoded message.

From Prosper: Have recruited hundreds of locals in the past few days. Request more arms drops. With your help out capabilities are limitless.

She couldn't keep a grin from forming. "Do you think they'll be able to supply us with enough guns?"

Gilbert shrugged as he started to code. "There's no harm in asking." He put on his headphones and tapped at his Morse key. After he'd finished, he sat back in his chair, relaxing, before reaching across to a nearby rose bush. Carefully he removed a flower and handed it to Andrée, who placed it behind her ear.

His reciprocating grin quickly disappeared and his eyes grew wide. Andrée could only assume someone was replying to him. Indeed, Gilbert began to move his pen rapidly across a square card. After the sender had finished, Gilbert took off his headphones and expertly decoded London's reply.

Andrée picked up the copy and read it aloud. "*We hear you Prosper and echo your enthusiasm STOP Request information on Chaingy trans- former station.*"

"Only Buckmaster would be that exuberant," she commented. "What's Chaingy?"

"It's one of the primary links for power for the Paris/Orléans railway."

"They didn't actually reply about the arms drops."

"They never do." Gilbert retrieved the card and held it over a candle. They both watched in silence as the paper caught fire. He blew it out before the flames reached his fingers and then buried the charred remains in a nearby rose pot.

"Oh," Gilbert said, as if suddenly remembering something. He checked his watch. "Just in time for the arrival of the new recruits."

As they left the greenhouse, Andrée noted that the grounds hadn't lost their luster in the orange glow of the setting sun. They walked in silence to the back of the property, their boots crunching over the gravel. They were relatively free from any prying ears, so there was no need to be quiet, but Gilbert had become sullen, possibly pouting over the fact that Buckmaster hadn't promised them any additional guns.

As they approached an iron gate, she had the feeling they were being watched. Indeed two dark figures stepped out from the shadow of a large tree.

"Can I get some lighter fluid?" one of them called out in perfect French.

"You mean petroleum." Gilbert answered the coded query as he unlocked the gate. "Welcome to the Prosper network," he said when the two men entered.

The shorter of the two shook his head. "I'm the Air Movements Officer for north-central France. I don't necessarily work for Prosper."

"Every agent stationed in north-central France works for Prosper," Andrée replied, taking in the man's muscular form. It was obvious he hadn't been subject to French rationing for quite some time, if ever.

"Well, *I* surely will be part of the Prosper network." The tall man stuck out his hand to Andrée. "Jack Agazarian, your new wireless operator."

Gilbert gave him a confused look as Jack turned to shake his hand. "I'm Gilbert Norman, Prosper's original operator. I wasn't aware he requested another one."

Jack gave him a wide smile. "I just do what I'm told."

"So you're Gilbert," the other man stated. "They told me my code name is to be Gilbert, but you can refer to me by my real name, Henri Déricourt."

The authentic Gilbert rubbed his forehead. "Sometimes Buckmaster's decisions seem to make no sense." He motioned for them to walk back with him. "Did you arrive with any ammunition or guns?"

"Yes." Jack fell in step with Gilbert.

"How many canisters?"

"Four."

Gilbert shot a look at Andrée before declaring, "That's not enough. We need more, much more, if they want us to keep supplying our would-be saboteurs."

"Maybe they're having trouble with the drops," Jack suggested. "It *is* the middle of winter."

"The weather has been perfect," Gilbert retorted dryly. He pointed upward. "Take tonight… not a cloud in the sky."

Jack seemed to be the eternal optimist. "Well, since organizing drops is Déricourt's job, maybe there will be more now."

"We have plenty of men 'organized' and they have been ready and waiting," Gilbert told him. "But the SOE isn't keeping up with demand."

Jack didn't seem to have a reply to that.

When they reached the main house, they found Prosper, Vanderwynckt, and Balachowsky indulging in a pre-dinner drink. After introductions, Déricourt poured two glasses of brandy and handed one to Andrée. "So that's your boss, the infamous Prosper."

"Yes," Andrée replied proudly.

He stared at Prosper for a few moments, clearly sizing him up. "He looks more like a cavalry officer than a spy."

It was Andrée's turn to size up Déricourt. She surmised that Miss Atkins hadn't given him her eagle-eyed inspection before he'd left England. If she had, she would have demanded he cut his shaggy brown hair, which was so long it curled up at the base of his neck. "Prosper is a born leader," Andrée said. "Can you say the same about yourself?"

He shrugged. "I'm just here to coordinate departing and arriving aircraft."

She tried to meet his guarded blue eyes, but he took a long drag of his drink instead and then shook his empty glass. "Time for another. You need one?" He was still refusing to look at her straight on.

"No."

"Suit yourself," he said as he walked away.

I certainly will.

Gilbert sauntered over to her and stood in the same spot Déricourt had just vacated. "What do you think of the new men?"

"Jack's a little clueless, but he'll learn. His character seems fine, but I don't know if I can say the same of Déricourt."

"He's not so bad. Besides, you might want to be nice to him— he's in charge of dispatching messages that are too large to send over the wireless along with other intelligence, like photographs and blueprints of buildings. He's already promised to get a letter to Prosper's wife back home." Gilbert's voice took on a tone of fake nonchalance. "Is there anyone in London you'd like to contact?"

Andrée shook her head. "No one."

"Good," Gilbert replied quickly before draining his glass.

Andrée watched as Déricourt poured himself a double and then stuffed his face with bread. "Still, there's something about the new Gilbert that rubs me the wrong way. He seems quite full of himself."

Gilbert laughed. "Didn't you think the same of me?"

She turned to him, a grin forming. "Was I wrong?"

"Not at all," he replied before taking her arm and leading her into the dining room.

CHAPTER 21

YVONNE

*W*hen Yvonne and Pierre returned from their latest drop, a rather embarrassed Madame Flamencourt informed them she would be having company for the holiday and asked that Yvonne and Pierre move out temporarily.

They found housing with Henri Ruhiere, a kindly old man who took to calling Yvonne, *chérie.* He lived only a few miles away from the Flamencourts and, like them, sometimes housed Resistance members or men evading the *Service du travail obligatoire.* The best part was that the old widower had two extra bedrooms, which meant Yvonne and Pierre could have separate rooms.

Shortly after they'd moved in with Monsieur Ruhiere, Pierre asked Yvonne to sew a couple of missing buttons on his shirt.

She looked up from the map of Paris she had been studying. Although Pierre often referred to her as "his right-hand woman," her position in the Adolphe subcircuit had never been officially clarified. "Do it yourself. I'm not your housekeeper."

He held up a line of black thread. "Can't you do it just this one time? People might think it strange that we are supposed to be husband and wife, and here I am with white buttons sewn on— poorly I will add—with black thread."

"If anyone asks, tell them your wife refuses to sew buttons when her husband has ten perfectly working fingers." Yvonne went back to her map.

The three of them celebrated New Year's Eve with a couple of bottles of red wine that Monsieur Ruhiere dug up from his cellar. "It's not the finest I've ever served," he told them regretfully as he passed them the glasses.

"But it's very much appreciated," Pierre replied.

"My wife and I used to host grand parties every December," Monsieur Ruhiere continued. "She was a wonderful hostess."

"How long has she been gone?" Yvonne asked.

Monsieur Ruhiere closed his eyes, counting. "Seven years now. I'm almost glad she was never around to see the Boches enter France."

"My mother was living in Paris at the time and still is," Yvonne said. After a moment, she added, "I often wonder what she thinks of all of the swastikas flying everywhere."

"I hate them." Pierre was vehement. "I hate their flags, I hate their jackboots, I hate everything about Nazis."

Yvonne took a sip of wine. "I can see why you joined the Resistance."

Pierre gave an ironic chuckle. "You'd think it would have been that easy, but it wasn't in the early years. I wanted to be a pilot, but at that time the French Air Force didn't accept applications from men who wore glasses. So I enlisted in the infantry and was posted to Belgium only a few months after I married Ginette."

Yvonne's hand shook a little, spilling a dollop of wine. She had never heard Pierre mention his wife by name. "Is that when you were captured and sent to the POW camp?"

"Yes. I tried to leave Dunkirk by sea, but the boat had a rotten bottom. I couldn't swim and probably would have drowned if the Germans hadn't gotten there first."

"You are lucky you managed to get out of their prison camp," Monsieur Ruhiere said as he grabbed the bottle of wine.

"Indeed. A friend I'd made told them I'd come down with thyrotoxicosis. The Boches didn't know what it was, but they were convinced it was massively contagious. Really I was suffering from depression from the loss of my wife." Pierre nodded as Monsieur Ruhiere held up the bottle.

"How long were you married?" Monsieur Ruhiere asked after he'd finished pouring.

"Less than a year," Pierre replied. "You?"

"Forty. I was married to my darling wife for forty years." Monsieur Ruhiere's gaze was unfocused as he stared off in space. Yvonne imagined he was remembering some cherished moment with his wife.

Pierre broke the silence as he asked Yvonne, "What about you? You said you were separated from your husband, but you must have loved him once, right?"

She sighed as she set her glass down. "I don't think so. I married him mainly to get away from my mother." After Yvonne's father died, Madame Cerneau had completed the transition from overbearing to downright oppressive, at least in her daughter's opinion. When Yvonne decided to move to England for a fresh start, Madame Cerneau wasn't about to let her only surviving daughter go 'traipsing around a foreign country unchaperoned.' Though the marriage to Alex Rudellat had been one of convenience, it had produced one of the great loves of Yvonne's life: her daughter, Constance.

Her other great love had arrived ten years into her farce of a marriage. His name was Michael O'Sullivan, an Irishman. He too was married and, for the most part, their affair had consisted of late-night phone calls and affectionate notes until, at the start of the war, he had been compelled to return to his wife for reasons too painful to recount.

Yvonne faked a yawn before getting up to collect the empty wine glasses. "I'll do the washing up." Neither Pierre nor Monsieur Ruhiere replied.

She went into the kitchen and turned on the sink to fill the basin, hoping to drown out the memory of Michael leaving her. The water flowed for less than ten seconds before it stopped abruptly, just like their affair.

She shut off the faucet and turned it back on again, but nothing happened. "Damn," she said aloud then called to Pierre, "I think the pipes have frozen. Can you get some from the well so I can finish up?"

Even from the kitchen she could hear Pierre's heavy sigh. The weather had been poor the night before and there were several inches of snow on the ground.

"I'll help you," Monsieur Ruhiere offered.

While she waited, Yvonne dipped a cloth into the little trickle of water in the basin to scrub at a dot of wine on her culottes. She dropped the cloth when she heard Pierre shout. From the urgency in his voice, she knew something was desperately wrong.

She ran out of the house, not bothering to put on shoes or a coat. She found Pierre bent over Monsieur Ruhiere, who was lying face down in the snow next to the well.

"I don't know what happened," Pierre said, his voice barely audible. "He just fell all of a sudden."

Yvonne held two shaking fingers to Monsieur Ruhiere's wrist and then to his neck. "He's dead."

Pierre met her eyes. His were stricken. "What should we do?"

"We have to go, now."

He shook his head. "We can't leave him here."

Yvonne adjusted Monsieur Ruhiere's neck so that his head was in a more natural position. "We could call the authorities, but do you want to stick around and answer their questions as to why we, perfect strangers, have been staying with Monsieur Ruhiere?"

"No. You're right."

Together they went back to their rooms and threw their meager belongings into suitcases. They met in the hallway and started down the stairs, but then Pierre stopped abruptly.

"What is it?" Yvonne asked.

"I gave Monsieur Ruhiere 50,000 francs to store safely in a lockbox."

"Should we break into it? I don't think he has any use for the money, and from what he told me, he didn't have much family around here."

"No." It was Pierre's turn to convince her. "We'd better just leave."

Yvonne grabbed a small glass flower from the mantel, thinking it must have once belonged to Madame Ruhiere. She put it in the dead man's coat pocket before they fled the grounds.

CHAPTER 22

NOOR

*A*fter Noor finished her instruction at the Drokes, Kim Philby informed her that Major Buckmaster wanted to see her in his London office.

Noor searched Philby's face for any hint of emotion, but his expression was as inscrutable as always. She was aware that Major Buckmaster was the head of F Section, and though she had never met him, she had the sense that the man knew everything that happened within his branch of the SOE. She could only hope that his summons was routine. Perhaps he was going to offer congratulations on her exemplary performance, though in truth Noor wasn't sure she had even passed the training program.

She took a bus to London's West End and walked to the address she was given, which was just off Baker Street. The innocuous limestone exterior of the building gave no hint of the secret operations she imagined were being plotted within.

A tall man in an equally innocuous gray suit answered the bell. Noor expected him to ask for her name, but he didn't say anything as he gestured for her to come in. She followed him down a hallway cluttered with Art Deco knick-knacks until he stopped at a gilded door, which he unlocked with a flourish. He marched into the apartment and turned into a side room. "You will wait here," he told her in a deep voice.

Noor looked around, startled. *Some waiting room.* The massive black onyx bathtub in the corner gave away the fact that she was in a bathroom. Without another word, the tall man left her alone.

She sat on a corner of the bathtub and took a deep breath, convincing herself that Buckmaster wouldn't have personally invited her here if he was going to kick her out of the program.

A few minutes later, the door flew open. A slender man with bright blue eyes stood at the threshold.

"Major Buckmaster?" Noor guessed.

"Call me Buck." He waved at her to follow him to his office.

Noor sat down in one of the chairs facing his desk. Buckmaster's mannerisms gave no hint of anything being amiss, but maybe his nonchalant attitude was a cover.

After a short exchange of pleasantries, he got down to business. "The reason I called you here was to go over your latest reports. It seems you have become quite the controversy within F Section."

"Me? Why?"

Buckmaster indicated the papers on his desk, which had been organized into two stacks. "This pile," he tapped the top of the left one, "are the commendable reports, from Kim Philby, Adele, and a few earlier ones from Wanborough. But this one," he gestured to the other heap, which looked slightly higher to Noor, "contains arguments against you going to France. For instance," he picked up the first paper. "Colonel Spooner says that you 'aren't overburdened with brains.'"

Noor's face grew hot. She'd never been accused of being unintelligent. *Clumsy? Maybe. A dreamer? Certainly. But never dumb.*

Buckmaster waved his hand. "I think what Spooner wrote is nonsense, and I'd also add that we don't need our agents to be overburdened with brains, anyway."

She tilted her head, wondering how to reply to that.

"What Major Buckmaster means is that agents shouldn't overthink things."

Noor looked up to see a trim woman wearing a tailored tweed

suit standing in the doorway. "Instead, you should rely on the instinct your training has instilled upon you." Her thin lips stretched into a smile that didn't reach her eyes. From her posture and supercilious attitude, Noor decided she must be a woman of rank, though she wore no insignia.

Buckmaster waved for the woman to come in. "Nora, I'd like you to meet Miss Atkins. She oversees all the women agents, and most of the men, for that matter."

"Hello, Nora." Miss Atkins sat primly in the chair across from Noor. "How is your mother?"

"As well as can be expected, thanks," Noor replied.

"And your brother Vilayat? How is he enjoying the Royal Navy?"

Noor was taken aback by the depth of Miss Atkins' knowledge of her family. But then again, she supposed it was the woman's business to know everything about her agents. "I'm not sure. I haven't heard from him in weeks."

"Well, I'm sure Claire will write to you soon with more information." Miss Atkins folded her hands in her lap and looked at Buckmaster expectantly.

He cleared his throat. "Seeing as there is still some lingering doubt about your qualifications, we decided we are going to move you to a country house at Chalfont Saint Giles in Buckinghamshire with a few other agents. It will give you time to warm up to living under your new alias—we want you to get to the point where your cover story literally becomes second nature so that..." another throat clear, "in the event you are ever captured by the Gestapo, we won't have a repeat performance of your practice interrogation."

Noor refrained from hanging her head. "I understand."

"You will also be able to keep up with your Morse instruction," Miss Atkins added.

Buckmaster reached into a drawer and pulled out a file. "We've decided that you will become Jeanne-Marie Renier, a children's nurse."

"We thought that particular false occupation would best suit your temperament." Clearly Miss Atkins liked to finish Buckmaster's thoughts.

"Indeed," he agreed. "Your SOE call sign will be Madeleine."

Noor suppressed a sigh of relief. They were sending her to do more training, but at least they weren't firing her. She leaned forward as a thought occurred to her. "Can I say good-bye to my mother in person before I leave London? Her apartment is only a few stops away on the bus."

Miss Atkins recrossed her legs. "Don't you think that would just make it harder? You've already said good-bye once. As far as she knows, you've been in Africa for the past couple of months."

Noor opened her eyes as wide as they would go and tried not to blink, knowing that if she did, the tears that had formed would spill over. She recalled the painful day, which now seemed so long ago, when she'd had to say good-bye to Mams and Claire. As much as it pained her not to be able to see her mother one last time, she knew that Miss Atkins was right. "When do I leave?"

CHAPTER 23

FRANCINE

*A*fter her training was complete, Francine moved into a flat in Bayswater while she received her final instructions. She was ecstatic to learn that it would only be a few weeks before she saw Jack again.

She met with Buckmaster in his Orchard Court office to go over her cover story: she was to be a former shopkeeper whose store had been confiscated by the Wehrmacht. Her alias would be Madame Francine Fabre.

"That way Jack can still refer to you by your real first name, not that he'd struggle to remember a fake one," Buckmaster told her. "He's one of the best we've got."

Francine beamed.

"You'll be a courier for Prosper," Buckmaster continued. "He has several of them now, his network has expanded so much." He nodded satisfactorily to himself. "But you should refrain from associating with anyone but Prosper and Jack. The less contact you have with other agents, and particularly with other networks, the better. That way, if you get caught, you can't give the Gestapo too much information." His blue eyes momentarily lost their twinkle. "From what I hear, it's awfully hard to keep quiet once they get their talons into you. We don't need all of our circuits to fall like dominoes from the arrest of one agent."

"Yes, sir."

He patted his front pocket absently before spying his pipe lying in front of him on the desk. As he lit it, Francine was pleased to sense his easy-going manner return. He passed her an envelope. "Here are 50,000 francs, and some blank identity and ration cards. Prosper or Andrée Borrel will know what to do with them."

"Yes, sir." Francine had heard of the fearless Andrée, Prosper's original courier, during training.

"And now for the pills." Buckmaster pulled a small pouch out of a drawer and emptied it onto his desk, unveiling an assortment of different-sized tablets. He picked up one of the green ones. "These are Benzedrine, a stimulant. Take them when you need to stay up all night."

Francine nodded.

"The tan ones are downers—you can slip them into someone's drink and they'll sleep for hours. The white will produce violent stomach problems, as if your insides are breaking down. Once again, useful for thwarting the enemy or if you yourself need to feign illness. It's not the most enjoyable experience, but, should a doctor need to examine you, it'll get the point across."

"What about that brown one?" Francine asked, noting there was only one of them.

"Ah." He picked it up. "This is cyanide. We call it the 'L' tablet; L as in lethal. Once chewed, it will kill you in a matter of 15 seconds."

Francine was taken aback. "You're talking about suicide?"

"Obviously it would only be used as a last resort." He dropped it back into the pouch. "If you do get captured by the Gestapo and you're not sure what you might be encouraged to say under torture, then this little pill can help." He set his pipe down to scoop the rest of the pills into the pouch as Francine picked up her purse.

His pipe was back in his mouth as he held the pouch out to Francine, who gingerly accepted it.

. . .

After Francine's meeting, Miss Atkins took her shopping to ensure that everything she took with her would be authentically French. The SOE had hired a tailor who'd escaped through the PAO line and specialized in fitting second-hand clothes donated by other refugees. He also boasted that he had a wealth of French labels that could be sewn onto newly-made outfits in an absolute pinch.

Though Miss Atkins paid for the clothing—a red sweater made from an itchy material, a couple of blouses, and a pair of pleated culottes—Francine was displeased. "Can't I have at least one new dress?" she asked.

"No." Miss Atkins set her lips in a firm line.

"But…"

"Francine, according to your cover story, you—like most women in Occupied France—have no money to spare. Your clothing should reflect that."

Desperate, she showed Miss Atkins the fine blouse she was wearing. "May I at least be permitted to take this with me? I bought it in France before I left."

Miss Atkins fingered the silk. "Well, you must have had to replace the buttons along the way, because they're clearly English-made. The Gestapo can pick up on little things like that, just as I did. Do you want to risk your mission—and your life, for that matter—for a blouse?"

"No," Francine replied. But while Miss Atkins was busy inspecting the rest of her belongings, Francine convinced the tailor to replace the buttons. It wouldn't do to see Jack again, after months apart, wearing the dregs Miss Atkins had picked out. The worst was the underwear: giant bloomers made of thick fleece.

"Coal is scarce in Paris, and it gets very cold," Miss Atkins declared when she handed them to Francine.

"How very practical," she replied, holding the bloomers at arm's length. She resolved to pack just one pair of her lacy satin underwear. *For Jack's eyes only.* No Gestapo officer would ever have to know of their existence.

·   ·   ·

The next stop was a lawyer's office so that Francine could make out her will.

"Who is your next of kin?" the lawyer asked, his pen poised.

"Jack Agazarian," Francine answered.

Miss Atkins reached out to touch Francine's hand. "I would also have another person, just in case..."

In case neither of you returns from France, Francine finished to herself.

The lawyer then asked if she had any children.

Francine shook her head. She gave him the last known address of her brother, who had joined the RAF.

"It's better that you don't have a lot of family," Miss Atkins stated as they left the lawyer's office. Something in the way she said it sounded to Francine as though she were also trying to convince herself. "You wouldn't be able to contact them from the field, anyway. The agents there are effectively cut off from everyone they know and love back home. They live a life of deception, with a false name, false papers, and a false backstory, all designed to protect them." She paused to look at Francine. "I can't imagine it's easy."

"I suppose I'm lucky in that way," Francine replied in a soft voice. "I'll have Jack."

"Yes. It was Major Buckmaster's idea to send you both over." Though it was clear Miss Atkins didn't entirely approve of Buck's decision, she took Francine's hand and squeezed it. "I'm sure everything will work out for the best."

CHAPTER 24

YVONNE

*Y*vonne and Pierre returned to the Flamencourts, but Yvonne couldn't help being uneasy at the death of Monsieur Ruhiere. The old man's demise had most likely been caused by something unpreventable, like a heart attack, but she couldn't shake the feeling that their presence was putting the Flamencourts and the others at Petit Aunay in danger.

When she expressed this to Pierre in their shared bedroom, he agreed with her. "At any rate, we've managed to set up a competent arm of Adolphe here, one who will be able to manage without us. We need to move on to another nearby town and recruit more locals."

"Any ideas?"

He rubbed his mustache. "Édouard once introduced me to a power supply manager named Julien Nadau."

"Power supply? So he would know the best places to stick time-pencils to literally keep the Boches in the dark?" Yvonne grinned at her own joke.

"That and he's allowed a car to travel around his territory." Pierre tapped his forehead. "I remember what you told me about the benefits of recruiting civil servicemen who can move about without triggering the Gestapo's suspicions."

"Do you think this Nadau would be willing to help us?"

Pierre raised his eyebrows. "It's worth a shot."

Nadau indeed proved trustworthy and found them a small cottage to rent in the Sologne region, a remote area between Orléans and Tours, bound by both the Loire and Cher rivers. The land was dotted with a multitude of lakes, and, in between, marshland and forests, making it a perfect hiding spot.

The soil in the region was too sandy to grow much besides asparagus, and most of the Solognots were poor, with tiny houses and the occasional lone goat. Yvonne had initially assumed that such people were too busy trying to feed their families to worry much about rebelling against the Germans. However, she underestimated their hatred for the *Service du travail obligatoire* and other atrocities committed by the Germans. Here too, the sons who had gone into hiding had formed *maquis*. The spark of vengeance was lit, and all Pierre and Yvonne would need to do was fan the flames with British guns and ammunition.

Nadau knew the location of every remote cottage that housed people willing to join the Resistance. Consequently, soon after they'd arrived, Yvonne and Pierre set off with Nadau one morning by bicycle. Their destination was the house of André Gatignon, a wine merchant, who, as Nadau had explained to them, smuggled Jewish refugees across the River Cher to the Unoccupied Zone in his wine barrels.

Yvonne couldn't help fretting as she pedaled. The Germans had recently increased their reward for any information leading to the capture of British agents in France. Not only that, it was rumored they were sending anyone who refused to reveal such knowledge to their work camps in Germany. As a result, any potential new recruit could turn out to be a treacherous liability for the Adolphe subcircuit.

Yvonne reached into the little basket strapped to her handlebars and touched the cold metal of the pistol she'd hidden underneath a bundle of asparagus for reassurance. She hoped she wouldn't need to use it on anyone, for it would be a difficult task to dig a hole deep enough in the frozen soil to encase the body of a German. *But then again*, she reasoned, *perhaps the sandy asparagus beds would make for decent burial grounds...*

The sight of the charming château finally brought her out of her revelry.

"We're here." Nadau led them onto the estate and parked his bicycle against a large pine tree. "I must warn you that the Gatignons are currently billeting two Boches."

"Krauts?" Yvonne's mouth dropped open. "Surely—"

Nadau shook his head. "They sleep in the drawing room, but they leave very early in the morning. I am sure they are not here now."

"Right." Pierre put his hands in his pockets. "It wouldn't do to try to recruit saboteurs in the presence of the very enemy we are trying to destroy."

Yvonne took the pistol from the bicycle basket and shoved it into her culottes as Pierre and Nadau walked toward the main house, which was surrounded by square buildings, presumably housing wine barrels.

A pretty middle-aged woman greeted the trio and introduced herself as Madame Gatignon. She led them into the drawing room, where about a dozen men were gathered. Yvonne noted with relief that none of them wore a German uniform. Madame Gatignon took a seat beside a short, bearded man, and gazed at Pierre expectantly.

He cleared his throat. "Good morning. I am sure Monsieur Gatignon has recruited you here with purpose, so I will spare you the details and just let you know that we are different from most local Resistance outfits in that we have backing from London."

"What do you need from us?" Monsieur Gatignon asked.

"Mainly storage," Pierre replied. "We are expecting many supplies to be dropped by air in the coming months, and will need a place to store them until the Allies arrive in France. In addition, I will need your help in finding suitable landing grounds for these drops, as well as attending them and bringing the provisions to the safehouses."

"They have been trained by a secret office in England for these purposes, and will teach us all they know," Nadau added.

"I was not trained myself," Pierre countered. "But my partner here, Jacqueline, was." He nodded at Yvonne, who stepped forward.

She began to pace the length of the room. "We know what we are asking is not easy. If they," she gestured toward the Boches' pile of blankets and pillows in the corner of the room, "catch you, you will most likely be sent to a work-camp in Germany, or else killed immediately, if you are lucky enough not to be tortured." She focused her gaze on Madame Gatignon as she continued, "You must weigh the risks carefully and think of your family, your children, before you move forward."

This was met with mumbling from the men, but Madame Gatignon simply nodded.

Pierre clapped his hands and the room fell silent again. "Now who is ready to help us?"

Madame Gatignon was the first to shout an enthusiastic, '*Moi.*' Her husband raised his hand, and the rest of the room gave their affirmatives.

Pierre glanced at Yvonne, a smile forming under his mustache. "Mission accomplished," he told her.

"Indeed," Yvonne replied.

The next step was to establish a new drop zone. When Monsieur Gatignon suggested a large, wooded field in between Pontlevoy and Contres, Pierre borrowed Julien Nadau's car to check it out. After he found it satisfactory, he went to Gatignon to have Gilbert Norman inform the SOE.

Pierre did not look happy when he returned.

"What's wrong?" Yvonne asked as they sat down to dinner. She still refused to do Pierre's sewing, and now cooking, but a few of their new recruits had taken pity on them and were more than willing to supply them with home-cooked meals. Tonight's dinner consisted of rabbit stew and a few raw carrots, the irony of which was not lost on Yvonne.

Pierre cracked a carrot in half. "London hasn't been responding to Prosper's repeated requests for more arms."

"Why not? How are we supposed to prepare for an Allied landing if we don't have enough guns and explosives?"

He paused his chewing to reply, "Your guess is as good as mine."

A few days later, a cyclist dropped off a message to the cottage. Jack Agazarian finally had confirmation that the SOE would be dropping canisters at the new field in two nights' time, during the full moon. Pierre decided this would be an ideal time to train the newest members of Adolphe.

On the night of the drop, Pierre and Yvonne had some more stew, this time coupled with stale bread, while they listened to the radio. The SOE had made arrangements to send messages to their agents over the airwaves, buried in the BBC's *les messages personnels*. To the average listener, they were nonsense, but to the right ears, they were notices of air drops, parachutages, or other pieces of news from London. Tonight's coded message was 'The microscopic hand starts off the operation.' As soon as he heard it, Pierre jumped up. "They're on their way."

The DZ was near enough to a main road. Most of the new drop zone committee arrived by bicycle, though Monsieur Gatignon brought a large van full of empty wine barrels to hide the canisters in.

Yvonne hid her bicycle under some branches and took stock of the surroundings. The moon was bright enough for her to see that the field sloped from the road into a deep ditch. On the far end was a bog surrounded by a copse of oak trees.

Pierre got to work instructing the new contacts how to determine the direction of the wind and set the flashlights accordingly. "And you have the most important job of all," he told Monsieur Gatignon as he handed him the last flashlight. "You're the one who is going to flash the Morse code."

"What about you?" Monsieur Gatignon checked the batteries and then turned the flashlight on.

"Remember, this is a training exercise." Pierre pointed toward one end of the ditch. "Jacqueline and I are going to observe from over there. Let us know if you have any questions."

Monsieur Gatignon clicked off his torch with shaking hands and nodded, his eyes wide.

Yvonne and Pierre were only meters from the ditch when they heard unfamiliar voices approaching from the road. "More recruits?" she whispered.

She could see Pierre's shoulders raise and fall in confusion as he rushed toward the ditch. She followed, just in time to see that the voices belonged to bicyclists, who were clearly out on a leisurely night ride and not part of their group. She held her breath as she knelt down, thinking it would be a few seconds until they passed by. When she heard the squeak of brakes, she shot Pierre a confused look. He gave her another shrug.

She listened hard for any hint of what the cyclists were up to, but there was only the sound of trickling water. She patted her culottes, thinking maybe she had mistakenly sat in a creek, but her bottom was still dry. She then glanced up to spot a stream of water shooting down from somewhere above her head. It took her a further moment to realize that one of the cyclists was urinating into the ditch. Luckily the sound drowned out Pierre's low chuckle.

The bicyclists finally got on their way, and a mortified Yvonne was able to scoot away from the offending puddle.

It was only a few minutes before the plane's droning could be heard. Pierre held up his hand and crossed his fingers. Yvonne peered over the top of the ditch to watch the parachutes float down. "Why are they coming from way over there?" she asked.

Pierre scrambled out and began running toward them. "Something's wrong," he called over his shoulder.

Yvonne followed him, though she paused when she realized that the landing signals had been placed back to front. Instead of heading toward the empty, flat field, the parachutes were bearing toward the bog.

The February night was already bitterly cold, but the team had no choice other than to dive into the swampy waters to retrieve the canisters.

Yvonne was a decent swimmer but didn't relish the thought of getting into the dark, dank marsh. Without pausing to reconsider, she plunged in. The chest-deep water was indeed freezing.

A circuit member near her said loudly in an English accent, "*Merde*, it's so cold."

"You! Englishman," a disembodied voice shouted. "If you are going to swear, you'd better swear in French."

Yvonne glimpsed a short, stout form standing in the woods. The figure, a woman Yvonne decided, lifted a gnarled finger. "You are English, right? It's high time you came back to do your part, considering how you let our boys down at Dunkirk."

Pierre, who was rolling a canister onto the shore, glanced back at the group, a bewildered look on his face. It was now Yvonne's turn to shrug. She saw him reach into his pocket, probably to grab his gun, but the woman shook her finger at them one more time before marching off.

Somehow the party managed to retrieve all the canisters, a total of eight this time. They loaded them into Monsieur Gatignon's van before wrapping their still-soaking wet pant legs around their bicycles and heading back to their warm beds.

"What did you think of the new recruits?" Pierre asked as he and Yvonne pedaled toward their cottage.

"Well, they laid the signals wrong," she replied. "But they did show heart, and I don't think they'll make that mistake again."

"No," Pierre agreed. "Next time we're going to find a field much further from the road."

"And away from any bodies of water," Yvonne added.

CHAPTER 25

ANDRÉE

*A*s Prosper's courier, Andrée traveled all over north-central France, picking up messages from a myriad of Resistance associates, which she then passed on to Gilbert—or Jack Agazarian when Gilbert wasn't around—to be transmitted back to London. One of her favorite letterboxes was that of the Tambour sisters, the women who had been so hospitable when Andrée first arrived in France, at 38 Avenue de Suffren.

Germaine was almost always the one to greet her, with a requisite glass of brandy, and usually a tidbit or two of information to convey to Prosper. The Tambour apartment was the meeting ground for other agents as well. Andrée had run into Adele there once (though she heard that she'd recently returned to England), and Yvonne on another occasion.

This time there were two unfamiliar men sitting in Germaine's living room.

"Andrée, I'd like you to meet some of the men from the Donkeyman circuit." Germaine gestured toward a man with faded blonde hair and weathered skin. "This is Raoul Jean Kieffer—"

"Call me Kiki," he interrupted, holding out his hand. After

Andrée shook it, Kiki indicated the other man. "This is Roger Bardet."

"We were just leaving," Bardet stated. His eyes were such a deep brown they almost seemed black.

Germaine handed him an envelope. "Please pass this on to Paul Frager," she said before seeing the two men out.

Andrée got comfortable on the worn couch, noting the bottle of brandy and empty glasses on the coffee table.

"What's the latest?" Germaine asked when she'd returned.

Andrée shrugged. "You probably know more than I do."

Germaine smiled coyly. "I suppose you are too busy now with the gorgeous Gilbert Norman to keep up with all the news."

Andrée rolled her eyes. As clandestine as the Prosper circuit was to the Gestapo's prying ears, it seemed that gossip spread like wildfire among its members.

"Maybe after a couple of sips of brandy, you'll be willing to spill what it's like going to bed with such a gorgeous man. In the meantime…" Germaine retrieved a newspaper and handed it to Andrée.

The paper was in German, which meant it was unintelligible to Andrée. "What's this?"

"Another German was murdered in the subway the other day." Germaine sat across from Andrée and poured them both some brandy. "It could be all propaganda, but the article implies it was someone with a Sten gun."

"A communist?"

Germaine raised her eyebrows. "Maybe. Maybe not. But I think we can agree on where that gun came from."

"There will be reprisals. The Germans will make the French pay in blood."

Germaine shrugged. "While I don't wish to sacrifice any of my countrymen, especially the women or children, you and I both know the Germans' reprisals only stoke the flames of Resistance."

Andrée folded up the paper. "We need more guns. Dozens, hundreds more, if we want to do some real damage."

"I know you think that. But that's why I wanted to show you the story. There's at least one dead German as the result of a Prosper-supplied weapon."

"I wish I could shoot them myself," Andrée said, the longing in her voice obvious. "But of course, that would destroy everything we've worked for. Still..." she clenched her fist, thinking of those well-fed Boches trampling through the streets of Paris.

"What if you *could* do more?" Germaine asked. "Not by killing them, but by hitting them where it counts."

Andrée stared at her. "What do you mean?"

"Well…" Germaine set her empty glass down. "Have you heard of Chaingy?"

Déricourt was late. Andrée drummed her fingers on the table of the Café de Flore, her briefcase snug against her leg. Inside was a folder full of intelligence on the Chaingy power station; Paul Frager, head of the Donkeyman circuit, had entrusted it to Germaine, who had then passed it on to Andrée. Its contents were much too extensive to be transmitted over the wireless, which was why she had to arrange a meeting with Déricourt.

She glanced around, taking in the art nouveau decor, which was nearly hidden by a thick cloud of cigarette smoke. It never ceased to amaze her how the hustle and bustle of the French café was one tradition that had remained fairly unchanged despite the Occupation. Gilbert encouraged fellow Prosper members to use them for rendezvous because, as he said, 'a crowded café was a safe café.' At any rate, it was a welcome distraction to the silence of the streets.

Andrée had chosen a table in the corner next to a large, gilded mirror so she could see everyone who walked in. After half an hour, three cigarettes, and two cups of ersatz coffee, she finally spotted the muscular frame and unruly hair that could only belong to Déricourt.

She flagged him down. He paused to peer into the mirror, smoothing a cowlick, as Andrée pointedly checked her watch. "You're late."

"I had other, more important, things to do." He arranged himself in the chair opposite her. "What do you have for me?"

She retrieved the folder from her briefcase and handed it to him.

He tucked it into his valise without looking at it. "Is there a message to accompany it?"

"Yes, but I still need to code it." Andrée took out a pencil and a square coding card.

Déricourt snatched the paper from her. "You can't do that here." He glanced furtively over his shoulder. "People will get suspicious."

Andrée calmly took the card back. "You're the one acting suspicious. It's a wonder they don't arrest you just for being you."

He leaned forward. "I have a drop scheduled for tonight and I'll be sure to hand the message directly to the pilot. It will be in the hands of Buckmaster in a matter of hours. There's no need to put it in code."

She ignored him and set up a poem code. After she'd finished, she set her pencil down as a thought occurred to her. "Do you not encrypt your messages?"

He shrugged. "My courier has yet to be trained by the SOE."

"What courier? You're not a circuit leader, so what gives you the right to hire a courier?"

He gave her an oily grin. "I have too much on my plate to handle all of it myself. I hired an old friend, Julienne Aisner, to help me out."

"Did Prosper okay this?"

"Prosper is out of town. I didn't see the need to get his permission."

Andrée drained her coffee cup before replying. "Prosper likes to oversee every detail he can."

"Well, maybe he's been overextended. At any rate, I've known Ju-Ju for years. She's trustworthy." He pointed at Andrée's work. "You done yet? I have to leave."

She handed it to him. "You said the drop is this evening?"

"Yes." Déricourt folded the paper and tucked it into the front pocket of his bag. "It's Jack's wife who is arriving tonight, actually."

Andrée narrowed her eyes. "Should you be sharing that information with everyone?"

He shrugged. "She's going to be another of Prosper's couriers, so I figured you'd already know."

"As if Gilbert had been informed about Jack coming? Besides, the network's been expanding so fast, I can't keep track of every new recruit."

"If you say so. Francine is going to stay with Ju-Ju for a few days to get acquainted and then I'll have her contact you." He touched his hand to his temple in mock salute. "I've got to get going."

As Andrée watched Déricourt saunter away, she couldn't help thinking that his questionable security only served to heighten her distrust of him. She made a mental note to ask Germaine Tambour what she thought of Julienne Aisner—and Déricourt himself—for that matter.

CHAPTER 26

FRANCINE

*T*he train was very crowded, Francine noted as she made her way down the aisle, looking for a seat.

A tall man in a grayish-green uniform and heavy black boots stood up, causing her heart to hammer. It was only her first full day in France—was she about to get caught already? "You may have my seat, madame," the German soldier told her.

She managed to give him a tiny smile before sitting down. He was forced to perch next to her in the aisle, a little too close for comfort.

Francine refrained from wrapping her arms around the suitcase on her lap, knowing that, if the German discovered it contained a .32 revolver and ammunition, she'd be arrested right away, and taken to Gestapo headquarters. And if they performed a body search, they'd find a cloth belt hidden under her clothes containing the banknotes and blank ration cards Buckmaster had given her. Not to mention the transmitting crystals, intended for Jack, that had been sewn into the sleeves of her black dress by Miss Atkins herself.

The soldier's guttural attempt at French interrupted Francine's thoughts. "Are you headed to Paris?"

"Yes," she answered quickly. "I work in Poitiers but I'm going to see my aunt." In fact, she'd arrived by Lysander the previous day. A man named Déricourt had greeted her and given her the train ticket and instructions to report to Paris.

"And your husband?" The German's tone had taken on a hopeful tinge.

She dropped her gaze downward before replying in a soft voice, "The *Service du travail obligatoire.*"

He nodded, a guilty look flashing across his face before he focused his attention elsewhere on the train.

Francine adjusted a crystal so that the lump on her sleeve would not be so obvious. *Being in France wouldn't be that hard*, she decided.

At first glance, Paris seemed like the city that she used to know. The corner cafés were still crowded with people and the streets and sidewalks thronged with bicycles. But, as Francine made her way to her destination, she realized that there weren't many cars, and the few that did drive by were all the same: black Citroëns. And from every public building flew Nazi flags with black spider-like swastikas, the sight of which made her stomach turn.

When she reached the address Déricourt had given her, 1 Rue de Berri, off the Champs-Élysées, she took the elevator to the top floor. The lettering on the door of 10B declared it to be the office of Hérault Films.

She was greeted by a small woman who was almost as short as Francine herself, with liquid brown eyes set into a round face. "You must be Francine." The woman stuck out a manicured hand. "I'm Julienne Aisner."

She chatted animatedly as she showed Francine into an elegantly decorated room and then stopped abruptly at a bookcase full of circular metal disks.

On closer inspection, Francine realized they were projector reels. "What is Hérault Films?"

"It is my husband's film company. Or rather, I should say, my ex-husband's." Julienne's voice dropped to a whisper, though as far as Francine could tell, they were the only ones in the office. "He was a Jew, so he fled to America." Her voice grew louder. "Now he's working in Hollywood, advising them as to what it's like living under

Nazi Occupation. He consulted on that American film, *Casablanca?*"
She paused to see if any of her name dropping had an effect on
Francine. It didn't so she continued, "Harry asked me to help him in
his operations, knowing this would be a good safehouse for the
agents he's helping to get into France. Do you need any ration cards
or identification documents?"

"No." Francine patted her pocketbook. "The SOE provided me
with papers before I left."

"The SOE." Julienne nodded to herself. "Harry wants to send
me to London to become an official agent." She peered at Francine.
"I can see you are small, like me. Did you think the agent training
was difficult?"

Francine finally figured out that 'Harry' must be Déricourt.
"Yes, but my husband helped a lot, especially with the physical
portions."

"You must be talking about Jack then. I wondered about your
last name."

"Have you met him?"

"Yes. I was able to get him a fake X-ray that showed his lungs
were in poor shape, to keep him out of the German service."

"Where is he?"

"I don't know right now. He comes and goes. But Harry told me
to find you an apartment with a full bed, so maybe you'll see Jack
soon."

Francine breathed deeply. "I certainly hope so."

CHAPTER 27

YVONNE

*I*n just a few weeks, Pierre and Yvonne managed to set up Resistance guerilla groups throughout the Sologne. Their initial recruits from the Gatignon château all drafted more, who also drafted more; it seemed every person they encountered knew someone else who was willing to join the network.

The phony couple's remote, single-story cottage was known to the locals as 'Le Cercle' because of the fire pit in the back ringed by a circle of tree stumps. Though void of luxuries such as indoor toilets, it did have electricity, which they needed to listen to the BBC broadcasts, and an oven, which they never used. The scant furniture had been donated by members of their circuit. Yvonne made sure she and Pierre had their own bed, each complete with an old parachute as a bedspread.

She had at first balked at the lack of running water, but after Pierre had told her, "There are plenty of trees in the forest," she reasoned that the seclusion would be beneficial for their operations. She found a small vase to use for washing up, though every time she went out to the well, she had a vision of poor Monsieur Ruhiere lying dead in the snow. Fortunately there wasn't that much laundry: Yvonne had only the one pair of stained culottes, a couple of shirts, a vest, and a wool sweater for cooler weather. Pierre, she knew, had an equally meager wardrobe, not that she ever offered to do his laundry.

The frequency of arms drops had finally increased in the spring of 1943, and Yvonne and Pierre found themselves with more arms and explosives than either they or Prosper could distribute. They stored the volatile Nobel-808 in small ditches hidden among the trees of Le Cercle but because the Sologne was so humid, they couldn't leave the time-pencils, grenades, or guns out to rust in the open air. Instead Pierre scaled the rickety ladder to the small attic above their living quarters while Yvonne gingerly handed him the treacherous goods, thinking it was enough to blow all of Le Cercle —and possibly a good chunk of the rest of the Sologne—to bits. Sometimes Yvonne would lie awake at night and stare up at the ceiling, imagining a stray lightning bolt striking the attic and incinerating them. But then she would console herself by picturing a similar fate for all things Nazi, which would hopefully be the ultimate destination of the explosives.

One night Pierre and Yvonne were quietly planning their next mission when there was a loud pounding on the door.

"Open up!" a deep voice commanded.

"Who is it?" Pierre called as Yvonne shot him a startled look.

"What are you doing in this house?" the voice demanded.

Pierre marched over to his bed and pulled a pistol out from under the pillow. He motioned for Yvonne to hide, but there was no place to go, save for the armed attic and she had no desire to hole up among the gunpowder. She took a seat in an armchair and clutched the well-worn leather arms.

Pierre checked to make sure there were bullets in the gun before cocking it. He opened the door only part-way so as to hide his pistol. "Can I help you?"

"I want to know why you are in my cabin."

Pierre relaxed his arm. "*Your* cabin? We are here on the authority of Julien Nadau. He rented this to us, care of the Romorantins."

"The Romorantins don't own this cabin. *I* do."

Pierre tucked the gun into the back of his belt and opened the door wider. "Please come in." He motioned to Yvonne. "We're refugees from Brest."

The man had the courtesy to bow toward her. "I didn't mean to startle you."

"It's not a problem." Pierre went over to a chest of drawers and pulled out a wad of francs. "I can pay you the rent right now."

The man's eyes widened. "Why do you have so much cash?" His eyes darted back and forth across the room.

Yvonne's heart, already beating fast, picked up speed. She supposed her partner had been trying to bribe the man, but it seemed the would-be landlord wasn't going to fall for it. *Now you've really done it, Pierre.*

"Are you...?" The stranger lifted his arms and wiggled his fingers downward. "I've heard about you."

"What do you mean?" Yvonne was now genuinely confused. It looked like he was motioning raindrops, which didn't make sense.

He repeated the gesture. "You know..." he went over to the bed and fingered the parachute bedspread.

"Oh..." Yvonne glanced at Pierre, who shrugged. "Yes," she said finally.

"Me too," the man's voice dropped to a whisper. "I think I've just been recruited into your circuit by Albert le Meur, a friend of Julien Nadau."

Pierre breathed a heavy sigh as Yvonne began to laugh. "We're very sorry about the mix-up," she said when she'd finished giggling, "but as Pierre told you, we're more than willing to pay you the rent we owe."

"No." The man held up his hands. "I could never accept payment from you. Indeed, it is I, and all of France, who is in your debt."

Pierre put the money back in the drawer and shoved it shut. "Well, if that's the case, would you care for a drink?"

. . .

A few days later, there was another knock on the cabin door. This time Yvonne answered it to find two familiar figures standing on the porch.

"Andrée! It's so good to see you." Yvonne gave her friend a kiss on each cheek.

"Remember me?" Gilbert asked as he stepped inside.

"Of course," Yvonne replied. "I never forget a face, especially one as handsome as yours." From the way Andrée blushed, Yvonne knew that the relationship between the two had become more than a working one.

Gilbert held up his suitcase. "Do you mind if I set up my aerial? I need to make my afternoon sked."

"Not at all." Yvonne waved toward a window. "The trees give us good cover, but will they be a problem for your transmissions?"

He started unloading the contents of the case on the kitchen table. "Shouldn't be an issue."

"Prosper told us about your new accommodations," Andrée said. "We're in the area to investigate some RAF bombings."

As Andrée spoke, Yvonne studied her friend. She looked fresh-faced and happy. Her polka-dot dress was faded but still flattering to her figure and she'd touched up her blonde hair.

Yvonne was suddenly struck with inspiration. "Gilbert, can you do me a favor and ask London to send me some new clothes?"

He glanced at her ratty outfit with a raised eyebrow.

"Look at what they expect me to wear." She demonstrated how her vest barely closed at the waist. "Trust me, with all this rationing, it's not because I've gained weight. It's because these awful French fabrics that Miss Atkins insisted we wear have shrunk with washing."

"I can try," Gilbert said as he took out a pencil and silk code.

"Where's Pierre?" Andrée asked.

Yvonne shook her head. "He's outside. He had the brilliant idea that we should booby-trap the grounds in case anyone 'unfriendly' happens by. I tried to convince him there were enough explosives in the house already but he didn't listen."

"You two are like an old married couple."

Yvonne settled into what had become her customary armchair. "You're right about the old part."

Andrée took a seat in a rickety chair. "Oh stop. Do you remember meeting Jean Worms?"

Yvonne scrunched her eyes in concentration before nodding. "Short Jewish guy? Head of…"

"Juggler," Andrée finished. "Yes, that's him. He told me after he'd met you, he guessed you were in your early thirties."

Yvonne waved her hand. "Please."

"It's true," Gilbert called from his spot at the kitchen table. "You're looking younger and younger in your old age. This type of work obviously suits you."

Yvonne recalled those lonely, terrified nights she'd spent cowering from the bombings in her London basement. Since her daughter had gotten married and moved out, and she'd long kicked Alex out of the house, there had been no one to join her in what could have been her last hours on Earth. Even though the work she was doing was as equally threatening, at least she had the network now. And Pierre. "I'm just trying to do my part."

Gilbert carefully began packing his equipment back into his suitcase. "Now that that's finished, what do you have to eat around here?"

Pierre joined them for some leftover stew. This time, their dinner had the added benefit of some croissants Andrée had brought from Paris.

"So why did you two travel all the way out here?" Pierre asked through a bite of the chewy stew.

"We're here to meet up with some of the members of the Juggler circuit," Gilbert replied.

"Jean Worms is the leader," Yvonne added helpfully.

"Yes." Andrée tore off a piece of croissant and dipped it in the stew. "Worms has a new courier, a beautiful young girl. I believe from her dark hair and coloring that she is also Jewish. Sonia something or other. She's not SOE-trained."

"That's not such a big deal." Pierre stated. "I've given up asking to be transported to London at this point. Learning on the fly worked well enough for me."

Gilbert pushed his empty bowl away. "And also we're here to discuss Chaingy."

"Chaingy?" Yvonne asked. "Why? Is there a new branch of Prosper there?"

"No," he replied. "It's a transformer station that provides the electricity for the railways in northern France."

Pierre grunted in agreement. "The lines are all electric. If you destroy the station, you wipe out the power, which means the trains bringing German troops and supplies to France won't run." He stabbed at a stalk of asparagus.

Yvonne caught on. "And neither will the ones deporting French men—and Jews—to Germany." Noting that Pierre still had the asparagus dangling from his fork, she gently reminded him to eat it.

"Oh yes." He gazed wonderingly at the stalk before shoving it into his mouth. Clearly his mind had been focused elsewhere.

"Right," Gilbert said, eager to continue. "We sent plans to London, hoping that the RAF could blast the Chaingy station from here to kingdom come. But the bombs were only able to hit a few power lines before all the planes were brought down."

"And the pilots?" Yvonne asked.

Gilbert shook his head slowly. "Not only did the Germans slice their knives through them, making sure they were dead, they left them to rot in the middle of the town square for four days."

Yvonne's mouth dropped open. It sounded so cruel, even for the Nazis. "So what are we going to do?"

"Bomb the hell out of Chaingy, this time from the ground," Andrée replied.

"You can count us in," Yvonne told her.

Andrée smiled at her friend. "I knew you'd say that."

CHAPTER 28

FRANCINE

*J*ulienne set Francine up in a flat in the Rue du Colonel Moll. It was dreary, with only a lone window in the living room to let in light, and lacking in furniture. The couch was shabby and the 'full bed' that Julienne had told her about seemed ready to fall apart at any moment. All in all, the apartment was in stark contrast to Julienne's warm and inviting one, but, with the added restrictions of rationing, there wasn't much Francine could do to liven it up.

Near dusk the second evening after Francine had moved in, she heard a knock at the door. When she answered it, she found Jack standing there, holding a brown leather suitcase. "The concierge invited me to look at this apartment. I'm told it's for rent?" He strolled in and paused at the window.

"Jack?" Francine asked uncertainly. "What's got into you?"

"This appears quite suitable." He set his case on the table, and then turned to Francine, his wide grin revealing both dimples.

She ran straight into his open arms. "Oh Jack, I've missed you so much."

"Me too, Francie." He stroked her hair, his breathing heavy.

She broke away to peer at him. He looked mostly the same,

maybe with another crinkle or two around his eyes. She moved her hands across his chest. It was still muscular, and she couldn't see any bruises…

"I'm perfectly okay, Francie." He kissed her on the lips. "How was your flight?"

"It was fine. No incidents. A man named Déricourt was part of my reception." She filled in the rest of the details of staying with Julienne.

"We have quite the welcoming party in Prosper now." Jack pulled her to the couch and sat down.

"Are you tired?" Francine's backside sank into the threadbare cushions. "Have they been overworking you?"

"Yes, but it's to be expected. We're preparing for the Allied landings, and at least London has finally started supplying more ammunition. We were worried there for a while."

She grasped his hand and brought it to her heart. "Well, I'm here now. There's nothing to worry about."

He put his other hand on her cheek and caressed it before asking, "Are you ready to hear about your first mission?"

"Mission? I've only just got here."

"And there's much afoot. Starting tomorrow, in fact."

She closed her eyes and sighed. "Okay, I'll be willing to listen in a few minutes, but first…" she laid back on the couch, thinking it had to be sturdier than the bed, and pulled him on top of her.

The next morning, Jack and Francine set off for the Palais-Royal garden. Upon arrival, she could see why it would be a fitting spot for a rendezvous between secret agents. It was secluded, with double rows of trees along two sides of the garden, and the maze of shops on the ground floor of the old palace provided an easy escape from any overly watchful eyes.

Jack paused at a bench facing a marble fountain, which, due to wartime austerity, wasn't operating. Francine sat beside him, her arms folded over her chest. She turned her back to Jack, pretending to be fuming at him, which gave him the opportunity to scan the crowd.

"Here they come," he said faintly.

Francine kicked at the gravel beneath her feet, knowing she shouldn't stare, though she was dying to get a good look at the famous Prosper. She glanced up as Jack walked closer to the fountain, whistling. He stuck his hands in his pockets and stopped a few feet away from a dark-haired man and his companion, who was even taller than Jack. She assumed they were exchanging information, but the gentle breeze carried away any hint of what they were saying.

When Jack returned to the bench, he told her he had to leave.

Francine didn't have to pretend to be perturbed this time. "Why?"

"I have to make my sked. They want to be sure Buck knows about our efforts today."

"Can't Gilbert do it?"

Jack shrugged. "I think he wants to be in on the action." He patted her hand. "It's not a big deal. Prosper and Gilbert will show you how it's done, and then we can celebrate tomorrow." With that, he strode off, leaving Francine no choice but to join the men at the fountain.

"You must be Francine," the shorter man said. He turned to study her face. "I assume you know who I am."

The confidence in his voice could only mean she was talking to Prosper. "I do."

The tall man reached out to shake her hand. "I'm Gilbert Norman."

"I'm glad to finally meet both of you," Francine stated as they began to walk away from the fountain.

"And Jack has informed you of our plans for this afternoon?" Prosper asked.

"A little."

"Gilbert here can fill you in on everything on the way to Orléans." Prosper led them to a small black car. The front passenger side was filled with paper products, so Gilbert sat in the back with Francine.

"How did you manage to obtain a car?" Francine asked as Prosper started the engine.

"One of our circuit members donated it." He nodded at the goods next to him. "And those too. I travel under the guise of being a paper salesman, though we only use the car for special occasions."

Gilbert took one of the pads of paper and a pencil and began to sketch. "These rails to the southwest of Paris are all electrified. If we cut the powerlines, then the German supply lines would be crippled, at least for a few days."

"Probably less than that, though," Francine said, recalling what De Wesselow had told her about pylons not being the greatest target.

Gilbert's pencil stopped moving. He glanced up at Prosper, who was frowning in the rearview mirror.

"You just finished your training, didn't you?" Prosper asked. The question felt biting, intent to put Francine back in her place, but his tone was not altogether unkind.

"Jack did say that Francine still has a lot to learn," Gilbert acknowledged.

Francine bit back the retort that was on her lips, thinking Jack would not appreciate it if she made enemies with his new colleagues. "I'm sorry. I know there are a great many things I don't understand, but I'll get them in time."

Prosper nodded. "See that you do." This time the warning in his voice was unmistakable.

Gilbert returned to his sketch. "It's not just a few pylons. It's over twenty of them. They usually have 300,000 volts flowing through them, and it's our job to make sure that they don't anymore. We have multiple teams working at the same time. Andrée and Jean Worms took a train out to Orléans last night and are biking to Chaumont-sur-Tharonne as we speak, and Yvonne and Pierre are going to do their part in the Sologne." He tilted the pad toward Francine. "I made a scaled-down model of the whole set-up, and the best places to put the charges are here, here, and here." He tapped his pencil at each spot. "We've learned that you should only destroy three of the legs; if you go for all four, then the pylon just falls, but is still functional. This way it will collapse and wreck the whole circuit."

Prosper checked his watch. "If it's as easy as you say, we can be back in Paris this evening so I can pack."

"Where are you going?" Francine asked. Her heart skipped as the car slowed, but Prosper was merely stopping at a stop sign, and the country road was void of any other cars.

"Buckmaster has something he wants to discuss with me back in London."

Francine wanted to ask what it was, but didn't want to seem overly nosy. Luckily Gilbert rescued her from dying of curiosity. "You think it's about the Allied landing, boss?"

"Your guess is as good as mine," Prosper replied.

CHAPTER 29

ANDRÉE

*A*ndrée heaved a heavy breath as she paused her bicycle by the side of the road to let her companion catch up. Neither of them was accustomed to pedaling long distances—especially not when wearing a cumbersome backpack overstuffed with explosives —but Andrée wasn't nearly as winded as Jean Worms was.

"I think your backpack is heavier than mine," he managed to gasp out. "Do you want to switch?"

Her gaze traveled over the short-legged, pudgy Worms, thinking his masculine gallantry was wasted on her. "No, that's okay. I'm getting used to the weight."

"The weight, huh. The contents don't bother you?"

She shook her head as she remounted. In truth she preferred to perform acts of sabotage at night, under the cover of darkness, but Prosper insisted this one had to be done during the day so they could place the charges just right. Still, she was more excited than nervous, picturing with glee how angry the Boches would be when they realized their power had been cut.

A short time later, they reached their destination: a deserted field bordered by several enormous metal pylons. They got to work attaching the Nobel 808 to three legs of a nearby pylon before moving to the next one. Andrée coughed as the wind blew a whiff of the strong almond smell into her face.

"All right, I think they are all in place," Jean said after they'd finished setting the explosives on the third tower.

She handed him a time-pencil. "Do you know how these work?"

He used his other hand to push a piece of dark hair off his sweaty face. "I think so."

"Once you break the copper tubing, we won't have much time before the acid disintegrates the wire and causes the striker to detonate it."

"Got it."

Andrée finished with the first detonator before Jean and quickly walked over to the third pylon. She used a pair of pliers to crush the end of the tube and then held it up to peer through the inspection hole. To her dismay, it appeared blocked. She searched her backpack for another time-pencil, but she'd only brought three. *This one will have to do.* She tried scraping her nail along the hole but that did nothing to clear the blockage. She closed her eyes before shaking the whole thing vigorously, hoping she wasn't about to blow herself up. This time when she looked, she could see straight through, which meant the countdown had started. Taking one last deep breath, she removed the brass safety strip which held back the striker. Her usually steady hands were shaking this time, but she managed to attach the pencil to a block of Nobel 808.

"Time to go!" she announced to Jean, and the two of them raced back to their bicycles.

As Andrée pedaled away, it occurred to her that the time-pencil could very well have exploded in her hand. She wasn't afraid of death, necessarily—it would be hard to be in this line of work if she was—but a small, niggling piece of her couldn't help from being curious if anyone would miss her if she were gone. She hadn't had contact with her family since the war began and, though Maurice had been in her life longer than most men, she never pictured herself marrying him. And now there was Gilbert. They'd talked about what they would do when the war was over, but she wasn't sure how serious he was about her. Or if she was serious about him. Did she love him? Not having ever said those words to anyone, Andrée had no idea.

She was so wrapped up in her thoughts she'd almost forgotten about the detonators until the ground shook beneath her bicycle. She and Jean both halted. They were only a few kilometers away and could see the blast clearly enough. She gave a little shout of triumph as the first pylon fell in a sea of wires and blue flames. Black smoke filled the air. The second tower, the one Jean had ignited, soon followed in a similar manner until the blackness smothered the electrical fire.

"The sparking stopped," Jean stated.

"They must have cut the power."

"What about the third pylon?" That was the one that was supposed to be detonated by Andrée's faulty time-pencil.

Her heart sank, remembering de Wesselow's customary admonition during explosives training: *the demolition must never fail.* "I don't know," she replied, putting her foot back on the pedal as she caught sight of a black Citroën zooming across the field toward the conflagration. "But we probably shouldn't stick around here to find out if it blows or not."

There were no trains back to Paris that afternoon, so Andrée stayed with Jean in Orléans. He took her to dinner at a black-market restaurant. The Juggler courier, Sonia Olschanezky, joined them. She was accompanied by a tall, elegant man whose bright blue eyes contrasted with his fading blonde hair.

"This is my fiancé, Jacques Weil," Sonia informed Andrée as the waiter seated them at a corner table.

Jacques grinned at Andrée. "Don't say it—I already know I'm old enough to be her father."

"You're not old," Sonia told him affectionately. "I'm just young."

Andrée gazed at the diminutive, dark-haired girl. "How old are you anyway?"

"Nineteen."

Even Andrée was surprised at that.

"And don't ask about *my* age," Jacques said. "I was raised in Switzerland, but I've been a resident of Paris since before Sonia was born."

Andrée couldn't help wondering if the blue-eyed Swiss was Jewish, like Sonia and Jean. It was one thing to be a British agent in Occupied France, but she couldn't imagine also living under the ominous threat of deportation to an unknown destination because the Nazis didn't approve of your religion or race.

"Baker Street considers Jacques my second-in-command," Jean proclaimed. "Though I would argue that he is the real head of Juggler and Sonia is his second. Even as a young lady of nineteen, she's one of the best we've got."

Sonia's black eyes flashed at the compliment.

Jean shook out his napkin. "I keep hounding Déricourt to get them on a plane back to London for training, but…"

Jacques waved his hand. "I've been there often enough as a businessman. And besides, what could I learn there that I haven't already picked up during my own experience in the Underground?"

They fell silent as a waiter approached.

Sonia leaned closer to Andrée. "You'll find the food better here than some places in Paris, where the meat is most likely to be horse."

Andrée nodded her approval.

"Steak for everyone, and two bottles of your finest wine," Jacques told the waiter. "And please give the bill to me." He waited until after the waiter was out of earshot and then said, "The SOE is always offering me money, but I prefer to pay my own way. It makes me feel as if I'm contributing something to the war effort."

"Contributing something?" Jean raised his eyebrows before he turned to Andrée. "Jacques and Sonia were part of the crew that laid charges on the railway tracks this afternoon. They destroyed an entire car full of German soldiers."

Andrée's eyes grew wide. Remembering where she was, she cast a surreptitious glance around the restaurant. It was mostly empty, but there could be prying ears anywhere.

"It's okay," Jean told her. "We come here often. The servers don't listen, and even if they did, they're all sympathetic to our cause."

As if on cue, the waiter returned with the wine. No one said anything as he opened the bottle and then poured four glasses. He shot Andrée a shy smile before he left the table again.

Jacques, clearly an expert on wine, swirled his glass and then tasted it before nodding approvingly. "The destruction of the train, in addition to the electricity interruption, should really confound the Boches for at least a little while."

"Yes, but one of our pylons didn't blow," Andrée said.

"No, it did," Sonia countered. "We were riding down a backroad on the way back to Orleans when we saw two officers get out of a Citroën and approach the fire, just in time for the last explosion. It threw the lead man a few feet in the air, and the other one ran back to the car."

Jean nudged Andrée. "It would have been fine with just the two towers, but I'm awfully glad we managed to kill, or at least seriously maim, a Boche as a bonus."

"Me too," she replied, pleased that the demolition hadn't failed after all. She held up her glass. "Cheers to…" Even though they'd assured her the restaurant was a safe zone, Andrée couldn't bring herself to say, "defeating the Boches," aloud. "Cheers to our health."

"Hear, hear," Jean agreed. "May our luck ever spread."

CHAPTER 30

YVONNE

"*D*o you think it's enough?" Pierre asked, gazing at the pile of explosives he and Yvonne had gingerly stacked in Jean Nadau's trunk.

It was filled to the brim, but Yvonne replied, "It doesn't matter. We could completely obliterate dozens of pylons and the Boches would be able to restore the power in a few days. As it is, it won't be anything to write to London about."

"Prosper only said the two pylons."

She shut the trunk door. "Whatever Prosper needs, we'll do, though he should know better than to target electricity towers."

"Besides," Pierre climbed into the backseat of Nadau's car. "The French citizens are always cheered by acts of sabotage, even if it is an inconvenience to them."

Yvonne arranged herself in the passenger seat. "I just hope the Germans don't decide to harm those same citizens because of our actions."

"Indeed," Nadau agreed as he started the car.

They'd only driven about ten kilometers in the direction of Vernou-en-Sologne when Yvonne could feel the car slowing.

Nadau eased his foot off the break. "Damn."

"What is it?" Yvonne squinted, barely making out a dark mass several meters ahead of them.

"Roadblock," Pierre said in a low voice.

Nadau turned off onto a dusty side road. "I have my papers, but I wouldn't want to risk it."

Yvonne grinned. "I can just imagine the expression on the Boches' faces should they dare open the boot and see our Nobel 808."

"Théo Bertin's house is not far from here," Nadau said. "I'm going to head there and we can figure out what to do next."

Yvonne sighed to herself. Prosper would not be pleased at the delay in their mission, but sometimes obstacles like German road-blocks couldn't be avoided.

Théo did not seem overly surprised to find the three of them on his doorstep and ushered them in. His living room was what one would expect from a poacher—abundant fur rugs carpeted the floors and dead animal heads covered every available wall space. Yvonne sat in an overstuffed armchair and looked down as a little brown dog rushed over, wagging its tail.

Théo whistled at it. "Louki, meet my friend."

"A dachshund?" Yvonne asked. "Why did you, as a veteran of the First Great War, choose a German breed?"

Théo shrugged. "He's a good hunter, not to mention a terrific watchdog."

She reached down to pat Louki's head. "What is our plan?"

"The Feldgendarmerie has set up numerous checkpoints throughout the region in the past few days," Théo told them.

"Why?" Nadau demanded.

"Hopefully just as a precaution," Théo replied.

Pierre rubbed his mustache, obviously deep in thought. "It does complicate things. Still…" he dropped his hand. "Orders are orders, and I wouldn't want to disappoint Prosper."

Nadau nodded to himself, as if making a decision. "I'll go out on my bicycle and see if I can find another route. There's a pub a few miles away from our target. If I can make it there without being stopped, I'll telephone to let you know."

As Théo got up to show Nadau where he kept his bicycle, Pierre leaned back on the couch and shut his eyes. Yvonne picked up a half-chewed ball and threw it near Louki, who growled and went to fetch it.

"Do you want a drink?" Théo asked when he returned.

"Just tea," Yvonne replied. "I'm working," she added when he raised an eyebrow.

He busied himself in the kitchen. "Actually, I'm glad you two are here. I'm not sure if you were informed about the incident last week…"

"Incident?"

"With Déricourt." Théo set a tray on the table in front of Yvonne, surprising her with his unexpected domesticity.

She nudged Pierre awake as she asked in a loud voice, "What has Déricourt done now?"

Pierre's eyes flew open. "What?"

"I was part of the reception committee for one of Déricourt's landings," Théo said as he stirred his tea. "There were two planes expected that night. The first one touched down fine, but as the second one came in, we men on the ground heard a loud, booming sound. The plane hit a tree."

"Was it damaged?" Yvonne asked.

"A bit. The propeller was dinged up for sure. The pilot was none too happy and blamed the whole thing on Déricourt. Some words were exchanged, ones not fit for me to repeat in the company of a lady."

"I've heard them all anyway," she stated dryly.

"The plane was able to get back to London all right, as far as I know, but the pilot said he was going to file a report against Déricourt and I don't doubt that he did."

Yvonne exchanged a perplexed glance with Pierre before asking Théo, "Do you think it was Déricourt's fault?"

"I couldn't say for sure. They don't turn their landing lights on till they're right above the ground, so… maybe it was an error by the pilot."

. . .

A few hours later, Nadau called to say he had arrived safely. Théo offered to join Yvonne and Pierre, but insisted they use his family's bicycles instead of taking the car. Théo and Yvonne each loaded a few blocks of Nobel 808 into their baskets while Pierre carried the time-pencils in his pocket.

They found the field without any trouble, even though every time they'd turned a corner, Yvonne expected to be stopped. However, the pylons were so spread apart that they only had time to cover one with charges.

"Don't you want to watch the results of your handiwork?" Théo asked her.

"No," Yvonne replied as she connected a two-hour time-pencil to a brick of 808. "We wouldn't want any of those men at the road-block to get suspicious." She pointed to the darkening sky. "It's bad enough we'll be out after curfew." She dropped her arm before grinning at Théo. "But trust me when I say I'll see the explosion in my dreams."

CHAPTER 31

NOOR

*N*oor couldn't help arriving early for her lunch appointment at Manetta's. She'd been extremely tense ever since that last talk in Buckmaster's office, when she'd felt sure they were about to fire her, and the anticipation of this meeting was enough to break anyone. She took a seat on the red leather couch near the door and clenched her fists to keep from picking at her nails.

Precisely at noon, the door to the restaurant flew open and Miss Atkins, clad in gray tweed, breezed in. "Nora, thanks for meeting with me. Come, come," she gestured before marching to the hostess stand.

Noor trailed behind Miss Atkins as the hostess led them through the clamorous dining area to a table in the corner.

Noor followed suit as her companion took her time spreading her napkin across her lap. "Do you like working for us?" Miss Atkins finally asked.

Noor reached out to straighten the silverware. "Yes, of course I do."

"I'm glad." Miss Atkins signaled the waiter and requested two waters. Noor felt her stomach grumble. During her SOE training the past few months, Noor had gotten used to being fed well. However, Miss Atkins' even-more-brisk-than-usual manner made it clear that they were not meeting here to dine.

As Noor had predicted, Miss Atkins waved the waiter away after he delivered the drinks. She turned back to Noor. "I wanted to let you know that I've heard from several people who don't think you are suitable for the position you are about to undertake."

"Again?" Noor looked pleadingly at her boss. "Who said that?"

Miss Atkins pulled an envelope out of her purse and displayed the return address to Noor. It was the Chorleywood apartment she'd been staying in with two other agents. "They wrote to you?" Noor asked.

"Yes." Miss Atkins returned the letter to her bag. "They say you've been acting melancholy and pessimistic, as though you were overtaxed—"

"I'm not." Noor rarely ever cut people off, but she wanted to assure Miss Atkins that she was prepared for the task ahead of her. "Trust me."

"Nora, you know, if you are having doubts, it's not too late to back out. I can rearrange every detail—get you transferred to another sector where you wouldn't have to travel abroad."

Noor shook her head.

Miss Atkins reached across the table and placed her hand over Noor's. "There's only one crime in our line of work: letting the other members of the circuit down."

She refrained from yanking her hand back. "I would never do that."

"Is it your family you are worried about?"

Noor covered up a pang of sadness with a gulp from her water glass. "Yes. As you suggested, I told my mother I was going to Africa. I've never lied to her before. Or anyone."

Miss Atkins took a tiny sip. "What you call 'lying' is essential to your job. If you lie to your mother about where you're going, it's not because you are a bad daughter, it's because you're a good agent." When she sensed her words did little to comfort Noor, she asked, "Is there anything I can do to help?"

Noor was about to shake her head again, but then something occurred to her. "If something bad were to happen to me... if I go missing, I would like it if you wouldn't tell my mother anything until you knew for sure that I was... not coming back. I wouldn't want to worry her unnecessarily."

"You have my word," Miss Atkins replied. "In the meantime, I'd like you to meet with Leo Marks, our coding extraordinaire. I think he can help you with your confidence, and reassure Major Buckmaster and myself that you are ready."

"Yes ma'am."

CHAPTER 32

ANDRÉE

*A*ndrée uncapped a tube of lipstick and leaned forward to peer into the tiny dorm room mirror.

"You don't need that," Gilbert told her from his perch on the bed. "You're already beautiful."

She pursed her lips and then checked to make sure she didn't have lipstick on her teeth. "And then there's my hair." Her hand went to her tangled coiffure.

He gave her an indulgent grin. "Happens when you roll around in bed all afternoon. Now come on," he patted the bed, "stop primping and get over here."

After nearly a week of not seeing Gilbert, she'd met up with him in Grignon at the agricultural college. Dr. Vanderwynckt had invited them to dinner but she couldn't help feeling nervous at the thought of interacting with all of the intellectuals, afraid they'd pick up on the fact that she wasn't one of them.

Gilbert leaned back on the bottom bunk with his hands behind his head. "Chaingy go okay for you?"

"Yes." She decided to leave out the part about the warped time-pencil. "You?"

"Fine, except Jack's wife was a bit nervous and needed help with her charges."

Andrée ran a brush through her hair. "She's new. Give her some time to acclimate."

"That's what I told Prosper, but he seems to think everyone should be as competent as him."

"Yet no one can be."

"No. Especially not Déricourt, who's been recalled to London because of the plane/tree incident."

She wrinkled her nose. "Maybe Buckmaster will make him stay in England. There's something about him I don't trust."

"I haven't had a problem with him so far."

She swatted him with the hairbrush. "You like everyone."

He grabbed her hand and pulled her to him. "Especially you."

Their lips met in a long kiss. When they finally broke, Andrée asked, "Have there been reprisals for Chaingy?"

"Back to business again." He began massaging her shoulders. "No, the Boches haven't really done much, other than setting an earlier curfew for Blois and temporarily closing its cinemas."

"That's not bad. They've done worse, much worse, in the past."

"I agree. I heard that members of another circuit, in no way connected to Prosper, have recently been captured." He paused, his palms lying flat against her body. "It is my understanding that they're the ones who took the blame for Chaingy."

"Well, that was awfully nice of them."

"The Gestapo was probably torturing them. If they're going to confess, they might as well own up to other crimes to keep their fellow Resisters out of the spotlight." Gilbert dropped his hands as someone banged on the door.

Without waiting for a welcome, Prosper strolled into the room. "They've arrested the Tambour sisters."

"No!" Andrée exclaimed in disbelief. Germaine and Madeleine Tambour's Avenue de Suffren apartment was frequently used both as a safehouse and a letter box. "Why?"

Prosper shut the door. "No one seems to know, but I have a

terrible suspicion the Germans have finally started closing in on those Carte contacts they stole from Marsac's briefcase back in November. Germaine was Carte's former secretary and must have been on the list. Why they waited this long, I don't know."

"What are we going to do?" Andrée recalled meeting the two men from Frager's circuit—Kiki and Roger Bardet—at the apartment. "The Tambour sisters not only know about our network, but many others as well."

"Indeed, especially Germaine," Prosper's eyes landed on the tangle of sheets at the foot of the bed before they returned to Andrée. "I can't imagine the old gal being able to withstand any of the Gestapo's usual interrogation tactics."

"We've got to get them out of prison then," Gilbert decided.

"How?" Andrée demanded.

He put his arm around her. "You know as well as I do that everything in Paris is for sale… if you pay the right price."

"You're talking about giving the Boches money." She shrugged him off. "Bribing them, like a collaborator or a racketeer. What if the Allies find out? You could be tried as a war criminal."

"All the same, we need to get them out," Gilbert told her. "We all know Germaine could topple the entire F Section if she talks."

Prosper nodded. "Be sure to tell London to cancel the letterbox —we obviously can't use their apartment as a safehouse anymore. I'll start gathering funds. Jacques Weil knows a police officer at Fresnes. He might be able to help us find a 'friendly' guard who wouldn't mind extra pay."

Andrée began another protest. "But—"

Prosper held up his hand. "You've made your opinion clear, but I can't think of any other solution." This time there was a challenge in his brown eyes. "Can you?"

She couldn't recall another time where Prosper had spoken to her so harshly. Wordlessly, she shook her head.

The plan to rescue the Tambour sisters was swiftly put in place, thanks to Jacques Weil and the Juggler circuit. The sisters were to be brought to the Château de Vincennes as though they were being transferred from Fresnes Prison. Once the corrupt officers had received the SOE-provided down-payment of one hundred thousand francs, they would hand over Germaine and Madeleine to the Resistance and then later claim their car had been hijacked.

On the afternoon of the planned exchange, members of both the Prosper and Juggler circuits waited for the sisters at a café near the Metro. It seemed less suspicious to be in pairs than alone, so Jacques Weil joined Prosper at an outside table under the green and white striped awning, while Andrée and Gilbert sat a few tables away. Jean Worms stood across the street pretending to read a German newspaper. Though it was a warm day, most of the other Resistance members sitting inside or wandering the street wore long trench coats in order to hide their Sten guns and hand-grenades.

To Andrée, Prosper looked as cool and calm as always, but there was still a nervous energy permeating the air. He glanced up suddenly and Andrée followed his gaze. A black Citroën slowed down as it approached the café. When it came to a stop, two men in uniform got out from the front seat to open the back doors. They appeared again momentarily, escorting two blonde women.

Andrée narrowed her eyes. The women's clothing was ill-fitting and they appeared ashen-faced and exhausted, as if they'd been in prison for years instead of weeks. She bit back a gasp as she realized they were not the Tambour sisters.

Prosper had also apparently recognized the mistake. From her vantage point, Andrée could hear him shouting, but could not make out what he was saying.

The women looked bewildered as he walked up to them waving his arms wildly. One of the uniformed men shook his head before holding out his hand. Andrée's mouth dropped open as she saw Prosper hand over the money.

"I think the boss just paid a hundred thousand francs for the most overpriced prostitutes in all of France," Gilbert whispered from behind his menu.

"What about the sisters?" Andrée shot back.

He put the menu down and shrugged.

Jacques leaned over to hiss, "What is happening?" It was obvious he'd never met the Tambour sisters.

"They're not the right women," Andrée replied in a low voice.

He sighed. "Well, they are at least French girls. We can't let them go back to Fresnes." He got up from the table to approach the little group. He put a calming arm around Prosper before speaking to the guards. After a minute, one of the guards shook his hand before he and his companion left.

Despite the circumstances, Andrée couldn't help smiling when the women, clearly overjoyed to be released from prison, started kissing Jacques and Prosper. Jacques broke away to whistle loudly. A burly man materialized at his side. Jacques nodded at the women and soon the burly man was escorting the women to the Metro station.

"What happened?" Gilbert asked as Prosper seated himself at their table.

"A mix-up. The guards claim it's because Fresnes is so over-crowded. But Jacques is going to renegotiate and try again."

"Maybe we should just cut our losses, boss," Gilbert said. "This game of breaking out the Tambour sisters is getting too dangerous."

"No." Prosper was adamant. "We're not giving up."

This time Jacques's contact demanded two million francs, with half up front, claiming it was "danger money."

When Prosper entered Andrée and Gilbert's apartment and opened his suitcase, Gilbert gaped at the contents. "That's a lot of cash to put down for the possibility of another pair of working girls."

Andrée still didn't agree with bribing the enemy, but she grinned as an idea came to her. "They want half up front, we'll give them half up front." She went into the kitchen and came back with a pair of scissors. She picked up a bill and cut it down the middle. "We'll give them half now, and then the other half when the Tambours are exchanged."

"That's not going to make them happy," Gilbert said wryly, gazing at the destroyed francs.

"Does it matter?" Andrée asked.

He reached out and took her hands in his. "I don't want you to come this time. I have a bad feeling about this."

She squeezed his hand before letting it go. "It's fine. What are they going to do?"

"Probably nothing," Prosper said.

"All the same, I'd rather you not be there," Gilbert told her.

On the day of the new exchange, Andrée, forced to stay back, waited restlessly for Gilbert to return. There wasn't much to do. She tried to read an old, pre-war *Vogue*, but the fashion was hopelessly out of style. As she flipped through an article entitled, "Spring Collections Designed to Please Your Man," she glanced down at her fingernails, which had been bitten to the quick. She wasn't used to being nervous, especially not on behalf of someone else. In fact, she rather hated that she missed Gilbert so desperately and refused to think of what might happen if he didn't come back.

She had just shut the magazine, wishing that she and her fellow women wouldn't feel the need to please anyone with their wardrobe, when the door burst open.

She jumped to her feet. "Well?"

Gilbert shook his head. "Instead of a Citroën, they drove up in a 'Black Maria.'" *A Gestapo transport van*, she quickly translated. "Twenty men with guns filed out. Luckily we were waiting inside and managed to escape out the back door, but…"

"They didn't bring the Tambour sisters," Andrée answered for him.

"No." His eyes were dark with sadness. "They're probably in Germany by now. But the good news is that those dirty Boches didn't get the money this time."

"I guess we can tell Buck we have two million francs in reserve now."

He gave her a wry smile. "Just as soon as we reassemble all the bills."

Even with the help of Sonia and Jacques, it took them three days to tape the rest of the francs back together.

CHAPTER 33

NOOR

*L*eo Marks' office was extraordinarily messy. While Noor waited, she tapped a coding pencil against the table, trying not to focus on the possibility that this might be her last chance to prove her worth to the SOE.

Someone entered the room. He was shorter than Noor but carried himself as though he were tall. "You must be Nora," he said as he sat behind the desk. "I'm told you need some last-minute coding practice." He pushed a square pad of gridded paper toward her. "Why don't you try to compose a message of at least 250 letters and then encode it?" His voice, though commanding, was not unkind.

"Right." She began writing out a message saying the circuit had successfully blown up a train carrying Hitler, but then thought it was too far-fetched. She crossed out 'Hitler' and then wrote 'Hermann Göring.' *But instead of the circuit using explosives from the inside of the train, perhaps it should be the RAF destroying it from the air.*

"Nora?"

The sound of Marks' voice startled her. "What?"

"Pretend London is on air and waiting for that information." He tapped his watch. "You'd better encode it now."

"Right." Noor reached for her purse to grab her poem code. In an effort to impress Marks, she told him, "I wrote this poem myself."

He nodded. "Good. I'm always telling Buckmaster that it's safer if agents use original poems that aren't easily recognizable to the Boches. Though really they should have abandoned poem codes altogether and taught you WOK keys."

Noor chose her five words from the poem and wrote the indicator group on the side of the paper. She speedily numbered the key-phrases before picking up her message. It was still not right, so she crossed out the letter 'a' in front of 'train' and replaced it with 'the.'

"Nora?" Marks asked gently. "You haven't finished encoding."

"Sorry." Noor shot him an apologetic smile. "I'm a bit nervous."

"It's alright." He nodded at the card, and Noor set to work again.

When she triumphantly announced she was done, Marks told her to decode it.

"But I'm the one who coded it."

"Just try it," Marks replied.

After twenty minutes, Noor still wasn't able to decode her own message. She felt a lump forming in her throat as she told Marks, "I don't know what I did wrong."

He picked up her card and stared at it. "You've made fewer mistakes than most, but the ones you have made are pretty inventive."

She shook her head. "I can't imagine how."

"Coded messages have one thing in common with monkeys." Marks put the card down. "If you jump too hard on them, you'll break their backs—just like you've done to this message. I doubt Brahmadatta himself could decipher it. I guarantee my monkeys in the code room couldn't."

Noor's eyes grew wide. Brahmadatta was one of the characters in the short story, "The Monkey Bridge" from *Twenty Jataka Tales*—the book she'd written before the war.

"I greatly enjoyed your book," Marks stated. "It taught me a lot about you."

She could hardly believe that was true. "Such as?"

"That you despise lying." He pointed to her coded message. "But you've told me a lie, Nora, and you made the code tell a lie."

She got to her feet. "No I didn't."

"You gave the wrong indicator-group. How is that not a lie?"

She sat back down.

Marks moved the pad so it was directly in front of her. "This makes a total of six lies and one half-truth. We'd have to try 100,000 attempts at decoding this before Buckmaster could read it—and even that might not be enough."

She hung her head. "I'm sorry. I told you I was nervous—clearly my nerves got the better of me today."

"Every time you encode a message, think of its letters as monkeys, trying to cross a bridge between Paris and London. If they fall off, they'll be caught and shot… but they can't cross by themselves, and if you don't help them, giving them all your thoughts and protection, they'll never reach the other side. When there's a truth to pass on, don't let your code tell lies."

She took a deep breath before nodding.

"Now try again."

This time she went slower and took more care. After she'd finished, she closed her eyes and ran her finger over the letters she'd written, as if they were her monkey subjects and she was their protector. None of the monkeys cried out in alarm, so she handed the card back to Marks.

He raised his eyebrows as he examined it. "This is perfect—absolutely no mistakes."

"I hoped it would be," she said quietly.

He folded his hands under his chin as he looked at her. "Do you think you will be able to keep it up?"

"Yes, Mr. Marks, I promise you I will."

"Okay, good. Now we have to discuss your security checks." He picked up her file. "Because you're still using the poem code, I take it they gave you a bluff and a true check?"

"Yes, sir." The true check was used during every transmission. It consisted of three otherwise meaningless 'dummy' letters inserted into the message in random places. The SOE kept a record of each agents' checks, and the absence of them might mean the agent had been captured.

He blew out his breath. "It would be easier to use a WOK. That way you don't have to worry about safety checks, but..." Noor sensed he understood the WOKs they'd tried to teach her at Beaulieu had been beyond her comprehension. "Never mind." He changed tactics. "You realize that, under interrogation, you must never reveal your true check to the Nazis, right?"

"Of course. That's what the bluff is for." The bluff check was another set of letters that could be given to the enemy.

"Otherwise they may torture the true check out of you and pretend their messages are coming from you, and we'd never know you'd been caught. If they ask you, you have to lie."

Her voice was hesitant. "To stop them from lying to you."

"Yes."

"But what if there was a better way—suppose I refused to tell them anything at all, no matter how often they ask?"

Again his curious eyes scanned her face. "You'd rather they break your back than tell a lie?"

"I—"

He leaned forward excitedly. "I've got an idea. I'm going to give you a security check that's completely new, and you'll never have to lie about it because no one else but you and I will know it exists."

Noor smiled. She hadn't been so sure about Marks at first, but he had clearly sized her up and, unlike many of her other SOE instructors, was willing to accommodate her unique moral compass.

"All you have to do is remember not to choose a key-phrase with eighteen letters. You can have it be seventeen, or nineteen, but never eighteen. If you use eighteen, I'll know you've been caught."

Her smile grew wider. "Eighteen happens to be my lucky number. I can do that."

He ran a hand through his wiry black hair, making it stand even higher. "I almost wish you would have been a complete failure at this, and then I could write a bad report on you."

Her hand clenched involuntarily at her side. "Why would you want to do that?"

"To stop you from going to France," he replied softly.

She rose. "I promise you I won't forget my security check, or anything else you've taught me, Mr. Marks. I appreciate everything you've done for me."

As she turned to leave, he called out, "Nora…"

"Yes?" she asked, her hand on the doorknob.

"Good luck."

"Thank you, Mr. Marks."

CHAPTER 34

FRANCINE

*E*ver since the debacle over rescuing the Tambour sisters, Francine's nerves had been growing increasingly frayed. Sometimes when she was delivering messages to the various letter boxes throughout the city, she felt as though someone was watching her. She'd been taking extra precautions lately—such as circling the block and ducking in and out of buildings—in case she did indeed have a tail, but it did little to soothe her uneasiness.

It didn't help that Jack had also been stressed. Ever since Déricourt returned from London, he'd been using Jack as his wireless operator, which in turn displeased Prosper. It was almost a relief when Prosper left by a Déricourt-arranged Lysander for a meeting with the SOE in London.

In Prosper's absence, the work had slowed, and Francine and Jack took advantage of their leisure time to meet up with Andrée and Gilbert at 10 Square de Clignancourt, one of their safehouses, to play poker. Jack built a fire in the fireplace, which quickly warmed the small room. For the first time in weeks, Francine relaxed, comforted by the presence of Jack and the other agents. She pushed Major de Wesselow's warning—that it was unwise to congregate with other Resistance members—out of her mind.

"So I take it Déricourt was cleared of any wrongdoing with the plane crash?" Andrée asked as she dealt the next round of cards.

"I guess so," Jack replied. "He didn't say anything to me about it." He rearranged the cards in his hand. "Besides, with the European Allied landing coming soon, they're going to need all the help organizing the supply drops they can get."

"Prosper told me they're now calling the landing 'D-Day,'" Gilbert said.

Francine and Andrée started to ask the same question. "What does the D stand for?" Andrée finished.

"I have no idea." Gilbert threw some chips in the middle of the table. "I'll raise you four."

Francine took stock of her cards and then counted out four chips. "Do you think they'll tell Prosper the date of this D-Day?"

Jack made a face. "I'd say Buckmaster himself doesn't even know. He doesn't have that type of clearance, as much as he would wish it were so." His frown grew deeper as he studied his cards. "I fold."

"Same." Andrée set her cards down.

"I bet it all." Francine pushed the rest of her meager pile of chips into the middle of the table.

Jack raised his eyebrows at her. "Are you sure, Francie?"

"Sure as I'll ever be," she replied as Gilbert called the game. She fanned her cards face up on the table. "Two aces."

"Hah!" Gilbert threw his hand down. "Three kings."

Francine crossed her arms over her chest. She should have known better than to make such a reckless bet. "I thought you were bluffing."

"Sometimes I do. But not this time." Gilbert gathered his winnings with his broad hands. "Another round?"

Jack winked at Francine. "I'll lend you some of my money if you want to play."

"No, that's okay."

"I don't want to play another round either," Jack replied quickly, though Francine could tell he felt the opposite. He nodded at a stack of papers. "I need to decode those before my sked tonight."

"I'll do it." Francine picked up a paper and a pencil. She smiled at her husband. "You play."

"If you're sure…" He gave her a quick peck on the cheek.

"Will you two stop flirting?" Gilbert said as he started dealing. "Makes some of us sick."

"Oh you," Andrée gave him a playful nudge.

All four of them froze as someone knocked at the door. "Are you expecting anyone?" Andrée asked Gilbert quietly.

"No." His gaze traveled around the room as he got up from the table. Francine had already stashed the papers she'd been decoding inside a photo album. "Looks perfectly innocent to me," he declared before leaving to answer the door.

Francine tried to squelch a wave of uneasiness as she heard a gruff voice ask, "Can we speak to Gilbert?" She supposed she would never stop being nervous any time things seemed out of the ordinary. At least not until the war was over and she and Jack were back home safe in London.

"You are speaking to him. Would you like to come in?" Gilbert offered. He entered the room with two rather confused-looking men.

"We're here to ask about a flight to England…" one of them started to say in an unfamiliar accent.

"But we can see you are busy," his partner finished. "We can come back."

"No, no," Gilbert told them. "I think you must want to speak to Henri Déricourt, whose code name is Gilbert. He is the one in charge of flights. Gilbert just also happens to be my first name—my SOE code name is Archambault."

"Do you know where we can find this Déricourt?" the first man asked.

"No," Andrée replied. "But I can tell you he definitely won't be dropping by here anytime soon."

"I know how to contact him," Jack cut in. "However, there won't be a full moon for another few weeks. You'll have to wait till then if you want a plane."

The second man thrust his hands into the pocket of his suit coat. "So be it."

Gilbert showed them both to the door. "That was strange," he said when he'd returned.

"What kind of accents were those?" Francine asked.

"I think one of them was Dutch," Andrée said. "Best I can guess for the other is Belgian."

Gilbert reached out to twirl a piece of her hair. "A Belgian accent? Like Prosper's? Isn't Belgian code for 'not really French but trying to be?'"

Andrée shrugged. "It's either that or he was German attempting to pass off being French."

Francine, who'd been retrieving the papers from the photo album, paused and looked up. "Do you really think…"

Andrée waved her hand. "Kidding."

"Ha ha," Jack replied in a humorless tone.

CHAPTER 35

YVONNE

*I*n the late spring of 1943, the frequency of the air drops increased greatly. Even Yvonne became worn down from the endless long nights. Pierre was determined to expand the Adolphe subcircuit even further to prepare for the Allied invasion, which he thought might come soon. He decided to use their latest drop, which was to take place in the Neuvy region, as a training exercise for the newest recruits.

"Are you sure you want to have so many people from different subcircuits?" Yvonne asked as she packed the basket of her bicycle.

Pierre scratched his mustache. "I don't see a problem with it. We have to get them trained—there's no way you or I can keep up with all these drops by ourselves."

"I'm definitely not getting any younger," Yvonne agreed.

He gave her a sharp glance. "Are you feeling all right?"

"Just a bit tired. Why?"

He pointed to her bicycle. "Don't you think using that to tie the basket is a tad obvious?"

Yvonne looked down. The basket had come loose a few days ago, and she'd used a piece of string she'd found lying around the cabin to reinforce it. In the sunlight however, she realized the string was actually a parachute cord. "Sorry," she murmured as she started to untie it. "Maybe we should take the car instead." A Romorantin garage owner had recently given them a car left behind by fleeing refugees. Ironically it was a Citroën, the kind preferred by the Boches.

"It's only for special occasions, not general use," Pierre replied. "The DZ is only a few kilometers away. You can make it, can't you?"

"Of course." Yvonne tucked the cord into the pocket of her culottes before throwing her leg over the bicycle. "I told you I'm just a little tired."

The landing zone was near two roads, and most of the Resistance members came in pairs or small groups on their bikes, though Georges Fermé, a grocer from Montrichard, brought his van in order to transport the canisters.

Albert Le Meur, a hotelier, was tasked with leading the mission so Pierre and Yvonne sat down near a large tree to watch and wait.

The Halifax came in range around 1:30 am, circling once as it released its cargo. Yvonne counted nine parachutes in all. But as the first container touched ground, there was a blinding light which flashed as bright as daylight before it was gone.

"Get down!" Pierre shouted.

Yvonne threw herself to the earth, feeling it vibrate as a loud explosion reverberated through the forest. For a moment, she was thrown back in time to the Blitz in London, when her apartment building had been destroyed. When she had never felt so helpless.

But I'm not helpless now. She got to her feet in time for the next explosion, which she could feel under her boots. There was only one explanation: the Germans were bombing them.

"Run," she told Pierre, who was lying next to her. "We've been betrayed."

"No, wait…" he started to say, but she darted off.

Most of the Resistance members had scattered at the explosion, but she could see two of their men standing near the road. She stopped to catch her breath when she reached them before shouting, "We must go now!"

Their wild eyes stared back at her incoherently, but they did not move.

"What happened?" Pierre asked as he came upon them.

"I don't know," one of the men replied. He showed them his arm, which was bleeding. "It gave me a piece of shrapnel but I don't think it was the Boches."

"There were two explosions," Yvonne stated, calmer now. "Did they come from the plane?"

Pierre was obviously winded from his sprint as well, and his words came out in gasps. "Whatever it was, it's clear we need to load these containers and get out of here."

Albert Le Meur had already put out the flames from the blast, which had consumed all the evidence. Yvonne still thought it had been sabotage, but whether it was by the actual Boches or someone in London, she wasn't sure.

She mulled over the possible reasons behind the explosion all the way back to Le Cercle but could not come to any conclusions. She and Pierre did not speak as they rode home, and the silence was only broken once, by an ear-piercing siren coming from Romorantin, probably sounding the alarm. *Well, if those bombs weren't from the Boches, they definitely know about them now,* Yvonne thought darkly.

CHAPTER 36

FRANCINE

A few weeks after the Dutchmen interrupted their poker game, Jack arranged a rendezvous between them and Déricourt at Café Capucines. When Déricourt cancelled at the last minute and asked Jack to go in his place, Francine decided to tag along and meet Andrée for coffee. To save coal, the Boches had ordered that electricity be shut off from 3 to 5 every afternoon, and Francine had no desire to stay in the dark apartment until Jack returned.

"I think the only thing worse than ersatz coffee is cold ersatz coffee," Andrée remarked, making a face as she set down her mug.

"Agreed." Francine glanced across the room to where Jack sat waiting for the Dutch agents. Most of the other wicker chairs were empty this late in the afternoon. Jack caught her gaze and gave her a tight smile as the two men entered the café.

Francine picked up her coffee cup, pretending not to be interested in the goings-on in the corner.

"Are you feeling any better?" Andrée asked.

Francine took a gulp of the bitter liquid. "Not really. I still have this awful premonition that something is going to go wrong."

Andrée leaned forward. "Did you hear what happened to Yvonne in Neuvy?"

"No."

"A container exploded when it hit the ground."

"Exploded?" Francine covered her mouth as she looked around. A few more people had filed in after the Dutchmen, but they were well out of earshot. She waited while a man in a black trench coat strolled past and seated himself on the outside terrace, before stating in a quieter tone, "I didn't know containers could burst into flames on their own."

"Well, they are full of rather volatile materials, but I've never heard of that either. Pierre thinks it was just an accident, but Yvonne is not so sure. According to Gilbert, the pilot flew back to London with no idea anything was amiss."

Francine couldn't help but be envious of the pilot in his warm cockpit, heading back to the comforts of England. "Was anyone hurt?"

"No, just bruises and scratches, but as you can probably imagine, Yvonne is a bit shaken up."

Francine nodded. "I can indeed imagine."

Both women looked up as a low whistle sounded. A Wehrmacht soldier in a grayish-green uniform stood in the doorway of the café. "We need to see everyone's papers."

Andrée and Francine automatically reached for their purses. Out of the corner of her eye, Francine saw one of the Dutchmen get up from the table and head toward the door, walking too fast to go unnoticed. The soldier noticed him too and nodded at the man in the trench coat on the terrace outside, who shouted something at the Dutchman as the door opened. Half a dozen men surrounded the would-be escapee and took him out of Francine's view.

"Madame?" The soldier snatched the papers from Francine's hand, glanced at them, and then returned them with an oily smile. Not wanting to displease him, she turned her own lips slightly upward, but Andrée didn't deign to even look at him as she set her papers on the table.

Francine held her breath as another officer approached Jack's table. She knew that his Prosper-network supplied documents would be fine, but she wasn't so sure about his companion's. Even from across the room, Francine could see her husband was nervous, but she prayed the soldier wouldn't ask any questions. She finally let out her breath as the soldier walked away from the table. They'd passed!

"Let's get out of here," Andrée hissed. "We'll go across the street."

As Francine stood and gathered her things, she once again caught Jack's eye and touched her arm with her finger, pointing in the direction of the Café Napolitain. They'd move to yet another, hopefully more friendly, café.

This time Francine ordered a stale piece of bread to go along with her cold coffee. She picked at it without eating while she waited for Jack.

When he finally arrived, Andrée didn't wait to exchange pleasantries. "They arrested the Dutch agent."

"Yes," Jack said. "I'm not exactly sure what happened, but I gather Arend knew his French wasn't good enough to fool the Nazis, so he tried to leave. Most likely he's at Gestapo headquarters on Avenue Foch now. His friend took off after the Boches checked our papers, presumably to see if he could find out what happened."

Andrée shook her head. "This Arend saw all of us, including Gilbert, at the poker game. He had a flight to England and he knows about Déricourt." She put her head in her hands. "We have to tell Prosper."

"We can't wait for Prosper to return." Francine grabbed Jack's arm. "We have to go back to London. Now. Something bad is going to happen—I can feel it in my veins."

Jack placed his other hand over hers. "Francie, it will be fine. The Dutchman won't crack under pressure, you'll see. The Nazis don't know anything."

"No. I want to go home," Francine insisted. "This isn't what we signed up for. It's become too dangerous."

"You're wrong, Francie," he replied in a gentle tone. "This is exactly what we signed up for."

"Let's just take a break, for a little bit." Francine hoped it would be long enough for the widely expected Allied landing to happen, and then the war would be over. "You get a hold of Déricourt and tell him we want seats on the next flight out."

Jack managed a smile. "I guess with this latest arrest, there will be an extra spot on the plane." He glanced at Andrée, who'd been pretending to be interested in her coffee during their exchange.

Andrée put her hands in the air. "There's no room for me on the flight, and besides, I have to stay here and wait for Prosper."

You mean you have to stay here with Gilbert, Francine corrected her silently, but she didn't blame her friend for wanting to be with her lover. She tightened her grip on Jack's arm.

"Go," Andrée told Jack. "Get some rest. Maybe after Francine's nerves are settled, you can return. We'll always need good wireless operators. I have an inkling that Gilbert's going to be even more busy when Prosper gets back."

Jack shot a guilty look at Francine, probably feeling responsible for the mountain of work that would be piled on Gilbert in his absence.

Francine stood up and brushed her hands free of crumbs before extending one to Jack. "Let's go find Déricourt."

CHAPTER 37

NOOR

*N*oor's legs were unsteady as the gray-uniformed man led her up the stairs to Buckmaster's office. Once again she'd been summoned to meet with the head of F Section.

"Nora." Buckmaster's tone was as ebullient as always. "Come in, come in."

She sat down in the chair he indicated.

He lit a cigar before peering at her. "I don't suppose you know why you are here."

"Is it about my meeting with Leo Marks?"

"No. Well, in a way." He took a puff of cigar. "Marks thought you were grand, by the way. Actually, I called you here because we need a new wireless operator in Paris. You'll be the first woman sent into France in that role."

"You want me to go to France now?" Noor uncrossed her legs and leaned forward in a rather un-ladylike fashion. "I still have a few more weeks to go at Chorleywood."

"You're ready." He waved at the cloud of smoke. "But I have to warn you, Paris is the most dangerous city in all of Occupied France —the Gestapo are everywhere."

"I think I would be fine in Paris. I'm quite familiar with the city."

"I knew you would say that." He set the cigar down in a tray. "The next full moon is in a few days. Will you be ready by then?"

She knew better than to ask to see her family again. "Yes, sir."

Buckmaster pushed a large file folder across the desk. "You'll be working with the Phono circuit, an offshoot of the Prosper network. Prosper, though he doesn't know it yet, has just lost his wireless operator, so you'll probably tag along with Gilbert Norman for a while. Your SOE call sign will be 'Madeleine,' and of course, you've memorized all there is to know about your alias..." he looked at her with raised eyebrows.

"Yes, sir."

"You'll arrive to a reception committee prepared by Henri Déricourt." Buckmaster put the smoldering butt of his cigar back into his mouth, so his next words came out unclear. In an effort to hear him better, Noor leaned so far forward she almost fell over. "When you get to Paris, your contact will be Emily Garry, at 40 rue Erlanger."

"Emily Garry, 40 rue Erlanger."

"Right. And be careful of your filing of your messages." To Noor's relief, he stabbed out the butt before reaching into his desk drawer. "Now for the pills." He showed her pills of different shapes and colors as he rattled off what each was used for.

"I'm sorry, did you say cyanide?" Noor interrupted.

He stared back at her, the lethal pill still between his fingers. "I imagine something like that is against your religion, but it could save many others' lives should you feel unable to resist the Gestapo's torturing ways."

She shut her eyes, trying not to think of what her brother Vilayat, or her mother for that matter, would say if they knew she was carrying such a pill around in her purse.

"Here, look." Noor opened her eyes to see Buckmaster holding up a tube of lipstick. He unscrewed the bottom of the tube and inserted the pill before handing the tube to her. "Put it in your pocketbook and forget about it. Hopefully there will never be a time when you have to consider using it."

Noor dumped the lipstick into her purse with shaking hands.

Buckmaster glanced at the clock on the wall. "I think that's about it. Do you have any questions?"

Noor stood. "I think I've got it all."

He nodded at the file folder. "You'll want to memorize the contents of that and then burn it."

"Yes, sir."

"Good luck, Nora."

CHAPTER 38

YVONNE

*A*fter the incident with the explosive container, the German presence in the Sologne region intensified. They set up roadblocks and dispatched inspection teams, most likely searching for the hundreds of arms depots that members of the Adolphe subcircuit had hidden. At Yvonne's urging, Pierre sent a request via Gilbert Norman's wireless for London to pause the air drops for a few weeks.

"Did they agree?" Yvonne asked when he got back to Le Cercle.

"No." Pierre went into the kitchen and fetched himself a plate of food. "In fact, they told me Prosper is parachuting in tomorrow evening and he's requested us to receive him."

"Why not Déricourt? And didn't Prosper hurt his leg the last time he parachuted?"

Pierre sat down wearily. "He probably doesn't trust Déricourt any more than the rest of us do."

She sighed. "I don't really want to go back there. The Germans are everywhere."

"I agree with you, but Prosper's the boss. We have no choice. Besides, we should take his reception party nomination as a compliment."

"Choosing us over Déricourt?" She harrumphed loudly. "I wouldn't call that much of a compliment."

After the BBC's message, *the bicycles of the lord of the manor are worth nothing*, Yvonne and Pierre set out for the field. In honor of Prosper's return, Pierre decided to use their new car, though Yvonne had objected at first because of all the roadblocks. To her relief, Pierre kept the reception party small this time, the only others being Théo Bertin and Albert Le Meur. They were already at the DZ when Yvonne and Pierre arrived.

Prosper and his companion, France Antelme, a great big bear of a man, landed without incident. There were only a few containers and none of them exploded, so the six of them managed to get them loaded into Théo's van in record time.

Antelme left to catch a train for Paris while Pierre and Yvonne drove Prosper back to Le Cercle.

Prosper appeared exhausted—he was thinner and had more gray hair than Yvonne remembered. "Can I get you anything?" Yvonne asked as he sank into the armchair.

Pierre looked up, surprised at her uncharacteristic offer of hospitality.

"I wouldn't object to a cup of tea," Prosper replied. "But can you put the milk in first?"

"You are so English," Yvonne told him as she set the cup down in front of him.

"I have good news," Prosper stated after he'd taken a sip. "Adolphe is now on record with the SOE as an official circuit." He nodded at Pierre. "You are named Commandant, with Yvonne as lieutenant."

"It should probably be the other way around," Pierre said.

"Well, at any rate," Prosper continued, "I wanted to acknowledge the excellent work you two have been doing. I'm told there are guns and ammunition hidden all over the region, just waiting for the day the Allies need them."

"Thank you." Yvonne modestly decided to change the subject.

"What did old Buck have to say about the arrest of the Tambour sisters?"

"Not much." Prosper set his teacup down. "In fact, he didn't have much to say about any of the goings-on here, except to warn that the network might be growing too big, too fast. But I don't really think they get the full picture, how necessary the work we're doing is."

Yvonne stayed silent. She herself was beginning to think the Prosper network was becoming too extensive. Every new recruit was another person who could betray them all.

"Speaking of which…" Pierre cleared his throat. "I wanted to talk to you about relaxing the pace of the drops. They've been accelerating lately—for good reason, of course—but with the incident a few weeks ago, the area has grown hot."

Prosper shook his head. "Now is certainly not the time to back down. We need to have more supplies for D-Day, when the Second Front opens up. The Allies could literally be dropping parachute divisions on top of our heads any day now."

Yvonne recalled the fear she'd experienced after the explosion, and then she thought of Monsieur and Madame Gatignon, the Flamencourts, and poor Henri Ruhiere. *May he rest in peace.* She turned to Prosper. "I think it would be ill-advised to underestimate the Boches. You must remember that the people working for the Resistance in this region of France have their families with them."

Prosper narrowed his eyes. "If Reseau Adolphe refuses to take part in any more parachutages, I will bring in another circuit to do them."

Pierre sighed. "I still consider myself a soldier. If I am given an order, I will obey it."

"Yes," Prosper replied. "You will get the order for more drops. And you will carry it out."

CHAPTER 39

NOOR

*N*oor spent her last few days in England in constant anxiety. She filled her time by writing long letters to Claire and her mother, asking them not to worry if they didn't receive news from her for a while. She ended both letters by promising that the next time they were all together would be 'bonny and beautiful' and they would celebrate with pink champagne.

She penned even more pages to her older brother, Vilayat, whom she hadn't seen for over a year.

We will meet again someday, somewhere, when the war is over. And what a day it will be. There will be so much to tell each other. Duty can pull us to different ends of the world, but the ties between us will only be strengthened. For now I shall see you in my dreams, facing the wind and standing noble on your Navy ship. I feel so awfully proud of you. I wish you luck and know you do the same for me. Victory will be ours very soon. With all my love... Tallyho, Babuli.

When she wasn't writing letters to her family, Noor practiced being Jeanne Marie Regnier. Some of Jeanne Marie's backstory was familiar: she had an American mother and had studied at the Sorbonne. But unlike Noor, she was neither a writer nor a musician. Jeanne Marie's father was equally as mundane: a philosophy professor who had been killed in the Great War right after the birth of his non-existent daughter. It was as if Jeanne Marie was merely a shell of Noor, polished on the surface, but with all the meaty innards taken out.

Finally, on the afternoon of June 16, 1943, Miss Atkins called on Noor and told her it was time to leave. Noor grabbed her carefully packed bag and transmitting suitcase and loaded them into the car.

It was a lovely summer day and the scent of honeysuckle drifted through the open-top car as Miss Atkins drove through the Sussex countryside. Noor was occupied with her own thoughts. She was happy to note that the combination of the car's engine and the wind whipping their hair made it impossible to carry on a conversation.

Dusk had fallen when they reached their destination: an ivy-covered cottage opposite the RAF station in Tangmere. Noor was startled by the sudden silence when Miss Atkins turned off the engine. Though it was still quite warm, no one was outside and all of the windows to the cottage were shut tight.

"I don't allow them to open them—I don't want anyone passing by to know what we do here," Miss Atkins told Noor as she slid a key into the heavy door.

The house was filled with cigarette smoke, causing Noor to cough. They could hear the sound of male voices laughing in another room. "You shouldn't meet any of the boys," Miss Atkins said as she led Noor upstairs. "We'll wait up here. Don't look around too much," she cautioned. "These rooms are the pilots' sleeping quarters, and they might not be as neat as we'd like them to be."

Noor tried to shield her eyes the best she could, but she couldn't help but settle her gaze on a book by the bedside table. It was called *Remarkable Women*. She picked it up. "Do you suppose the pilot chose this as his reading material, or is the novel supply so limited here?"

Miss Atkins looked thoughtful. "I'm not sure. But I can tell you that there will have to be a sequel written someday soon, when you girls have finished your duties over in France. The ones I've met from F Section might just become the most remarkable women of them all."

Noor gave the normally icy Miss Atkins a grateful smile.

"Come then, Nora. Let me do a last-minute check."

Noor kept her arms by her side as Miss Atkins dug through her pockets, looking for anything that could give her away as British—cigarettes, receipts, coins. She was so close that Noor could smell her shampoo. She focused her gaze on the lapel of Miss Atkins' tweed suit, where a small silver bird was pinned.

Miss Atkins caught her looking at it as she straightened up. "It's a quail."

"I wrote a story once about quails." Noor was eager to talk about anything else than her impending trip. "A man was hunting them by throwing a net over them, but the King Quail told them all to fly away and they managed to escape from the net by landing under a thorny bush."

"Is that so? I'd heard you were a writer, but I haven't had the chance to check out your book." After a moment, Miss Atkins undid the pin and extended it toward Noor.

"Oh, no, I couldn't," she insisted.

"Take it." Miss Atkins' thin lips stretched into a smile. "It will bring you good luck. I hope a net never closes in on you, but just in case…"

"Thank you." Noor leaned forward as Miss Atkins pinned it on her. As soon as she had finished, there was a quick knock and then a handsome man in uniform opened the door. "Are you ready?"

"Yes," Noor replied.

The Lysander loomed large and black against the night sky. Noor found the sight of its stationary propellers eerie, as if they had been frozen in time.

As she exited the car, she was surprised to see her friend from training, Cecily Lefort, standing next to the plane, a suitcase at her feet. Noor refrained from embracing her, knowing that Miss Atkins wouldn't approve of fellow agents acknowledging each other.

Cecily apparently had no such qualms. "'Allo, Nora," she called gaily.

"Bonjour," Miss Atkins corrected pointedly.

Cecily waved her hand dismissively. "We're not in France, yet."

Miss Atkins gave a long sigh.

Another woman with big brown eyes stepped forward. Her fair hair was tied back in a low ponytail, complete with a plaid bow. "I'm Diana Rowden."

Miss Atkins sighed again. "Diana, didn't we talk about that bow?"

Diana removed the bow and handed it to Miss Atkins before shaking Noor's hand. Noor couldn't help thinking that, despite all of Miss Atkins' administrations, Diana still appeared very proper, very English.

A young man in uniform ducked underneath the tail of the Lysander and saluted Miss Atkins. "All set?"

"This is your pilot, Bunny Rymills," Miss Atkins stated.

"The best pilot in the RAF," he added.

After shaking Bunny's hand, Cecily reached into her purse and pulled out a pack of cigarettes.

"It's probably not the smartest idea to smoke near the plane," he told her. "And probably an even worse idea to smoke English cigarettes."

"Really, Cecily?" Miss Atkins put her hands on her hips. "Girls, did we not talk about this? Making mistakes like these in occupied territory could get you killed."

"I was going to finish all of them before I got to France," Cecily insisted.

Miss Atkins held out her hand and Cecily placed the nearly full pack into it. Miss Atkins put it into her coat pocket and then waggled her finger for Diana to step forward. She searched through her bag and coat for any last-minute British possessions and did the same to Cecily before turning to Noor. "I expect you'll be writing the sequel to *Remarkable Women* when you return." She reached out to touch the silver pin. "Good luck."

"Thank you," Noor replied.

Miss Atkins nodded at Diana and Cecily. "And good luck to you girls as well." Her face crumpled and for a moment Noor thought she saw tears form in the prim lady's eyes. "God speed."

"It must have been a trick of the light." Even though the three girls were nearly sitting on top of each other in the cramped fuselage of the Lysander, Cecily had to shout to be heard about the plane's engine.

"What was?" Noor shouted back.

"I thought Miss Atkins shed a tear. But that would mean she actually had a heart after all."

Noor shrugged. "She's always been nice to me."

"What are you going to be doing in France?" Cecily asked. "I know we're not supposed to talk about it, but it's not like the Boches can hear us now."

"I'll be heading to the Jura to work with the Acrobat circuit," Diana replied.

Cecily nodded. "I'll be in the southeast, with Jockey." She paused briefly before nudging Noor. "What about you, Nora?"

"Paris," Noor said, so softly that Cecily commanded her to speak up. "With Phono."

"Where do they come up with such names?" Cecily asked. Apparently it was a rhetorical question, for after a moment she leaned in to ask the pilot where they were. For the next half hour, Bunny pointed out landmarks to her and Diana, with only the black terrain and a compass to guide him.

Noor closed her eyes and took a deep breath. To distract herself from the dangerous mission she was about to undertake, she thought of all of the children sleeping warm in their beds back in England. Maybe some of them had been put to bed with one of her stories from *Twenty Jataka Tales*. Maybe someday those same children would indeed grow up to read a book penned by Noor Inayat Khan about tales of remarkable women and what they did during the war. Just as soon as it all became unclassified, of course.

· · ·

When they arrived in France, Noor was helped down from the Lysander's hatch by a handsome man with blue eyes. He met her gaze with a surprised one of his own. "What is the SOE thinking? You are far too exotic-looking to not stand out in a crowd."

Noor yanked her hand out of his grasp. "I'll take that as a compliment."

"Don't. The Gestapo are wise to everything." He touched her hair. "If I were you, I'd cut and dye this. Make yourself unattractive —and therefore, unnoticeable by German officers—as soon as possible." He extended his hand to Cecily. As she jumped down from the Lysander, Noor heard the dark-haired man say, "You'll do."

"Ignore him." Noor turned to see a pretty woman standing next to a clean-cut man who towered over her. The woman leaned closer. "And when I say ignore him, I really mean it."

Noor didn't know how to take her cryptic remark—the tone of her voice made it sound as if it were a warning. She debated whether to ask for clarification, but the woman pulled her companion toward the airplane.

"Who was that?" Noor asked aloud, temporarily forgetting that they weren't supposed to have contact with other agents.

"Francine Agazarian," the dark-haired man replied. "She and her husband couldn't take the pressure of living with the Boches breathing down their necks, so they are running back to England with their tails between their legs."

"And who are *you*?" Noor demanded. She'd never heard anyone at the SOE talk so bluntly.

He gave her a mock salute. "Henri Déricourt, Air Movements Officer. And you must be..." he consulted a list in his hands. "Madeleine."

Noor's reply was drowned out by the noise of the Lysander taking off. She watched it climb, taking its passengers back to the safety of England. She felt a slight panic rise in her chest at the thought that she was now in enemy territory without a way to escape.

Diana collected their parachutes and walked over to a pile of shovels.

"Is that a good idea?" Cecily pointed to Déricourt's list. "Having all our names written down like that…"

"You're in the same amount of danger whether or not your name is on here," Déricourt replied quickly. "Anybody who opts for this job gambles on being arrested."

"Yes, well, better go our separate ways then." Cecily indicated a spot behind a copse of trees, where Noor could make out a metallic gleam. "Those our bikes?"

"Yes. It's a little over ten kilometers to the station in Etriche. There you can find your own trains." He nodded at Noor. "The one for Paris leaves early in the morning, so you'll have to pedal fast."

"No problem." Noor followed Cecily to where the bicycles were parked.

Déricourt's deep voice cut through the silence of the night. "Monique?"

Noor turned back. In the bright moonlight she could see Déricourt staring at them expectantly. "I think he means you," she hissed at Cecily.

"Monique. Right," Cecily said, and then cleared her throat. "Yes?"

"Your train doesn't leave until later. It will be less suspicious if you girls ride to the station alone. In the meantime," he pointed toward Diana, who was digging a giant hole, "you can help bury the evidence."

Cecily gave Noor a quick hug. "I guess this is it."

"Good luck," Noor replied, taking in her friend's sturdy figure and no-nonsense expression as if it were the last time she would ever see her. To stave off the unwelcome premonition, she added, "Until we meet again."

CHAPTER 40

ANDRÉE

*A*fter another week of not seeing each other, Andrée met up with Gilbert in Grignon. As they strolled through the gardens, the scent of pine and lilies filling the summer air, she filled him in on what had happened with Jack and the Dutch agents. "I'm convinced Déricourt knows more about the Nazis' operations than he owns up to. Why else would he have sent Jack to the rendezvous instead of going himself?"

"I don't know, but I agree that Déricourt is not entirely trustworthy."

As Gilbert finished his sentence, Andrée heard footsteps approaching. She stopped walking and pretended to admire a plant while she glanced surreptitiously behind her. Luckily the figure was more than familiar. "Prosper! You're back."

She wasn't sure if it was the lack of sun or something else, but Prosper's coloring and general demeanor had turned gray during his brief sojourn to England. "I have no new information about D-Day, other than it's coming," he said by way of greeting. His voice was grim as he added, "And Buckmaster didn't take my warning about Déricourt seriously."

"Why not?" Gilbert demanded.

Prosper's frown turned deeper. "I don't know. It was Bodington mostly; he tried to make light of everything I told them about Déricourt."

"Nick Bodington?" The way Gilbert spat out the name, Andrée gathered he was not a great admirer of Bodington.

Prosper nodded. "I heard that he and Déricourt were friends before the war. Buckmaster told me in confidence that Paul Frager had similar complaints to mine about Déricourt's lack of security—that Déricourt asked too many questions for Frager's liking—but even that didn't convince them."

Andrée threw up her hands. "What do we do now?"

"If the Allied invasion is coming this summer, the SOE probably wouldn't have time to find a replacement for Déricourt, even if they had believed Prosper and Frager," Gilbert said.

Prosper ran his hands through his thinning hair. "I guess we'll just have to deal with him. But don't send anything *en claire* from now on. Make sure everything you give him is encoded and labeled 'For Buckmaster's Eyes Only.' I'll try to get London to do the same, but I really don't think they have any idea how treacherous Déricourt may be."

The implication was too great for Andrée to completely comprehend. "You don't think he's really working for the Germans, do you? If he got word of the date of the invasion—"

Prosper interrupted before she could finish her thought. "And that's exactly why he can't."

"I'm worried about Prosper," Andrée remarked to Gilbert when they'd returned to the privacy of their room.

She expected him to reply with one of his usual optimistic remarks, but all he said was, "Me too."

She sat heavily on the bed. "I don't get it. I heard that he insisted Yvonne and Pierre carry on with their air drops despite the increased presence of the Boches in the Sologne, yet Prosper himself recognizes how dangerous this is getting. It's as if he suspects there's a traitor among us but refuses to slow down."

"Because he knows D-Day will come eventually, and then it's only a matter of time before the war is over."

"You're right." She picked at a loose thread on the bedspread. "This is exactly what we've been working toward, and it would be foolish to slow down now." She tried to push the image of her boss's downtrodden face out of her mind. "Once we've opened a second front, the Nazis won't be able to keep up this fight for long." She wrapped the thread around her finger and pulled until it broke off with a satisfying snap. "What will you do after the war?"

Gilbert seemed grateful for the change of subject. "Actually, I've been thinking about that a lot lately." He reached into his bag. "I think the better question is, what will *we* do after the war?" He knelt down beside her and held up his outstretched palm. In it was a gold bracelet.

"What's this?" Andrée asked, taking the bracelet.

"I know it's not a ring, but it's all I have right now. Buck gave it to me as a symbol of good luck before I left England." A dimple appeared in his cheek. "At any rate, I'm asking you if you'll marry me."

"Marry you?" She nearly dropped it. "I didn't…"

The dimple was gone as Gilbert stood. "If this is just a war-time fling, you probably should have told me a long time ago."

"I never considered it a war-time fling. In fact…" Andrée wrapped the bracelet around her wrist. It was much too big for her, but it didn't matter. "Maybe I will marry you." She held her arm out to Gilbert expectantly.

He fastened the clasp, clearly relieved. "Maybe?"

"If we survive the war, I suppose I don't have any other plans than to become your wife."

He grinned. "Oh, we'll survive the war. I have new motivation to do so."

"Me too." She stood up and met his lips for a lasting kiss, marveling at how someone who had once seemed so different from herself could have brought so much joy into her life.

CHAPTER 41

NOOR

*P*aris wasn't exactly the same as Noor remembered. The streets, which once had been busy with cars, were now clogged with bicycles and horse-drawn carts, reminding her of when her family went on pilgrimage to Delhi when she was younger. And as Buckmaster had warned, German soldiers in grayish-green uniforms were everywhere, their guns obvious in the holsters hanging off their hips.

There hadn't been room in the Lysander for either her suitcase or her radio, so Noor was told to meet her contact at 40 rue Erlanger, in the swanky 16th Arrondissement, to help her make the next arrangements. She could only assume that Emily Garry was an elderly lady, so Noor stopped at a street vendor to buy a posy of carnations for her. She felt her face heat up as a German officer passed by, but luckily he didn't so much as glance at her.

After Noor knocked on the door to an apartment on the 8th floor, she was greeted by a tall man with dark, curly hair. His face was clean-shaven, revealing a well-defined jaw, and his soft brown eyes reminded Noor of her father's. "Yes?"

Since she had not anticipated a man, let alone someone so

handsome, her voice came out in a sputter. "I believe I am expected."

The man gave her a bewildered look but opened the door wider and gestured for her to come inside.

Noor decided that the man must be her contact's grandson. Or nephew. She grew even more confused when a pretty young woman entered the room.

The man rubbed his chin before nodding at the woman. "This is my fiancée, Marguerite Nadaud."

Not Emily then. Noor gave a little curtsy under the curious gaze of Mademoiselle Nadaud, who invited her to sit down. Silence followed while Noor waited for the elderly lady to appear.

The man seemed at a loss for words. "Cigarette?" he asked finally.

"No thank you." Noor waved the pack away.

He lit a cigarette and took a long drag. "I'm Émile Garry. People call me Cinema because they think I look like Gary Cooper." He gazed curiously at her, as if weighing her reaction to this new information.

"I'm sorry, I don't really watch many motion pictures."

He raised his eyebrows and exchanged a bewildered look with his fiancée. Both were clearly puzzled by Noor's presence.

She shifted on the couch. Something was not right. They must have somehow been associated with the Resistance, for why else would they have invited a stranger into their flat? But her orders were to say the password only to her contact.

"I'll get some tea," Mademoiselle Nadaud said, rising from the couch.

As soon as she was out of earshot, Garry leaned forward. "Are you from London?"

"Yes." Noor wondered if she should inquire about Emily.

"Don't you have something to ask me?"

Noor's mouth dropped open. After a moment, she stammered out the awkwardly long code phrase. "I come from your friend Antoine in search of news about the company's building."

Garry nodded. "The case is up to the courts now."

"You *are* my contact!" Noor exclaimed. "I thought you would be an old lady."

He threw his head back in laughter. When he was suitably calm, he asked, "There are no old ladies here, just Marguerite, myself, my sister Renée, and occasionally Antelme. Why would you think that?"

"I…" Noor thought back to her briefing, recalling how the cigar in Major Buckmaster's mouth had obscured his words. She smiled sheepishly at Garry, not wanting to admit she'd mistaken Émile for Emily. "I don't remember."

Mademoiselle Nadaud returned and set the tea on the table. She glanced at her fiancé. "All better now?"

"Yes. Our friend here…" he stopped and looked expectantly at Noor.

"Madeleine," she filled in.

"Madeleine is indeed our 'friend,' despite a little misinterpretation."

Noor realized she was still clutching the bouquet of carnations. She extended them to Mademoiselle Nadaud. "These are for you," Noor said.

"Are you hungry?" Mademoiselle Nadaud asked as she accepted the posy.

Noor put both hands over her stomach as it grumbled loudly. She hadn't had anything to eat since she'd left England. "I paid for the flowers with cash, but I wasn't sure how to use the ration coupons they gave me at the market. Besides there was such a long queue to get in."

"Welcome to Occupied France," Garry replied.

"Let me fix you something to eat." Mademoiselle Nadaud went back into the kitchen.

Garry stretched his arm over the spot his fiancée had vacated and focused on Noor. "The SOE never showed you how to use the ration book?"

"No."

He rolled his eyes. "I'm obviously not SOE-trained. My code

name is Cinema, but I don't have an alias since I'm a native Frenchman."

"But you do work for Prosper? My instructions were to…"

"Yes, I work for Prosper: I run the Phono circuit, which is part of his network. My identity card states that I am an engineer with the Société Electro-Chime of Paris. I often carry messages from Paris to Le Mans and back. Marguerite," he nodded toward the kitchen, "works for the Ministry of Food and Agriculture. She can teach you everything there is to know about ration coupons."

Noor clasped her hands together. "That would be much appreciated."

He sat up, as if something had suddenly occurred to him. "Did they give you a safehouse or somewhere to stay?"

Noor shook her head.

Mademoiselle Nadaud set a steaming plate of noodles down in front of Noor. "You will stay here, of course."

"Yes, please do," Garry agreed. "Tomorrow I will give you directions to find Archambault, Prosper's wireless operator."

The food filling Noor's stomach and the warmth from the fire made her feel sleepy. Although she'd spent so many years in pre-war Paris, it felt alien to her now and she was grateful to have found such accommodating contacts, especially ones who could help navigate this strange new world.

As Noor's head began to bob from exhaustion, Mademoiselle Nadaud touched her on the shoulder and said, "I'll go make up your bed now."

CHAPTER 42

YVONNE

A few weeks after Prosper returned, Yvonne and Pierre headed out in the Citroën to pick up two more new arrivals. They had landed near St. Aignan two days prior, to a reception party organized by the Ramorantins.

"We both got our parachutes caught up in trees," one of them, a tall man with blonde hair and blue eyes, told Yvonne in a rather awkward accent.

"The Ramorantins should have probably picked a field with fewer trees," Pierre said.

"Oh, it was fine," the other one replied, his accent as inept as his companion's. "They cut us down right away."

"Which is a good thing." Yvonne nodded at the blonde man. "With your coloring, you might have been mistaken for a German parachutist."

"You can put your bags in the boot of the car," Pierre told them. As soon as they were out of earshot, he turned to Yvonne. "What was Buckmaster thinking?" He shook his head. "With those accents, they'll never be able to pass themselves off as French."

"I think they're Canadian," Yvonne hissed. "Their syntax is a bit off."

"Did the SOE run out of French people to recruit as agents?" Pierre stood straighter as the men reappeared. He held out his hand to the tall blonde man. "I'm Pierre Culioli, and this is my partner Jacqueline."

"John Macalister. And this is Frank Pickersgill. Buck always referred to us as Pick and Mac."

"You've been to France before?" Yvonne asked as they settled into the car, the two newcomers sitting in the back.

"I have," Pickersgill said. He appeared to be the same age as Mack—early 30s—but had dark hair and wore tortoiseshell glasses. "I went to school here, and taught myself French. I found that the only way to learn the bloody language is to talk yourself blue to anyone who will put up with it."

Yvonne thought to herself that he could have used a bit more practice.

"I'm from Toronto," Macalister said. "I went to Oxford. My wife is French—we met on holiday when I was in Cannes."

"And you are Canadian, too?" she asked Pickersgill.

"Yes. I'm originally from Winnipeg."

Yvonne rubbed her forehead. Their grammatical mistakes were so blatant that even an ear as poorly tuned as a French-speaking German could pick them up. She couldn't help wondering the same thing Pierre had earlier. What *was* Buckmaster thinking?

Pierre drove them all back to the Gatignons' chateau and they celebrated Pick and Mac's safe arrival with a few bottles of wine graciously provided by Monsieur Gatignon.

Yvonne's opinion about their poor accents did not change much, but—linguistic gaffes aside—the men said all the right things, especially when the Allies' victories in Africa were brought up. By the end of the night, they had convinced her they were intelligent and certainly had the same determination as most Resistance agents.

"What did the SOE say is your main objective?" Yvonne asked.

"I'm to be the leader of a new circuit in the Ardennes area,"

Pickersgill replied. "Macalister here is going to be my wireless operator."

"But first we must go to Paris to meet with Prosper," Macalister added.

"We can drive you to the train station," Pierre said. "Jacqueline and I are supposed to have a meeting with Prosper as well."

Madame Gatignon, who had been refilling Pierre's glass, paused. "Jacqueline, would you like to borrow one of my outfits for your trip?"

Yvonne glanced up. Madame Gatignon was nearly the same size as herself. "Thank you, that would be wonderful." She touched one of the many stains on her culottes. "I've been trying to get London to send me new clothes for months, but apparently it's not a priority for them."

"I've got just the thing." Madame Gatignon left the room and returned a few minutes later with a light gray, summer-weight jacket and skirt.

Yvonne picked up the skirt. It was well-made and very clean. She felt unexpected tears forming. It had been so long since she'd been able to wear such lovely clothes. "Thank you," she repeated, feeling embarrassed by the intensity of her emotions, especially in front of Pierre and the new arrivals.

Madame Gatignon gave Yvonne a quick hug. "Considering all that you've accomplished for France, it's the least I could do. You deserve to be pampered."

"I'll take good care of the suit," Yvonne promised.

Pierre glanced at his watch. "We should get going. The train leaves early tomorrow morning."

Yvonne stood up and gingerly draped the suit over her shoulder. "Sleep well, boys," she told the Canadians.

CHAPTER 43

NOOR

The morning after her arrival, Émile Garry provided Noor with the address of a place out in the country, near Versailles. She was sad to leave him and Mademoiselle Nadaud, but ready to fulfill her instructions.

The address turned out to be a college in Grignon. After Occupied Paris, the greenhouses and arboretums were a welcome sight, not to mention the enormous brick wall that surrounded the estate, which gave it at least a perception of safety. She wasn't sure exactly where on the extensive grounds she'd find Archambault, but her eyes landed on an aerial on top of one of the greenhouses.

The musty smell of dirt combined with the fresh fragrance of jasmine filled her nostrils as she entered the greenhouse. She found a tall, dark-haired man bent over a transmitter on the far side of the room and figured she must be in the right place. "Are you Archambault?"

The man jumped, smacking his hand against the transmitter. "Ouch!" he shouted before putting his bleeding finger in his mouth.

"I didn't mean to startle you." Noor tore a leaf off a nearby aloe plant, broke it open, and extended it to him.

"Yeah, well, everything is startling nowadays," he said, accepting the aloe leaf.

"I was told I would find Archambault here."

"That is indeed me, but most people call me Gilbert." As he put the gel from the leaf on his cut, Noor noticed that he had strong, steady hands.

"I'm Nora Baker, code name Madeleine. I'm to be Cinema's wireless operator." He seemed confused, so Noor added, "Cinema is the Gary Cooper lookalike."

"Ah, yes. The Prosper network has gotten so big it's impossible to keep track of everyone." He glanced down. "I see you don't have your equipment yet."

"No. If possible, do you mind if I use yours? I'd like to send a message to London letting them know I arrived safely."

"No problem." He handed her a pencil and notebook and Noor got to work coding her first message from France. She kept it simple: *landed without incident and met all contacts.* She ended by stating that she was still awaiting her transmitter and personal suitcase.

The reply came back quickly. "Well done, Madeleine. We believe you've set a new record for time between arrival and the first field transmission. Your things will arrive tonight; please arrange for pick-up." The rest of it was coordinates for a landing site.

"Do you know this place?" Noor asked Gilbert, handing him the decoded message.

"Yes. It's a farm not far from here. I'll have Balachowsky take care of it." He put the card down. "I have to say, you are quite efficient with your work. And, as they said, it takes most people weeks before they manage to send a message to Baker Street."

Noor was pleased at the compliments. "Thank you."

"I wasn't aware they were hiring women as W/T operators."

"I am the first one." Remembering Alice Wood, her friend in training, Noor added, "But I don't think I'll be the last."

"At any rate, I'm starving." Gilbert put away his Morse key and shut the transmitting suitcase. "Let's go to the main house and get something to eat."

"Sounds like a plan."

Gilbert hid the case behind a large potted plant before leading her out of the greenhouse. "I can't help thinking that you look familiar."

"I was thinking the same thing."

"Did you go to Lycée Saint Cloud?"

"Yes!" Noor exclaimed. "I graduated in 1931."

"I was in 1933. I'm two years your junior." His eyebrows furrowed. "Yet you look so much younger."

She gave him a shy smile. "Lack of life experience."

He put a friendly arm around her shoulders and guided her down a path through a garden. "Something tells me you're about to get all the life experience you'll ever need."

The main house turned out to be more of a castle than anything else, with a grand ballroom-turned-parlor that was filled with people. Gilbert introduced Noor to the occupants of the room: the director of the college, Dr. Vanderwynckt, his wife and two daughters, and Professor Balachowsky and his wife.

After a few minutes of polite banter, Madame Balachowsky asked Noor if she wouldn't mind helping her make a tea tray.

"Of course not," Noor said, following her to an enormous kitchen. Wanting to be useful, she picked up a tea pot and began to pour. Too late, she realized she'd done exactly what her trainer at Beaulieu had warned her not to: she poured the tea over the milk. In France, they do the opposite.

"You haven't been in France long, have you, dearie?" Mrs. Balachowsky asked gently.

"No," Noor replied.

"But you are aware those types of mistakes can get you killed, right?"

She nodded sheepishly.

"You are in Occupied France and must understand that the Gestapo and the Milice are everywhere. You must assume that everyone you meet is your enemy and act accordingly."

"Yes, madame." Noor knew it was most prudent to think the

way Madame Balachowsky suggested, but it seemed an awfully lonely way to live.

When Noor returned to the parlor, she saw there were two new people: a thin man with graying hair and a pretty woman with dyed blonde hair and full lips.

Gilbert rose on seeing her. "Nora, I'd like you to meet Prosper and Andrée Borrel." He turned to the man. "This is our new wireless operator."

Prosper shook her hand, clearly distracted by something else.

Madame Vanderwynckt put her arm through one of her daughter's. "We will take our leave. I'm sure you have business to discuss." Soon the only ones left in the room were Prosper, Andrée, Gilbert, and Noor.

Andrée helped herself to some tea and a biscuit as Prosper walked the length of the room.

"We have two landings tonight," Gilbert stated. "One is Nora's radio, which I've arranged for Balachowsky to pick up, and the other is more agents." His voice took on an ominous tone. "Déricourt's in charge of that one."

Prosper paused his walking and sighed heavily. "Yvonne and Pierre just picked up two new men the other day. I'm starting to think the network is growing too vast. Every new recruit represents a danger. We still don't know if the Tambour sisters will crack under interrogation. And here is Old Buck not heeding my warnings about Déricourt, sending in more agents—and lining up countless others —all waiting to infiltrate France. It's too much."

In the silence that followed, Andrée and Gilbert both looked as defeated as Prosper's voice sounded.

"What can I do?" Noor asked.

"For now, you can go back to Paris," Prosper answered. "We'll make arrangements through France Antelme for the delivery of your radio. Until then, if you have any messages from Cinema, you can pass them on to Gilbert for transmission. You were given the address of a letter box, correct?"

"Yes." Noor closed her eyes in recollection. "38 Ave Suffren. 15e." Belatedly, she remembered another instruction. "I was supposed to perform reconnaissance there yesterday."

Gilbert blew out his breath as Prosper asked, his voice gravelly, "You were told to go there yesterday?"

Noor was afraid she'd made yet another mistake. "Yes, but Cinema insisted I come here to meet Archambault."

Prosper's hands clasped into fists. "It's just as well. Had you gone there, you might have met one of the many Gestapo investigators that frequent there."

"Ges-Gestapo?" Noor stumbled over the word.

"Yes. I told Buck that apartment had been compromised when the Tambour sisters were arrested. I don't know why he gave it to you as a letter box." He shot Gilbert a bewildered look. Gilbert's return glance was just as shocked.

"Gilbert, send a transmission ASAP to the SOE. Tell them we are cancelling all known letter boxes until further notice," Prosper said.

"Do we have alternatives?" Gilbert asked.

"Not yet," Prosper replied grimly.

CHAPTER 44

YVONNE

$\mathcal{P}$ ierre and Yvonne arrived to pick up the Canadians at seven in the morning on June 21, 1943. Macalister put his wireless suitcase in the trunk, along with a small box containing extra quartz crystals addressed to Archambault, before handing Yvonne a small parcel tied in brown paper.

"What's this?" she asked.

"Messages from London for Prosper and Archambault."

She read the label aloud. "Jacques Coutreau, POW?"

Macalister shrugged. "It's supposed to look like a package from the Red Cross."

"Okay." She stuck it in the glove compartment.

Pierre drove. Macalister and Pickersgill discussed plans for their new circuit in the cramped backseat as Yvonne, wearing her smart gray suit, gazed out the window. It was a peaceful day in the countryside, sunny, with barely any wind. In Yvonne's opinion, it was almost too peaceful. Recalling the rumors about increased Germans in the area, she asked Pierre if he had his Colt with him.

"Of course," Pierre replied.

"Can you get rid of it?"

"Now?"

"Yes."

As usual, Pierre didn't question her and pulled the car over. He took his revolver out of his pocket and stashed it under a bush. "I'll pick it up on the way back," he said when he got back in the car.

As they approached Dhuizon, Yvonne could see that a barbed wire barricade had been erected in the middle of the road. A truck was parked in front with men in grayish-green uniforms milling around it. She put her hand on Pierre's arm. "There's a road-block up there."

"It's probably just a routine check. And all of our papers are in perfect order. I examined the newcomers' myself."

Indeed the guard waved them through, but once they were past, they saw dozens of armed soldiers stationed about 10 meters apart on each side of the road. Dhuizon had been invaded.

Pierre gave a low whistle and slowed the car as another armed soldier motioned for them to stop.

This time after their papers were inspected, the soldier did not return them. "Get out," he commanded the Canadians.

They did as bid, and another soldier with a submachine gun got into the back of the Citroën. He directed Pierre to drive to the town hall as Yvonne tried to collect herself. It would do no one any good if the Boches caught onto how anxious they were making her.

Once there, Yvonne got out and smoothed down her skirt, her trembling, sweaty hands leaving marks. It was strangely quiet outside, as though even the birds were holding their breath.

The inside of the building was a stark contrast to the stillness outside. The sharp, acrid smell of perspiration permeated the modest town hall, which was packed with people in a similar state of nervousness as their papers were checked by German soldiers.

She glanced over at Pierre, who appeared outwardly calm, though the knuckles clutching his briefcase had turned white. She knew he never traveled without the briefcase, but it contained a host of compromising papers that would denounce both of them as Resistance agents.

He met her gaze with worried eyes. She tilted her head, indicating an empty chair in the corner of the room. He walked over and, after looking around the room, put the case behind the chair.

The person who asked for Yvonne's papers wore plain-clothes, leading her to suspect that, rather than being a soldier, he was a member of the Gestapo, which flustered her more.

Luckily the man questioned Pierre first. "What brings you to Dhuizon?"

Pierre's voice was steady. "I'm a civil servant, and this is my wife. I know I am not supposed to travel for pleasure, but I had some business to conduct here and my wife needed to get out of the house."

The inspector hailed a well-dressed man standing nearby. "Are you acquainted with this man?"

"Yes, of course," the other man answered. "I see him around town lots. He delivers mail."

The inspector shrugged. "If the mayor knows you…"

Yvonne glanced at the stylish stranger. Pierre had never mentioned meeting the mayor of Dhuizon, but she supposed the man was only trying to help a fellow Frenchman.

Pierre held up both arms as the inspector patted him down. Yvonne gave an inward sigh of relief that she had asked him to get rid of his Colt only an hour before. The inspector turned to the baggage they had taken from the Citroën and pointed to the package addressed to Jacques Coutreau. "What's that?"

"Charcuterie," Pierre replied. "It's meant for my wife's father. He is very ill."

The inspector nodded as he gathered their papers. "Just so you are aware, the requirements for identity cards have recently been changed." He tapped Yvonne's picture. "This image now has to be in profile and attached with rivets instead of staples."

She refrained from rolling her eyes. The Germans were always changing their rules. In her opinion there was no other reason than to keep the French citizens from becoming too comfortable. Still, that meant that non-citizens like herself and most of the others in F Section would need new cards.

The inspector handed back their papers before flipping open a small pad of paper. He scribbled something on it and then ripped it off the pad. "For your wife and yourself," he said, extending the sheet toward Pierre. "This is a pass stating you are both free to go."

Yvonne's relief turned to agitation as she watched Macalister and Pickersgill being led inside the building. "*Merde alors*," she cursed under her breath.

Pierre took her arm and they sidestepped the Canadians as they went outside, pretending not to know them.

Once Pierre had started the car, he turned to Yvonne. "What do we do now?"

"We can't leave them in there. Their accents will never pass, especially Macalister's."

"Maybe they'll let them go too." Pierre's voice sounded doubtful.

But just then a uniformed man ran out of the building, shouting. Though they couldn't hear him over the roar of the engine, Yvonne saw with horror that he was carrying Pierre's briefcase.

Pierre hit the accelerator hard and the car raced away. She glanced back to see the soldier had dropped the case and was now waving his arms frantically at the guards on the side of the road. She gasped aloud, her confusion churning into fear, as one of guards pointed his machine gun at them. She reached out and moved the steering wheel to the left, causing the car to swerve violently. The gun fired and both Pierre and Yvonne flinched, although no bullets hit the car.

She looked back again, noting that three black cars were now following them. Another shot rang out, but the Germans' cars were too far away to hit the Citroën. Her breathing slowed just a tiny bit when the narrow village street widened into a country road. *Maybe Pierre will be able to outmaneuver them*. She didn't dare to think what would happen if he couldn't. Her grip on the door handle tightened again as they passed the field where the explosion had occurred only a few weeks ago.

As they rounded a small bend near Bracieux, Pierre cursed as he caught sight of yet another barricade. Beyond that was a throng of soldiers who raised their guns and took aim at the Citroën.

The cars tailing them had decreased their distance and the Citroën was now being shot at from both forward and behind. "I'm sorry, Yvonne," Pierre shouted as he drove straight toward the barricade.

She had barely registered the bullet whizzing by Pierre's hat when a round hit the windshield, splintering the glass. The shards seem to fall in slow motion. She touched her bleeding leg as she heard a faint buzzing sound behind her coming closer. As the buzzing grew into a booming noise, she felt an intense pain in the back of her head.

And then… nothing.

CHAPTER 45

ANDRÉE

*A*ndrée shivered as she took a seat across from Prosper at the Café de Flore. Even though it was late June, the weather had turned cold and the sky was gray, as if the sun, too, was hiding from the Germans.

The dark circles under her boss's eyes had become even more pronounced. Andrée had heard that he had been wandering the streets after curfew and then showing up at other circuit members' apartments at dawn, nearly falling over with exhaustion. She was glad he at least had a moment to sit as he waited at the café for Yvonne and Pierre to deliver the newest agents, Pick and Mac. Besides receiving their instructions from Prosper, the men were to deliver new quartz crystals for Gilbert, who was currently back at Grignon with Nora.

After ordering two coffees, Andrée asked Prosper if he was feeling all right.

"It's not my health," Prosper said. "I can't tell you the trouble which weighs on my mind."

"I'm sure Yvonne and Pierre just got held up."

Prosper waved his hand dismissively. "I'm not worried about

them. I fear there are hard blows coming, and it is from London they will come."

"What do you mean?" When Prosper didn't reply, Andrée gently touched his sleeve. "Do you think there's a spy in the London office?" Recalling Gilbert's reaction back at Grignon, she added another question. "Is it Nick Bodington?"

"I don't know," he replied tersely. "I do know that if D-Day doesn't come soon, the strong morale we have right now in the Resistance may be crushed."

"But you said yourself even Baker Street doesn't have information about the Allied invasion."

Prosper slammed his fist down on the table. "If it doesn't happen this summer, Gilbert and I will provoke our own war."

"I'm not sure that's the right way to go about this..." Andrée trailed off, not wanting to directly contradict the leader of the greatest Resistance network in all of France.

Prosper seemed about to argue with her, but, after a moment, laid his hand over hers. "Whatever happens, I want you to know I think you are the best of us all."

There it was again, that gloomy tone. She had never heard him sound so unsettled. "Everything is going to be okay." She gave his hand a squeeze. "D-Day will come, eventually."

"I certainly hope you're right." He moved his hand to check his watch. "Well, I don't think they're coming today, and I've got to get going to prepare for an air drop tonight."

"Maybe you should have someone else cover for you," Andrée said. "I think it's more important that you get some sleep."

He gave her a tight smile. "There will be time to sleep when the war is over." He got up from the table. "Will you be here again tomorrow to wait for Yvonne and Pierre?"

It was standard procedure to meet at the same place the next day if a rendezvous failed the first time. "Of course."

CHAPTER 46

NOOR

A week after her arrival, Noor still hadn't received her wireless set. Luckily Andrée had lent her some essential clothing to get by with until her suitcase arrived. Because Prosper had canceled all of the safehouses, Noor had to travel to Grignon to transmit Garry's messages to London, under the helpful eye of the handsome Gilbert Norman. She told anyone she encountered she was a student at the agricultural college, and no one questioned her.

When she returned to Garry's apartment one night, a tall man with tanned skin almost as dark as Noor's stood as she entered the living room. "You must be Madeleine. I have your radio."

"It's Nora, actually." She took the suitcases he'd brought and set them on the coffee table. "Thank you so much." The case containing the wireless was intact, but the one with her personal items looked battered. She opened it to find her clothing was disarranged and rumpled and some of it was covered with dark green stains.

Antelme cleared his throat. "The professor didn't want me to tell you that there were some... issues with the landing."

"What do you mean?"

He gave her an embarrassed smile. "The suitcase got caught by a tree branch and opened, spilling its contents. It took quite a while for Balachowsky and his students to gather all of your things."

Her face grew hot as she imagined them collecting her under-garments from the clutches of a tree's branches.

"I'm sorry, I should introduce myself." He held out a bronzed hand. "France Antelme, head of the Bricklayer circuit."

"Nice to meet you."

Garry entered the living room. "Any word on what happened in the Sologne?" he asked Antelme.

"No."

"The Sologne?" Noor inquired.

Antelme took a mug of coffee from Garry. "Prosper was expecting two new men, Canadians I guess, to arrive with some of his most trusted agents in the Sologne region. It's been three days and they still haven't shown up."

"Oh," Noor said, for lack of anything else to say. "I hope nothing is wrong."

Antelme and Garry exchanged a worried glance. "Me too," Antelme replied.

CHAPTER 47

ANDRÉE

On yet another moonless night, Andrée and Gilbert found themselves tasked with creating new identity cards in one of the grandest houses Andrée had ever been in. It was owned by a childhood friend of Gilbert, Nicolas Laurent, who had proven to be a pleasant, accommodating fellow.

Andrée couldn't say the same of his wife Maud, who had been raised in England and had a sour-faced, privileged-British demeanor. Laurent didn't seem to mind members of the Prosper network coming in and out of the house at all hours of the day, but Maud would see to it that a housekeeper swept and mopped the marble floors after them.

Neither Laurent nor Maud ever asked questions, and of course, Andrée and Gilbert never volunteered what they were up to. It was safer for everyone that way.

That night they were undertaking the arduous task of forgery. The government had recently changed the rules for the *cartes d'itentité* in that the picture could no longer be facing front. This meant that all French citizens would have to visit their local town hall to obtain a new card, and that hundreds of false papers would need to be produced for members of the Resistance.

They'd been provided with an extensive list, which matched French aliases to SOE code names or, in some cases, real names. Andrée wrote the information on the cards, while Gilbert trimmed the pictures with scissors and attached them with metal rivets, for the new rules also dictated that the images could no longer be stapled to the card.

"Did Yvonne and Pierre ever show up?" Gilbert asked as he set a photograph on the table.

Andrée frowned. "No. I'm going to travel to the Sologne in the next few days to see what I can find out." She waved a card in the air to dry the ink. "Between you and me, I'm pretty worried about them."

"Same here."

She had just started on the card for François Desprez—Prosper's newest alias—when the doorbell rang. Laurent soon appeared in the doorway. "Are you expecting anyone?"

Both Andrée and Gilbert shook their heads. Andrée checked her watch. It was nearly midnight.

Laurent was back in a few minutes. "They are asking for you," he told Gilbert.

"Are you sure they want me and not Déricourt?" Gilbert asked as he rose.

"Pardon?" Laurent asked.

"Never mind." He looked at Andrée. "You okay here?"

She sighed as she looked at the mountain of paperwork, hoping it wasn't someone from the network needing Gilbert to send a message. Knowing it would put Laurent and Maud in danger, he never transmitted from their placc, which meant he might have to travel all the way to Grignon in the middle of the night. "It could be about Pierre and Yvonne," she said. As he turned to leave, she added, "Hurry back."

"I'll try."

As soon as Gilbert left the room, Andrée felt a knot form in the pit of her stomach. *Something was wrong.* She got up and went into the hallway. The night was pleasantly cool and a window to the garden had been left open, letting in a breeze scented with gardenias. She crept toward the window as she heard Gilbert's voice raise in inquiry.

A deep, strange voice answered, "I have the radio crystals you were expecting, courtesy of Pierre Culioli."

She breathed a sigh of relief and was about to join them to ask about Yvonne when, through the window, she watched Gilbert open the garden gate and a shadow crept past. To her horror, at least a dozen more shadows appeared, and then a nightmarish voice shouted, "You are under arrest by order of the Gestapo!"

No! Gilbert! Andrée wanted to scream at them to stop but knew it would be a vain attempt. She ran back to the room she'd just vacated and scooped the ID cards into the small box that previously held scissors and rivets. She put the box on an empty shelf on the bookcase and then picked up the list they'd been working with. There was no way she could let the Gestapo stumble upon hundreds of names of active Resistance members. She ripped the paper into tiny pieces and sprinkled a few of them behind the bookcase before shoving the rest into the pocket of her trousers.

After exiting the room, she looked desperately around. There were two staircases in the hallway, one leading down to the kitchen, and one leading to the garden. She figured the Secret Police had already gotten into the house and decided that fleeing into the garden was the safest bet.

As the cool night air surrounded her, someone shouted, "Halt!"

Only after she heard a gunshot did Andrée stop running.

"Put your hands in the air!"

She half complied by raising one hand. With the other, she crammed the rest of the master list into her mouth.

A pistol was cocked and pushed into her face. "Don't you dare swallow."

She tried to gulp as nonchalantly as possible. "Swallow what?"

The pistol was replaced by a flashlight. "Open your mouth."

This time she did exactly as bid. The owner of the flashlight gave a heavy sigh at her empty mouth. "What was that?" he demanded.

Andrée shrugged.

He raised his voice to a shadow behind him. "Here's another one. A woman."

"We'll bring her in too," the shadow replied.

It was only a few blocks to the Gestapo headquarters. Andrée was marched along the dark streets, a gun nuzzled in her back. Judging by the broad thoroughfare and the elegant buildings, she assumed they were heading down Avenue Foch, now sometimes derogatorily called "Avenue Boche" since the Nazis had confiscated most of the residences for their own purposes.

She was ordered to stop at Number 84, a light-colored building surrounded by a wrought iron fence. She was brought through a splendid lobby, the jackboots of the Boche behind her pounding on the marble floors. She was then shoved up an equally splendid staircase, the gun still in her back.

On the third floor, another man in plain-clothes was waiting next to a door, which he opened and then gestured for her to enter. The room was nearly empty except for a small table and two chairs. A crystal chandelier hung above the table, clearly a relic from its previous residents, though Andrée noted that the Boches hadn't bothered to dust it.

The new man had followed her and her captor in. "What is your name?" he demanded.

"Denise."

He nodded at the captor, who slapped her.

"That is your fake name," the new man, obviously a Gestapo interrogator, insisted. "I want you to tell me your real name."

"That is my real name."

"No." He gestured to the other man, who slapped her again.

Forty-eight hours, she told herself. That's what Major de Wesselow had drilled into them. If a captured agent could hold out for forty-eight hours without giving anything away, it would give the other members of the network a chance to escape.

Andrée shut her eyes, willing Prosper to pack up and leave town. As far as she knew, he was safe. Judging by how the Boche in the garden had mentioned Pierre, she figured the same couldn't be said about Yvonne.

Andrée didn't care what the Boches did to her personally, but tears sprang to her eyes when she thought about Gilbert and Yvonne being interrogated.

She tensed the muscles in her face in anticipation of another slap. When one wasn't forthcoming, she opened her eyes.

The interrogator shoved a picture in front of her face. "Who is this?"

It was a snapshot of Serge Balachowsky, the agricultural professor. "I've never seen that man before," Andrée replied.

"Liar."

The next picture was of Major Buckmaster. "We know this is your boss. What can you tell us about your organization?"

She tried her best to cover up her surprise. *How had they come to possess a photograph of Buck?*

Her refusal to answer was met with a kick to her shin.

"We are aware the Allies are planning an invasion. We'd like to know when."

"I don't know anything about an Allied invasion," she answered, which resulted in a kick to the other shin.

This went on for hours, with the one man asking questions, and when Andrée didn't answer or gave one he considered unsatisfactory, he had his partner batter a body part. Sometimes it was the same limb, sometimes it was a different one. Just when she thought her right shin had stopped throbbing, the guard delivered another swift kick with his jackboot, causing her to double over in pain.

"Have you had enough?" the interrogator demanded. "Are you ready to talk now?"

Andrée could feel her eye swelling and pictured the massive shiner that would soon develop. She lifted her head high and forced her cracked, bleeding lips into a smile. "The answer to both of your questions is 'no.'"

CHAPTER 48

NOOR

Gilbert Norman was late. Noor shifted impatiently on a garden chair. She was supposed to be meeting him at the college so she could practice transmitting on his wireless set, using the new crystals that were en route from London. She'd left her own radio at Garry's apartment so she didn't have to lug it all the way to Grignon.

She checked her watch again as Professor Balachowsky burst into the greenhouse. "My wife just got a phone call from Paris."

"Oh?" Noor used a rag to rub out a fingerprint on her Morse key, wondering if Gilbert was going to cancel. *Maybe he got held up.*

"Yes." Something in Balachowsky's voice made her look up. His face was pale. "The caller said that Prosper, Andrée, Jean Worms, and many others have been arrested."

"Arrested?" Noor's voice was hardly more than a whisper. She stared at the now spotless Morse key, his words echoing through her head as she tried to make sense of the news. "And Gilbert?"

"I don't know." Balachowsky shook his head. "But it's clear the Gestapo has compiled a great deal of information on the Prosper network and its officers. I think we can assume it's only a matter of time before they raid the college."

She jumped up and started loading Gilbert's transmitting suitcase. "We have to get rid of all of this."

"Yes." Balachowsky grabbed two shovels, seemingly glad to have something to do. "We'll bury it in the vegetable garden."

After the evidence was hidden, Noor fled back to Paris. Luckily, she found Émile Garry alone in his apartment. In a voice much higher than her usual, she filled Garry in on what she'd learned at Grignon.

"*Merde alors*," Garry said, sitting down heavily. He put his head in his hands, but, after a moment, gazed back up at Noor. "Do you think you were followed from the college?"

"No." Noor was more uncertain than she sounded. "But at any rate, I should probably find my own flat. I can't transmit from here, and Grignon is compromised."

"Transmit? You shouldn't transmit anything for a while. We have to lie low: we don't know how far the network's been penetrated."

"But if Gilbert's been arrested, I'm the only W/T operator left in the area."

Garry gaped at her. He was about to say something else, but shut his mouth as they heard a key being inserted into the lock. As the door opened, Noor stifled a scream: she'd had enough surprises for one day. But it was not the Gestapo: it was France Antelme.

As soon as he'd closed the door, Garry pounced on him. "Prosper's been arrested. Andrée and Worms too."

Antelme cursed as he dropped his suitcase. "I was supposed to meet Prosper for lunch tomorrow." He took a deep breath. "Thank God you warned me—I'm sure the Gestapo would have been waiting for me at the restaurant."

"What are we going to do?" Noor asked.

Antelme held up a finger as he began to pace up and down the apartment. "First thing is to relocate, and then we'll go into hiding until this blows over."

"Blows over?" Noor demanded. "The Prosper circuit has been obliterated. Our work is more important now than ever."

He paused his pacing and thrust his hands in his pockets. "I agree, but our lives are even more important."

"If Gilbert is still free, he might know what happened," Noor stated. "Plus, I still don't have the new crystals. If we are going to stay in touch with London, we'll need him."

Antelme scratched at his beard stubble. His gaze turned to Garry. "We don't know anything about Gilbert's whereabouts?"

"No," Garry replied.

"Professor Balachowsky told me that he might still be safe." An idea occurred to her. "I can go back to Grignon and find out who called Madame Balachowsky. Perhaps they have more information. At the very least, I can dig up Gilbert's transmitter and inform London about Prosper's arrest."

"No—" Garry started to reply, but Antelme cut him off. "All right, Nora. You can return to Grignon in the morning."

CHAPTER 49

ANDRÉE

*T*he morning after she was arrested, Andrée was transferred from 84 Avenue Foch to Fresnes Prison, an imposing penitentiary made of red brick. The guard accompanying her brought her through the massive iron gates, and then into an office. A trim woman with a permanent frown greeted Andrée by telling her in French to take her clothes off.

"Why?" Andrée demanded, shocked that a fellow country-woman could be so cruel.

"I need to inspect you for lice or open sores. We cannot have any infestations here."

"I can assure you I have neither."

The guard, probably sensing that he was no longer needed, departed.

The woman crossed her arms and looked impatient as Andrée reluctantly undid the top buttons of her soiled shirt. Too late, she forgot about the bracelet Gilbert had given her.

The woman's eyes widened at the glimmer of gold. "Give me that."

Andrée tried to cover the bracelet with her other hand. "No."

"I'll put it with your other..." she eyed Andrée up and down, her frown deepening, "things to return to you, if you are ever released."

"*When* I am released."

The woman came toward her, holding out hands with nails that looked more like claws. Andrée had no choice but to give up the bracelet.

After a humiliating inspection, where the woman searched her every crevice, Andrée was taken to a dark, dank cell.

Andrée's first day in Fresnes melted into a blur of loneliness and fear, marked only by a guard coming in the evening to deliver cold, watery coffee—which tasted far worse than ersatz—and a stale piece of bread.

At night she lay atop a stained mattress, attempting to sleep, though her bruised body ached. Her thoughts naturally traveled to the fate of the Prosper network. Gilbert was a lost cause, for surely he must also be imprisoned. But Prosper might still be free. If he caught wind of her arrest, he would have known to get out of town and contact London as soon as possible. Perhaps another circuit— not Déricourt's of course—had arranged for his safe escape to England. There he would help plan D-Day himself with Buckmaster and Miss Atkins. And then there was the new W/T operator, Nora. Maybe she was safe as well.

The niggling thought—the one that had been threatening to surface since she was arrested—finally formed. *What about the ID cards?* Prosper's picture had been printed on the card she'd made with his new alias. What if the Gestapo had found the box of ID cards and could recognize Prosper by sight?

She pushed that thought away as quickly as it had come, but the next one wasn't any better. *What about Gilbert?* Andrée couldn't bear to think of what the Gestapo might be doing to him at that very moment. Instead, she focused on what he'd said when he proposed to her. She closed her eyes and whispered to the empty room, willing her lover to hear her: *Gilbert, remember you promised to survive the war. No matter what happens, just do your best to survive.*

. . .

In the morning, Andrée was summoned once again to 84 Avenue Foch. An SS officer drove her in a black, windowless van.

Once again she was taken to the room with the chandelier, but this time there was a new man waiting for her. His civilian clothes hung loosely on his thin frame and the lenses in his glasses were so thick they almost seemed comical on his narrow face. Andrée looked around the room to see if he had a henchman huddled in the corner, for it didn't appear this milksop would be able to apply the same torture methods she'd been exposed to before.

As though reading her mind, the man said, "I'm not going to hurt you. My name is Ernest Vogt. My job is mostly to act as an interpreter for the senior officers."

"Are you a Nazi?"

He blinked a few times behind those heavy glasses. "Not especially."

"Then why did they send you in here to talk to me?"

He shrugged. "Sometimes when their tactics don't work, they try me. I can help you—if you cooperate, I can get them to treat you as a prisoner of war, not a convict. You will have access to privileges not usually obtainable to people charged with espionage."

"I don't need any privileges from you, and besides, I haven't been charged with anything yet."

Vogt shrugged again. "Suit yourself. Many of your comrades in the SOE have realized that resisting us does not make sense. We Germans are superior to you in every way: intellectually, creatively, and physically." When she didn't respond, he added, "We have a fine kitchen and dining room here. I could get you out of Fresnes and moved back to Avenue Foch if you tell me what I need to know."

In lieu of a reply, she pursed her lips and slumped in a chair with her arms folded across her chest.

He eyed her with interest, as if she were an insect he wanted to inspect. "We already have a great deal of information about your operations."

Andrée sat up. "Is that so? That's what your friend, the one who did this to me…" she lifted the leg of her pants to display her shin, which was nearly black with bruises, "thinks too, but I assure you, you know nothing."

He opened a desk drawer and took out a fat file folder. "We have a spy in your midst, what some people might call a 'double-agent.' How else do you think we got this?" He took something out of the folder and handed it to her.

It was a negative photostat. Andrée squinted to read the white print off the dark background. It was a letter, addressed to 'My darling wife.'

It seems ages since I left you. I keep on thinking of all the things I should have said to you—I hope my next visit won't be in the same rush.

Feeling slightly guilty at reading someone else's personal mail, she scanned down to the bottom. It ended with, 'All my love,' and then the unmistakable signature of Francis Suttill. She dropped the photostat and hid her shaking hands under the desk. *How did the Gestapo manage to get a hold of one of Prosper's letters to his wife?*

"That's not all—we have many more copies of your mail. Would you care to see any more?"

"No."

He put the photostat back in the file before reaching into his drawer again. This time he displayed a map of central France marked with white X's. Andrée felt like crying when she realized the X's marked the Prosper and Adolphe networks' dropping zones.

"We are aware that someone named Madeleine has just arrived. And though we haven't found her yet, trust me when I say that we will."

So Nora was still safe. "I trust nothing that you say."

He leaned closer, the glare from the chandelier on his spectacles obscuring his eyes. "You are a spy, and must suffer the fate of one, unless you disclose everything." He tapped at the map. "If you ever want to see daylight again, tell me where the arms from these dropping zones have gone."

"I don't know anything about that."

He sat back in his chair and put his hands behind his head. "I understand. You are doing what you consider your patriotic duty. It speaks well to your sense of honor. But these weapons could get into the wrong hands, given to terrorists who will use them for their own corrupt purposes. These criminals do not have the best interests of their country at heart and will not bring glory to France."

She assumed he was talking about the communists they'd been supplying. "I don't know anything."

He stood up. "I'm sorry to hear that, Ms. Borrel." She looked up, startled at the use of her real last name. "Feel free to return here if you suddenly remember any details you think would be beneficial to our investigation." He left her alone in the room, pondering how they'd manage to acquire so much intelligence on the Prosper network.

When Andrée was escorted out of the building, she found the afternoon had become stiflingly hot. Upon arriving at Fresnes, she was informed that the guards were allowing some of the female prisoners to try to cool off in the prison courtyard.

The cement-floored courtyard, surrounded on all sides by the towering prison walls, felt positively boiling. As sweat beads formed on her forehead, Andrée shielded her eyes against the sun to take stock of the prisoners.

Someone was walking toward her. She hoped against hope that it would be the tiny figure of Yvonne. It seemed strange to think that the chilly day when she had waited in vain with Prosper for Yvonne and Pierre had only been a week ago—it felt like years.

But the large-framed woman approaching was not Yvonne. Andrée nodded in recognition at Germaine Tambour, not wanting to call out her real name in case she'd given a code name to the Boches.

Germaine paused close enough to talk to her in a low voice, but not close enough to appear suspicious to the eagle-eyed guards. "So, did all of the circuit fall or was it just us?"

"I think a lot," Andrée replied, the regret obvious in her voice.

"Well, it will soon be more."

"Why?" Andrée asked, recalling how worried Prosper was about the Tambour sisters talking during interrogation.

Germaine glanced around her. "It's Gilbert. You've got to stop him. He's helping the Gestapo send messages to London, asking for drops and agents."

Andrée couldn't help how loud her reply was. "What?"

"He's going to betray everyone."

"No." Andrée shook her head. "I don't believe you. Not Gilbert."

A guard shouted for Germaine to keep moving. As she passed Andrée, the older woman hissed, "Not all of us can handle the pressure put on us by the Gestapo. I don't blame him. I just think if anyone can stop him before it's too late, it's you."

Andrée watched as Germaine walked away. It was clear from her painful limping that the Gestapo had been employing their usual mistreatment upon her.

There had to be another reason why Germaine had said those things. Maybe she was trying to pin the blame for her own betrayal on Gilbert. Maybe the Gestapo had told her falsehoods about Gilbert in order to get her to confess. Anything would make more sense than what she'd claimed. Gilbert could not willingly be feeding the Gestapo information about the Prosper network. He would never do such a thing. Andrée kicked at a piece of gravel, trying to repress the question that was taking shape in her head. *Would he?*

CHAPTER 50

NOOR

*A*s soon as she arrived at the École Nationale d'Agriculture, Noor knew something was wrong. She hid her bicycle in a clump of bushes and then approached the main building from the side, keeping herself hidden just in case. As she was nearing the entrance, she saw a man in a dark gray uniform walking across the lawn and nearly gasped out loud. She sought the cover of a large elm tree as she saw more men in dark uniforms accompanying Dr. Vanderwynckt. She blinked twice as they led him off the school grounds. A few minutes later she heard a volley of gunshots.

She covered her hand with her mouth, tears forming in her eyes. Her first instinct was to retch into the bushes, but she was afraid someone would hear her. She swallowed hard. *What do I do now?* There were yet more gunshots, and she realized she had to leave immediately: there was nothing she could do to help the man who'd been so helpful to the Resistance, and kind to her.

She hopped on her bicycle and pedaled away as fast as she could. She headed for the Balachowskys' house, which was a few kilometers away from the college.

. . .

Madame Balachowsky answered the door. "Nora?" She ushered her in. "What are you doing here?"

Noor was out of breath from her frantic ride. "Dr. Vander-wynckt," she managed to gasp out.

"And Serge too."

Noor fell into a chair. "He was arrested?"

"Yes. This morning." She shook her head. "You shouldn't be here. It's far too dangerous—they are probably watching this house. I'm lucky they didn't arrest me too."

"You're right." Noor was sorry to leave the comfortable chair to go back out there, where the Gestapo might pounce on her at any moment. "I will go back to Garry's apartment."

"You might want to telephone to make sure everything is okay there."

"It was fine this morning."

"That doesn't mean it's fine now. The Gestapo are everywhere. Now that they've arrested all the leaders of the Prosper circuit, they're closing in on the fringe members. Like Serge and Dr. Vanderwynckt." Her voice broke. "And you and me."

After a moment of thought, Noor realized Madame Bala-chowsky knew far more about being under surveillance than herself. Noor walked over to the telephone stand and reached for the receiver.

Madame Balachowsky stopped her. "Not here. They could be tracing the phone call. Call from a pay phone and tell whoever answers that you are a friend of Garry's. If they ask more questions, hang up and assume Garry's been compromised."

Noor was grateful for the advice, especially since, when she called Garry's apartment from a pay phone in Paris, an unfamiliar voice answered. She hung up quickly and went to see if she could locate France Antelme.

CHAPTER 51

FRANCINE

The SOE helped the Agazarians arrange a holiday in Somerset—Buckmaster had agreed that Francine's nerves needed time to recuperate. She and Jack spent a few days just lounging around, enjoying introducing themselves with their real names to fellow guests at the hotel, and eating hearty meals. Now that they were back in the safety of England, Francine wanted to bring up having a baby again, but decided to wait until the time was right. If Jack still wasn't ready, it might have ruined the rest of their holiday.

They returned to a small flat in London near Baker Street, once again courtesy of the SOE. It was a little too close to the F Section's headquarters for Francine's liking, and she was even more displeased when Jack was called in for a meeting one afternoon.

When he arrived back at their apartment, it was as if he'd seen a ghost: his face was white and he seemed agitated.

"What's wrong?" Francine asked.

Jack rubbed his forehead. "There's been bad news from Paris."

"Is everything okay? Is Andrée—"

"Arrested. Prosper too."

Francine sat down heavily on the couch, thinking of Andrée,

with her pretty face and strong will. The Gestapo would never get her to talk, no matter how hard they tried. No matter what interrogation methods they used. She blinked back a tear for her friend, hoping she'd survive whatever they decided to put her through. She felt slightly guilty about her next thought: *Thank God we got out when we did.*

Jack started pacing the length of the living room. "They think Gilbert is free—he's sending radio transmissions, but as Buck said, his last one was missing his true security check."

Francine wrinkled her nose. "Gilbert wouldn't make that mistake."

"No." Jack rubbed the stubble on his face. "I don't think so either, but that could only mean…"

"The Germans are forcing him to send messages." Francine stood up. "That's what the security check is for, right?"

"Yes, unless they somehow got a hold of his codes and are sending their own transmissions. Either way…" he stopped walking and his eyes met Francine's. She had never seen fear reflected back in them before. "It means Gilbert is in trouble."

Her legs felt as if they were going to give way. "What is the SOE going to do?"

Jack's face relaxed in a wry smile. "They're going to send me back."

"No." She sank into the couch. "You can't go back. We've only just left there."

"I have no choice. They need me to accompany Nick Bodington. I'm the only one who can pick up the pieces of what remains of the Prosper Network. If Gilbert is gone, then Madeleine is the only wireless operator left in Paris."

"*We're* the ones that are left. You can't go back—you'd be descending right into the mouth of the lion. Nick Bodington is a high-up in F Section. If the Gestapo caught him and tortured him into talking, any remnants of the Resistance would be obliterated."

"Francine, you know I'm no fan of Bodington. But I have to find out what happened. Gilbert and Andrée need me. France needs me."

She grabbed his arm as though she were drowning and Jack was her only lifeline. "I'm coming with you."

"No, Francie, you can't. You know how dangerous this is. I will try my best to keep safe, but I can't do that and look out for you at the same time. Stay here and wait for me."

"I can't just sit around waiting for you and thinking the worst."

"Then go back to the SOE. I'm sure they could use you in the signals room." His familiar grin returned. "That way you'll know what I'm up to."

She relaxed her grip on his arm, knowing there was nothing she could say to convince him not to go. Her heart felt heavy and every centimeter of her wanted to scream, "Don't do it!" but she knew Jack's sense of duty to the SOE was even greater than his obligations as a husband. And she couldn't begrudge him—one of the many reasons she married him was because of his honor.

She covered his face with kisses, trying to memorize every little imperfection and wrinkle so she could picture him each time she closed her eyes. She prayed it wouldn't be the last time she'd ever see him.

CHAPTER 52

ANDRÉE

A few days after Andrée talked to Germaine Tambour in the courtyard, she was awakened by a guard. "Sturmbann-führer Kieffer commands your presence in the dining room at Avenue Foch."

Andrée folded her arms across her chest. "You can tell him I'm not hungry."

The guard put a hand on his gun. "He'd like you to come now."

With a sigh, Andrée got out of bed. She gave her face a quick rinse before allowing the guard to handcuff her.

When they arrived at 84 Avenue Foch, Andrée was once again led through the opulent lobby. A sturdy-faced man with dark, curly hair sat at an elegantly dressed table in the dining room.

"Denise," he said, standing up. "Welcome. If you would please have a seat."

"I would rather stand," Andrée replied.

He shrugged. "If that's the way you prefer to eat."

A uniformed waiter brought in a tray of pastries and bread.

Andrée's mouth watered as she spied what appeared to be real butter in a silver dish.

"Would you care for some toast?" the man asked.

She shook her head.

"Coffee then?" He poured himself a cup of rich, black liquid. The smell of genuine coffee beans permeated the room and made Andrée weak with hunger. She had no choice but to drop into a chair.

The man nodded at the waiter, who filled her coffee mug up to the brim.

She took a cautious sip. It tasted as good as it smelled. She set it back down, splashing black liquid on the cream-colored tablecloth. *Don't fall for their trap.* Andrée figured they were trying to give her a false sense of security by plying her with food and coffee.

The man also put his cup down. "I'm Sturmbannführer Kieffer, but you may call me Hans."

"Mr. Kieffer," Andrée threw a napkin over her coffee cup. "Did you need something from me, or can I be escorted back to my cell?"

"Well, actually," he cleared his throat. "I was hoping you could provide us information about the arms drops you've been running via Prosper."

Andrée blew out her breath. "I don't know anything about any arms drops."

Kieffer's eyes narrowed. "I think you do, and you are also aware that most of these weapons end up in the hands of communists. I think it would be in both of our interests to not let that happen again."

"I wouldn't agree, even if I knew where these so-called arms drops took place. Any enemy of Hitler is an ally of mine."

He stood up and approached her. "Give us the location of where the guns and explosives from London were dropped and you can keep everything else to yourself. The people we arrest—your people—will not be executed, only interned until the end of the war. This is the arrangement we have made with your former boss, Francis Suttill."

So Prosper had indeed been captured. "I want to hear this from him," Andrée stated.

"No." He stuck a fat finger in her face. "I want to make clear that we'd already been told about some of the locations of your ammunition stores. Luckily, the villagers gave up easily, otherwise there would have been fire and bloodshed." He put one leg up on a chair and leaned against it. "Now about the others..."

The others. Andrée knew there were hundreds, maybe even thousands, of recruits, from Le Mans to Saint-Quentin, the Sologne to nearly Belgium. Many were French citizens, local people recruited into the Prosper network to act as reception committees or to store guns and ammunition in preparation for the invasion. There was no way the Gestapo could possibly find them all, unless someone gave them the information. It certainly wouldn't come from her. "I will reveal nothing until Prosper tells me too."

His narrowed eyes descended into slits. "Prosper is currently... unavailable, but perhaps you would like to hear from his second-in-command, Gilbert Norman."

At this Andrée sat up straight. She tried to keep her expression neutral, not daring to let the German see the effect his name had on her. She nodded her consent at Kieffer.

He walked over to the door and shouted at someone in the hallway. "Get me Gilbert Norman." He turned back to Andrée and folded his arms across his chest. "He'll convince you to talk, you'll see."

Andrée's reply was simple. "No."

"You two were lovers."

She focused her gaze on the waiter as he cleared the table instead of replying. *How did Kieffer know that?*

"At any rate," he put his hand on the doorknob. "I'll leave you two alone, so that you can get... reacquainted and Norman can explain what he and I have discussed."

After a few anxious minutes, Andrée heard shuffling in the hallway. The door was opened and a guard led Gilbert into the room. His arms were handcuffed in front of him. Though he was free of bruises, she also noted his normally confident swagger had disappeared.

"They didn't listen," he said as he sat down at the now bare table. "I tried to warn them, but they didn't listen."

"Who didn't?" she asked, bewildered.

He glanced around before leaning forward. "Buck. He actually responded to the Germans' message, pointing out that I'd forgotten my true security check and that I must never do it again."

Andrée closed her eyes. "Which means they now know we have separate checks." The absence of a true check was rule number one in the wireless rulebook for alerting London that something was wrong. Not only had Buck seemingly not realized that Gilbert was in trouble, but he'd also compromised the situation even further.

"It's not worth hiding anything anymore. The Germans know all," Gilbert said.

Her eyes flew open. She had never heard him so defeated. Still, she recognized that defeat—she'd felt the same thing when they showed her Prosper's letter to his wife. "You've seen the photostats then?"

He nodded. "They must have come from Déricourt."

"But they're just copies of mail. It doesn't mean the Boches know everything about the circuit. We can't tell them other names." *Nora. Please tell me you haven't said anything about Nora.*

Gilbert leaned forward, the chains between his hands rattling. "The best thing is to tell them all you know. They have promised everyone's lives will be spared. Prosper said to confess in order to save yourself."

"Prosper would have never agreed to such a thing." She wished she could say the same thing of Gilbert, but something told her she'd be wrong. *Germaine had been telling the truth.*

"We've made a pact with them. They won't hurt anyone if you tell them where the arms are hidden." His voice grew mournful. "They've gotten a hold of my new crystals and they've been sending messages back to London under my name, asking for supplies. The

Germans will be the victors of this war. Ours was a grand adventure, but now it's over."

"No." She reached out and put her hand over his. "It's not over, not until the Allies win. What we've sacrificed cannot be for nothing."

"That's just it!" He stomped his chained foot on the floor. "Sacrifice, Andrée. Are you willing to give up your life for the cause?"

"Yes," she replied simply, withdrawing her hand. "If it means that…" she looked around the room. The only guard was in the corner, pretending not to listen. She lowered her voice. "If by dying, I'm protecting the others, then yes, I'm willing to die."

"Well I'm not. We made a pact—tell them what you know, and our lives—and the lives of hundreds of others—will be spared."

"Gilbert, they are liars. What makes you think they will keep their word after you reveal everything? Have you forgotten what happened when we tried to rescue Germaine and her sister?"

He paused, seeming to consider what she had said. "At any rate, they are stronger than us."

They might be stronger than what you've become, but they wouldn't have been stronger than who you were before. Andrée resolved to not let them get the best of her. "Living as a traitor, knowing you gave in to their demands, is not a life worth living."

He nodded at the guard before getting heavily to his feet. "Then I guess we have nothing left to say to each other."

"No," Andrée agreed. "Only goodbye. Goodbye, Gilbert."

"Goodbye, Andrée."

CHAPTER 53

NOOR

France Antelme found Noor a new flat at 1 Square Malherbe. It was owned by a woman, Madame Aigrain, who spent the majority of her time at her lover's apartment in the same building. While Antelme continued his inquiries into what happened to the Prosper circuit, Noor stayed holed up in the apartment, though she did occasionally go out for necessities.

One evening she decided to dye her hair in case the Gestapo had a description of her. She chose a deep red, which, with her dark skin tone, probably wasn't the most flattering but at least she looked a bit different to herself in the mirror.

The next morning, Antelme told her that Émile Garry had sent a message saying he'd fled to Le Mans with his fiancée. Noor sighed with relief when she heard they were safe. She'd been in France for less than a month and had seen almost all of the Prosper network topple. Day after day, Antelme brought news of Gestapo raids on hidden arms depots in remote regions and the arrests of minor members of Prosper.

"How do they know so much?" Noor asked Antelme after he'd told her that George Darling, the head of a subcircuit in Gisors, was killed by the Gestapo.

"I don't know," he replied. "It's as if someone is supplying the Nazis with all of this information."

Noor tried to not reveal that her fear, which she had done her best to control since she first heard of Andrée's capture, was bubbling over. She nearly screamed aloud when someone knocked at the door to the flat.

Antelme held up his hand. "That will be Jean Savy, another member of Bricklayer." He opened the door to reveal a short man with graying hair.

"Jean's a Parisian lawyer with massive connections," Antelme told Noor, stepping aside to let the man in. "He's helped raise a great deal of money for the Resistance."

"Nice to meet you." Noor held out her hand, and Jean shook it. To her surprise, she saw that his left arm was withered and hung immobile at his side.

"We were hoping you would know of a place where Madeleine could transmit to London," Antelme said as he led the way into the living room.

"I can't do it from this apartment, obviously," Noor added. "Buckmaster told me that the Prosper network would provide me with safehouses, contacts, etc., but now I'm on my own."

Savy sat down heavily. "I'm afraid I can't help you. The Gestapo raided my flat the other day, and I've been staying with Robert Gieules." He rubbed his forehead before looking up at Antelme. "Gieules has a contact who said Émile Garry's place had been searched. The Gestapo has gotten hold of your food card. Though Mademoiselle Nadaud tore your name off the card, they have your picture and your old address."

"Which means they have a description of Antelme," Noor surmised.

"You should get out of France as soon as you can," Savy told him before locking eyes with Noor. "Both of you."

"No." Noor looked at Antelme. "You go. I'll stay. Someone has to have a link with London."

"You don't even have a safehouse to transmit from," Antelme replied. "There's nothing left for you here. Come back with me."

"No," Noor said again. She stood up. "I will start making arrangements for your return with Déricourt. Maybe he can help me find a safehouse."

CHAPTER 54

YVONNE

*Y*vonne could still hear the buzzing and feel the car swerve. *It's coming.*

"What's coming?" a disembodied voice asked.

She opened her eyes. *Did I say that aloud?*

"Jacqueline."

Who is Jacqueline?

An intense light was shone into her eyes and she blinked rapidly. The voice asked, "Can you see me?"

"Yes, I think so." Images were appearing. A man, wearing white. A window. She perceived she was lying down. *Not in a car then.* "Am I dead?"

"Not yet." The man went over to raise the blinds. "You were shot. The bullet went into the back of your head but did not pass through your skull. However, the kinetic energy from the bullet was transferred to your brain, causing concussive injury."

"Bullet, bullet…" Yvonne tried to focus.

"I didn't remove it. In my opinion, it would be best to keep it there for now—it's sterile from the heat of the gun and not doing harm. It would be better than undergoing surgery."

Yvonne could hear the words, but nothing made sense. She

265

touched the back of her head, which felt warm and wet. She tried lifting her legs to look at her feet, but they wouldn't respond. *Am I paralyzed?* She glanced down at her hands, which were now folded across her chest. The fingers of her right hand were covered in a red, sticky liquid.

The man was still droning on, oblivious to Yvonne's inner turmoil. "You will eventually recover, but in the meantime, you might have some minor memory loss, and remain in a state of confusion from the brain edema." He leaned closer to her. "Which might not necessarily be a bad thing considering that you were arrested…"

The man's voice faded into more buzzing and everything grew dark again as Yvonne shut her eyes. In a moment, there was nothing but blackness. And silence.

CHAPTER 55

NOOR

*O*nce Antelme had left for London, Noor was truly on her own. Since she still hadn't found a place to transmit from, she left Madame Aigrain's flat one very warm day in July to search for a suitable locale. It need not be an entire house—even a closet would do as long as it had a window near trees on which to fix the aerial.

As she walked along the streets, she felt even more sweaty than she should. She sniveled and then cleared her throat, which felt sore. It wouldn't surprise her if she was coming down with a cold, or even the flu, with all the stress she'd been under in the past two weeks. Whatever it was, she couldn't let an illness stop her.

She wandered the city, her straw hat pulled down over her eyes and her gaze focused on the ground. It made her feel safer to not see the German soldiers on the street. When the cobblestones started to look familiar, Noor finally glanced up. As if by rote, her feet led her to the house belonging to Mademoiselle Renié, her former harp teacher.

She rang the doorbell as she did so many times before, when she used to live in Paris a decade ago.

"Yes?" Mademoiselle Renié asked guardedly. She stood blocking the door, clearly wary of strangers. She looked thin and frail, and her once gray-streaked hair had gone completely silver.

Noor took her hat off and gave her old teacher a shy smile, wondering if she'd be able to recognize her with her hair dyed red.

"Noor?"

"Shh." She ducked her head. "May I come in?"

"Of course." Mademoiselle Renié's stance relaxed as she moved aside to let her in.

The hallway was dark and cool, and brought back many fond memories. Noor stretched out her fingers, practically feeling a harp's strings underneath them.

Mademoiselle Renié shut the door. "What are you doing back in Paris?"

"I'm here with the Red Cross."

Mademoiselle Renié's eyes narrowed and Noor could tell she hadn't fooled her old teacher.

"Do you know of any rooms for rent?" Noor asked.

"You need a place to stay? Why Noor, you can stay with me."

"No," she answered quickly. She wouldn't want to put Mademoiselle Renié through the hazard of hosting either herself or her radio.

Mademoiselle Renié fiddled with a stray curl as she looked Noor up and down. Her gaze landed on her wireless suitcase, as if she could sense what was inside. "Whatever it is you are doing, you are risking your life. The Gestapo are everywhere."

"I know." She set down the case to hug Mademoiselle Renié. "And now I must leave, for I would not want to cause any trouble for you."

"Noor, wait."

But she was already bounding down the steps. She turned and gave Mademoiselle Renié a little wave before she turned a corner. Once out of sight, Noor leaned against a wall, breathing hard. It had felt so nice to see a familiar face, but even the simple act of entering Mademoiselle Renié's house could have put the old woman in jeopardy. *I must not slip up like that again.* Not now.

. . .

Dejected, Noor made her way back to Madame Aigrain's. As she put her suitcase next to the bed, she looked out the window. There were plenty of trees. What was stopping her from sending a transmission from the flat? Madame Aigrain wasn't in. The only person Noor would really be putting in danger was herself.

She checked her watch. If she didn't get set up soon, she'd miss her sked again, and it would be another 24 hours before she could get in touch with London. She lifted up her suitcase and took out the aerial. *Just this once,* she promised herself. In the morning, she'd go out again to find a safehouse.

She got to work coding a message, knowing there was no time to find the right words to let the SOE know the Prosper network had fallen.

CHAPTER 56

FRANCINE

*M*iss Atkins arranged for Francine to work in Room 52 in Norgeby House, the SOE's signals room. The restricted access area could only be reached via a blocked-off corridor. Francine estimated that she had to show her ID card no less than four times to reach the room, which was cramped with dozens of seated women dressed in FANY uniforms, most of them wearing headphones. Since heavy blackout curtains covered the few windows, blocking all the natural light, the room was lit by buzzing fluorescent bulbs.

Francine walked over to the central blackboard, which contained information on the agents' call-signs and schedules. Under the heading 'Paris,' Jack's code name, *Marcel*, had been crossed off and there was a giant question mark next to the word, *Archambault*. Underneath those, the name *Madeleine* was printed in large letters, and Francine saw that her sked was coming up soon.

"Francine, welcome."

She turned to see Miss Atkins entering the room.

"I didn't expect to find you here," Francine said.

"Yes, well, this is where all the action happens." Miss Atkins spread her long arms wide. "I'd rather hear bad news straight from the horse's mouth than to wait for it to reach F Section headquarters." She walked over to a desk. "Many of the operators here are assigned to one agent, and their workdays revolve around their specific agent's sked."

Francine nodded. Though the FANYs would get to know their field operator's typing rhythm on the Morse key well, most would never actually meet the man—or woman—behind the messages. To them, their wireless operator would just be another faceless name written in block letters on a chalkboard. But those W/T operators had been very real to Francine—Jack, of course, and Gilbert Norman, and the exotic-looking new girl who'd just arrived in France, whom she suspected was Madeleine. "When will Jack be transmitting?"

Miss Atkins frowned. "His official assignment is not to be a W/T operator this time."

"Why did he have to go back, then? Bodington could have gotten anyone to accompany him."

"For whatever reason, Nick wanted Jack to go with him. At any rate..." Miss Atkins shot her an apologetic smile. "I think you and I can both agree that you are not fast enough to be officially assigned to an agent."

"I was trained to be a courier, not a wireless operator," Francine retorted.

"Of course. But at the same time, none of these FANYs," she swept her arm around the room, "have field experience. You're going to be considered the resident expert on any information related to the Prosper network. If any new intelligence comes in, I've asked the girls to consult you first to see if it's important, especially if I'm not around."

Francine followed as Miss Atkins walked over to a desk in the corner of the room. 'Madeleine' was printed on the chalkboard above the FANY's head.

"We haven't heard from Nora in quite a few days," Miss Atkins said. "I'm hoping everything is okay."

As if on cue, the FANY operator held up a finger with one hand while placing the other over her headphones. Francine decided only a W/T operator with a message coming through would be so impertinent as to tell Miss Atkins to be quiet.

Indeed, after a few seconds, the FANY hissed, "It's her."

Both Miss Atkins and Francine watched as the operator took down the code. Once the card was filled, Francine took it from her. She picked up the paper that had Madeleine's—or rather Nora's—poem code on it, and began to translate the message. Miss Atkins peered over Francine's shoulder as she worked.

When she finished, the message read: *Prosper arrested. Andrée too. Many others either arrested or in danger. STOP.*

Miss Atkins sucked in her breath before grabbing the arm of a FANY who was passing by. "Let Buck know Nora's on the line. He's in the War Office on the first floor." Miss Atkins let go of her. "Now," she added, causing the FANY to rush out of the room.

The wireless operator took off her headphones and gave Francine a curious look. Belatedly, Francine realized she'd been biting on the pencil. She took it out of her mouth and casually discarded the gnawed wood in a nearby trash can. Miss Atkins paced the length of the room, her normally inscrutable face wrinkled with worry.

When Buck came in, Miss Atkins handed him the message. He scanned it before stating, "We know that already." He crumpled up the paper and threw it across the room, aiming at the trash can, which he missed. "Ask her what she knows about Gilbert."

The W/T operator coded quickly before putting her headphones back on and typing out the letters on her Morse key. Nora's answer was that she had no new information, but that Gilbert was "presumed arrested."

"She doesn't know that for sure." Buckmaster's gaze focused on the blackout curtains across from them, as if he could see something the rest of them couldn't.

"Sir?" The FANY operator tried to get Buck's attention. "How should I respond to Madeleine?"

He closed his eyes in thought. "Tell her to get the hell out of there. It's far too dangerous. We'll get Déricourt to arrange a flight home."

"I can't," was Nora's reply. "I'm the only wireless operator left. It's up to me to rebuild Prosper."

"Is she crazy?" Buckmaster stormed.

Once again, Francine recalled the girl who'd gotten off the same Lysander on which she and Jack had departed France. *Jack was about to go back there, and if Nora wasn't around, then he'd never be able to communicate with London.* "Sir," Francine gently touched Buck's arm. "She's right. She's the only connection we have with Paris right now."

He exchanged a desperate glance with Miss Atkins, who nodded.

"Jesus." Buckmaster sat down in an empty chair. "What has the world come to? My best men, as well as some of my best women, have been arrested and all that's left is a little Sufi girl who trembles at the mere mention of the word 'Gestapo.'"

"I agree with Francine," Miss Atkins said. "Nora's our only hope right now. She may be a bit timid, but she's more than capable of operating a wireless."

"Okay." Buckmaster nodded at the operator. "Tell her to lie low and keep her daily sked for listening to further instructions only. She is not to transmit for a while in case they are looking for her signals. With her and Gilbert being the only radio operators in the area, it wouldn't take long for the detectors to find her."

"Yes, sir," the operator replied.

Buckmaster rubbed at his chin. "Lying low is probably the only 'lying' Nora will ever agree to." Seemingly to himself he added, "She has no idea of the danger she's in."

CHAPTER 57

YVONNE

*T*he man in white was back. He was trying to talk to Yvonne, but the buzzing noise in the back of her head mostly drowned him out. Only one word managed to sink in: *Gestapo.*

She tried to sit up, but found she couldn't.

"No, don't strain yourself," the man in white said. "Nurse?"

A woman wearing a habit and carrying a syringe came to Yvonne's bedside as two tall men in suits entered the room.

"It's time for her medicine," the man in white informed the newcomers. "She won't be able to answer any questions at this time. In fact..." the man in white gestured for the suited men to follow him. Yvonne watched them walk out of the room before she fell back asleep.

CHAPTER 58

FRANCINE

"Francine, come over here," Miss Atkins commanded. She was standing in front of the desk of a FANY operator.

As Francine did as bid, Miss Atkins handed her a pair of headphones and a pencil. "I want you to take down this message."

Listening intently, Francine wrote down the letters as they came in. After a long pause, she took off the headphones.

Miss Atkins gave the card to the FANY operator to decode. "What did you think about the rhythm?" she asked Francine.

"It was a little slow, maybe the mark of a new operator or one uncertain of the message they were sending. Was it Nora?"

"No," Miss Atkins replied. "It was under Archambault's call sign."

Francine shook her head. "There's no way that was Gilbert Norman. I was there sometimes during his sked. He always transmitted with the same confidence he did everything else."

"I agree. Gilbert would never be that hesitant."

"Did he use all of his security checks correctly?"

"Well," Miss Atkins took Francine's arm and led her away from the desk. "There's been a slight snafu regarding the security checks."

"What do you mean, 'snafu?'"

Miss Atkins looked around before she answered in a low voice. "It was suggested that Gilbert Norman might have been captured along with Prosper and Andrée."

Francine's gaze landed on the chalkboard listing the field operator's skeds. Archambault's transmission had come through right on time. She also noted the question mark next to his name had been erased. "That would mean that he's transmitting with the Boches sitting next to him," she surmised. "Jack mentioned as much before he left."

"Or the Germans got a hold of his crystals and codes."

"No matter what, he still would have had to tell them his skeds."

"Right." Miss Atkins sighed. "When I suggested something similar to Major Buckmaster—that maybe Gilbert revealed his transmitting schedule and codes under torture—he replied that Gilbert would have rather shot himself. Major Buckmaster refuses to acknowledge the possibility that Gilbert's radio is in the wrong hands, and when he forgot his security check, Buck kindly reminded him to not forget it next time."

Francine was flabbergasted. How could Buck have been so pig-headed in revealing the true check to whoever was operating Gilbert's radio? She shut her eyes, recalling the sluggish rhythm she'd heard over the radio waves. Buckmaster may be convinced that the sender was Gilbert, but she knew he was wrong. And from the expression on Miss Atkins' face, Francine could tell she felt the same.

CHAPTER 59

NOOR

*N*oor rode the elevator to the top floor at 1 Rue de Berri. She paused before she knocked, wondering why she had been sent to a film company. Major Buckmaster had told her during her last sked to meet someone named Nicholas Bodington at this address.

An impeccably dressed, petite woman answered the door. "Yes?"

"I'm looking for Major Bodington."

"That's me," a voice called from the living room.

The woman gave her an encouraging smile. "I'll make some tea."

Noor entered the living room to find a bespectacled, balding man sitting on thc sofa. He didn't rise to greet her. His thin lips barely moved under his clipped mustache as he said, "You must be Madeleine."

"Yes." She set her wireless case on the coffee table. "I was told that you would need a W/T operator."

"Yes. I'm just in from London." He looked her up and down. "I'm Buckmaster's second-in-command."

She took a seat across from him. "I always thought Miss Atkins was his second."

"Vera?" Bodington guffawed. "No, she's just a secretary."

Noor fingered the silver bird pinned to her bodice. "She was very helpful to me."

"Nonetheless," he clasped his hands together. "You have a regular sked with Buck, correct?"

"Yes."

"He's in contact with Gilbert Norman. Norman is going to give Buck his latest address this afternoon. London will then transmit this address to you, and you will pass it on to me."

"Gilbert? We haven't heard from him in weeks. Garry and Antelme are convinced Gilbert has been arrested."

Bodington heaved a sigh. "He couldn't have been, could he? How else would he still be contacting Baker Street?"

Luckily, Noor was saved from answering when the woman returned with the tea.

"Thanks, Julienne," Bodington said. As she poured three cups, he asked, "Have you two met?"

The woman set the pot down and extended her hand to Noor. "Julienne Aisner."

"It's nice to meet you," Noor replied. In the silence that ensued, she glanced around the room, her eyes landing on a bookcase full of projector reels.

Julienne followed Noor's gaze. "They belong to my ex-husband." She went over to put her hand on one of the reels. "He works in Hollywood now."

"Oh," Noor replied, wondering if Mr. Aisner had ever met Gary Cooper, Émile Garry's supposed lookalike. She set her unfinished teacup on the tray and then stood. "I'd better be getting back. I have to meet my sked."

Bodington checked his watch before nodding. "Report back here at noon tomorrow with the address the SOE provides you."

"Yes, sir."

. . .

When Noor returned the next day, another man was sitting in the living room with Bodington and Julienne. He looked slightly familiar. As he stood to greet her, Noor noted he was exceptionally tall.

"Jack Agazarian." He held out his hand. "I used to be one of Prosper's wireless operators."

"From the plane," Noor said. "I remember you and your wife. You just returned to England—what brings you back so soon?"

Jack rolled his eyes as Bodington stated, "Because I needed him to help me find out what happened to Prosper." He gestured for Noor to come closer. "Did you get the address?"

"Yes." Noor opened up her transmission notebook. "It's on the Rue de Rome." She read the address aloud and Bodington repeated it twice.

Noor shut her notebook. "If you don't mind me asking, is it safe for you to be going there?" She turned to Jack. "As I explained to Major Bodington, France Antelme and Émile Garry were under the impression that Gilbert Norman was arrested weeks ago. Is it possible that the Germans have gotten a hold of his radio and code book and are sending messages under the guise that it's Gilbert?"

"Whether or not it is indeed Norman, Jack and I have been given our orders," Bodington said. "Although," he addressed Jack, "I don't suppose both of us need to go. What do you say we flip to see who investigates the address?"

Jack rubbed his forehead. "I'm not sure…"

But Bodington had already produced a coin. "Heads you go, tails I do." He tossed it into the air. To Noor, it seemed to fall in slow motion until he caught it. "Heads," he declared.

"I guess that means me," Jack said, an ominous tone in his voice.

CHAPTER 60

YVONNE

The buzzing had greatly lessened the next time Yvonne woke up. But it wasn't the man in white who stood by her bedside, nor was it the Gestapo.

The name of the poacher who'd so often accompanied her and Pierre to the dropping zones seemed to come from somewhere deep in her brain. "Théo."

"Shh." He put a finger to her lips.

"How did you get in here?"

He smirked. "Breaking into a hospital room is not challenging for a man like myself." He leaned closer. "Can you walk?"

"I don't…" Yvonne looked at her feet, willing her toes to move. Nothing happened. "I don't think so."

His mouth turned downward. "We've got to get you out of here. We can dress you in disguise as a nun, but you have to be able to walk on your own."

"No, Théo, it's too dangerous. I don't want anything to happen to you." She stared at the buttons on his sturdy chest. Memories were exploding in her brain. She was in France, working as a secret agent. *Like Pierre.* But there was a black cloud around that memory. *Something bad had occurred.* "You're not arrested."

"No."

There were others. *The Flamencourts. The Gatignons. Julien Nadau.* "Did the circuit fall?"

His hesitation told her more than any reply.

It was all there now. Everything that had happened these past few months. She worked for Adolphe, a subset of the Prosper network. They had recruited so many people to work for the Resistance. And there were others, people being sent in from London. She could recall the busy town hall where the Canadians had been arrested and the ensuing car chase. They'd discovered Pierre's suitcase with all of his contacts. The Gestapo must have had a field day with all those names.

To her surprise, Yvonne found her voice was steady. "How did you escape?"

"I was away when they came to my house. My nephew was there and the Boches tried to intimidate him by forcing them to watch as they killed two rabbits he held in a cage." Théo shrugged. "The rabbits were meant for the pot anyway. My nephew gave nothing away."

"And Pierre?"

He gave a heavy sigh. "He's in a Paris hospital, but I heard they are going to transfer him to Fresnes Prison soon."

She straightened her spine as best she could. "Théo, you can't be here. If anyone saw you, they could connect you to Adolphe and arrest you."

As if on cue, a nun entered the room. "What are you doing to her?" she demanded, wielding a syringe as though it was a weapon.

Théo lifted his own empty hands. "Nothing."

The nun looked from Yvonne back to Théo. "You are a friend?"

"Yes," he replied.

She dropped the arm holding the syringe. "It's pentothal," she explained. "We give it to her when the Germans come. It makes her sleepy so they can't ask her any questions."

"Then you know who she is and what she's done for this country."

The nun shook her head. "I can't know too much, but I know enough to protect her."

"I am glad she is in good hands." Théo turned back to Yvonne. "I need to go now, but I will be back soon. Try to work on doing what we discussed." He nodded toward her feet and then touched his hand to his forehead in salute to the nun as he left.

CHAPTER 61

NOOR

The morning after Jack was supposed to meet with Gilbert, Noor awoke to a pounding on her door. She opened it to find Major Bodington standing there.

"What happened?" she asked sleepily.

"Agazarian never came back," Bodington said as he entered the apartment.

She shut the door, repressing the urge to say *I told you so*. "Do you think he was arrested?"

"I think it's safe to assume he's now in German custody."

Noor felt tears well up for the kind man and his poor wife waiting for him back in England. She blinked rapidly, willing her tears not to fall since she did not want to display any weakness in front of Bodington. "What should we do?"

"We have to let Baker Street know about this latest arrest, and that Gilbert Norman should be considered compromised."

Once again, *I told you so* was on Noor's lips, but she knew uttering the words aloud wouldn't help the situation. It wouldn't bring Jack back. "Buck told me not to transmit for a while," she said instead. "Besides, I don't have a safehouse."

"Well, I think it's time we find you one. With Gilbert gone, you're the only wireless operator left in Paris." With that, Bodington left Noor's apartment.

Once she was alone, Noor burst into tears, partly because of Jack's disappearance and partly out of sheer panic over the new burden she was being forced to bear.

CHAPTER 62

FRANCINE

Francine knew something was wrong the moment she entered Norgeby House.

"Major Buckmaster asked to see you straightaway," the guard told her after she'd produced her ID card. "He's in his office on the first floor."

Her heart hammering in her chest, Francine made her way to Buck's office. He was seated behind his desk smoking his pipe, though it wasn't quite nine in the morning. Miss Atkins sat primly across from him.

"Francine." Buck nodded at the empty chair next to Miss Atkins. "Take a seat."

"Is this about Jack?" she asked, still standing.

"Please sit down, Francine," Miss Atkins said.

As she arranged herself in the chair, Buck set his pipe down. "We've finally heard from Nora."

Francine leaned forward. "Did she have news of Jack?"

Buck and Miss Atkins exchanged a glance. "Yes," Buck said. "But it's not good."

Francine could feel tears forming. Her voice came out higher than she'd intended. "What is it?"

Miss Atkins put her hand on Francine's shoulder. "Jack never returned from the rendezvous."

"What rendezvous?"

Buck took another puff. He seemed to be expecting Miss Atkins to answer. When she didn't, he took the pipe out of his mouth. "Gilbert had given us an address where he wanted to meet with an agent. Bodington said Jack volunteered to go, but when he got there, it evidently wasn't Gilbert waiting for him."

Francine closed her eyes, letting the tears fall. After a moment, she stood, feeling angry all of a sudden. "I told you that wasn't Gilbert transmitting. Why would you let anyone go there, let alone my husband?"

"I'm sorry, Francine," Miss Atkins said.

The calmness in her voice caused Francine's anger to dissipate. "I'm sorry too." With that, she left Buck's office. She didn't bother to go to work. She didn't want to interpret any other agent's signals for a long time.

CHAPTER 63

NOOR

*A*fter Bodington found Noor a ground-floor apartment in Neuilly-sur-Seine, his next move was to purchase a café in the Place St Michel to act as a new rendezvous spot, with Julienne Aisner and her boyfriend as the proprietors. Noor was instructed to alternate between the café and the Neuilly flat for her transmissions.

With the last hopes of the Prosper network extinguished, including Jack Agazarian and Gilbert Norman, there wasn't much left for Bodington to do. He asked for Noor to arrange a flight back to London for him via Henri Déricourt.

Noor recalled that fateful day at Grignon when Prosper had said he'd tried to warn London about Déricourt. At the time, she had wanted to form her own opinion of the Air Movements Officer, but now, after Jack's disappearance, she realized it would be best to not trust anyone. "I must warn you," she told Bodington. "Some people have questioned Déricourt's loyalty to the Allies."

"Henri?" Bodington laughed. "I agree that his first loyalty will always be to himself, but if you are accusing him of being a double agent, you are mistaken. He's no more harmful than you or I."

She decided to change the subject. "Do you mind taking some

letters back with you? I have many for my family, and one for Miss Atkins as well."

"Sure," Bodington replied. "No problem."

Noor handed him the letters. She'd written to her mother, of course, and Claire and Vilayat. In the letter to Miss Atkins, she thanked her once again for the silver pin, telling her that it had indeed brought her good luck so far and would certainly continue to do so in the future.

Noor had also thought about writing to Jack's wife, but she didn't know what to say. She'd replayed that fateful scene back in Julienne's apartment over in her mind so many times. The ending was always the same: Bodington had his orders to send someone to that address, and there was nothing she or Jack could do to convince him otherwise.

As Bodington stuck the letters in his bag, he asked, "Are you sure you want to stay? You've already surpassed the six weeks they say is the average duration of a radio operator. Besides, if the Gestapo can catch Frank Suttill and Gilbert Norman, they can get anyone."

"I can't leave until they send a replacement," Noor insisted.

CHAPTER 64

ANDRÉE

The next time Andrée was summoned, it wasn't to Avenue Foch. Instead, she was brought down to a small room in the prison where a stocky man in a gray suit was waiting.

"Haven't you people given up yet?" Andrée asked. "You should know by now that I will tell you nothing, no matter what you do to me."

"I'm not with the Gestapo," the man replied. He took off his tortoise-shell glasses and cleaned them with his shirttail. "My name is Hugo Bleicher. I work for the Abwehr, a counter-intelligence department. Unlike the Gestapo and the SS, we are not directly affiliated with the Nazi Party."

"Well, in that case, do you mind?" She held up her bound wrists. "Your friends consider me a major threat, but there is nowhere for me to escape."

"I assure you, they are no friends of mine." Bleicher produced a key and unlocked her handcuffs. "In fact, Kieffer and I are quite the opposite."

Andrée rubbed her sore wrists. "Gestapo, Abwehr—the distinction means nothing, for you all demand things from me that you will not receive."

He shrugged. "I've made a few arrests of other circuits, namely Interallié and Spindle, but the SD believes the Abwehr to be mostly washed up now. You don't have to consider me a threat. I was here to visit another SOE woman earlier, and once I heard you were here, I wanted to meet you."

"Another woman from the SOE is here?" He couldn't mean Germaine—she had been a local recruit. *Was it Yvonne?*

Bleicher lit a cigarette. "Do you know a woman named Lise?"

Andrée shook her head.

"Exceptional woman. She worked briefly with a man who goes by the code name Louba." He took a deep drag of his cigarette. looking at her expectantly.

She shrugged. "I don't know Louba."

"His real name is Paul Frager."

She kept her expression neutral. "Never heard of him either."

"No?" Bleicher dug through his briefcase. "This was supposed to be his new ID." The card he displayed was familiar—it was one of the ones Andrée had been working on with Gilbert the night they were arrested.

"Where did you get that?"

He pocketed the card. "I think you know."

"The Gestapo…"

He shook his head. "We were able to search the house first—Kieffer was too distracted with his interrogation of Prosper to bother. They tortured him, you know."

Andrée's eyes filled with tears. "Where is Prosper now?"

"Germany, I expect. Like many of you Resistance members will be soon. They're clearing out the prison to make more room. I don't know if you know this, but a second continental Allied landing is expected any day now, and they want a place to put all the soldiers they capture."

She wiped her eyes, forcing her countenance to be as inscrutable as his.

His tone was conversational as he stated, "They'll probably put you all in their 'work camps,' which are not places you'll want to be."

"I don't care where I go. I'll survive."

"No." He stabbed his cigarette out. "I take it you haven't heard of the *Nacht und Nebel* policy?"

Andrée shook her head.

"The German poet, Johann Wolfgang von Goethe first used the phrase, in reference to crimes committed in the concealing fog and darkness of night. If you are sent away under the decree, no one who loves you will ever learn of your fate. The Nazis describe it as '*vernebelt*'—transformed into mist. Trust me, they know how to make you disappear."

Andrée rubbed at her temples, thinking of Gilbert. *Was he about to disappear or would his collusion with the Gestapo protect him?* Despite his betrayal to the SOE, she still hoped it would be the latter. No one deserved to perish without a trace, and—though she knew she and Gilbert could never be a couple again—she wanted to take comfort in knowing he'd at least survive the war.

She dropped her hands as another thought occurred to her. "What will you do with the ID cards from Laurent's house?"

"That's really up to you. I don't necessarily need to do anything with them if you can tell me how to get in touch with Paul Frager or anyone from the Donkeyman circuit."

"I can't help you."

"Not even if I offer you a deal?"

"No."

He let out a deep breath. "I figured as much. Lise said the same thing." He stood. "I admire your integrity, but wish you'd taken me up on my offer. I fear what's in store for you."

"You don't need to worry about me."

"No, I don't need to, but there will probably be a few moments where I will wake up in the middle of the night and hope that you and Lise are not suffering too much." He put his hand on the door. "I think you should know that both Hitler and Heimrich Himmler have taken a personal interest in the F Section. Berlin considered the Prosper network particularly dangerous, so there will most likely be some retaliation in store for you and your friends."

Bleicher presumably meant his words as a threat—or at least as a last-ditch effort to get her to comply—but they didn't have the right effect on Andrée. Instead of being alarmed, she was consoled at the thought of Hitler being troubled by the success of the Prosper network. The sacrifices she had made had indeed been worth something.

CHAPTER 65

YVONNE

*Y*vonne had a vague vision of Théo Bertin visiting her in her hospital room, but figured it must have been a dream. She couldn't imagine the poacher being able to pass the armed guards who stood outside her door all day and night.

One morning, she faintly heard a voice ask, "Madame Culioli?" The speaker, a man, stepped deliberately into her eyeline. "Are you Madame Culioli?"

The name sounded slightly familiar, but surely she would have immediately recognized it. "I don't know," she said. "My name might even be Mussolini. Or Hitler."

He sighed and flipped through her chart. "Well, whatever your name is, it has been requested that you be relocated."

"Who requested this?" she asked, thinking again, for some reason, of Théo Bertin.

"A…" his finger moved across the chart. "Colonel Bleicher of the Abwehr."

"Never heard of him." Yvonne closed her eyes.

"You'll probably want to get dressed now."

Yvonne's eyes flew open to see a nun holding a light gray jacket and skirt. "Those aren't my clothes," she told the nun.

The nun frowned. "This is what you were wearing when you were brought in." She indicated a brown stain on the collar. "We tried to get the blood stains out, but…"

Yvonne recalled Madame Gatignon loaning her the suit for the trip to Paris. *Paris. Pick and Mac. The town hall. Gunshots.* She sighed. "Give me the clothes."

The nun pulled back the bedsheet.

"I can put them on myself," Yvonne snapped.

CHAPTER 66

NOOR

*N*oor was exhausted. In addition to the Neuilly flat and Julienne's café, she'd found a place to transmit from in Suresnes. She traveled among all three spots on a daily basis to keep the Germans from locating her, carrying her hefty transmitter all the while.

In August, Émile Garry and his fiancée-turned-wife Marguerite returned from Le Mans. Noor occasionally stayed with them, though she wasn't overly fond of Garry's sister, Renée, who was tall and stout, with dirty blonde hair, and seemed to have an unexplained hatred for Noor.

Noor's only clue as to why came one day when she dropped by the apartment to pick up Garry's latest message for the SOE.

"Do you know what happened to that handsome man who used to come around—Antoine?" Renée asked by way of greeting.

Antoine was France Antelme's code name. "He had to go away for a little while, for his own safety," Noor replied.

Renée blinked rapidly, as though her heavy eye make-up was too much weight for her lids to bear. "He left because you are dangerous." She pointed a chubby finger at the notebook Noor always carried with her. "You shouldn't keep notes of all your transmissions."

Feeling snarky, Noor told her she was still in contact with Antelme, which was not a complete lie. London's transmissions often contained personal instructions from him, including contacts he suggested that she make.

"I don't believe you," Renée replied. "At any rate, I still think you are dangerous." With that, she traipsed off.

"I'm sorry about that," Garry said, entering the hallway his sister just left. "She's always been a bit full of herself." He gestured for Noor to follow him into the kitchen.

"It's no matter." She picked up a piece of paper. "Is this encoded?"

He shook his head. "Not yet."

After she'd pocketed it, he showed her a map. "Look at this." He tapped at a series of lines. "This is Orly, the Parisian airport. The Boches have fifteen Flak guns all pointing here," he indicated a spot north.

Noor nodded in understanding. "Waiting for the Allies to land."

"Don't you think the guns, not to mention the airport, would make an excellent target for the RAF?"

She grinned. "I do indeed. This should be on the next flight out to London." Her grin faded. "Which means I'll have to take this map straight to Déricourt."

Garry noted the change in her attitude. "Do you not trust Déricourt?"

"No, but we don't have a choice." She checked her watch. "I've got to get going soon. I have a meeting scheduled for the afternoon."

"Another of Antelme's contacts?"

"Yes. Robert Gieules. He's the one Jean Savy was staying with before he left. Like Savy, he's a lawyer and is compiling information on companies that are breaking the agreement of the Armistice, such as BMW and Renault."

Garry ran his hands through his hair. "Sounds very interesting, but we need more than just information. We need someone to fill the seat left by Prosper's arrest."

"Gieules has agreed to help rebuild the Prosper circuit as well. He said he has many Resistance contacts all throughout France."

"Besides us and Gieules, who else is left?"

Noor counted on her fingers. "Two local recruits named Vaudevire and Arrighi, who are working with the Free French, and someone called Pierre Viennot. He's employed by an electronics company and was able to repair my radio when it went on the fritz last week."

Garry folded his hands under his chin. "Have you met Sonia?" When Noor shook her head, he continued, "She's a courier with Juggler. Actually, with Worms arrested and Weil gone, she's the only one left from her circuit. She may have other contacts who can help us out."

"Let's hope so. I promised Buckmaster that Prosper would be back up and running soon. In the meantime..." Noor picked up the map of the airport, "this will be sure to impress them."

A few weeks later, Noor received instructions to meet two newly arrived F Section agents at a café on the Champs Elysées. Buckmaster had told her that the agents were Canadian and went by the names of Pickersgill and Macalister. They were stationed in the Ardennes and were to form a new circuit called Archdeacon.

The next day, Noor walked to the Café Colisée. It was a warm day, and the outside terrace was crowded. She strolled inside and asked the coatroom attendant for "Bertrand." The attendant nodded and led her to a basement room.

A short, stocky man introduced himself as Frank Pickersgill. His companion, who was even shorter and wearing a large hat, said his name was John Macalister.

The men, especially Pickersgill, spoke with odd accents. They didn't sound either French or Canadian to Noor. "We've been asked to organize a network north of Paris," Pickersgill said. Noor decided that perhaps his accent was Swiss as he continued, "We're looking for a man named Monsieur Desprez. Do you know him?"

He looked disappointed when Noor shook her head. "But," she added, recalling something Robert Gieules had told her in passing, "I think I might know someone who does."

Pickersgill shook her hand one more time and they arranged to meet a few days later at L'Étoile, another café. This time she would bring Gieules with her.

She was on her way to L'Étoile via the Métro when two German soldiers boarded the train. Though the car was exceptionally warm, she felt a chill run down her back when she caught them staring at her transmitting case. She contemplated getting off early, but they were standing in the aisle, blocking the exit.

The soldiers exchanged monosyllabic words with each other, and then, to her horror, approached her.

"What's in the case?" one of them asked.

Noor thought quickly. For some reason, Julienne Aisner and her collection of film reels came to mind. "A cinematographic apparatus."

"What? Let me see," the other one said.

Noor opened up the suitcase halfway, praying they wouldn't know what a wireless transmitter actually looked like. "See all the tiny bulbs?"

"Ah, yes," the first soldier said. He gestured to the other one. "My comrade here thought it was something else." The train pulled to a stop and he moved aside to let her through. "You may go. I hope we haven't inconvenienced you too much."

"It's not a problem," Noor called over her shoulder. She sighed to herself after the door had shut. She was still far away from L'Étoile, but at that point she would rather walk.

The two Canadians were waiting underneath a crimson awning outside the café. Macalister was still wearing his hat; this time it was pulled down even lower over his eyes. Noor hesitated before joining them. She glanced around and spotted the short, stout form of Gieules sitting at a table nearby. She nodded at him and he stood. He threw a few francs down and then joined her at the Canadians' table.

"This is my contact," she told them in a low voice before turning to address Gieules, "And these are the new arrivals."

Gieules reached out to shake their hands.

"I'm told you are acquainted with Maurice Desprez," Pickersgill said.

"I am."

"Can you take us to meet him?"

A muscle twitched in Gieules's cheek. "I can indeed." His smile turned apologetic. "But first, if you don't mind, I'd like to catch up with Mademoiselle Madeleine."

Pickersgill picked up his coffee cup. "Not a problem. We are not quite done here, anyway."

Gieules put a firm hand on Noor's arm and led her a few paces away. "If that man's Canadian, then I am Charlie Chaplin."

"I don't know what you mean."

"Where did you hear of these gentlemen?"

"From Buckmaster. He asked me to meet them, and they told me they needed to get in touch with Monsieur Desprez."

He relaxed his grip on her arm. "Are you certain they are who they say they are?"

"Yes. Pickersgill supposedly has a flair for language. He's probably trying to imitate a Frenchman to cover his Canadian accent."

Gieules rubbed his forehead. "If you vouch for them, then I will take them to Desprez."

"I do. The orders from Buckmaster were to accommodate them, so I think we should do just that."

"All right." Gieules's lips turned upward as he walked back to the table. Her duty done, Noor stood at her spot and watched Gieules gesture for the men to follow him. Once they'd gone, she checked her watch and realized she had a sked to make.

CHAPTER 67

YVONNE

*Y*vonne was taken to Fresnes prison and put in a cell with two other women, who told her they had belonged to the Resistance. Not knowing whether or not they'd been planted there by the Gestapo, Yvonne said nothing about her involvement with the SOE. Still, her cellmates treated her kindly and even attempted to wash the blood out of Madame Gatignon's gray suit, to no avail.

Occasionally men in uniform tried to interrogate Yvonne, but she stuck to her story that she could remember nothing. In truth, she was slowly getting better, though the back of her head constantly throbbed and she frequently got headaches.

After only a few weeks, Yvonne's cellmates were moved out and she was once again left alone. She had another one of her headaches—this time it was so bad the pounding seemed to be originating from outside her body. *Thud, thud, thud.* With a start, she realized it wasn't her head making the noise. There was a series of tapping sounds coming from the other side of her cell wall, some short, some long.

She closed her eyes, trying to recall the Morse code she'd

learned in training. The taps started over again. *Hello, hello is anyone there?*

She placed her palm flat on the wall before making a fist. She found it more difficult to recall which Morse sounds to tap out than to translate the ones coming in. She tried, "I am here," but, based on the prolonged silence on the other side, she was afraid she'd used the wrong letters.

Finally a reply came. "My name is..." but Yvonne's thought processes couldn't keep up with the tapping. "Again," she requested.

This time her brain worked faster, but she wasn't really sure she could believe what she heard. "Frank Pickersgill."

The Canadian. "I know you," Yvonne answered, her mind composing the letters rapidly now. "It's Jacqueline."

"Hello, Jacqueline. I thought you were dead."

"Not yet," she tapped back. "How long have you been in here?" What she really wanted to know was how long it had been since they'd been arrested. She'd lost track of time since emerging from her coma.

"Several months, though it feels like an eternity."

Agreed, Yvonne thought. She blinked rapidly to clear her mind in order to catch his next question, "Have you been to Avenue Foch?"

"No. What is that?"

"Gestapo headquarters."

Yvonne was starting to feel dizzy and her knuckles hurt. After a minute, Pickersgill continued, "Gilbert Norman is there. He is telling the Boches where the supplies from the arms drops are hidden."

"Why would he do that?" She was running out of strength. "Does Andrée know about this?"

Pickersgill responded that he didn't know, but whether it was in response to Yvonne's first or second question—or both—she wasn't sure. She was too tired to care anymore. She lay down on the cold floor of her cell and promptly fell into a deep, dreamless sleep.

CHAPTER 68

NOOR

A few days after the incident with the Canadians, Noor was supposed to have another rendezvous with Robert Gieules, but he never showed. She half-expected Pierre Viennot to not be waiting for her the next day at their scheduled meetup in the Tuileries. But sure enough, his tall, lanky form was stretched out on the middle of a bench when she arrived at the garden.

Viennot was an administrator at one of France's largest electronics companies, and in addition to helping fix her transmitter, he often provided her with information on which frequencies the Germans were using to communicate with submarines.

He moved so she could sit next to him. "Good morning, Madeleine."

"Good morning."

"If you don't mind me saying, you look exhausted."

"I am." She tucked her transmitting case under the bench. "I've been worried about Gieules. Have you heard from him?"

"No." Viennot uncrossed his long legs before meeting her gaze. Worry was etched on his handsome face. "You don't think he's been arrested, do you?"

"I don't know," Noor admitted.

He nodded toward a pay phone. "There's one way to find out."

With shaking hands, Noor dialed Gieules' number. To her relief, he answered, though he sounded tired.

"Where have you been?" Noor demanded.

"Busy," Gieules replied in a vague tone. There was a pause before he asked Noor to meet him the next morning near the Arc de Triomphe.

There was something odd in the way he spoke, Noor decided after she hung up. She confessed as much to Viennot.

"I'll come with you tomorrow," he offered.

The following day, Noor met Viennot on the same bench at the Tuileries and he led her to his car, a maroon coupe. Though Noor knew he worked for a prominent company, she couldn't help gaping, wondering how anyone could afford a car like that, let alone the petrol.

He smiled indulgently at her. "If only my boss knew what nefarious activities I use this baby for."

He drove slowly down the Champs-Élysées. Noor could see the stocky Gieules waiting on another bench near the corner of rue Tilsit. She moved her arm to wave at him, but Viennot took his hands off the wheel and grabbed her. "Wait."

Noor's eyes widened as she took in another man wearing a black trench coat sitting on an adjacent bench, his back to Gieules. Across the street was another man in similar clothes, and another one stood a few meters away. All in all there were six men besides Gieules, all dressed similarly, and all with an odd stillness about them, as if they were waiting for someone.

"It's a trap." Viennot drove slowly down the street, away from Gieules and the man.

Noor's mouth felt as though it were filled with sawdust as Viennot parked the car. She swallowed hard. "Do you think they are looking for me?" Most of the men had been situated on the driver's side, so maybe they didn't see her.

"I don't know." He shut the engine off and put his hand on the door handle.

"What are you going to do?"

"I have some friends I can call. They might be able to help."

She watched the too-casual men surrounding Gieules. Luckily, they didn't seem to notice Viennot as he made a call on a nearby pay phone.

"They should be here soon," Viennot said when returned.

"Do you think this has something to do with the Canadians I introduced Gieules to a few days ago?" Noor asked.

Viennot shook his head. "I don't know."

A few minutes later, a black Citroën pulled up near Gieules' bench.

"Are these your friends?" Noor asked hopefully.

Viennot held up his hand as the men behind Gieules walked up to him. One of them put his hands on Gieules' shoulders and then led him into the car. "No," Viennot replied finally as the Citroën drove off. More minutes went by as Noor's mind whirred. *Those civilian-clothed men must have been Gestapo, clearly alerted to Gieules' activity with the Resistance.* Was this all her fault?

Another black car pulled up near them. "These are my friends," Viennot said as he once again got out of the car. Four very large men wearing baggy suits and fedoras exited the car. They looked like gangsters. Noor had heard that members of the Corsican mafia had sided with the Resistance, but never had seen evidence, until now. *No wonder Viennot has such a fancy car.*

He exchanged a few words with one of the gangsters before they drove off. "Just a couple of minutes too late," Viennot said when he got back in.

Noor's voice came out shrill. "What are we going to do now?"

"We are going to hash this out." Viennot drove to the L'Étoile café. He helped Noor out of the car and led her inside, her steps sounding hollow on the black-and-white tiled floors. After he ordered two coffees, they sat in silence.

Noor took a sip of bitter coffee before saying, "Gieules set a trap for me. This is all my fault."

"No, it's not," Viennot replied. "But it's clear the Gestapo are on the lookout for you." He gave her a searching gaze. "Have you ever thought about dying your hair a different color?"

Her hand flew upward and touched a red lock of hair. "The strands are all ready to break from my last dye job. I don't think it could handle another home coloring."

"Gieules probably gave them a description of you."

"But I don't have the money for a salon coloring—I gave away the last of the SOE cash Antelme had given me." She pulled a notebook out of her purse and began to flip through it. She found the right page and traced her fingers across an entry. "On the 28th of September, I gave 500 francs to Gieules."

"Put that away," Viennot hissed.

As she did, he asked if she recorded everything in there.

"Yes," Noor replied. "Buckmaster told me to."

"Is he crazy? If the Boches got a hold of that, they would know every communication you'd ever had with London."

"It's not as if they can break into my apartment and find it," Noor retorted. "I keep it with me at all times."

"Even worse." He stretched out his hand. "Give it to me. I'll burn it."

"No." She held it to her chest with both arms crossed over it. "Buckmaster told me to be careful with my filings."

Viennot clenched his fist as if he wanted to grab the notebook from her. After a moment, he relaxed his hand. "If you don't have money to get your hair done professionally, I'll pay for it." His eyes dropped to her disheveled blouse. "And I'll buy you some new clothes while we're at it."

CHAPTER 69

FRANCINE

*F*rancine spent a few tearful weeks holed up in her tiny flat. Winter was looming and since the apartment was always freezing, she stayed wrapped in Jack's overcoat for warmth. Though it became filthy, she refused to wash it. She wanted the smell of Jack to linger on it as long as possible.

She spent the long, dark nights lying in bed, staring up at the ceiling, replaying what Buckmaster and Miss Atkins told her about Jack's last days in Paris. It didn't make sense to her that Bodington had told Jack to go to an unsecured address. When such scenarios came up in training, they had been instructed to recruit a local—someone with no ties to the Resistance—and pay them to investigate the location first. If Bodington had done that, he would have known it was crawling with Gestapo. *He should never have sent Jack there alone.*

Chills ran down her already cold back when she thought about whoever had been using Gilbert's radio to contact them. Buckmaster had finally been forced to close down communication with that frequency, but that didn't mean there weren't other strange things happening at the SOE. In the past few weeks, there had been more reports about Déricourt's faulty security measures from someone called Louba. And no had heard from John Macalister of the Archdeacon circuit in several weeks.

A loud knock roused Francine from her thoughts. She tightened the waist belt of Jack's coat before approaching the door. "Who is it?"

"It's me, France Antelme. Open the door, Francine."

She did as he asked.

Antelme had lost his ruddy coloring and his hair was more gray than black now. "I heard about Jack," he said as he stepped into the apartment.

Francine shut the door behind him. "It doesn't make sense."

"Nothing much does these days. But that's war."

She gestured for him to sit down while she made tea. "I'm glad you're back," she stated when she returned to the living room.

"It's only for a little while. It got too risky in Paris."

"I heard." She poured the tea into cups, relishing in the hot steam. Anxious to talk about anything but Jack's disappearance, she tried to change the subject. "How's Nora? I haven't been in the signals room for a while."

"She'll be fine." He took a sip of tea. "A lot of people underestimate her, but that girl's got it where it counts."

"Not like me." Francine rubbed at the bags under her eyes. "I couldn't handle it anymore." Her resolve to not speak of her husband failed. "But Jack…"

"Jack did what he needed to." Antelme set his cup down. "He might come back one day. You can't give up all hope."

"Actually, I can," she countered. "And I have."

"Francine." Antelme looked as helpless as he sounded. "You—"

She didn't give him a chance to finish. She hurled herself into his bewildered arms, crying hysterically for all she had lost.

After she was spent, she sat back up, feeling slightly embarrassed for her outburst. Antelme's cotton shirt was soaked through with her tears.

He touched her hand. "You should get back to the signals room. Nora needs you."

"I don't think I can, especially knowing all that has happened over there."

"The Prosper network's flame might have been extinguished, but there are still fires of Resistance burning all throughout France in anticipation of the day the Allies land. We can't give up hope." He tilted her chin upward, forcing her to look at him. "It's all we have left."

She moved her head away from his hand.

"Do it for Jack," Antelme pleaded. "Maybe someday a signal will come through and it will be him."

"No. Even if that happened, at this point I don't trust that any transmission is coming from the person it's supposed to." She sighed. "But you're right. I pledged to help England. I should go back. This time I'm going to do it for Nora." She picked up the remains of the tea and headed back to the kitchen, the cups and saucers clattering loudly in her shaking hands.

CHAPTER 70

NOOR

*I*n addition to buying Noor a new dress—a stylish blue one trimmed in white—and paying to have her hair cut and dyed in a salon, Viennot found her a new flat on the Rue de la Faisanderie, off the Avenue Foch.

"Isn't it rather close to the Gestapo headquarters?" she asked doubtfully as she stared up at the brick building.

"That's why it's a suitable place to transmit from—the gonios will never suspect someone would be broadcasting right under their noses."

"Gonios" was slang for the Gestapo's radio-detection vans. One of Noor's worst nightmares was that they would home in on her signal and find one of her hideouts.

She kept her eyes peeled for the vans as she walked to Émile Garry's apartment later in the week, but she didn't see a single one.

Garry wasn't home so she wrote her new address down and gave it to his sister, Renée. "Let Émile know that I keep an extra key under the doormat," Noor instructed.

"Whatever. If you get in touch with Antoine, tell him I said hello," the stocky woman called as Noor left.

The morning after she moved in, Noor's growling stomach woke her up. She was supposed to meet Viennot that afternoon to blow up a shed containing hundreds of Metox radar detectors. Since her morning was free and Viennot had also provided her with some spending money, Noor decided she deserved a little treat.

It was a pleasant fall morning, and though Noor relished being in the sunshine, she went into the bakery next door and purchased a stale croissant.

When she came back outside, something seemed amiss. As soon as she started walking, she got a sixth sense that someone was following her. She strolled straight past her apartment and paused in front of a storefront. Peering into the window, she could see two men in dark coats a few paces down. They had also paused. Now she was sure she had a tail.

She started whistling and quickened her pace, heading toward a large building. Once in the shadow of the building, she darted around the corner and ran into an alleyway. Knowing she couldn't outrun the men for long, she quickly took stock of the alley, searching for a place to hide, but there wasn't much there save for a couple of trash cans and a massive, open dumpster.

With no other options, Noor used one of the trash cans as leverage to heave herself into the dumpster. She held her breath and closed her eyes when she heard footsteps enter the alleyway, hoping they wouldn't have the acumen to peer into the dumpster.

To her relief, the footsteps finally retreated. She took a deep breath in, temporarily forgetting where she was until the vile scent of rotting garbage filled her nostrils.

After another minute of breathing through her mouth, Noor pulled herself up and scanned the area. Finding the alleyway empty, she climbed out of the dumpster.

Her new dress soiled and stinking, she went back to her apartment. She figured it would be safe since she had just moved in and hadn't even transmitted from it yet.

As soon as she unlocked the door, she regretted her carelessness. A giant man in a dark overcoat stood just inside her flat.

She didn't dare to hope he was with the Resistance and kicked out her foot, hearing an "oof" as she struck bone. The man attempted to capture her wrists, but she bit his hand.

"Du miststück!" he exclaimed, letting go of her to attend to his wound.

Noor tried to grab the door handle, but he pushed her back. She kicked at him again, though this time he was ready. He dodged her foot and then came up behind her, grabbing her shoulders and shoving her toward the couch. She lashed out wildly and managed to scratch his face with her fingernails.

He reached into his coat and pulled out a gun. "Keep still or I will shoot you."

Noor had never been in a physical fight before, but it was as if someone else, a wild animal maybe, had temporarily taken control of her body. She spread her hand out like a cat waiting to claw him. "Go ahead and try."

He cursed again before going to the phone, keeping his gun aimed at her head. As he barked orders in German into the receiver, Noor slumped into the couch. How could she have been stupid enough to go back to her flat when she knew she'd been followed? How could she have failed Buckmaster, Antelme, and all the others who had helped her?

A few minutes later, there was a loud banging on the door to the flat. Her attacker opened it to reveal more men in dark suit coats — thanks to the flat's convenient location near the Avenue Foch, it hadn't taken the Gestapo long to supply reinforcements.

As the men led her into an awaiting Black Maria, Noor noted with a slight bit of glee that her attacker's face and hands were bleeding.

CHAPTER 71

YVONNE

*O*ne morning a few weeks after she'd arrived at Fresnes Prison, Yvonne was awakened by a guard and told to get dressed. "What's happening?" she asked sleepily.

"You are being transferred," was the gruff reply.

She was taken to a train station and forced to board a cattle car packed with people. Luckily she was able to find a spot on the floor to sit, as she felt like she'd pass out from the heat.

When the train pulled away from the station, heading toward an unknown destination, someone in the car began singing *La Marseillaise*. Yvonne had trouble remembering the words and settled for humming along with the melody.

As it grew even hotter in the car, the singing turned into cries for water. Yvonne's intense thirst resulted in yet another pulsating headache. At one point she was so desperate she eyed the bucket in the corner meant for the discharge of bodily fluids, but changed her mind when the wind turned and she caught a whiff of the stench coming from the bucket.

. . .

It took three days to reach their destination, three days of sweltering conditions with little food or water. Yvonne slept most of the time, trying to build strength for whatever she would be forced to endure next. Her dreams were vivid and horrible, but it was hard to separate the imaginary nightmares from the real one she was experiencing.

When the train finally came to a halt, Yvonne awoke and stretched as best she could, thinking that the worst of her ordeal was surely over. A uniformed guard shouted at her in unintelligible German, but his meaning was made clear when he unshouldered his rifle: *Get out.*

The well-lit, immaculate station and fresh air were a welcome contrast to the filthy cattle car. That is until Yvonne caught sight of more guards waiting on the platform, some holding well-fed Alsatians, who barked at the prisoners as they walked off the train.

A guard demanded to know Yvonne's age while his dog strained at the leash, trying to paw her.

"Forty," she lied.

"Do you have any of the following?" He listed off a string of ailments.

"No," she replied to each one, including when he asked about headaches.

He directed her to stand in a line behind a hundred or so other women. Yvonne noted that not all of the people who disembarked were told to get in the line, especially the ones who had trouble walking. These were instead directed—or in some cases, shoved—into awaiting black lorries. After watching the guards drag a lifeless body off the train, Yvonne decided to keep her head forward.

Finally the women in line were directed to march north.

They walked about seven kilometers down a sandy road that cut through a pretty town, with rows of neat cottages surrounding a lake. It was past dawn now, and the sunlight sparkled over the cerulean water. *Wherever we are going, it can't be that bad,* Yvonne decided. She had deduced that they were being taken to one of the

German work camps and she hoped she might be assigned to cleaning the cottages.

Her hope turned to dread when a towering brick wall topped by a maze of barbed wire came into view. As the massive iron gates opened to allow the women entry, Yvonne had a vision of passing through the gates of Hell.

Hell, Yvonne quickly discovered, was in the form of Ravensbrück Concentration Camp, built strictly for the women prisoners of the Reich.

After the line had entered, they were told to form neat rows in a clearing just inside the camp and prepare for inspection. This meant stripping down to nothing, while a few skeletons in striped uniforms came around and picked through their things, seizing any jewelry, belts, or leather shoes and dumping them into a basket. The skeletons performed their duty half-heartedly, presumably with just enough effort so that the muscular women guards in heavy boots who patrolled the rows didn't kick them. The guards also kicked or slapped any of the newcomers who stepped out of line or begged to keep her things. A few male guards stood on the sidelines, leering at the naked women.

The skeleton who examined Yvonne's clothes picked up the still-bloodied gray suit and held it between her fingers but said nothing. For some reason, she reminded Yvonne of the marionette shows her mother used to take her to as a child, as though all the skeletal prisoners were being manipulated by invisible strings.

One by one the rows of women were told to pick up whatever remained of their belongings and go into a long building. When it was Yvonne's row's turn, she noted that some women were selected to stand in another line while a young, pretty woman in a green uniform shaved their heads. Yvonne managed to escape that fate.

Some women were given striped uniforms, but a female guard told Yvonne they had nothing in her size and she would keep wearing whatever clothes she'd come in with.

"Here." Another guard thrust a red, triangular patch and a

needle and thread into Yvonne's hands. "Make sure you sew this on your jacket."

Before leaving the building, the new prisoners were doused with water and then another woman in uniform dumped a white powder over them, which clung to both Yvonne's skin and clothing and smelled almost as bad as the cattle car. She decided it must be some sort of delousing powder.

Before she left the building, she was given a pink card with the letters "NN" printed on it.

Yvonne was placed in Block 17, a building situated in almost the exact center of the camp. Most of the other women who were sent there spoke a foreign language and wore brown triangles on their clothing.

"You are French?" one of them asked. When Yvonne nodded, the woman frowned. "You are soft then."

"I can assure you I am not soft," Yvonne replied, but the woman had turned away.

They entered a room filled with long rows of bunks on either side. Many of the women ran to claim their beds, some deciding to share with other women with whom they were clearly familiar.

Yvonne found an empty bed on a top bunk with a torn straw mattress. She considered it fortunate that the bed was situated next to a tiny window as she could only imagine what the cabin would smell like when the rest of its occupants returned from wherever they were.

She had just lain down on the filthy straw bed when she heard a deafening shrieking sound. She sat up, hitting her head on the ceiling.

A woman in a striped dress peeked her head into the cabin. "It's time for Appell," she said. "You must go to the Appellplatz to be assigned your work crew."

Yvonne rubbed her head before asking, "Where is the Appellplatz?"

"North," the woman replied before slamming the door shut.

Since her accident, Yvonne had trouble with directions, but she was able to follow the other women from Block 17 to a clearing a few meters away. Once again they were lined up, this time in rows of five.

"Jacqueline?" a surprised voice hissed a few women away from Yvonne. "Is that you?"

Yvonne turned her head as far as she dared. The woman spoke out of the corner of her mouth so as not to be heard by the guards who patrolled the rows, hitting or kicking any woman who moved. "It's me, Madame Flamencourt, from Petit Aunay."

The wife of the poultry farmer looked much older, her once bright blond hair now dulled with streaks of gray running through it. "I remember," Yvonne murmured. She watched as a heavyset woman carrying an accordion folder shouted at prisoners a few rows ahead of them. The women in the row then scattered in different directions.

"They are assigning work detail. Did they give you a pink card?" Madame Flamencourt asked.

"Yes," Yvonne replied.

Madame Flamencourt sighed audibly. "It's no matter. You can volunteer to do gardening with me. It is not as bad as some of the other work crews you could be assigned to."

The woman with the accordion folder was now in front of them. "*Was willst du?*" she demanded of the woman next to Yvonne, another newcomer who obviously didn't understand what the guard was asking. The guard hit the prisoner over the head with her folder and bawled something in German. The poor woman scurried away.

"Gardening!" Yvonne shouted when the guard raised her eyebrows at her.

She eyed Yvonne up and down and then pointed to the far end of camp with her fat finger. "*Schnell, schnell.*"

Yvonne walked slowly to give Madame Flamencourt time to catch up with her. She had so many questions to ask, especially regarding how her friend had ended up as a prisoner at a German work camp, but she knew this was no time to get them answered.

They passed many other long brick buildings until they reached a wire fence, beyond which were neat plots of black dirt. Madame Flamencourt entered through the fence's gate first, but when Yvonne tried to follow, another guard pulled her out of line. "You are too old. Weren't you given a pink card?"

Once again, the lie came smoothly. "No."

"We have enough gardeners here today," the guard stated. "Besides, you don't look like you are up to the task." Spittle flew out of her mouth as she added, "Go back to your bunk and clean it. There is plenty of work you can do there."

The other women left behind in Block 17 were old and frail. They must have sensed that Yvonne didn't feel as if she belonged with them and excluded her from conversation as they swept and mopped the floors. Yvonne tried to make herself useful by cleaning up the attached bathroom, ruining her gray suit even further.

Afterward, the women sat down in a circle and began knitting, using battered needles and thick greenish-gray wool.

"What is this for?" Yvonne asked.

"Socks for the Boche soldiers at the Russian front," another woman replied. She gave Yvonne a funny look. "Are you…?" she circled her finger around her head. *Crazy*.

"No."

"Can you knit?"

Yvonne shrugged. She'd done it a few times before the war, but that was before a bullet became lodged in her brain. Nowadays she struggled with any unfamiliar task.

"You can do the legs   heels and toes are probably too hard for you," the woman instructed. "Besides, who cares if you drop the stitches? Maybe the Boches will get frostbite."

As they worked, the other women gossiped in French about who'd been absent at that afternoon's Appell and whether they thought they'd been taken to the crematorium or transported to another camp. They mostly ignored Yvonne, who was predictably a much slower knitter.

After a particularly long discussion regarding which way of

cooking lobster was the best, Yvonne shouted at them to stop. Such talk made her already aching stomach growl even more.

One of the women paused her needles and focused on the red triangle at Yvonne's breast. "You think because you are a political prisoner you are more important than the rest of us?"

"No," Yvonne shot back. "I think I am more important because I don't gossip about useless things. Such talk helps no one."

After that, the women all knitted in silence. The click-clack of their needles did nothing to soothe Yvonne's aching head.

CHAPTER 72

NOOR

The Black Maria drove down the broad, tree-lined Avenue Foch and came to a stop outside number 84, a beige building accented by wrought-iron balconies. A still-fuming, hand-cuffed Noor was escorted through the high-ceilinged, marble-floored lobby and up to the fifth floor.

She was led to a tiny room which clearly had once served as servant's quarters. A thin man wearing civilian clothes and spectacles with thick lenses was waiting for her. Without introducing himself, he began to fire off questions. "Who did you work with after the collapse of Prosper?"

She blanched visibly at the name and then cursed herself for giving the man the satisfaction of getting a reaction from her. She tightened her lips instead of replying.

"Who provided you with safehouses?"

Again, Noor said nothing.

He was about to ask another question when she cut in. "Do you mind if I have a bath?"

The man's mouth shut in surprise before it opened up again, reminding her of a fish. "What?"

"A bath. I smell like garbage." She shifted closer to him in order to prove it. "I had to hide in a dumpster from your thugs."

The man glanced uncertainly at the guard at the door. "I guess… if you must. But Herr Bauer will be waiting outside."

When she walked into the bathroom, Bauer insisted the door be kept open a crack.

"Why, so you can watch me take my clothes off?" Noor demanded. "Even Nazis like you must have at least some morals and realize it is improper to see a woman naked."

Bauer had the grace to color slightly. "If you please Fräulein, I will let you undress in privacy, but I must insist you open the door before you get into the bath."

She shut the door in his face and then went to the bathroom window. To her surprise, it was unlocked. Without pausing to reconsider, she lifted it up and climbed out onto the narrow, rickety ledge. She bent her body, using the roof tiles to keep her balance as she carefully trode away from the window. She wasn't entirely sure what would happen when she reached the end of the ledge—her goal was simply to clamber away from view before the guard realized she was gone.

She had nearly made it to the edge of the roof when she heard someone say in a low voice, "Madeleine, don't be silly. You will plummet to your death, and then what would your mother say?"

She looked up to see her interrogator leaning out of a window. "Give me your hand," he commanded.

She looked down, contemplating falling to her death. At least it would ensure she would never give up her comrades. But the man was insistent. "Think of what would happen if your poor mother learned you committed suicide?"

Noor had no choice but to take hold of his hand. He grasped her shoulder with his other arm and yanked her inside.

Once she was back on solid ground, the man pulled out a gun and stuck it in her back. "Now let's go back to your new accommodations."

He led her back to the little room and deposited her there before slamming the door behind him.

Feeling deflated after such a rush of adrenaline, Noor sank onto the hard bed. Her shoulders felt heavy both from the man's touch and from the weight of the guilt that she had let everyone down—Buckmaster, Miss Atkins, Jack, Antelme, and everyone else in the Resistance. *The Allies.* She began to wail loudly. On top of the fear and disappointment, she felt angry at the Boches. And herself.

Someone knocked at the door, but Noor didn't stop crying. After a while, her tears dried up, but she still wailed as loud as she could, thinking it might make the guards uncomfortable to have a woman bawling in their presence.

Another knock and then someone called out. Noor paused. The voice sounded familiar.

The door opened a crack and, to her utter astonishment, Gilbert Norman peered through. "Nora?"

She raised her head. "Gilbert?"

He strolled in with all the confidence of the world. "I'm surprised you were able to hold out so long. Good job."

"I should have held out longer."

"With Déricourt running loose?" he scoffed. "You should be glad you're here—he's a traitor."

Noor sat up. "Is he really a traitor?"

"Yes. He's told them everything. It's no use trying to keep anything from the Germans—they know all. Just answer their questions and you'll be protected. I've made arrangements."

"Are you…" Noor searched for the right words. "Collaborating with them?"

"I wouldn't call it collaborating. More like making a deal to spare people their lives."

"You can't make deals with dirty Boches. You of all people should know that."

He tried reaching for her, but Noor moved away. "It will be fine, you'll see," he said, as if everything were perfectly normal. "You trust me, don't you? Remember we went to the same school when we were younger."

"Get out of my room."

"Nora—"

"No. I don't trust you and I never want to see you again. I can't believe they've done this to you, but I'm not going to go along with it."

He stood up. "Don't you see—"

"Get out!" Noor's voice rose in hysteria. "Get out, get out, get out!"

Gilbert finally left, slamming the door behind him.

A few minutes later—or was it hours?—the man who had pulled her in from the roof came back into her room. This time he was pushing a cart. On the top was a silver tray and Noor's stomach growled again in much the same way it had that very morning, when she had still been free.

The man lifted the tray's lid with a flourish, revealing a steak and mashed potatoes. "Care to dine with me?"

"I don't eat meat."

He used a knife to cut into the steak. "You aren't hungry?"

"No."

"Suit yourself." He stuck a large piece in his mouth and chewed. Noor hoped he'd choke on it, to no avail. "Tell me about Baker Street."

"I don't know what you are talking about."

"I know that the head of F Section is named Maurice Buck-master and that you agents trained at Beaulieu." Though he spoke with a trace of a German accent, he managed to pronounce the very English name correctly—'Bewley.'

She raised her shoulders in feigned non-recognition.

"And you received parachute instruction at Ringway."

This time she didn't have to lie. "I've never learned to para-chute." Still, the extent of his knowledge was disturbing. Was it all due to Gilbert's betrayal or had they known about this before they arrested him?

He stood up, replacing the lid on the now empty tray. He

retrieved a case from the bottom of the cart and sat on the bed next to Noor. "Let's see what we have here." He pulled out a few pieces of paper and handed them to her. Noor flipped through them with shaking hands. They were copies of letters she had given to Déricourt to deliver back to London, including the note to her mother and to Miss Atkins. "Where did you get these?"

"We have our ways." Next he took out her notebook, the one Viennot had told her to burn. "I was glad to discover you were using a poem code. So much easier to decode—I've already figured it all out."

"You couldn't possibly have—"

"You underestimate me, of course. Just as people have underestimated you your entire life. Buckmaster for one, your father for another."

"Stop." Noor shut her eyes. "Please stop talking."

To her surprise, the German stood. "That's all for now, then. Why don't you get a good night's sleep and we'll continue this in the morning?"

But sleep didn't come easily. Every time Noor closed her eyes, she had the sensation of falling. She saw herself standing on the ledge the way her interrogator must have seen her: frail and unsteady. Could she have made it to freedom? She would never know now.

However it went down, she vowed not to let the Boches get the best of her—she would not fold as she had in her mock interrogation during training. *I may have been captured, but I won't lose my footing this time.*

CHAPTER 73

YVONNE

*T*he long days at Ravensbrück turned into weeks, which blended into one another. It was easy for Yvonne to lose track of time since every new day seemed like a repeat of the last. Their rations never varied: in the morning they were given a weak, lukewarm liquid that was presumably intended to pass for coffee, and for lunch, watery soup. Dinner consisted of the same watery soup, this time with a slice of stale bread. Already thin, Yvonne grew bony and frail and the strength she'd been building since she left the hospital quickly dissipated.

It didn't help that the women were forced to stand at Appell for hours, three or four times a day. Occasionally she caught sight of Madame Flamencourt, but never got a chance to speak to her because Yvonne was always commanded to go back to her cabin for cleaning and sewing. She supposed it could have been worse—some of her cabin mates were sent to the fields to do hard labor all day and didn't return until just before lights out at 8 pm.

Yvonne had just shut her eyes after yet another long day of cleaning and standing at Appell when a shrill voice called, "Jacqueline Culioli?" She closed her eyes tighter, thinking it was one of the guards. She heard hushed whispering before the voice called again, this time much closer.

Yvonne peered down at a small woman standing next to her bunk. She wore the black-and-white striped camp uniform like many of the other prisoners, but, despite her emaciated frame, her chafed, red cheeks had managed to maintain their girlish roundness. "This is for you." The woman shoved something at Yvonne before retreating out of the bunk.

The little package was wrapped in cloth. Yvonne opened it to find a raw carrot. She quickly crammed it into her mouth before any of the other women could see what it was.

The next night the process was repeated. This time Yvonne received a small potato, which she ate like an apple.

On the third night, Yvonne met the woman at the door. "Who are you?"

"My name is Marie Moldenhawer. I work in the kitchen with a friend of yours, who asked me to deliver extra food to you. She's worried about you."

Yvonne wanted to reply that there was no reason to be worried, but she knew that would be untrue. "How long have you been here?" she asked instead.

"Five years."

Yvonne's mouth dropped open. She couldn't imagine surviving five weeks at Ravensbrück, let alone five months. "You could be beaten or killed for stealing food, not to mention entering another cabin." The female guards seemed to relish punishing the prisoners for committing even the slightest crimes, such as falling asleep at Appell. Just that morning a woman had been taken out of Yvonne's block before roll call. When the guards returned the woman in the afternoon, she was covered with bruises and could barely walk.

"I know that," Marie replied. She gave Yvonne a little wave before she walked away.

. . .

The nightly visits continued. One night Marie brought Yvonne a man's coat to replace her bloodied gray one. It was so long it nearly reached her knees, but it was a relief not to feel the wind at Appell.

Yvonne looked forward to the visits, not only because of Marie's gifts, but because she longed for some companionship. The other women in Block 17 had made it clear that they disdained her, but Marie seemed not to judge her.

One day Yvonne asked her why.

"I'm Polish," Marie shrugged. "The most hated race here. When I first arrived, the German guards told someone I gouged out the eyes of children, but really I was just a teacher at a primary school."

As Marie finished, another woman ran into the bunk, the door slamming shut behind her. "I heard there's going to be a surprise inspection tonight." She looked pointedly at Marie. "We're going to have to hide you, otherwise we'll all get in trouble because you broke curfew."

Marie climbed into the empty top bunk next to Yvonne's. She was so emaciated that her form was barely discernible under the blanket, especially when another prisoner put a bedroll at the base of the bunk.

Someone entered the cabin and began shouting at them. From her voice, Yvonne could tell it was the stocky blond guard from Appell.

The guard did little more than perform a cursory walk up and down the aisle way before she left again.

"Thanks," Marie said as she handed the bedroll back to its owner.

"Please don't come again," the woman said. "We will all be beaten if they find you here."

Yvonne gave Marie a heartbroken look.

"It's okay," Marie told Yvonne. "You could come to the Polish block during free time if you want."

Yvonne nodded. "I'll see you tomorrow."

. . .

The painful throbbing that had been in the back of Yvonne's head ever since she was shot had turned into a dull ache, but she still had trouble concentrating. Especially when it came to tasks she'd once been an expert at, like finding her way in the dark. Somehow, in spite of her new disabilities, she managed to locate the Polish block.

As she entered, Yvonne marveled at the illusion of safety it gave —the bunks were so crowded there that the guards couldn't walk between them for their inspections. This meant the women could hide precious goods—such as bread from the kitchen, extra socks, even a comb—under their mattresses.

"I like it better here," Yvonne said when she spied Marie. She was alone in her bunk, so Yvonne crawled in beside her.

"Yes, but there are so many women here, it's inevitable you'll lose more," Marie said. "My bunk companion died in the middle of the night a month before you got here. In the morning, I discovered her cold body."

"What did you do with it?" Yvonne asked, horrified.

"I dragged it to the center of the room, thinking the prisoners who clean the cabin would get rid of it, but they just dumped it in the corner of the bathroom. It took three days for the guards to finally remove it, which meant there were more rats in here than normal."

"That's awful."

Marie shrugged. "When you have been here as long as I have, nothing really shocks you anymore." She pointed at Yvonne's coat. "For instance, that jacket I gave you used to belong to a woman who was sent to the crematorium. Her husband gave it to her when they were moved from a Jewish ghetto. He was sent to the gas chamber as soon as he arrived at Buchenwald."

Yvonne shivered. She was too cold to take the coat off, but whispered a prayer for the previous owners. "Thank you for helping me," she said to Marie when she was finished. "Do you mind if I ask, why me?"

Another shrug. "Marguerite asked me to. She told me what you did for the Resistance."

"Who is Marguerite?"

"I think her last name is…" Marie scrunched her face in thought. "Flamencourt."

"Ah, yes that explains it."

"You seemed so helpless and confused when you first arrived. And besides, you remind me of my sister."

"What is her name?"

"Aurelia."

"What happened to her?"

"I don't know. We were both part of the Polish Army's Women's Auxiliary. I was caught trying to cross the border into Czecho-slovakia. Hopefully, we will meet again after the war." Marie was silent for a few minutes before she asked, "Who do you most want to see again when this is all over?"

"My daughter. She's in England."

"England? But aren't you French?"

"Yes." Yvonne hesitated, but something told her she could trust this woman. "I am a British agent. They trained me to help instigate the French Resistance."

Marie's eyebrows rose. "Really?" She ruminated over this new information for a moment. "No wonder you are so secretive: if the guards found that out, you'd probably end up in the crematorium."

"*Lights out!*" someone shouted, startling Yvonne. She'd almost forgotten they were surrounded by hundreds of other women.

"Will you say something in English?" Marie whispered, rolling over. "I visited Liverpool once when I was a Girl Guide, but I haven't heard the language spoken much since."

Yvonne looked around the darkened room before speaking in her most proper voice, "Very well then. I have to get going before they notice I'm missing from Block 17." She made her way to the edge of the bed.

"Good night, Jacqueline."

"Good night, Marie," Yvonne replied in her posh tone.

CHAPTER 74

NOOR

*E*very time they sent for Noor, she expected to be brought to the torture room she'd heard so much about in training. But so far the Boches had treated her with kid gloves. It was almost as if they had a grudging respect for her.

Her original interrogator, who went by the name of Vogt, usually started his sessions by asking questions about her family. He still thought her name was Nora Baker. The last thing Noor wanted to do was to reveal her real surname for fear of reprisals against her brother Hidayat, who still lived in France with his wife and young children.

If Vogt sensed she was getting comfortable, he'd reach into his file folder and pull out names of Resistance members and ask Noor if she had any information about them. Remembering what she'd told Marks about not wanting to lie, Noor said nothing at all.

One morning they gave her a break to use the bathroom. As she was washing up, her eyes landed on a broken porcelain tile next to the sink. Was it her imagination, or was there something stuffed inside the crack?

She dried her hands before carefully extracting what turned out to be a small piece of paper. With shaking hands, she unfolded it. It was a sketch of a beautiful, dark-skinned woman. She gasped aloud with the realization that she was looking at a portrait of herself.

When she returned to Vogt, he asked if there was anything he could get for her. He always asked that, and Noor almost always refused his offer, but this time she didn't.

"I would like some paper and a pencil."

"What for?" Vogt asked.

"I want to do some writing. I was an author before the war, and I'd like to be able to jot some of my thoughts down."

"Would you let me read some of them?" he asked unexpectedly.

"No. I don't like for anyone to read my work until it is polished."

He looked at her thoughtfully. "I think that can be arranged. Is there anything else?"

"No," Noor replied. "Not at this time."

A few hours later, a guard delivered a small notebook and a pencil to Noor's cell.

"Who are you?" Noor wrote in the first page of the book. "Are you a prisoner too?" She ripped the page out and folded it as small as it could go before asking a guard for permission to use the bathroom. She fit it into the broken tile and crossed her fingers.

The next day she found a response. "Cheer up. You're not alone. Perhaps we'll find a way to get out of here."

"I would very much like to get out of here," Noor wrote to her mysterious pen pal. "Do you have any suggestions?"

"No," was the only reply.

For some reason, that one little word felt like the final nail in the coffin of Noor's confinement. Alone in her room, she started crying, softly at first, but as the permanency of her situation hit, she began to wail.

She wiped her tears on her sleeve, trying to catch her breath, when she heard a small scratching noise. Thinking it was a mouse, or worse, a rat, she resumed her sniffling. But the scratching grew louder, into a knocking sound. There was something rhythmic about it, and Noor stopped crying to listen. With a start she realized that someone was tapping in Morse.

Noor grabbed her little notebook and took down the letters as they came through. *Are you with the Resistance?*

"Yes," she tapped back. "My name is Nora Baker."

"Léon Faye." There was a slight pause, and then the tapping asked, "Are they hurting you?"

"No."

"Then why are you crying?"

This time it was her turn to pause. "I want to escape from here, but I'm not sure how."

"I've been thinking about this too. There might be a way. Do you have bars in your ceiling?"

Noor looked up and then knocked, "Yes."

His reply managed to restore Noor's hope. "I think those bars protect an air shaft that leads to the roof."

"But how can we remove the bars?" she asked.

"I don't know yet. But I will think on it."

Noor flexed her hands. Her knuckles had become sore from all the rapping on the walls. "Please do. Good night."

"Good night."

The next morning, Noor was brought down to a small office on the second floor, where a tall man with white hair awaited. On the desk were her wireless set, Morse key and notebook.

"Come in, Nora," the man said. "My name is Dr. Goetz."

"What are you doing with my transmitter?"

"We are going to send a little message to London."

"No."

"I don't really need your help." He repositioned the Morse key and started tapping on it. "We were able to get many details of your skeds and signal plans because of the mail you sent 'en clair' through one of our double agents. And, of course, we have your notebook. You should have never kept such careful records of your messages and security checks, in case they fell into the wrong hands." He stretched out his arms and cracked his knuckles.

"You can't possibly think that London will believe it is me on the Morse key. You don't have my rhythm."

He continued tapping, and Noor had to admit that his timing was more in line with hers than not.

"We've done this quite a few times, using sets we seized from Gilbert Norman and John Macalister." He dropped his hands and met her steady gaze with penetrating brown eyes. "How else do you think we managed to arrest Jack Agazarian and your friend Robert Gieules?"

"No. Gieules and Macalister—"

"Surely you know they weren't the real John Macalister and Frank Pickersgill—we captured them months ago. The men you met were ours."

She sat down heavily. "That's why I was arrested."

"No. Gieules didn't give anything away. He insisted he didn't know your phone number or address." Goetz lit a cigarette. "And when you didn't fall for our trap at the Arc de Triomphe, we were afraid you'd slip through our fingers again."

"So how did you find me?"

"It was Renée Garry, Émile Garry's sister, who told us about you."

Bitch! Noor's father had always preached that the path to joy included not judging others and always being willing to forgive. Right now, however, forgiveness for Renée Garry seemed an impossible task.

"We paid her a hundred thousand francs. Half of it was awarded when she led us to your latest address, and the other half after your arrest. She even knew where you kept your spare key."

Noor buried her head in hands as she recalled giving Renée the note to pass on to Garry.

Oblivious to her plight, Goetz continued, "Stupid girl—she could have held out for more. It was only a tenth of what we usually pay informers for an SOE agent, not to mention Madeleine was very high on our wanted list."

Noor looked up. "You have my skeds and codebook. Why do you need me?"

"I was hoping you would help. I fear London is becoming the slightest bit suspicious with our *Funkspiel*, or radio game, lately."

Struck by sudden inspiration, Noor pretended that she wanted to negotiate. "What will you give me?"

"What do you want?'

"A meal. Pasta with tomato sauce." Noor still wasn't hungry, but Goetz didn't need to know that.

"Consider it a deal." He passed a square coding card to her.

She picked up a pencil. "First, the transposition key." She carefully wrote one that was 18-letters long, just the way Marks had instructed her to do if she were ever captured. She then coded a message saying that her old address was unsafe. She looked up at Goetz. "Do you have a new address for me to give them?"

Goetz looked through his rolodex before pulling out a card. "157 Rue Vercingetorix."

Noor coded it and then pushed everything toward him. "Can I use the bathroom?"

Once out in the hallway, Noor crossed her fingers that Leo Marks would somehow get her message and realize that she'd been compromised.

After washing and drying her hands, Noor extracted a note from underneath her skirt. It asked her mysterious pen pal if he too had bars on his window and if he knew of a way to remove them.

The next morning she had a reply. "Yes. I think we would need a screwdriver. I'll try to get one."

CHAPTER 75

FRANCINE

"Francine!" Miss Atkins rushed through the signals room. "We just got a transmission stating that Madeleine is in the hospital."

Not another one. Francine threw her pencil down. "That means she's been arrested."

"I am aware of that possibility." Miss Atkins impatiently thrust the message at Francine. "It came through from Jacques Weil in Switzerland. He said he got the news from someone called 'Sonia.' Who is she?"

"I don't know." Francine examined the message, but there wasn't much more than what Miss Atkins had just said.

"Should we assume this is legit and that Nora has been captured?" Miss Atkins asked.

"I don't know," Francine repeated. "I never met anyone named Sonia."

Miss Atkins took the paper and crumpled it. "Buckmaster's insisting that we've been getting genuine transmissions under Madeleine's call sign, but I'm not so sure it's her."

"Let me see those transmissions," Francine said.

The first read: *My cachette unsafe. New address 157 Rue Vercingetorix, Paris. This perfectly safe. Goodbye.*

The message seemed innocuous enough. "Did she include her security checks?"

Miss Atkins checked her notes. "She omitted her bluff check and included her true check."

"Then you'll agree with me that something's wrong. Maybe this Sonia is right and Nora's been compromised."

Miss Atkins frowned. "Leo Marks said he gave her a 'special' check. I'll see what he knows. In the meantime, were you aware that France Antelme was planning to go back to Paris?"

It was Francine's turn to frown. "No."

Miss Atkins stood. "I'll talk to Marks, and you convince Antelme not to go back."

Francine met Antelme for coffee that same afternoon.

"Don't do it," she stated, even before he had removed his coat.

"You know I have to."

"But Phono is blown. The Musician network's operator reported that Émile Garry was arrested a few days ago."

"Nora's been communicating just fine."

Francine shook her head. "No, she's not. I'm not sure who the SOE is talking to, but it's not Nora. She missed her security checks."

Antelme sat down across from her. "She probably forgot them."

"You and I both know she wouldn't do that." Francine put her hand over his. "I understand why you feel the need to go back. Just as Jack did." Her voice broke, but she forced herself to continue, "If you really have to go, then drop blind."

"I can't." He gave a heavy sigh and Francine let go of his hand. "They're sending me in with a radio operator and a courier."

"I just have such a bad feeling about this—something's not right with Phono and it hasn't been for a while. Nora's not..." she found she couldn't finish her sentence. "Like with Gilbert and Jack..." She wiped a tear with the back of her hand. "There's something fishy going on in France, and you're going to land right into the middle of it."

"That's why I have to go there. I'll figure it out, and… I'll see if I can find out what happened to Jack."

CHAPTER 76

NOOR

The escape plan was, of course, quite involved. Léon Faye, the prisoner in the cell next to Noor's, came up with most of the details, which he tapped on the wall in Morse to Noor. She then passed them on to her pen pal, George Starr, via the cracked tile in the bathroom. As the prison librarian, Starr was in favor with both Kieffer and Vogt and had managed to steal a screwdriver while he was trying to repair a vacuum cleaner. After he'd loosened the screws holding the bars in place, he delivered the screwdriver to Noor by hiding it behind the toilet.

But once Noor was in possession of the screwdriver, she still faced the problem of how to reach the iron bars. Her bed folded into the wall when not in use, so she couldn't push it underneath the bars and use it as a stool, as Starr told her he'd done. The best she could do was stand on her cot with one foot, and brace the other leg on the wall for leverage.

Both ends of the bars were embedded in thick plaster, and she chipped away at it at night for as long as she dared. To hide the evidence, she stuffed uneaten bread in the holes. Sometimes she mixed her dark face cream into the bread to help it blend better with the wall color.

One night she lost her balance and fell onto the floor. A guard raced into the room.

"I'm sorry," Noor told him in a shaky voice, hiding the screwdriver behind her back. "I must have rolled out of my bed while sleeping." She avoided looking above her at the half-loose bars and hoped the guard wouldn't notice in the dark.

Luckily he didn't, nor did he see the plaster pieces scattered near his feet. "Well, don't let it happen again."

Once the bars in Noor's room were suitably loosened, she passed the screwdriver to Faye. Starr thought it would be a good idea to escape during the Christmas holiday, figuring that the guards would be distracted by celebratory liquor. But both of his fellow conspirators wanted to leave as soon as they were ready and it was up to Noor to convince Starr. Finally he agreed and the date was set for November 24, 1943.

That night, Noor proceeded to scrape out the last bar from the plaster. It didn't come easily and she grew tired and sweaty, fearing she would be late for the rendezvous. She was supposed to meet Faye on the roof in a few minutes, and they would wait for Starr to join them.

The time came and went, and still Noor hadn't freed the bar. Her arms were sore from being held over her head for so long and she feared she wouldn't have enough energy to climb up to the roof once she'd worked the bar loose. What if she wasn't able to escape and Starr and Faye left without her? She couldn't bear another night at Avenue Foch.

To distract herself, she grabbed her pencil and drew a giant V for 'Victory' on the wall. Once the blood returned to her arms, she again took up the job of chipping away the plaster.

A voice came through the air shaft. "Need some help?"

Noor looked up as a mane of dark hair appeared.

"Let's see here." There was a clanking sound, and suddenly the freed bar was dangling over her head. "Hide this under your bed," the voice commanded.

Noor did as bid before resuming her spot on top of the cot. She reached her arms up and felt strong hands grasping both of her forearms.

"Thank you, thank you," Noor whispered after the man had pulled her into the air shaft. She couldn't help kissing him on the cheek. "Are you Faye?"

"In the flesh," he answered. "Let's get out of here."

Faye helped Noor tie her shoes around her neck, so they wouldn't echo as they navigated the air shaft. She took a deep, calming breath once they made it to the roof. Although the night was chilly, the stars were out and she could see the Arc de Triomphe quite clearly.

A short, bald man whom Noor recognized as the prison librarian appeared. "You made it!" Noor and George Starr embraced briefly before he turned to Faye to inquire, "Now what?"

"I had a chance to scout out the roof while I was waiting." Faye pointed to the rear of the building. "It's flatter over there and there's a balcony on the building behind it that looks as if it's within jumping distance."

"Sounds like a plan," Starr returned.

As the three of them tiptoed toward across the roof, a loud noise began to blare.

An air raid siren. Noor cursed aloud, though neither man could hear her. She knew the guards checked all the cells during an air raid to make sure the prisoners weren't trying to signal to the planes above. It was only a matter of time before the guards discovered the three missing prisoners and the busted bars. She flattened herself against the roof as a searchlight shone from below.

Faye took out the makeshift ladder he'd made from torn blankets and tied it to a post on the roof. He indicated for Noor to use it to climb down to the balcony across from them.

She shimmied down until she was close enough to jump onto the balcony. Faye and Starr followed suit, but Noor found that the glass door leading from the balcony into the building was locked.

"Where's your rope?" Faye shouted to Starr.

He sheepishly opened his pack, revealing an intact blanket.

"Never mind." Faye held his flashlight over his head and then smashed it into the glass door. They dashed into the darkened flat.

Noor led the way to the front door and out into the hallway. "What now?" she hissed.

Faye ran down the stairs, taking two at a time. Noor, with her shorter legs, followed at a slower pace. His curses were more than audible as he opened the door. Noor caught sight of a dozen men with flashlights wandering the streets before Faye slammed the door shut again.

"We should go back upstairs and hide," Starr said from behind Noor.

"No. I say we make a run for it." Without waiting for a reply, Faye opened the door and ducked out, trying to stay in the shadow of the building's overhang. A shot rang out and he crouched lower.

Noor threw herself against the wall of the lobby as another gunshot sounded and several soldiers ran toward Faye. Her eyes met Starr's. He motioned for them to go back upstairs.

As they bolted back up to the apartment they'd just vacated, a woman in pin curls appeared on the landing, staring at them open-mouthed.

Noor had just shut the door to the flat and was trying to catch her breath when the door was broken open. Rough hands grabbed Noor and forced her back to building 84.

Kieffer was waiting for them, along with a handcuffed Faye, purplish bruises already forming on his fine-boned face.

"Stand them up against the wall," Kieffer shouted at the guards. "I'm going to shoot all three of them."

"No, please don't." Starr tried to hold up his cuffed hands.

"How could you, Starr?" Kieffer seemed to soften as he shook his head. "I trusted you most of all."

"I give you my word that I won't try it again." He nodded at Noor. "It was her idea. I only went along because if London heard a woman had escaped from Avenue Foch and I hadn't the courage to join her, I'd never hear the end of it."

Kieffer turned his steely eyes to Noor. "And what about you? Are you willing to promise to never escape again?"

"No."

"Even if I send you to a prison in Germany?" Kieffer asked. "You know you had it good here."

"I will not give you my word," Noor reiterated.

Kieffer turned to Faye. "And you?"

"I consider it my duty to escape from whatever prison you put me in," Faye replied.

"Then both of you will be on the next train to Germany," Kieffer declared.

CHAPTER 77

YVONNE

That winter was one of the coldest Yvonne could remember. As the wind howled through the loose planks of Bunk 17, she decided she was no longer grateful to have a window next to her.

Despite the freezing conditions, the endless hours standing at Appell under the deluge of abuse from the guards continued. Yvonne's hands, already sore from all the cleaning and knitting, were always icy, and the winter chill seeped through her jacket. She wasn't sure how much longer she would be able to endure the frigid conditions and feared she'd end up like the countless women who collapsed in the snow. Sometimes, after Appell was over, she would have to walk over the still, lifeless bodies which had frozen to the ground.

On Christmas Eve, the guards held a drunken party in the administration building and the prisoners were allowed to move around the camp unbothered. Marie and Yvonne went to Bunk 37 where Madame Flamencourt—or rather, Marguerite—stayed.

The American Red Cross had delivered parcels containing canned turkey, fruit, and tiny star decorations made from straw, which the women of Bunk 37 strung around the room. The mood in the cabin was as jolly as it could be considering the circumstances, and the three friends sat together on Marguerite's bunk.

When the German women in the cabin started singing, 'Stille Nacht,' Yvonne joined in, belting out the lyrics she could remember in English, but stopped when she got to the words, "For now the hour of salvation strikes for us."

Marguerite reached over to pat Yvonne's arm. "Salvation is not upon us yet, but it will be someday soon. We cannot give up hope."

Marie broke the silence that followed. "What will you do when the war is over?" she asked. "I want to walk down the Champs-Élysées in a brand-new dress, feeling the sunshine on my shoulders."

Yvonne didn't have to pause to think. "I will go back to London. I think I have had enough of France for now. I yearn to see the lights of Piccadilly Circus again." She wondered if her ex-husband, Alex, was still serving the elite at the Piccadilly Hotel. It seemed like a lifetime ago that she had been married.

"Can I come visit you?" Marie asked.

"Of course."

Marguerite sat up straighter. "Well, I will make it a point to travel to America and tell the Red Cross—and anyone else who will listen—what happened here." Her voice dropped. "I feel it is my duty to not let them," she gestured toward a pile of three corpses next to the washroom, "die in vain."

Yvonne gazed at the bodies, wondering if their loved ones would ever get word of their fates. "One doesn't know who will succumb to death," she stated. "It could be anyone."

"Well, it won't be me," Marie declared.

"It might be me," Yvonne said. "I am very tired, but don't worry —I am not afraid of death. Nothing bad will happen to me then."

"Don't talk like that, Jacqueline," Marie said. "You have to have strength. What good is it for me to go through all the trouble of taking care of you if you plan on giving up?"

Yvonne gave her friend a tight smile. "For your sake I will try to live on. But just in case, I want you to know my real name—Yvonne Rudellat. If I do not survive the war, please contact my mother and my daughter."

"Of course," Marguerite replied. "I have to say, you've never struck me as someone particularly motherly. Until now," she added. She reached under her mattress and pulled out a piece of paper and a pencil and then dutifully recorded Yvonne's mother's address in Paris and Connie's last known address.

When Yvonne had finished dictating, Marguerite looked impressed. "Your memory has really returned." She put the paper and pencil underneath the straw mattress. "Don't worry, I will locate them. But you *will* live."

Marie took both of their hands in hers. "Let's pray that all of us —and our loved ones—will do the same."

CHAPTER 78

NOOR

*N*oor was taken away from Paris by train. She estimated her destination was somewhere in Germany, judging by the accents of the people around her when she arrived at a station in the middle of the night.

She was brought to a massive four-story prison and then led into a cream-colored cell. A guard barked at her to sit down on the only furniture: a rusted iron bed. Her hands had been cuffed together throughout her entire journey, but now the guard placed shackles around her ankles before running another chain between her hands and legs.

"Is this really necessary?" she asked.

The guard shrugged before replying in broken French, "I was told you were high risk for escaping."

Another uniformed guard entered carrying a bowl, which he set on the floor in front of Noor. He then pulled a spoon from his pocket and placed it next to the bowl.

"How am I supposed to eat this?" Noor demanded, her chains rattling as she lifted her hands.

The second guard looked at the first, who said, *"Nacht und Nebel."*

Noor's inquiry was even more shrill this time. "What does that mean?"

"It means," the second guard picked up a spoonful of liquid and held it up to Noor's lips, "that we can't take your chains off."

She swallowed the watery soup hungrily.

After the guards had left, Noor went to one of the walls and used the metal of her handcuffs to hammer out a greeting in Morse. When she did not get a reply, she moved to the other side of the room and tried again, but she heard nothing in return.

The days faded into one another. Because she remained chained, she was unable to perform the simplest tasks. She was fed twice a day by guards, one of whom took pity on Noor and told her she was in Pforzheim prison and had been placed in solitary confinement.

Once a week she was brought a change of clothes and a female guard washed her with a dingy sponge. There was no toilet—instead, Noor was forced to relieve herself using a grimy bucket, a task made infinitely harder by her shackled hands and feet.

She exercised by maneuvering as best she could around the cell, her ankle chains dragging on the ground. They were heavy and the shackles cut into her skin. Both her ankles and wrists were permanently covered in purple bruises.

Though she was in isolation, she took comfort in the fact that the cell was surprisingly bright, due to the wall color and the lone window, which was too high to see out of. But she could tell when a new day had dawned by the shifting of the little light she could discern. She made a makeshift calendar by using a sharp point on her manacles to carve into the plaster on the wall.

A few weeks after she arrived, on January 1, 1944, she marked her 30th birthday on the calendar by drawing a tiny candle. She spent it the same way she had spent every day since arriving at Pforzheim—alone and in chains.

CHAPTER 79

FRANCINE

*M*iss Atkins confirmed to Francine that Leo Marks also thought Nora had been compromised, but, once again, Buckmaster stubbornly refused to believe it. Antelme, his W/T operator, and a courier named Martine—a woman whom Miss Atkins claimed was the best she had in training at the time—were dropped near Chartres in February.

Nothing was ever heard from Antelme's radio operator, Lionel Lee, but a few days after they had landed, "Madeleine"—Francine could no longer consider the call sign as belonging to Nora—radioed that Antelme had taken a fall during landing and "severely damaged his head." Whoever was operating the wireless claimed he was lying in critical condition in a hospital.

"What are we going to do about this?" Francine demanded after Buckmaster read the message.

He didn't say anything for a long time. When he finally deigned to provide a reply, Francine found it unsatisfactory. "I don't think there's anything we can do."

"If you say so," she retorted. "It's only the lives of your agents at stake."

Buckmaster left the signals room without acknowledging Francine's last comment.

CHAPTER 80

ANDRÉE

The next time Andrée was taken to 84 Avenue Foch, she sensed something was different. She found herself half-hoping Bleicher would be waiting for her in the interrogation room, but instead found six other women all chatting amiably.

"Sonia!" she exclaimed upon spying the dark-haired girl sitting in the corner.

"Andrée!" Sonia returned, getting up to give her a hug.

"It's Denise in here," Andrée corrected. Before she could ask Sonia if she had any information on Prosper or Gilbert, one of the other women stepped forward. She had soulful brown eyes and fair hair tied back with a neat plaid bow. "I'm Diana Rowden."

She seemed so proper, and therefore, so British, that Andrée decided to ask, "Did you train with the SOE?"

"Yes," Diana replied. "I take it both of you did, too?"

Andrée nodded while Sonia said, "No. I was locally trained with the Juggler circuit."

"When were you arrested?" Diana asked Sonia.

"In January of this year."

"You made it a long time," Andrée said admirably. "I heard Jean Worms was picked up soon after I was."

Sonia frowned in remembrance. "Yes. After the fall of Prosper, Jacques went to Switzerland, but I stayed around."

"Who else did you work with?"

Sonia named a few names Andrée didn't recognize before she stated, "And I saw Nora sometimes."

"Nora," Andrée repeated, recalling the beautiful, shy girl. "What happened to her?"

Sonia shook her head. "I heard she was arrested in the fall. I tried to warn Baker Street, but never received a response from them."

Andrée looked around the room. "It seems all of the women of F Section are here except for Nora."

"I knew Nora, too," Diana said in a soft voice. "We arrived in France together, with Cecily." After a pause, she added, "Cecily's not here either."

"Well, we might as well get down to it," Andrée decided, pulling a chair closer to the other women. "They can't do anything worse than what they've done. Let's go around the room and state our names and which circuit we were associated with. I'm Denise and I was courier for the Prosper network. Sonia here was with Juggler. We were both mainly based in Paris."

A curly-haired woman who looked to be in her early 30s raised her hand. "I'm Yolande and I worked for Musician in Saint Quentin."

"I'm Eliane, with Monk in Marseilles," a pretty woman with captivating brown eyes said.

Next was a short woman in a tweed coat and skirt. She looked older than the rest of the women, though possibly not as old as Yvonne. "I'm Simone. I started with Inventor, but then we were sort of absorbed by Donkeyman."

"I thought you looked familiar," Andrée said. "What happened to Paul Frager?"

Simone shook her head. "I'm not quite sure, but I presume he was arrested eventually. We had at least one traitor in our group."

"Traitor?" a stocky woman with a heart-shaped face and dark hair repeated. "Of course there was a traitor. My crew parachuted right into the Boches' hands. The head of our circuit, Antoine, had been to Occupied France before, but this was my first time." She shook her head. "I was never given a chance."

"What was your circuit's name?" Sonia asked.

"Bricklayer."

Andrée recalled Germaine Tambour mentioning the circuit a few times, and figured it had been another offshoot of Prosper. "Who was supposed to pick you up?"

Martine's face crinkled in concentration. "I think his code name was… Gilbert."

"I'd heard Gilbert was a traitor too," Diana said. "He would sit at the front desk of Avenue Foch and name any SOE agents that were brought in."

"No," Sonia corrected. "You don't mean Gilbert Norman, you mean Déricourt."

The mention of Gilbert's name had nearly made Andrée wince in pain, but she focused on her anger. "Henri Déricourt," she repeated. "He must have told the Germans you were arriving by plane. I knew he was a double-agent." She put her head in her hands.

No one said anything for a moment. The door opened again and a small woman entered. She was pretty but frail and had clearly been in prison longer than some of the other women, like Yolande, who still appeared fresh-faced.

Grateful for the distraction, Andrée welcomed her. "I'm Denise. I worked for the Prosper network."

The woman's grasp was remarkably strong. "You're with the FANY?"

Andrée managed a smile. "Yes. And this is Simone, courier with Inventor, and Yolande, the radio operator for Musician." One by one, Andrée introduced the F Section women by their code names and circuits.

"I'm Lise," the new woman said. "With Spindle."

Lise. Andrée had heard the name before, but for the life of her, couldn't remember where. "When did you train?"

"In the spring of 1942," Lise answered.

Andrée nodded. "I thought so. You must know Adele."

"I did."

"We parachuted into France together," Andrée said. "Last I heard she'd gone back to help train new F Section recruits."

"She trained me," Martine piped up. "Before I left."

Andrée turned to Lise. "The Boches were waiting when Martine and the rest of her circuit landed."

Lise's mouth opened wide. "How do they know so much?" she asked when she'd recovered from her shock.

"I think there was at least one mole in the SOE," Andrée replied matter-of-factly. She was about to repeat her suspicions about Henri Déricourt, but the door burst open and the commandant entered. "You will be leaving for Germany in a few hours," he told them. "Are there any requests? Keep in mind this might be your last."

"Yes," Lise replied quickly. "We could all use some tea. And," her eyes traveled over the other F Section women, "be sure to make it in the English way, with milk and sugar."

The commandant's eyes narrowed before he stormed out of the room. A few minutes later, an aide entered the room carrying a tray with a tea pot and eight china cups.

Andrée grabbed the tea pot. This time, for the first time in a long time, she put the milk in first. As the women drank their tea, they chatted animatedly about their Resistance adventures and when they thought the Allied landing would be.

Yolande had a tube of lipstick with her, and all the girls passed it around. When Simone handed it to Andrée, she paused. An image of Gilbert teasing her about her putting on lipstick at Grignon materialized in her mind's eye. Feeling as if she'd just been punched in the stomach, Andrée passed the tube to Diana.

"You don't want any?" Diana asked.

Andrée shook her head, overwhelmed by the memory of Gilbert. Though she had been in solitary confinement in Fresnes for so long—and had at first welcomed the chatter of the other women—now all she wanted to do was be alone to think. To run through all the possible reasons why Gilbert had betrayed so many of their circuit.

"Have any of you been condemned to death?" Lise asked.

Andrée shook her head, bringing herself back to the present.

"Have you?" Yolande asked.

"Yes." Lise's lipsticked lips stretched into a smile. "Twice, in fact."

Andrée wanted to ask the other women if they'd heard about the *Nacht und Nebel* policy, but the commandant returned with more men and more instructions. "You will be handcuffed in pairs. If any of you attempt to flee, you will be shot immediately."

"Where would we go?" Lise asked.

Andrée was wondering the same thing. She'd already assessed the situation and decided there was no way she could escape: there were at least ten armed guards for eight defenseless women.

"I don't know," the commandant replied, "but my superiors aren't taking any chances." He snapped a handcuff around Andrée's wrists and then attached the other cuff to Simone.

Two by two, the women were joined together. As they were led downstairs, Martine started singing *Le Chant Des Partisans*, the unofficial Resistance song, until one of the guards told her to shut up.

There were several black vans waiting outside with their engines running. Andrée squinted in the bright sun to take one last look at 84 Avenue Foch. As far as she knew, Gilbert might still be there, his tall frame wandering through the halls. She gave a little wave to the building with her free hand. As she moved her wrist, she realized she'd never gotten her gold bracelet back from the wardress at Fresnes. *It's no matter,* she convinced herself—that chapter in her life had closed.

Though she'd already said her goodbyes to Gilbert in person, Andrée couldn't help mentally saying them again. *Goodbye, Gilbert. I hope someday you will be able to come to terms with what you did.*

The Germans had reserved two second class train compartments. Andrée and Simone were seated across from Lise and Yolande while a woman in an SS uniform took the seat behind them. A male guard was placed near the door of their cabin.

"Do you think they are taking us to Germany?" Simone asked Andrée.

"I don't know."

Simone peered out the window. Andrée looked over her shoulder, noting the still-smoldering landscape with satisfaction. Clearly the RAF had been hard at work, most likely because of information provided by the Resistance.

"My real name is Vera Leigh," Simone whispered after a while. "If we get separated and something happens, please tell Miss Atkins you saw me. She'll know how to get in touch with my family."

"And I'm Andrée Borrel." She touched Vera's arm with her free hand. "But don't worry. They can't possibly do much more than put us in prison for the duration of the war."

Vera gave her an encouraging smile. "I hope you're right."

Their destination was Karlsruhe, Germany. Andrée and the other F Section women were unloaded and escorted, once again by armed guards, through the train station while a few passers-by stopped to stare.

"I have to use the bathroom," Vera whispered to Andrée. "Do you suppose they will take these cuffs off?"

"No," Andrée replied simply.

Someone shoved at her back with the butt of a rifle, forcing her toward an awaiting taxi. She and Vera awkwardly clambered inside as a guard, presumably the one that hit Andrée with his rifle, sat up front.

They drove for a few minutes in silence before arriving at an enormous, orange-bricked building.

"What's this?" Vera asked.

"A civilian prison," the guard remarked.

To Andrée, the Karlsruhe prison didn't appear nearly as intimidating as Fresnes.

The guard walked up to the double doors and pulled at a huge bell rope. A tall, thin woman appeared. Given her haggard appearance, Andrée decided she must be the wardress. They were led inside the prison and into a small room, which must have functioned as the wardress's office.

"Can you please take these off?" Andrée asked, holding out her wrist. The guard finally acquiesced.

Andrée and Vera took turns using the dirty public bathroom before being strip-searched and inspected for lice.

When the endless check-in process had finished, the women were taken to separate cells, placed as far away from each other as possible in order to cut off all contact. Still, Andrée took consolation in the knowledge that she wasn't alone. Somewhere in the depths of the large prison were seven other SOE women. Perhaps they all would be able to overcome whatever fate waited for them.

CHAPTER 81

FRANCINE

The day Prosper and Gilbert Norman had so long awaited finally happened on June 6, 1944. The Allies landed in France.

Francine arrived at Norgeby House at the usual time to find a flurry of activity. Hundreds of messages had come through—the active networks that remained were asked to commit acts of sabotage, and most of the reports were that the deeds had been performed successfully. The Pimento circuit had cut all of the railway lines between Toulouse and Montauban, and Francis Cammaerts of the Jockey circuit relayed that they had done something similar in Marseilles.

On a whim, Francine walked over to the FANY operator assigned to John Macalister, a Canadian W/T operator who had been sent into France last summer, soon after she and Jack had returned.

"Did you get anything from the field?" she asked the FANY.

The operator's eyes were wide. "Yes. Something just came in. I think Buckmaster himself needs to read it." She handed the card over to Francine with shaking hands. "It was sent *en clair* and signed by the *Geheime Staatpolizei."* Though she stumbled over the words, the meaning was clear: the Gestapo.

"Merde alors," Francine exclaimed. She gestured wildly to Miss Atkins, who grabbed Buckmaster's arm as she rushed over.

Francine read the message aloud:

Many thanks: large deliveries arms and ammunitions sent during long period all over France. Have greatly appreciated good tips concerning your Intentions and Plans. Unavoidable we had to take under the care of Gestapo your friends of French Section Such as Max, Cinema, Theodore, Antoine, etc. STOP

Very pleased to have your visit for which we have prepared everything.

"Who is that from?" Buckmaster demanded.

The FANY operator looked down as Francine answered, "The Gestapo." She cleared her throat, feeling tears forming. Cinema had been part of Nora's circuit, and Antoine was France Antelme's code name.

The FANY scribbled furiously as Buckmaster blasted off a reply:

Sorry to see your patience is exhausted and your nerves are not as good as ours STOP Sorry we gave you so much trouble in collecting containers but we had to carry on until our officers had been able to make bigger and better friends STOP Expense and stores no object STOP Incidentally we suggest you change your S phone operator we don't think much of his English STOP Auf Wiedersehen

When he'd finished, Francine stepped directly into his eyeline so that he could no longer ignore her. "Now do you believe that Macalister's radio, and probably a host of others, including Nora's and Gilbert's, have been compromised?"

Buckmaster refused to meet her gaze. "Yes."

CHAPTER 82

ANDRÉE

*A*ndrée stayed in Karlsruhe for only a few nights. One morning in early July, she was told to get dressed before being led out of the prison by a guard with an ever-present rifle. A Black Maria was waiting in the prison driveway, its engine running.

"Andrée!"

She turned to see Sonia being shoved outside by another guard. The hollows around the young woman's eyes had grown deeper, but Andrée was pleased to see that her friend appeared otherwise unharmed.

When they climbed into the car, they found Vera Leigh and Diana Rowden. Both women also looked relatively unscathed, though Diana must have lost her hairbow somewhere along the way.

"Good morning," Andrée called in the most cheerful voice she could muster. As the car started, she turned to the back window and watched as the prison disappeared. All in all, Karlsruhe hadn't been that bad: the food was better than Fresnes and she'd been allowed an hour outside to exercise every day, though it was never with any of the other F Section women.

After an hour or so of silence, Sonia asked, "Where do you think we are going?"

"Judging by the sun, we are heading west," Andrée replied.

"Maybe they are bringing us back to France," Diana said, the hope obvious in her voice. "Maybe they've given up now that the Allies are in France."

Andrée raised her eyebrows. "The Allies are in France?"

"Yes," Diana said. "A woman I was in the cell with told me. The Allies finally landed and the war will be over soon."

Sonia glanced at their driver, a man in an SS uniform, and inquired something in German. She translated his reply for the rest of the women. "He says we're going to a camp to do agricultural work."

"A work camp?" Vera asked. "I heard about them from another woman in Fresnes. They're supposed to have deplorable conditions."

Sonia shrugged. "It can't be that bad if they are going to let us work outside."

A few minutes later, Sonia gazed out the window as the car began climbing a steep hill. "I think this is Natzweiler."

Vera leaned over to point at something. "That's the Hôtel Struthof. I came here on a skiing holiday once."

"But it's so green." Andrée couldn't imagine the landscape covered in snow. Here and there, flowering trees were dotted along the dark green landscape and crimson poppies lined the side of the dirt road. She hoped the Boche driver wasn't lying when he said the women were there to do agricultural work—she wouldn't mind getting her hands dirty if it was in the black soil of the Alsace region.

As the Black Maria made a left turn, Andrée's thoughts went from cautious hope to despair. Ahead was an imposing wooden gate covered in barbed wire. Its posts, sharpened on the end like medieval torture devices, rose 10 meters high. *Konzentrationslager Natzweiler-Struthof* was painted in ominous black letters on a sign that spanned the width of the gate.

The Black Maria paused as two armed guards opened the gates.

Andrée could see several squat wooden buildings set into the mountainside. Beyond them was more barbed wire and then… nothing. It was as if they were at the edge of the world.

"What is this place?" Diana asked, the panic obvious in her voice.

"We're on top of a mountain," Andrée stated, not necessarily in reply to Diana's question. The conversation she had with Bleicher suddenly came to mind. What better place for people to disappear?

"*Aussteigen,*" the driver told them in a gruff voice as he cut the engine.

Sonia opened her door, nearly falling out of the car. There were hardly any trees at this high altitude, and the sun beat down on Andrée as she exited. The driver released the latch on the Black Maria's trunk before strolling to a group of squat buildings.

The women pulled their purses and suitcases out of the trunk and then gazed at each other uncertainly.

"What do we do now?" Vera asked.

"I guess we wait," Andrée replied.

There were no benches anywhere, so they stood in the blazing sun. Andrée took in a deep breath, noting that an underlying odor tainted the fresh mountain air. It was the scent of something burning. Covering her eyes, she scanned the area near the brown wooden buildings. One had a sizable chimney with black smoke coming from it. *I guess that explains the burning smell.*

An emaciated man in a striped uniform approached them. "Cigarette?" he offered.

Andrée gratefully accepted it.

The man's skeletal hand trembled as he tried to flick the lighter. Andrée took it from him and lit his cigarette first.

He took a deep drag and moved his head to blow the smoke away from them. "You are women," he said finally.

Andrée didn't know how to reply to that.

"We don't see many women here," he continued. He pointed to his chest, on which was sewn a red triangle. "I am a political prisoner. You too?"

The other girls nodded. "We were with the French Resistance," Sonia added.

"You look familiar," the man said to Andrée.

She couldn't say the same of him. In addition to having seemingly colorless eyes that sunk into his gaunt face, the man's hair was shorn and his scalp was sunburned.

"Did you work on the PAO line?" the man asked.

"Yes," Andrée replied, surprised.

He tapped his chest. "I'm Albert Guérrise."

Andrée nearly dropped her cigarette. Guérrise, aka Pat O'Leary, had been the head of the line during the time she and Maurice had worked it.

"What are you doing here?" Andrée asked.

"I was betrayed by someone else on the line. Now they force me to act as an interpreter for the guards." He stabbed his cigarette out. "At least it gets me out of manual labor, most of the time."

Their driver reemerged from the building. This time he was accompanied by two other men. "Let's go," one of them told the women in French. They grabbed their bags and followed the men.

The four women were marched down a paved slope that served as the camp's main road. Though the camp was concealed among the mountains, Andrée quickly discovered that everything that happened within was in plain sight of its occupants. Her grip on her purse tightened as a sea of skeletons with shaved heads stopped what they were doing to stare at them. Their observers were all male and it was obvious from their slack jaws that they hadn't seen women in a very long time. Though they all wore the same striped uniform, some of them had a yellow star sewn on their uniforms, indicating they were Jews, but others bore triangles in different colors: pink, blue, green, and red.

The women were led toward the low wooden buildings Andrée had spotted earlier. One of the guards unlocked a door and ushered them inside. The only window in the room was covered in metal bars.

"Stay here," the guard said before slamming the door shut again.

The women exchanged glances as they heard a rustle of keys. They were locked in.

A few minutes later, someone tapped on the window. Andrée was able to open it a bit by squeezing her hand between the bars and saw that Guérrise was standing outside.

He tossed a packet of cigarettes through the window. "Are all of you French?"

"Most of us."

Diana joined Andrée, declaring that she was English.

Guérrise rubbed at an open sore on his arm. "I was told that curfew will be at seven tonight instead of eight. That's never happened before."

"Do you think it has something to do with us coming?" Andrée asked.

He nodded as his gaze dropped to the ground. "I fear the worst."

Diana's grip on the steel bar tightened. "Do they hurt you here?"

"Sometimes." He put his hand on his sore again, which was now bleeding. "But I don't know what they'll do to you—they've never brought women here."

"I'm scared," Diana said in a low voice so that Vera and Sonia didn't hear.

Instead of replying, Andrée searched for something to give Guérrise in return for the cigarettes. "Take this." She pushed a tobacco pouch filled with money through the window.

He peered inside the pouch. "Are you sure you don't want to keep this cash?"

Andrée glanced at Diana, whose face looked stricken. "I'm not sure I will have a use for it," Andrée replied quietly. After a moment, she added, "If anything happens to us, please get word to Vera Atkins at the SOE."

Guérrise saluted her. "I will."

CHAPTER 83

NOOR

*J*n the summertime, Noor had new friends visit her: flies. Because she'd had no contact with any other breathing being besides her guards for—by Noor's estimate—nearly eight months, she welcomed the intruders, letting them land on her cheeks and legs. She pretended they were the fairies of her youth, abandoning their flower homes to let her know of their existence.

One day Noor was watching a fly crawl up her arm when she heard singing in the hallway. Temporarily forgetting the fly, she crept closer to the door. Women's voices, chanting a tuneless song with no real rhythm, were being carried through the vent above the door. Noor realized they were trying to communicate with her by pretending to sing. The words she heard included, "Allies, Paris, liberation," and she surmised that the Allies must have landed in France.

Noor opened her mouth to call out, but nothing came out except a hollow groan.

Someone yelled, *"Halt die Gosche!"* in the hallway, causing the singing to stop. Noor heard shrieking and then several footsteps retreating before her door was thrown open.

A guard Noor had never seen before stomped into her cell.

"*Das Miststück!*" He wound up his arm and she saw it come toward her face in slow motion. When it finally made contact, she fell to the floor, her jaw vibrating. She hadn't experienced such pain in all her life.

She felt as if she was going to faint as she saw him unbuckle his belt. *Please, please don't let him rape me,* she begged to herself.

But the guard had other things in mind. He whipped the leather belt across her legs and then her torso before he switched it up by using the metal buckle. Noor tried to distract herself by keeping count of his blows, but after eight, she lost track.

A few days of endless pain went by before Noor could crawl to her calendar again. Since she had been in and out of consciousness and couldn't keep track of the sun's movements, it was hard to know how much time had passed. By her best guess it was July 14, Bastille Day.

It took her hours to scratch *Vive la France libre* onto the wall because she had to give her bruised arms frequent breaks. Finally she took stock of her handiwork. She paused again before adding two tiny flags—one British and one French—next to the date.

As she was finishing, the wall beneath her hand trembled. She drew her arm back and glanced at the door, hoping it wasn't the stomping of a guard's jackboots that shook the walls.

But the tremors were originating from somewhere outside the prison. *The RAF.* The Allies were coming. Noor recalled the day in Garry's kitchen when he told her about the German's guns at Orly airport. It comforted her to know the world hadn't ended with her arrest—there were still other Resistance members out there, providing information for the RAF's next targets.

She closed her eyes, picturing whole German towns being obliterated by Allied bombs. After a moment, her eyes flew open. What was she thinking? She could not possibly be gleeful at the thought of other humans suffering.

She moved a pant leg to look at the bruises covering her shin as words from one of her father's sermons drifted into her mind:

The root of anger is arrogance. In order to arrive at true nobility of spirit, one must be prepared to forgive the imperfections of human nature—the best expression of love is that love which is expressed in forgiveness.

She wasn't supposed to harbor hate in her heart, not even for the guard that had done this to her. For that matter, she shouldn't be wishing tragedy to strike Renée Garry, who had gotten her into this mess. Who knew why Renée had felt the need to disclose Noor's identity to the Gestapo? Maybe she had needed the money, or maybe there was some other explanation for her betrayal. Whatever it was, it was not Noor's place to judge, only to forgive.

For her part, the suffering Noor was being forced to endure might one day turn out to be a blessing. After all, she thought with a faint smile, once upon a time she'd wanted the kind of life experience she could write about in a literary novel. Now, at only thirty years old, she'd had enough to fill hundreds of pages.

She folded her broken body into her bed, once again trying to sleep away the pain.

The next morning, one of the guards woke Noor up by shaking her. "You are going."

"Where?" she asked sleepily.

But the guard did not answer her. He produced a key and undid her chains. Noor waggled her arms wondrously—they felt longer than she remembered and seemed to move on their own accord, like a bird that had been suddenly released from a cage and didn't know how to fly. The silver pin Miss Atkins had given her popped into her mind. Unlike the quails that had listened to their king in *Twenty Jataka Tales*, Noor had been caught. But maybe, like most of the creatures in her book, there was a chance that she could still live happily ever after.

She flexed the fingers of her right hand, letting the blood flow through them completely, before crossing the first two behind her back for good luck as she followed the guard into the hallway.

CHAPTER 84

YVONNE

*C*amp life changed drastically in the spring as the population of elderly women at Appell dwindled more every day. Marie heard that they were being taken to the abandoned youth camp near the grounds of Ravensbrück, but no one knew much more than that.

One evening, a hefty blonde guard demanded that the 'knitters' stand for inspection outside Block 17. "*Schnell, schnell,*" she told a woman that looked to be in her early 40s but had feet that were so swollen she could no longer walk.

The guard strolled down the line, directing some prisoners, including Yvonne, to go back inside, and others to pack and then stand in yet another line outside the block. Those unfortunate women, some of them crying, gathered up their meager things and did as they were told. In a few minutes, an enormous black lorry arrived and Yvonne never saw any of them again.

At Appell, one of the SS guards, who was almost always drunk, started using a long, curved stick to yank women out of line by their neck. These women would not appear at Appell again. Marie nicknamed the guard, 'The Hangman,' though Yvonne personally thought 'Grim Reaper' would have been more apt.

Word began to spread that a crematorium had been built near the youth camp and could fit up to 150 women. As the days grew warmer and longer, the elderly and sick women continued to disappear and thick black smoke blanketed the camp. It was obvious that those prisoners who were unable to work were being selected as victims for the new crematorium.

Yvonne, fearing she would be next, asked Marie to get her some charcoal from the kitchen. She tried to darken her hair with the coal and make herself look younger, but it was no use. She settled for wearing a scarf over her head to hide her gray tresses.

One day, Marie and Yvonne were walking to Appell when they paused to let an open-backed lorry go by. Yvonne gasped when she realized it was filled with corpses. She tried to avert her eyes, but couldn't. As the lorry stopped at an intersection in front of them, she saw a hand move out from under a pile of bodies. "Help me," a voice croaked.

Yvonne started toward the hand, but Marie yanked her back. "Don't. If you go near that lorry, it will be suicide."

Yvonne forced herself to look away, convincing herself that someone else would step in and save the poor creature.

"Don't invite danger," Marie commanded as they began walking again. "We're in enough as it is." She pointed toward the enormous, L-shaped prison block known as the Bunker, where it was rumored the conditions were even worse than they were in the rest of camp. Prisoners in striped uniforms were being led out of the building by the dozens. "Whatever you do, you must stay away from the Bunker." Marie gripped her arm. "Yvonne, do you hear me? You have to watch where you are going when you are walking around camp. You cannot get confused and end up there."

"I will try, but sometimes I have trouble telling which direction is which."

Marie released her grip. "I know, but please tell me you will be careful."

"I will."

The Polish block consisted mostly of young, working women, and Yvonne thought it was safe from the Hangman, but he appeared one day when she was visiting Marie. Yvonne was able to escape through a window as the guard shouted for all the residents to line up outside.

Once she had fled the cabin, she had no idea where to go. She recalled that there had been a transport of women a few days ago. They'd been put in a makeshift tent and basically forgotten.

Yvonne headed off in the direction she thought the tent was, but flinched when she saw the brick exterior of the Bunker. As usual, a line of women was waiting to board an ubiquitous black lorry.

"You there," a guard called to Yvonne. "Get back in line."

She tried to protest, but he aimed his rifle at her. "I said get back in line."

She had no choice but to do as told.

CHAPTER 85

NOOR

*N*oor was taken by train once again, this time to a station in Stuttgart. When she got off the train, she found three other women waiting along with the requisite SS guards. She immediately recognized the cherub-cheeked Yolande Beekman from her SOE training, but wasn't sure whether to acknowledge her.

Yolande had no such qualms. "Nora!" she exclaimed, hugging her gingerly. She squeezed Noor's upper arm. "You were always thin, but my god, Nora—you're like a skeleton now!"

"You've lost weight too," Noor remarked.

Yolande, whose once partially tamed curls had become unruly, waved her hand. "I was at Avenue Foch for a bit and then they transferred me a few weeks ago to Karlsruhe."

"I was at Avenue Foch too, but I've been in solitary confinement in Pforzheim for nearly a year," Noor replied.

"Oh Nora," Yolande gave her another hug.

The other two women approached. The first one was not as emaciated as Yolande, and had short, dark hair. "I'm Martine."

"And I'm Eliane," the other one said. She was petite and pretty, with eyebrows that somehow had managed to stay perfectly symmetrical.

"*Pardonnez-moi.*" One of their guards cleared his throat and then said something in German.

Yolande translated for him. "It seems the train has been delayed."

"Was it an Allied bomb?" Noor asked hopefully.

Yolande repeated the question to the guard. His forehead furrowed before he shot back a reply.

"He only knows it will be a few hours," Yolande told the other women with a shrug.

Noor looked up at the sky. It was a pleasantly warm, sunny day. "I don't mind waiting."

"I'm going to ask him if they have any food, since some of us have been clearly kept on starvation diets," Yolande said.

The guard gave an uncertain look to his companion, who shrugged and muttered something unintelligible. In unison, they dug through their packs, producing bread, sausages, and cigarettes.

"Where are we going?" Noor asked the second guard in broken German. He exchanged another glance with the other man before stating out of the corner of his mouth, "Munich."

When the train finally arrived at the station, the guards led the women to an otherwise empty compartment. Noor sat next to Martine and the guards half-heartedly handcuffed the two women together. Noor's shackles were loose enough that she could have slipped out, but there was nowhere to run. Besides, after being alone for so long, she cherished being in the other women's company.

"Were you a courier too?" Martine asked Noor.

"No. I was the first woman W/T operator in the field." She couldn't help the little bit of pride that snuck into her voice.

Martine's eyes grew wide. "Then you are Madeleine. I heard about you in training."

"It's Nora, actually."

Martine did not acknowledge that comment. "When were you arrested?"

"In the autumn of 1943."

Martine sunk her head into her hands. "We landed in February 1944—our drop zone had been set based on field communications from someone called Madeleine. Or should I say the Gestapo. They were waiting for us."

Noor opened and shut her mouth but nothing came out.

"It wasn't your fault," Martine told her. "I just..." she stopped and tried again, "Antelme..."

"Antelme? Are you referring to France Antelme?"

"Yes." Martine shook her head. "He was to be my leader. We all parachuted in together."

"Where is he now?"

"Arrested," Martine replied softly. "Just like myself and Lionel Lee."

Noor was indignant with anger. "How could Buckmaster have done that? How could he have sent you in? That wasn't me on the wireless. Goetz was imitating my rhythm, but Buckmaster should have known. He..."

Martine's hand closed over Noor's. "It's okay. We're the ones who took the risk. We were trying to help England. After that, it is all white noise."

Noor shut her eyes in an effort to get a little sleep, but she was awakened a few minutes later when Eliane asked Yolande to inquire what they would be doing once they got to Munich.

Yolande leaned into the aisle and tapped the shoulder of the guard in front of her. He opened a piece of paper and read it before replying.

"He says we're to go to a camp in the south where we will farm," Yolande translated. "He says the weather there is good, so maybe they'll keep us outdoors most of the day."

Noor didn't understand much of the German language, but she knew enough about music to detect the hesitation that had been in the guard's reply. "Ask him if you can see his order."

Yolande did as bid, but the guard crumpled the paper before sticking it back in his pocket. She looked at Noor and shrugged.

Noor felt frozen. There was something in his behavior that seemed ominous, but she didn't want to relay her fears to the other girls. She simply smiled back at Yolande.

They arrived at Munich station in the early evening. The two guards led the four women on a three-kilometer walk, which took less than an hour. They paused at the entrance to a concrete-building complete with massive iron gates.

The words *Arbeit Macht Frei* were etched into the iron scrollwork of the gates. "Work will set you free," Yolande said.

"You see?" Martine's eyes were also focused on the gate. "We will do their bidding and they will release us soon, when the war is over."

The portentous feeling in the pit of Noor's stomach intensified, but she didn't want to argue. "Gardening won't be so bad," she told Yolande. "I think we can all use a bit of sunshine in our lives."

CHAPTER 86

ANDRÉE

*A*t dusk, Andrée and the other three newly-arrived women were sent for and then taken into a large, cavernous room. A man in civilian clothes stood in the corner, next to a set of beds with gray sheets.

"This is Dr. Rohde," one of the guards said as the doctor took out a syringe filled with a clear liquid.

"What's that for?" Andrée demanded.

"For typhus," Rohde replied.

"You are going to give us typhus?" Sonia asked.

"No." The doctor's repugnant lips twisted into an evil grin. "It's to inoculate you against it. The disease runs rampant through these camps. It's your only chance of survival."

Sonia glanced at Vera, who shrugged and held out her arm.

"No…" Andrée started to say, but it was too late. The doctor had already stuck his needle into Vera. He led her over to a bed and helped her lay down. "The vaccine makes you sleepy, but it's only temporary."

"Something's not right," Andrée stated under her breath. "He's not giving us a typhus vaccine."

"It's doubtful," Diana whispered back. "But whatever it is, it's probably better than dying of starvation, or worse, at this camp."

"No," Andrée said as the doctor approached them again. He drove the needle into Diana's arm and then turned to the remaining two women.

"We are both going to pass on the vaccine," Sonia told him. "Thank you anyway."

"You're not going anywhere," the doctor said. He dragged Diana to another bed as the guard picked up Vera and threw her still body over his shoulder.

Andrée met Sonia's gaze and mouthed the word "Run."

Andrée took a cautious step toward the door, which opened suddenly and three new men walked in. The doctor pointed to Sonia, who tried to back away, only to be stopped by one of the men. He grabbed her from behind and wrestled her to the ground.

Another man attempted to do the same to Andrée but she squirmed out of his reach. She had almost reached the door before he tackled her.

The doctor was much quicker now. He stabbed Sonia with the syringe, and then moved to Andrée. "There's not enough left in there," she managed to choke out before the guard covered her mouth. She bit his hand.

"*Miststück!*" the guard shouted as he put his hand to his mouth.

Andrée felt a sliver of satisfaction before she was again seized from behind. She turned her head to see the guard who had assaulted Sonia now held her arms in a vice grip.

Andrée tried to squirm, but she was overpowered. As if in slow motion, she watched the needle come closer. "That's not a vaccine, is it?" she asked, her voice shrill.

"No." The doctor inserted it into her shoulder. "It's phenol, designed to knock you out so we can throw you into the gas oven."

Now everything seemed to slow down and the world became sluggish. When she asked, "Why?" her voice sounded deeper and almost unintelligible, even to her own ears.

"*Nacht und Nebel, du französischer Abschaum,*" the doctor replied. "Good riddance."

"You will all pay for this someday," Andrée said before she blacked out.

CHAPTER 87

NOOR

*A*fter Noor spent the night in her own cell—a tiny, windowless room with ceilings so low she could not stand up—a guard summoned her around nine in the morning. He led her out into the fresh air, where the other three women were waiting.

A tall blond man in a grayish-green uniform soon appeared. He was accompanied by a shorter man, whom Noor assumed was the prison commandant.

The blond man reached into his pocket and pulled out a piece of paper, which he read aloud in German.

After he'd finished, Yolande's eyes grew wide with tears.

"What did he say?" Noor asked.

"He said," Yolande's voice broke and she took a deep, shaky breath. "He said we've been sentenced to death."

"Ask him if we can appeal it," Martine demanded.

When Yolande inquired, the commandant's reply was a simple, "*Nein.*"

"What about a priest?" Eliane asked.

This time the blond man said in French, "There are none here."

376

"This is a world without God," Martine commented under her breath.

"No," Noor replied. "God is everywhere." She tilted her head upward, relishing the warm sunshine on her face. "The birds are still chirping, and somewhere beyond this fence, there are flowers blooming. And the birds will chirp and flowers will bloom when we are gone."

"How can you be so brave?" Eliane asked in a trembling voice.

"I am prepared to die without regrets," Noor said.

Yolande stepped forward to grasp Noor's hand. The tears filling her eyes spilled over. "You're right, Nora. We did what we were asked, nothing more, nothing less. And someday soon, the Allies will win the war and the world will once again be free."

Noor squeezed Yolande's hand. "We did our part. We are not to die in vain."

The blond man spoke again in French. "But you *will* die, you English swine."

Noor's own words—words she'd written long ago in the monkey story from *Twenty Jataka Tales* Leo Marks had mentioned to her——popped into her head and she said them aloud. "I do not suffer in leaving this world, for I have gained my subjects' freedom. And if my death may be a lesson to you, then I am more than happy."

She saw Eliane reach for Martine's hand.

"I am ready," Noor declared.

As one of the men ordered *"Descendez!"*, Noor followed Yolande's lead by sinking to her knees. A mound of dirt lay just in front of them and beyond that, a gaping hole where their lifeless bodies would be dumped when this was over.

Noor closed her eyes as a rifle was cocked behind her. Knowing it was the last chance for her voice to be heard on Earth, she summoned the strength to shout, *"Liberté!"*

CHAPTER 88

YVONNE

*Y*vonne was taken to another camp. This one was in northern Germany, near the town of Bergen, where the prisoners—men this time as well as women—were in even worse states of starvation. Most of them had yellow stars pinned to their striped uniforms.

At Ravensbrück, they had been at least somewhat discrete with the dead and dying. A corpse might linger a day or two in a bunk, but it would eventually be removed. At this new camp, which someone said was called Belsen, the bodies just piled up, dozens high, most of them naked. The ones at the bottom were in an advanced state of decomposition, with blackened skin that peeled away from their bones.

Occasionally, when Yvonne was led down the main walkway on her way to Appell, she could see a still-breathing body on the ground next to the piles, but she could do nothing to help. She couldn't even help herself.

Once again, Yvonne was made to suffer mercilessly. The food at Belsen was even less substantial and her already depleted energy stores almost disappeared entirely. Appell was much the same, with the SS guards taking pleasure in any humiliation they could bestow onto the prisoners. Yvonne had to look away when a guard forced a skeletal man to run on his knees while pushing a wheelbarrow.

She'd grown numb to the world since leaving Marie and Marguerite. At first she was ashamed that—by getting lost and ending up at the Bunker—she'd done exactly what Marie had warned her not to. But even that shame disappeared, taken over by apathy toward the war, to her surroundings, to life itself.

As spring made its relentless march toward summer, Appell, which had already been unbearably long, was extended by hours—sometimes the morning session would last all day. Yvonne would grow weak both from hunger and the overpowering stench that clung to every molecule of air. When she had first arrived, there had been working latrines, but then something happened to the water supply and access to running water ceased. Many prisoners just went to the bathroom whenever it felt convenient, and the bare ground that wasn't covered with dead bodies was filled with human excrement.

There was no other work detail, except for digging open pits at the far edges of the camp or moving the corpses to said pits using bedraggled leather straps. As Yvonne could do neither, she usually just wandered around the camp aimlessly after Appell, doing her best to avoid stepping on anything besides the muddy ground.

It was almost a relief when she came down with typhoid fever and had to be quarantined in the hospital block, a brick building near the burial pits. Her headaches, which had lessened with time, came back full force, along with nausea, though her hunger pains had been replaced by delirium caused by the high fever.

Day after day and night after night, people around Yvonne gasped their last breaths and passed away. No one came to remove them, and they remained in place, rotting, until more sick prisoners arrived. In need of beds, the newcomers used the last of their strength to push the dead onto the floor and claim their bunks.

Once again, Yvonne was helpless. In her delirious state, she wished she'd died back at Ravensbrück, where she actually felt like a human and could have had a more dignified death surrounded by her friends.

She recalled the countless times she'd set detonators to undermine the Germans' infrastructure. Maybe she could have accidentally perished then.

No. Giving it more thought, she realized that there was not one act of sabotage she would have sacrificed to allow for her own demise. She would not take back any of the time she'd spent working for the Resistance—when she had felt young and free, with boundless energy. When she had felt respected by her peers and not debased by Boches, who would rather she die than have to deal with her.

One day Yvonne woke up feeling less overheated, as if her fever might have abated a bit. It took most of her remaining strength to promise herself she would not rot to death from the inside out. She would be saved from the worst ending possible.

"I agree," a soft voice said from the bunk next to her. "No one should draw their last breaths in a place like this."

Yvonne worked up the energy to turn her head. A skeleton with a shaved head had taken the place of the man that had been there last night. "Was I speaking aloud?"

"Yes," the skeleton—a woman, Yvonne decided—answered. "You said, 'No one should be forced to die like this,' and I agreed."

"Oh," was all Yvonne could reply.

"I'm Lucile," the woman said.

"Yvonne." She barely heard Lucile respond, "Nice to meet you," before she fell back asleep.

CHAPTER 89

FRANCINE

*A*fter D-Day, Francine didn't spend much time at Norgeby House and she took a position escorting Polish agents to the RAF field at Tempsford. One day her commanding officer informed her that her presence had been requested at Baker Street.

She entered the building, hoping that it had something to do with a wireless message and not bad news regarding Jack, though she didn't dare let herself hope they had found him alive.

She was escorted to Miss Akins' office. Since most of their previous meetings had taken place in the signals room or Major Buckmaster's office, Francine had never been there before. It was surprisingly messy, with papers and files stacked haphazardly on any available surface. Francine noticed the major was absent as she sank into a chair opposite the desk.

For once, Miss Atkins' no-nonsense manner was a godsend. "I'm going to get right to the point." She straightened a stack of papers. "I've called you in on a personal matter. Since D-Day, it has become my duty to compile intelligence on the dozens of agents who are still missing in action and communicate whatever I find to their family members."

Francine nodded her understanding. "Is this about Jack?"

"I'm afraid so." Miss Atkins opened a file folder containing only a single sheet of paper. "I've received word that Jack had been taken to a work camp in Flossenbürg."

Francine couldn't help interrupting. "Where is that?"

"Near Bavaria, on the Czechoslovakian border. The Americans liberated it a few weeks ago. While they were able to get some information on the prisoners, it seems the SS destroyed nearly all the records of their British captives, especially those who were associated with the SOE."

"What can you tell me?"

Miss Atkins reached across the desk to put her hand on Francine's. "All I know is that he is gone."

Francine started sobbing quietly as Miss Akins continued, "A Dutch agent who was in the cell next to him said that he and Jack had been communicating by thumping Morse code on the walls with their knuckles. On his last day, Jack tapped that he knew they were coming for him and requested the agent find you. His last words were, 'Tell my wife I love her.'"

The words were not much consolation to Francine, who continued weeping. Finally drained of her tears, she looked up as a thought occurred to her. "How did they kill him?"

Miss Atkins withdrew her hand. "I don't know, but even if I did, I don't think it's something you'd like to hear. I'm not sure how familiar you are with these German camps, but they're..." she paused, looking unsure if she wanted to go on. "Quite brutal."

Francine sniffled audibly. "He shouldn't have gone to France."

"What if we said that about all of our agents? Then none of what the Resistance did to speed up the end of the war would have occurred. I know it's not going to sink in now, but maybe someday you will realize what Jack—and all of the others—did for the war. What they did for freedom."

"You're right, I don't understand." Francine rose. "If you'll excuse me, I have to go make arrangements for my husband's memorial. If there's one good thing to come out of this, it's that I can finally let go of the hope that he's ever coming back."

"Let me know if you need any help," Miss Atkins offered. "Ever." As Francine began to walk out of her office, Miss Atkins called, "I do pray that one day you *will* understand."

CHAPTER 90

YVONNE

For a few days, it seemed as if Yvonne was turning a corner. Though there were no thermometers in the hospital block, she could tell her fever had broken. Here and there she was able to exchange snippets of conversation with Lucile and some of the other prisoners, who informed Yvonne that British soldiers were approaching the camp.

The SS guards must have evacuated the camp in anticipation of the arrival of the Allies, for the food stopped coming. Lucile was able to get out of bed and forage through the trash cans. She found moldy potato peelings, which she forced Yvonne to eat.

The effort of chewing almost finished her completely, and Yvonne realized that her renewed vigor had only been a brief deception. She was dying.

It could have been days or only a few hours later when she was awakened by a burst of sunlight. She blinked as a large, well-fed form filled the doorway of the cabin.

"We are from the 11th Division of the British Army," the form said. "We have come to free you."

Yvonne blinked again as more sturdy men in khaki uniforms filed in, moving among the comatose bodies and overflowing the dank, dark room with their boundless energy.

Two soldiers with stretchers paused between Lucile and Yvonne's beds. "Take her," Yvonne said, using the last dregs of her strength to point to Lucile.

One of the soldiers lifted Lucile and placed her gently on the stretcher. She was able to move her arm so that her fingers touched Yvonne's before they carried her away.

"We're going to take you to the hospital now," another young man in a khaki uniform told Yvonne in broken French.

"No," Her breath came out in gasps. "Don't waste... your efforts... on me. Save them... for another."

The young man glanced uncertainly at another soldier, who shrugged.

She could feel her heartbeat slowing. At Ravensbrück, she had once told Marie and Marguerite that she wasn't afraid of death. She still wasn't—she had always done exactly what she'd wanted and had lived a life full of adventure, love, and most importantly, friendship. *Until the Boches took it all away.* But at least now she could die like a human being, knowing that the Allies were going to do what they could for the people left in this hell the Nazis had created.

"Is there anything else I can do for you?" the young man asked gently.

"Please take care of Lucile … and please... let the world know what they did to us."

"I will."

"Thank you."

The young man stroked Yvonne's hair as she closed her eyes and went to sleep for the last time.

CHAPTER 91

FRANCINE

Unlike most of the rest of the country, Francine didn't feel much like celebrating the end of the war—at least in the European theater—on VE-day. Major Buckmaster, the eternal optimist, had remained convinced that almost all of the captured F Section agents would be coming home. "We have every reason to believe that they will be recovered," he told Francine when she went to his office to collect an award on Jack's behalf. Unfortunately, this was a hope Francine didn't share.

As the world waited on tenterhooks for the official announcement on the cessation of the bloodshed in Europe, Francine did her best to avoid all of the news outlets. She wanted no more information, unless it involved Jack coming home.

"It will be a new life," she heard someone declare on the street as she got into her car. *Indeed, it will be a new life,* Francine agreed. No more air raids. No more rationing. *No more Jack.* Her eyes filled with tears. Even though her husband had been gone for more than two years, she had never felt as alone as she did now.

· · ·

As Francine drove, she reflected on what she knew of her husband's fate. After the Americans had liberated Flossenbürg, Miss Atkins had done her best to try and recover Jack's body, to no avail. The Germans had been determined to bury every trace of his existence.

In Francine's mind, she had only wanted to avoid the London crowds, but when she arrived at the coast, she realized she'd chosen it as her destination because she wanted to be as close as possible to where Jack had died.

She parked her car and then walked to the edge of a cliff and stood, contemplating the vastness of the ocean. After a few minutes, she kicked at a pile of gravel, watching as the small stones tumbled down to the water. They barely made a ripple in the tide. *Would the fish lurking below have sensed their impact?* Would the stones' existence ever have a significant influence on anything whatsoever?

She knew it wasn't really the stones she was thinking about. Her mind was begging to justify the loss of Jack. The loss of her future.

Once France had been freed in the months after D-Day, those few agents who'd survived arrest returned to London and, like Miss Atkins, they insisted the Resistance had made an impact in shortening the war. At first, Francine had taken no comfort in these reassurances, but now she had no choice but to do so.

Francine hadn't known anyone amongst the handful of remaining F Section agents; in any case, she wasn't sure she'd be able to recognize anyone from the starved, feeble beings she occasionally spied at Baker Street. Now that the concentration camps had been liberated, stories were abounding of the torture and humiliation endured by the prisoners.

Francine refused to think of Jack or Andréc—two of the most courageous people she'd ever known—being subjected to that kind of suffering. It was better to remember them at their finest, such as when they were sabotaging the Boches' railways and machines of war.

Francine picked up a bigger rock and held it above her head before hurling it at the ocean with all her might. This time it made a satisfying splash, almost as if it were exploding. *Like the electrical pylons at Chaingy.*

She cast another rock into the swirling water below. *That's for Andrée.* Another one, for France Antelme. More for Prosper, Gilbert, Nora, and the dozens of others of agents who hadn't returned. *And for the soldiers who died at the front. For the people whose entire way of life had been uprooted and had lost so many loved ones in the process.* Francine tossed every rock she could find, until she'd exhausted herself and was forced to collapse at the cliff's edge.

She laid down, staring at the sky and breathing heavily. After a while, she sat up again and shielded her eyes as she looked across the endless expanse of ocean. On the other side lay France. She took consolation in the thought that well-fed soldiers in grayish-green uniforms no longer haunted the streets of Paris. Someday, not soon, but maybe someday she'd return to the Continent to visit the places she still had fond memories of. The safehouse at 10 Square de Clignancourt, where she and Jack had spent hours playing poker with Gilbert and Andrée. The little apartment with the rickety bed where she and Jack had sought solace from the turbulent reality of Occupied France. One day she would go back to the Café Capucines and drink real coffee and toast the memories of her lost husband and their friends. Maybe she'd even travel to this mysterious Flossenbürg and try to find more information on what had happened to Jack.

Francine managed to convince herself that she had no need for revenge, only for understanding. How had the world come to endure six years of war and the loss of millions of good people like Jack and Andrée? A whole race of people had nearly been exterminated while the notion of a free world had been threatened to its core.

But it was almost over. Soon other husbands—though not hers, of course—would be coming home and restarting their lives. Jack would have been elated to hear the Allies had finally won the war. *His sacrifice must never be in vain,* Francine vowed. The world should never be allowed to reach such a point again.

There was one last pebble left on the ground. She picked it up and kissed it before letting it fall into the depths below.

Goodbye Jack. I'll love you forever.

EPILOGUE

The fall of Prosper has been considered by many historians to be the worst single disaster in the history of the French Resistance. In addition to Noor, Andrée, and Yvonne, many of the other members did not survive the war. In fact, of the 470 SOE agents sent to France, between 25-33% were killed or interned in concentration camps. More than fifty of them had been captured because of the radio games, or *Funkspiel*. They included Gilbert Norman, who was executed at Mauthausen on September 6, 1944, and Émile Garry and the Canadians Frank Pickersgill and John Macalister, who were killed at Buchenwald a few weeks later. France Antelme was executed at Gross-Rosen at the same time as his radio operator, Lionel Lee, and Alec Rabinovitch from Spindle (Peter Churchill's network). Francis Suttill, AKA Prosper, managed to survive until March 23, 1945, when he was hanged at Sachsenhausen. Jack Agazarian and Jean Worms died at Flossenbürg less than a week later and only a few days before the Americans liberated the camp.

. . .

Although **Yvonne Rudellat,** who still had a bullet lodged in her skull, contracted typhus and dysentery from the putrid conditions at Bergen-Belsen, she survived until its liberation in April 1945.

She had been recommended for a Military Cross in 1943—most likely by Prosper himself during his brief sojourn to London—but was found ineligible since it was not awarded to women at that time. She was later made an honorary Member of the British Empire (MBE). Since the award is not given posthumously, it was backdated to April 23, 1945, the last date she was known to be alive.

Andrée Borrel was awarded the Croix de Guerre and the Médaille de la Résistance by France and the King's Commendation for Brave Conduct by England.

Noor Inayat Khan was also awarded France's Croix de Guerre and was Mentioned in Dispatches in October 1946. In addition, she was one of three F-Section* women to receive Britain's George Cross, awarded for "acts of the greatest heroism or of the most conspicuous courage in circumstances of extreme danger," which her brother Vilayat and sister Claire accepted in Noor's honor in 1949.

*The other two women awarded the George Cross were Odette Churchill and Violette Szabo.

Francine Agazarian, one of the very few survivors of Prosper, died June 24, 1998, at the age of 85. As Vera Atkins said, Francine was never able to free herself "entirely from grief" over the loss of her husband. Francine finally traveled to Flossenbürg in the late 1960s to see where Jack had spent his last hours on Earth. She was Mentioned in Dispatches in 1946 for her "courage and sense of duty shown for a period of three months under most dangerous and exacting conditions."

· · ·

It has long been assumed that **Henri Déricourt**—who also managed to survive the war—was a double agent. For more on him and Sonia Olschanezky, sign up for my mailing list and be first to hear of the release of the next book in the Women Spies in WWII series: *The Embers of Resistance*!

For more information on the fates of the characters in this book, be sure to visit https://www.kitsergeant.com/?page_id=732

Read on for a sample of *L'Agent Double: Spies and Martyrs in the Great War*

SELECTED BIBLIOGRAPHY

Basu, Shrabani. *Spy Princess*. The History Press, 2011.

Binney, Marcus. *The Women Who Lived for Danger*. Harper Collins, 2004.

Foot, M. R. D. *S. O. E.* Random House, 2014.

Fuller, Jean Overton. *Noor-Un-Nisa Inayat Khan: Madeleine*. Omega Publications, 2019.

Helm, Sarah. *A Life in Secrets: Vera Atkins and the Missing Agents of WWII.*. Anchor, 2008.

---. *Ravensbrück: Life and Death in Hitler's Concentration Camp for Women*. Anchor, 2015.

King, Stella. *"Jacqueline," Pioneer Heroine of the Resistance*. Arms & Armour, 1989.

Kramer, Rita. *Flames in the Field: The Story of Four SOE Agents in Occupied France*. CreateSpace, 2010.

Magida, Arthur J. *Code Name Madeleine: A Sufi Spy in Nazi-Occupied Paris*. W. W. Norton & Company, 2020.

Marks, Leo. *Between Silk and Cyanide: A Code Makers's War, 1941-45*. The History Press, 2013.

Marshall, Robert. *All the King's Men*. A&C Black, 2012.

O'Connor, Bernard. *SOE Heroines*. 2018.

Riols, Noreen. *The Secret Ministry of Ag & Fish*. Pan Macmillan, 2013.

Rose, Sarah. *D-Day Girls: The Spies Who Armed the Resistance, Sabotaged the NAZIS, and Helped Win World War II*. Crown, 2019.

Suttill, Francis J. *Shadows in the Fog*. History Press Ltd, 2014.

L'AGENT DOUBLE PROLOGUE

OCTOBER 1917

The nun on duty woke her just before dawn. She blinked the sleep out of her eyes to see a crowd of men, including her accusers and her lawyer, standing just outside the iron bars of her cell. The only one who spoke was the chief of the Military Police, to inform her the time of her execution had come. The men then turned and walked away, leaving only the nun and the prison doctor, who kept his eyes on the dirty, straw-strewn floor as she dressed.

She chose the best outfit she had left, a bulky dove-gray skirt and jacket and scuffed ankle boots. She wound her unwashed hair in a bun and then tied the worn silk ribbons of her hat under her chin before asking the doctor, "Do I have time to write good-byes to my loved ones?"

He nodded and she hastily penned three farewell letters. She handed them to the doctor with shaking hands before lifting a dust-covered velvet cloak from a nail on the wall. "I am ready."

Seemingly out of nowhere, her lawyer reappeared. "This way," he told her as he grasped her arm.

Prison rats scurried out their way as he led her down the hall. She breathed in a heavy breath when they were outside. It had been months since she'd seen the light of day, however faint it was now.

Four black cars were waiting in the prison courtyard. A few men scattered about the lawn lifted their freezing hands to bring their cameras to life, the bulbs brightening the dim morning as her lawyer bundled her into the first car.

They drove in silence. It was unseasonably cold and the chill sent icy fingers down her spine. She stopped herself from shivering, wishing that she could experience one more warm summer day. But there would be no more warmth, no more appeals, nothing left after these last few hours.

She knew that her fate awaited her at Caponniére, the old fort just outside of Vincennes where the cavalry trained. Upon arrival, her lawyer helped her out of the car, his gnarled hands digging into her arm.

It's harder for him than it is for me. She brushed the thought away, wanting to focus on nothing but the fresh air and the way the autumn leaves of the trees next to the parade ground changed color as the sun rose. Her lawyer removed his arm from her shoulders as two Zouave escorts appeared on either side of her. Her self-imposed blinders finally dropped as she took in the twelve soldiers with guns and, several meters away, the wooden stake placed in front of a brick wall. *So that the mis-aimed bullets don't hit anything else.*

A priest approached and offered her a blindfold.

"No thank you." Her voice, which had not been used on a daily basis for months, was barely a whisper.

The priest glanced over at her lawyer, who nodded. The blindfold disappeared under his robes.

She spoke the same words to one of the escorts as he held up a rope, this time also shaking her head. She refused to be bound to the stake. He acquiesced, and walked away.

She stood as straight as she could, free of any ties, while the military chief read the following words aloud:

By decree of the Third Council of War, the woman who appears before us now has been condemned to death for espionage.

He then gave an order, and the soldiers came to attention. At the command, *"En joue!"* they hoisted their guns to rest on their shoulders. The chief raised his sword.

She took a deep breath and then lifted her chin, willing herself to die just like that: head held high, showing no fear. She watched as the chief lowered his sword and shouted *"Feu!"*

And then everything went black.

A Zouave private approached the body. He'd only been enlisted for a few weeks and had been invited to the firing squad by his commander, who told him that men of all ranks should know the pleasure of shooting a German spy.

"By blue, that lady knew how to die," another Zouave commented.

"Who was she?" the private asked. He'd been taught that everything in war was black and white: the Germans were evil, the Allies pure. But he was surprised at how gray everything was that morning: from the misty fog, to the woman's cloak and dress, and even the ashen shade of her lifeless face.

The other Zouave shrugged. "All I know is what they told me. They say she acted as a double agent and provided Germany with intelligence about our troops." He drew his revolver and bent down to place the muzzle against the woman's left temple.

"But is it necessary to kill her—a helpless woman?" the private asked.

The Zouave cocked his gun for the *coup de grâce*. "If women act as men would in war and commit heinous crimes, they should be prepared to be punished as men." And he pulled the trigger, sending a final bullet into the woman's brain

L'AGENT DOUBLE CHAPTER 1

M'GREET

JULY 1914

"*H*ave you heard the latest?" M'greet's maid, Anna, asked as she secured a custom-made headpiece to her mistress's temple.

"What now?" M'greet readjusted the gold headdress to better reflect her olive skin tone.

"They are saying that your mysterious Mr. K from the newspaper article is none other than the Crown Prince himself."

M'greet smiled at herself in the mirror. "Is that so? I rather think they're referring to Lieutenant Kiepert. Just the other day he and I ran into the editor of the *Berliner Tageblatt* during our walk in the Tiergarten." Her smile faded. "But let them wonder." For the last few weeks, the papers had been filled with speculation about why the famed Mata Hari had returned to Germany, sometimes bordering on derision about her running out of money.

She leaned forward and ran her fingers over the dark circles under her eyes. "Astruc says that he might be able to negotiate a longer engagement in the fall if tonight's performance goes well."

"It will," Anna assured her as she fastened the heavy gold necklace around M'greet's neck.

The metal felt cold against her sweaty skin. She hadn't performed in months, and guessed the perspiration derived from her nervousness. Tonight was to be the largest performance she'd booked in years: Berlin's Metropol could seat 1108 people, and the tickets had sold out days ago. The building was less than a decade old, and even the dressing room's geometric wallpaper and curved furniture reflected the Art Nouveau style the theater was famous for.

"I had to have this costume refitted." M'greet pulled at the sheer yellow fabric covering her midsection. When she first began dancing, she had worn jeweled bralettes and long, sheer skirts that sat low on the hips. But her body had become much more matronly in middle age and even M'greet knew that she could no longer get away with the scandalous outfits of her youth. She added a cumbersome earring to each ear and an arm band before someone knocked on the door.

A man's voice called urgently in German, "Fräulein Mata Hari, are you ready?"

Anna shot her mistress an encouraging smile. "Your devoted admirers are waiting."

M'greet stretched out her arms and rotated her wrists, glancing with appreciation in the mirror. She still had it. She grabbed a handful of translucent scarves and draped them over her arms and head before opening the door. "All set," she said to the awaiting attendant.

M'greet waited behind a filmy curtain while the music began: low, mournful drumming accompanied by a woman's shrill tone singing in a foreign language. As the curtain rose, she hoisted her arms above her head and stuck her hips out in the manner she had seen the women do when she lived in Java.

She had no formal dance training, but it didn't matter. People came to see Mata Hari for the spectacle, not because she was an exceptionally wonderful dancer. M'greet pulled the scarf off her head and undulated her hips in time with the music. She pinched her fingers together and moved her arms as if she were a graceful bird about to take flight. The drums heightened in intensity and her gyrations became even more exaggerated. As the music came to a dramatic stop, she released the scarves covering her body to reveal her yellow dress in full.

She was accustomed to hearing astonished murmurs from the audience following her final act—she'd once proclaimed that her success rose with every veil she threw off. Tonight, however, the Berlin audience seemed to be buzzing with protest.

As the curtain fell and M'greet began to pick up the pieces of her discarded costume, she assured herself that the Berliners' vocalizations were in response to being disappointed at seeing her more covered. Or maybe she was just being paranoid and had imagined all the ruckus.

"Fabulous!" her agent, Gabriel Astruc, exclaimed when he burst into her dressing room a few minutes later.

M'greet held a powder puff to her cheek. "Did you finalize a contract for the fall?"

"I did," Astruc sat in the only other chair, which appeared too tiny to support his large frame. "They are giving us 48,000 marks."

She nodded approvingly.

"That should tide you over for a while, no?" he asked.

She placed the puff in the gold-lined powder case. "For now. But the creditors are relentless. Thankfully Lieutenant Kieper has gifted me a few hundred francs."

"As a loan?" Astruc winked. "It is said you have become mistress to the *Kronprinz*."

She rolled her eyes. "You of all people must know to never mind such rumors. I may be well familiar with men in high positions, but have not yet made the acquaintance of the Kaiser's son."

Astruc rose. "Someday you two will meet, and even the heir of the German Empire will be unable to resist the charms of the exotic Mata Hari."

M'greet unsnapped the cap of her lipstick. "We shall see, won't we?"

Now that the fall performances had been secured, M'greet decided to upgrade her lodgings to the lavish Hotel Adlon. As she entered the lobby, with its sparkling chandeliers dangling from intricately carved ceilings and exotic potted palms scattered among velvet-cushioned chairs, she nodded to herself. *This was the type of hotel a world-renowned dancer should be found in.* She booked an apartment complete with electric Tiffany lamps and a private bathroom featuring running water.

The Adlon was known not only for its famous patrons, but for the privacy it provided them. M'greet was therefore startled the next morning when someone banged on the door to her suite.

"Yes?" Anna asked as she opened it.

"Are you Mata Hari?" a gruff voice inquired.

M'greet threw on a silky robe over her nightgown before she went to the door. "You must be looking for me."

The man in the doorway appeared to be about forty, with a receding hairline and a bushy mustache that curled upward from both sides of his mouth. "I am Herr Griebel of the Berlin police."

M'greet ignored Anna's stricken expression as she motioned for her to move aside. "Please come in." She gestured toward a chair at the little serving table. "Shall I order up some tea?"

"That won't be necessary," Griebel replied as he sat. "I am here to inform you that a spectator of your performance last night has lodged a complaint."

"A complaint? Against me?" M'greet repeated as she took a seat in the chair across from him. She mouthed, "tea," at Anna, who was still standing near the door. Anna nodded and then left the room.

"Indeed," Griebel touched his mustache. "A complaint of indecency."

"I see." She leaned forward. "You are part of the *Sittenpolizei*, then." They were a department charged with enforcing the Kaiser's so-called laws of morality. M'greet had been visited a few times in the past by such men, but nothing had ever come of it. She flashed Griebel a seductive smile. "Surely your department has no issue with sacred dances?"

"Ah," Griebel fidgeted with the collar of his uniform, clearly uncomfortable.

Mirroring his movements, M'greet fingered the neckline of her low-cut gown. "After all, there are more important issues going on in the world than my little dance."

"Such as?" Griebel asked.

The door opened and Anna discreetly placed a tea set on the crisp white tablecloth. She gave her mistress a worried look but M'greet waved her off before pouring Griebel a cup of tea. "Well, I'm sure you heard about that poor man that was shot in the Balkans in June."

"Of course—it's been in all of the papers. The 'poor man,' as you call him, was Archduke Franz Ferdinand. Austria should not stand down when the heir to their throne was shot by militant Serbs."

M'greet took a sip of tea. "Are you saying they should go to war?"

"They should. And Germany, as Austria's ally, ought to accompany them."

"Over one man? You cannot be serious."

"Those Serbs need to be taught a lesson, once and for all." Upon seeing the pout on M'greet's face, Griebel waved his hand. "But you shouldn't worry your pretty little head over talk of politics."

She pursed her lips. "You're right. It's not something that a woman like me should be discussing."

"No." He set down his tea cup and pulled something out of his pocket. "As I was saying when I first came in, about the complaint—"

"As *I* was saying..." she faked a yawn, stretching her arms out while sticking out her bosom. The stocky, balding Griebel was not nearly as handsome as some of the men she'd met over the years, but M'greet knew that she needed to become better acquainted with him in order to get the charges dropped. Besides, she'd always had a weakness for men in uniform. "My routine is adopted from Hindu religious dances and should not be misconstrued as immoral." She placed a hand over Griebel's thick fingers, causing the paper to fall to the floor. "I think, if the two of us put our heads together, we can definitely find a mutual agreement."

He pulled his hand away to wipe his forehead with a handkerchief. "I don't know if that's possible."

M'greet got up from her chair to spread herself on the bed, displaying her body to its advantage as a chef would his best dish.

"Perhaps we could work out an arrangement that would benefit us both," Griebel agreed as he walked over to her.

Griebel's mustache tickled her face, but she forced herself to think about other things as he kissed her. Her thoughts at such moments often traveled to her daughter, Non, but today she focused on the other night's performance. M'greet always did what it took to survive, and right now she needed the money that her contract with the Berlin Metropol would provide, and nothing could get in the way of that.

M'greet was glad to count Herr Griebel as her new lover as the tensions between the advocates of the Kaiser—who wanted to "finish with the Serbs quickly"—and the pacifists determined to keep Germany out of war heightened throughout Berlin at the end of July. Although Griebel was on the side of the war-mongers, M'greet felt secure traveling on his arm every night on their way to Berlin's most popular venues.

It was in the back room at one such establishment, the Borchardt, that she met some of Griebel's cronies. They had gathered to talk about the recent developments—Austria-Hungary had officially declared war on Serbia. M'greet knew her place was to look pretty and say nothing, but at the same time she couldn't help but listen to what they were discussing.

"I've heard that Russia has mobilized her troops," a heavyset, balding man stated. M'greet recalled that his name was Müller.

"Ah," Griebel sat back in the plush leather booth. "That's the rub, now isn't it?"

Herr Vogel, Griebel's closest compatriot, shook his head. "I'd hoped Russia would stay out of it." He flicked ash from his cigar into a nearby tray. "After all, the Kaiser and the Tsar are cousins."

"No," Müller replied. "Those Serbs went crying to Mother Russia, and she responded." He nodded to himself. "Now it's only a matter of time before we jump in to protect Austria."

As if on cue, the sound of breaking glass was heard.

M'greet ended her silence. "What was that?"

Griebel put a protective hand on her arm. "I'm not sure." He used his other arm to flag down a passing waiter. "What is going on?"

The young man looked panic-stricken. "There is a demonstration on the streets. Someone threw a brick through the front window and our owner is asking all of the patrons to leave."

"Has war broken out?" M'greet inquired of Griebel as she pulled her arm away. His grip had left white marks.

"I'm not sure." He picked up her fur shawl and headed to the main room of the restaurant. Pandemonium reigned as Berlin's elite rushed toward the doors. Discarded feathers from fashionable ladies' hats and boas floated through the air and littered the ground before stamping feet stirred them up again. M'greet wished she hadn't shaken off Griebel's arm as now she was being shoved this way and that. Someone trampled over her dress and she heard the sound of ripping lace.

She nearly tripped before a strong hand landed on her elbow. "This way," the young waiter told her. He led her through the kitchen and out the back door, where Griebel's Benz was waiting. Griebel appeared a few minutes later and the driver told him there was a massive protest outside the Kaiser's palace.

"Let's go there," Griebel instructed.

"No." M'greet wrapped the fur shawl around her shoulders. "Take me home first."

"Don't you want to find out what's happening?" Griebel demanded, waving his hand as a crowd of people thronged the streets. "This could be the beginning of a war the likes of which no one has ever seen."

"No," she repeated. It seemed to her that the Great Powers of Europe: Germany, Russia, France, and possibly England, were entering into a scrap they had no business getting involved with. "I don't care about any war and I've had enough tonight. I want to go home."

Griebel gave her a strange look but motioned for the driver to do as she said.

They were forced to drive slowly, as the streets had become jammed with motor cars, horse carts, and people rushing about on foot. M'greet caught what they were chanting as the crowd marched past. She repeated the words aloud: "*Deutschland über alles.*"

"Germany over all," Griebel supplied.

The war came quickly. Germany first officially declared war on Russia to the east and two days later did the same to France in the west. In Berlin, so-called bank riots occurred as people rushed to their financial institutions and emptied their savings accounts, trading paper money for gold and silver coins. Prices for food and other necessities soared as people stocked up on goods while they could still afford them.

Worried about her own fate, M'greet placed several calls to her agent, Astruc, wanting to know if the war meant her fall performances would be cancelled. After leaving many messages, she eventually got word that Astruc had fled town, presumably with the money the Metropol had paid her in advance.

She decided to brave the confusion at the bank in order to withdraw what little funds she had left.

"I'm sorry," the teller informed M'greet when she finally made it to the counter. "It looks as though your account has been blocked."

"How can you say that?" she demanded. "There should be plenty of money in my account." The plenty part might not have been strictly true, but there was no way it was empty.

"The address you gave when you opened the account was in Paris. We cannot give funds to any foreigner at this time."

M'greet put both fists on the counter. "I wish to speak with your manager."

The teller gestured behind her. M'greet glanced back to see a long line of people, their exhausted, bewildered faces beginning to glower. "I'm sorry, fräulein, I can do nothing more."

She opened her mouth to let him have the worst of her fury, but a man in a police uniform appeared beside her. "A foreigner you say?" He pulled M'greet out of the bank line, and roughly turned her to face him. "What are you, a Russian?"

M'greet knew her dark hair and coloring was not typical of someone with Dutch heritage, but this was a new accusation. "I am no such thing."

"Russian, for sure," a man standing in line agreed.

"Her address was in France," the teller called before accepting a bank card from the next person.

"Well, Miss Russian Francophile, you are coming with me." For the second time in a week, a strange man put his hand on M'greet's elbow and led her away.

M'greet fumed all the way to the police station. She'd had enough of Berlin: due to this infernal war, she was now void of funds and it looked as though her engagements were to be cancelled. She figured her best course of action would be to return to Paris and use her connections to try to get some work there.

When they arrived at the police station, M'greet immediately asked for Herr Griebel. He appeared a few minutes later, a wry smile on his face. "You've been arrested under suspicion of being a troublesome alien."

M'greet waved off that comment with a brush of her hand. "We both know that's ridiculous. Can you secure my release as soon as possible? I must get back to Paris before my possessions there are seized."

Griebel's amused smile faded as his lip curled into a sneer. "You cannot travel to an enemy country in the middle of a war."

"Why not?"

The sneer deepened. "Because..." His narrowed eyes suddenly softened. "Come with me. There is someone I want you to meet." He led her to an office that occupied the end of a narrow hallway and knocked on the closed door labeled, *Traugott von Jagow, Berliner Polizei.*

"Come in," a voice growled.

Griebel entered and then saluted.

The man behind the desk had a thin face and heavy mustache which drooped downward. "What is it, Herr Griebel? You must know I am extremely busy." He dipped a pen in ink and began writing.

Griebel lowered his arm. "Indeed, sir, but I wanted you to meet the acclaimed Mata Hari."

Von Jagow paused his scribbling and looked up. His eyes traveled down from the feather atop M'greet's hat and stopped at her chest. "Wasn't there a morality complaint filed against you?"

M'greet stepped forward, but before she could protest, Griebel cleared his throat. "We are here because she wants to return to Paris."

Von Jagow gave a loud "harrumph," and then continued his writing. "You are not the first person to ask such a question, but we can't let anyone cross the border into enemy territory at this time. People would think you were a spy." He abruptly stopped writing and set his pen down. "A courtesan with a flair for seducing powerful men..." He shot a meaningful look at Griebel, who stared at the floor. "And a long-term resident of Paris with admittedly low morals." He finally met M'greet's eyes. "We could use a woman like you. I'm forming a network of agents who can provide us information about the goings-on in France."

M'greet tried to keep the horror from showing on her face. Was this man asking her to be a spy for Germany? "No thank you," she replied. "As I told Herr Griebel, I have no interest in the war. I just want to get back to Paris."

Von Jagow crossed his arms and sat back. "And I can help you with that, provided that you agree to work for me."

She shook her head and spoke in a soft voice. "Thank you, sir, but it seems I'll have to find a way back on my own."

"Very well, then." Von Jagow picked up his pen again. "Good luck." His voice implied that he wished her just the opposite.

L'AGENT DOUBLE CHAPTER 2

MARTHE

*M*arthe Cnockaert didn't think anything could spoil this year's Kermis. People had been arriving in Westroze-beke for days from all over Belgium. She herself had just returned home from her medical studies at Ghent University on holiday and had nearly been overcome by the tediousness of living in her small village again. She gazed around the garland-bedecked Grand Place lined with colorful vendor booths in satisfaction. The rest of Europe may have plunged into war, but Belgium had vowed to remain neutral, and the mayor declared that the annual Kermis would be celebrated just as it had been since the middle ages.

The smell of pie wafted from a booth as Marthe passed by and the bright notes of a hurdy-gurdy were audible over the noise of the crowd. She had just entered the queue for the carousel when she heard someone call, "Marthe!"

She turned at the sound of her name to see Valerie, a girl she had known since primary school. "Marthe, how are you? How is Max?" As usual, Valerie was breathless, as though she had recently run a marathon, but it appeared she'd only just gotten off the carousel.

Marthe refrained from rolling her eyes. "Max is still in Ghent, finishing up his studies." Valerie had never hidden the fact she'd always had a crush on Marthe's older brother, even after she'd become betrothed to Nicholas Hoot.

Valerie sighed as she looked around. "There's nobody here but women, children, and old men. All the boys our age have gone off to war and now there's no one left to flirt with."

"Where is Nicholas?"

"He was called to Liége. I suppose you've heard that Germany is demanding safe passage through Belgium in order to get to Paris."

"No."

Valerie shrugged. "They are saying we might have to join the war if Germany decides to invade. But the good news is some treaty states that England would have to enter on our side if that happened."

"Join the war?" Marthe was shocked at both the information and the fact that Valerie seemed so nonchalant about it. There were a few beats of silence, broken only by the endless tune from the carousel's music box, as Marthe pondered this.

"Ah, Marthe, I see you have returned from university." Meneer Hoot, an old friend of her father's, and Valerie's future father-in-law, was nearly shouting, both because he was hard of hearing and because the carousel had started spinning.

"Yes, indeed. I am home for a few weeks before I finish my last year of nursing school," Marthe answered loudly. "Glad to see you are doing well. How is your wife?"

"Oh, you know. Terrified at the prospect of a German invasion, but aren't we all?"

Marthe gave him and Valerie a tentative smile as the church bell rang the hour. "I must be getting home to help Mother with dinner."

. . .

Marthe knew something was wrong as soon as she entered the kitchen. "What is it?" she asked, glancing at her father's somber face.

"It's the Germans. They have invaded Belgium."

Marthe fell into her chair. Mother stood in the corner of the room, ironing a cap.

"Belgium has ordered our troops to Liége." Father sank his head into his hands. "But we could never defend ourselves against those bloody Boches."

Mother set her iron down and then took a seat at the kitchen table. "What about Max? Will he come home from Ghent?"

Father took his hands away from his face. "I don't know. I don't know anything now."

"I suppose we should send for him," Marthe said.

Mother cast a worried glance at Father before nodding at her daughter.

For the first time Marthe could remember, Kermis ended before the typical eight days. That didn't stop the endless train of people coming into Westrozebeke, however. The newcomers were refugees from villages near Liége and were headed to Ypres, 15 kilometers southwest, where they had been told they could find food and shelter.

Max sent word that he would be traveling in the opposite direction. He was going to Liége, a town on the Belgian/German border that was protected by a series of concrete fortifications. The Germans were supposedly en route there as well. Both Father and Mother were saddened by Max's decision to enlist in the army, but Marthe understood the circumstances: Belgium must be defended at all costs. She wrote her brother a letter stating the same and urged him to be careful.

As Westrozebeke became a temporary camp, Marthe's family's house and barn, like many of the other houses in the village, were quickly packed with the unfortunate evacuees. Soon the news that Liége had fallen came, and not long after, the first of the soldiers who had been cut off from the main Belgian army arrived.

Marthe stood on the porch and watched a few of them straggle through town. Their frayed uniforms were covered in dark splotches, some of it dirt, some of it blood. Their faces were unshaven, their skin filthy, but the worst part was that none of them were Max.

Upon spotting Nicholas Hoot's downtrodden form, Marthe rushed into the street. "Have you heard from Max?" she asked.

Nicholas met her eyes. His were wide and terrified, holding a record of past horrors, as though he had seen the devil himself. "No."

"C'mon," Marthe put his heavy arm over her shoulders. "Let's get you home."

Mevrouw Hoot greeted them at the door. "Nicholas, my son." She hugged his gaunt body before leading him inside.

After his second cup of tea, Nicholas could croak out a few sentences. After a third cup and some biscuits, he was able to relay the horrific conditions the Belgian soldiers had experienced at Liége, especially the burning inferno of Fort de Loncin, which had been hit by a shell from one of the German's enormous guns, known as Big Bertha. De Loncin had been the last of the twelve forts around Liége to yield to the Boches.

"Do you know what happened to Max?" Marthe asked.

Nicholas shook his head. "I never saw him. But it was a very confusing time." His cracked lips formed into something that resembled his old smile. "The Germans are terrified of *francs-tireurs* and think every Belgian civilian is a secret sniper out to get them." The smile quickly faded. "The Fritzes dragged old men and teenagers into the square, accusing them of shooting at their troops. It was mostly their own men mistakenly firing upon each other, but no matter. They killed the innocent villagers anyway." He set his tea cup down. "The Huns are blood-thirsty and vicious, and they are headed this way. We should flee further west as soon as possible."

Mevrouw Hoot met Marthe's eyes. "I'll tell Father," Marthe stated before taking her leave.

Mother was ready to depart, but Father was reluctant, stating that if Max did come home, he would find his family gone. Marthe agreed and disagreed with both sides. On the one hand, she wanted to wait for her brother, and judge for herself if the Germans were as terrible as Nicholas had said. On the other hand, if he was indeed correct, they should go as far west as possible.

The argument became moot when Marthe was awakened the next morning by an unearthly piercing noise overhead. The shrieks grew louder until the entire house shook with the crescendo, and then there was an even more disturbing silence.

Marthe tossed on her robe and then rushed downstairs. No one was in the kitchen, so she pulled Max's old boots over her bare feet and ran the few blocks to the Grand Place. She could see the mushroom cloud of black smoke was just beginning to clear.

She nearly tripped in her oversized boots when she saw someone lying in the roadway. It was Mevrouw Visser, one of her elderly neighbors. She bent over the bloodied body, but the woman had already passed.

The sound of horse hooves caused Marthe to look up. She froze as she saw the men atop were soldiers in unfamiliar khaki uniforms.

"Hallo," called a man with a thin mustache and a flat red cap. He stopped his horse short of Mevrouw Visser. "Met her maker, has she?" The way he ended the sentence with a question that didn't expect an answer made Marthe realize the British had arrived. The men paused at similarly lying bodies, giving food and water to those who still clung to life, but after an hour or so, they rode off.

Marthe went home, her robe now tattered and soiled, her feet sweaty in her boots. "What now?" she asked her father, who was seated at the kitchen table, also covered in perspiration, dirt, and blood.

"Now we wait for Max."

A knock sounded on the front door and Marthe went to answer it, fearing that she would greet a Hun in a spiked helmet. But the soldier outside was in a blue uniform. "The bloody Boches are on their way," he stated in a French accent. "You must flee the village, mademoiselle."

She glanced at Father, who was still sitting at the kitchen table. "I cannot."

The French soldier took a few steps backward to peer at the second floor before returning his gaze back to her. "Our guns will arrive soon, but we are only a small portion of our squadron, and cannot possibly hope to hold them for long. We are asking the villagers to allow us access to their homes in order to take aim."

She nodded and opened the door. He marched into the kitchen and spoke to her father.

Marthe went outside, and looked up and down the street, which was now dotted with soldiers in the blue uniforms of the French. The sound of hammering permeated the air. The soldier she had spoken to went upstairs to pound small viewing holes into the wood of the rooms facing the street. She helped Father barricade the windows and front door with furniture.

Marthe and her parents sequestered themselves in her bedroom, which faced the back of the house. Although half of her was frightened, the other was intensely curious as to what would happen. She used her father's telescope to peer through a loophole in the wood-barricaded window.

"I see them!" she shouted as a gray mass came into view.

"Marthe, get down!" her father returned.

She reluctantly retired the telescope, but not before she peered outside again. The masses had become individual men topped by repulsive-looking spiked helmets. There were hundreds of them and they were headed straight for the Grand Place.

The windows rattled as the hooves of an army of horses came closer. Marthe knew that many of those carts were filled with the Boches' giant guns.

The French machine guns, known as *mitrailleuse,* began an incessant rattling. *Rat-a-tat-tat:* ad infinitum. Marthe couldn't help herself and peeped through the hole again, watching as the gray mob started running, men falling from the fire of the *mitrailleuse.*

Mother's face was stricken as a bullet tore through the wood inches above her daughter's head. Wordlessly Father grabbed both of their hands to bring them downstairs. At the foot of the stairs was a French soldier rocking back and forth, clutching his stomach. Father tried to pull Marthe toward the cellar, but she paused when she saw the blood spurting from the soldier's stomach. All of her university training thus far had not prepared her for this horrific sight, his cntrails beginning to spill out of the wound, but she reached out with trembling fingers to prop him against the wall. "You must keep still."

His distraught eyes met hers as he managed to croak out one word. "Water."

Marthe knew that water would only add to his suffering. The sound of gunfire grew closer, and Father yanked her away.

They had just reached the cellar when a shell sounded and a picce of plaster from the wall landed near Father. He struck a match and lit his pipe. "Courage," he said. "The French will beat them back," but the defeated tone of his voice told Marthe that he did not believe it to be so. Nothing could stay that rushing deluge of gray regiments she had spotted from the window.

When the *mitrailleuse* finally ceased its firing, Marthe crept upstairs to retrieve water. The man at the stairs had succumbed to death, and there seemed no sign of any live blue-clad soldiers anywhere in the house. The hallway glistened with blood and there were a few spots where bullets had broken through the exterior wall. An occasional shot could still be heard outside, but it sounded much more distant now. Marthe glanced at her watch. It was only two o'clock in the afternoon.

The front door burst open and she turned to see a bedraggled young man standing in the doorway with his eyes narrowed. Something in the distance caught the sunlight and she glimpsed many men on the lawn, their bayonets gleaming. Marthe marveled that the sun had the audacity to shine on such a day.

The soldier before her holstered his revolver and spoke in broken French. *"Qui d'autre est dans cette maison avec vous?"* He marched into the room, a band of his comrades behind him. Marthe assumed he was the captain, or *hauptmann*. The men outside sat down and lit cigarettes.

She felt no fear at the arrival of the disheveled German and his troops, only an unfamiliar numbness. She replied in German that her parents were downstairs.

"There are loopholes in the walls of this house," the captain stated. "Your father is a *franc-tireur.*"

Marthe recalled what Nicholas had said about the Hun's irrational fear of civilian sharpshooters. "My father is an old man and has never fired a shot at anyone, and especially not today. The French soldiers who were here were the ones shooting but they have gone."

"I have heard that story many times before. Yours is not the first village we have entered."

You mean demolished, Marthe corrected him silently.

"Fourteen of my men were shot, and the gunfire from this house was responsible. If those men who were with him have run, then your father alone will suffer."

"No, please, Hauptmann." But the captain was already on his way to the cellar. Two other burly men stalked after him. Marthe was about to pursue them when the first man appeared on the steps, dragging her mother. The other soldier, a sergeant judging by the gold braid on his uniform, followed with her father, who held his still smoldering pipe.

The soldiers shoved her parents against the wall of the hallway. Marthe bit her lip to keep herself from crying out in indignation, knowing that it couldn't possibly help the situation they were in. She cursed herself for her earlier curiosity and then cursed fate for the circumstances of having these enemy men standing in her kitchen, wishing to do harm to her family. If only they had left when Nicholas gave her that warning!

"Take that damned pipe out of your mouth," the sergeant commanded Father.

The soldier who had manhandled Mother grabbed it from him, knocking the ash out on Father's boot before he pocketed the pipe with a chuckle.

"Old man, you are a *franc-tireur*," the captain declared.

Father shook his head while Mother sobbed quietly.

"Be merciful," Marthe begged the captain. "You have no proof."

"You dare to argue with me, fräulein? This place has been a hornet's nest of sharpshooters." He turned to one of the men. "Feldwebel, see that this house is burned down immediately."

The sergeant left out the door, motioning to some of the smoking men to follow him to the storage shelter in the back of the house, where the household oil was kept.

"Hauptmann—" Father began, but the captain silenced him by holding up his hand. "As for you, old man, you can bake in your own oven!" He dropped his arm. "Gefreiter, lock him in the cellar."

The corporal seized Father and kicked him down the steps, sending a load of spit after him.

"Filthy *franc-tireur*, he will get what he deserves," the corporal stated as he slammed the door to the cellar.

Mother collapsed and Marthe rushed to her. "You infernal butchers," she hissed at the men.

"Quiet, fräulein," the captain responded, taking out a packet of cigarettes. "Our job is to end this war quickly, and rid the country-side of any threats to our army, especially from civilians who take it upon themselves to shoot our soldiers. "

The feldwebel and two other men entered the house carrying drums of oil. Mother gave a strangled cry as they marched into the living room and began to pour oil over the fine furniture.

The captain nodded approvingly before casting his eyes back to Marthe and her mother. "You women are free to go. I will grant you five minutes to collect any personal belongings, but you are not permitted to enter the cellar. Do not leave the village or there will be trouble." He lit his cigarette before dropping the match on the dry kitchen floor. It went out, but Marthe knew it was only a matter of time before he did the same in the living room where the oil had been spilled.

Marthe ran upstairs, casting her eyes helplessly around when she reached the landing. *What should she take?* She threw together a bundle of clothes for her and Mother, and, at the last second, took her father's best suit off the hanger. She shouldered the bundle and then went back downstairs, grabbing Mother's hand. They went outside to the street to gaze dazedly at their home where Father lay prisoner in the cellar.

The German soldiers walked quickly out of the house, carrying some of the Cnockaert's food. Gray smoke started coming from the living room. Soon reddish-orange flames rose up, the tongues easily destroying the barricaded windows. Marthe put her hands on the collar of her jacket and began to shed it.

"What are you doing?" Mother asked, her voice unnaturally shrill.

"Father's in there. I have to try to save him."

Mother tugged Marthe's jacket back over her shoulders. "No," was all she said. Marthe lowered her shoulders in defeat. As she stared at the conflagration, trying not to picture her poor father's body burning alive, she made a vow to herself that she wouldn't let the Germans get the best of her, no matter what other horrors they tried to commit.

Eventually Mother led Marthe away from the sight of their burning home and down the street to the Grand Place. The café adjacent to the square was filled with gray-uniformed men who sang obscene songs in coarse voices. A hiccupping private staggered in the direction of Marthe and Mother as the men in the café jeered at him. Marthe pulled her mother into the square to avoid the drunken soldier.

The abandoned Kermis booths had now become makeshift hospital beds for wounded Germans. The paving stones were soaked in blood and perspiring doctors rushed around, pausing to bend over men writhing in pain. In the corner was a crowd of soldiers in bloodied French uniforms. Marthe headed over, noticing another, smaller group of women and children she recognized as fellow

THE FLAMES OF RESISTANCE

villagers. She had just put her hand on a girl's forehead when a German barked at her to move on.

"Where should we go?" Mother asked in a small voice.

Marthe shook her head helplessly, catching her eye on Meneer Hoot's large home on the other side of the square. They walked quickly toward it, noting the absence of smoke in the vicinity. Marthe reached her fist out to knock when the door was swung open.

Marthe's heart rose at seeing the man behind the door. "Father!"

"Shh," he said, ushering them into the house.

"How on earth—" Marthe began when they were safely ensconced in the entryway of the Hoot home.

"I took apart the bricks from the air vent. Luckily the hauptmann and his men were watching the inferno on the other side of the house."

Mother hugged him tightly, looking for all the world like she would never let him go. Father brought them into the kitchen, where Meneer and Mevrouw Hoot greeted them. Several other neighbors, including Valerie, were also gathered in the kitchen, and they waited in a bewildered silence until darkness fell.

Meneer Hoot finally rose out of his chair. Taking the pipe from his mouth, he stated, "We have had no food this morning, and I'm sure it is the same for you all. Unfortunately," he swung his arms around, "the bloody Boches ransacked our house and there is nothing to eat here." He put the pipe in his mouth and gave it a puff before continuing, "I am going to get food somehow."

Mevrouw Hoot clutched his arm. "No, David, you cannot go out there."

Father also rose. "I will join you."

Meneer Hoot shook his head. "No, it is safer for me to go alone."

Mother gave a sigh of relief while Mevrouw Hoot appeared as though she would burst into tears. Meneer Hoot slipped a dark overcoat on and left through the back door.

An eternity seemed to pass as they sat in the dark kitchen, illuminated only by the sliver of moon that had replaced the sun. The silence was occasionally broken by Mevrouw Hoot's sobbing.

Marthe was nodding off when she heard the back door slam. Someone lit a candle, and Marthe saw the normally composed Meneer Hoot hold up a bulky object wrapped in blood-stained newspaper. His rumpled trousers were covered in burrs and his eyes were wild-eyed. He tossed the bulk and it landed on the kitchen table with a thud.

Mevrouw Hoot unwrapped the package to reveal a grayish sort of meat from an unfamiliar animal.

"I cut it from one of the Boches' dead horses," Meneer Hoot told them in a triumphant whisper. He lit a fire and put the horse-meat on a spit. Marthe wasn't sure if she could eat a dead horse but soon changed her mind as the room filled with the smell of cooking meat. Her stomach grumbled in anticipation.

Just then the kitchen window shattered. Marthe looked up to see a rifle butt nudging the curtain aside. The spikes of German helmets shone in the moonlight beyond the window. The Hoots' entire backyard teemed with them.

"We must get downstairs, now!" Meneer Hoot shouted. He grabbed his wife and rushed her into the hallway. Father did the same with Mother, and Marthe followed, stumbling down the steps to the Hoots' cellar.

To Marthe's amazement, she saw the large room was already nearly filled with other refugees—men, women, and children of all ages—with dirty, tear-stained faces.

The sound of many boots thundered overhead and it wasn't long before the Germans once again stood among them. One of them pointed his rifle at the opposite wall and shot off a clip, the bullets ricocheting around the room, followed by wild screaming. Somebody had been hit, a child Marthe guessed sorrowfully by the tone of its wail.

She wanted to go aid the poor creature, but she felt the sharp point of a bayonet at her chest. "Get upstairs," the bayonet wielder sneered.

The soldiers lined up the cellar's occupants outside, and separated out the men. Without allowing a word of parting, the Germans led the men of the village down the hill, and Marthe watched Father's lank form until she could no longer see him. The remaining soldiers shepherded the women and children back down into the Hoot's now blood-covered cellar.

L'AGENT DOUBLE CHAPTER 3

ALOUETTE

AUGUST 1914

The smell of gasoline and the wind in Alouette's hair was as intoxicating as ever. She eased back on the stick of her Caudron, enjoying the adrenaline rush that always ensued when the plane rose higher. The French countryside below appeared just like the maps in her husband's office: the rivers, railroads, even the villages seemingly unchanged from her vantage point. The world beneath her might soon be engaged in combat, but, a few thousand meters above the ground, she was alone in the sky, the universe at her beck and call. She flew along the Somme Bay at the edge of the English Channel, marveling at the beautiful beaches and marshes that must be thronging with wildlife.

After half an hour, she began heading back to the Le Crotoy aerodrome to land, using the coastline as a navigation guide. She held the tail of the Caudron low and glided downward.

. . .

Alouette found the aerodrome in a state of commotion, with men running all about on the ground. As she turned the engine off, Gaston Caudron, the inventor of the plane, climbed up the ladder to stare into the cockpit.

"What's going on?" Alouette shouted over the noise. It sounded as though every plane in the aerodrome was running.

"We're taking the planes to the war zone."

"Okay." Alouette refastened her seatbelt and tilted her head, indicating she was ready for Caudron to spin the prop to start the plane up again.

His eyes, already jaundiced, bugged out even more. "You can't possibly think you can go to war."

"This is my plane."

He held up a hand to his mouth and coughed. "As I recall, I designed it for your husband."

"You know that Henri lets me fly it any time I want to." She tapped the ignition switch with impatience.

"Still, civilians can't fly planes during wartime." His voice softened. "You wouldn't want to hurt the war effort, would you Madame Richer?"

Alouette's hand dropped to her side. "No. No I would not."

Caudron stepped as close as he could to the edge of the ladder as she climbed out of the plane. "I guess I'll see about my motor-car in the garage at Rue," she said, navigating down the ladder as Caudron arranged himself in the cockpit.

"You'll find it a challenge to get back to Paris—all the petrol supplies have been requisitioned for the army."

"I'll be able to get as far as Amiens," she said, jumping down to the ground. "After that I shall find a way to manage, somehow."

"Good luck," Caudron replied ominously as he started the engine.

She saluted as he pulled her plane out of the aerodrome.

Alouette estimated that her car had enough petrol to carry her 30 miles, figuring she could stop at the aerodrome in Amiens, or at least a garage somewhere along the route to Paris. But near Picquigny, the car began to sputter and soon stopped completely. Alouette walked a few miles and was relieved to find a garage, albeit looking abandoned. She knocked on the closed shutters of the attached house.

A woman's hand opened the window a sliver. "Yes?"

"Can you please tell me, madame, where the mechanic is?"

The woman opened the window enough to eye Alouette up and down, from the lace neckline of her fashionable dress to the flower-trimmed hat she had donned after changing out of her flight gear. "He's gone to war," the woman finally replied.

Alouette got a similar response from the next garage she tried. One elderly woman seated on her porch did not appear as hostile and Alouette called out to her. "Do you have any vehicle I could use to take me to Amiens? My car has stalled and I need to find a mechanic."

The woman appeared likely to flee back into the house, so Alouette pulled her wallet out of her purse. "I can pay you."

Alouette soon found herself in the back of a hay cart pulled by reluctant horses, and being jolted from side to side at every rut in the road. They had to pull into the ditch almost every mile, at least it seemed to Alouette, as regiment after regiment of soldiers passed them, heading north. They drove by several villages in turmoil, the residents packing every belonging they owned onto motor-cars, rickety carts similar to the one Alouette found herself in, or even on the backs of donkeys.

"Why are you leaving?" Alouette called to one man as he balanced his rocking chair on a small wagon.

"The Germans are advancing toward the Marne," the man replied, the terror obvious in his voice.

Alouette tipped her flowered hat and focused her eyes on the road ahead of them. She had to get back to Paris as soon as possible.

The farm woman pulled back on the reins when they reached

the aerodrome, about half a mile outside of Amiens. "You sure this is where you want to be?" she asked, eyeing the aerodrome. The doors had been left open, revealing its nearly empty chambers inside.

"Yes, madame." Alouette placed a few extra bills into the farm woman's hand. "If you could just wait a minute."

The farm woman gave a deep sigh before nodding her acquiescence.

When Alouette entered the practically deserted cavern, she heard someone call, "Madame Richer! Whatever are you doing here?"

As she turned, she caught sight of the well-built Captain Jeanneros. "Oh, Captain, is it possible for you to send a mechanic to help me with my car? It has stalled on the road."

The captain threw his head back and laughed. "Only such things could happen to you, Madame Richer. The Germans are pushing toward here and I only have a few litres of petrol left. Of course, you can have some if you need it. But as for the mechanic, I cannot spare one. I'm very sorry, but I'm the last of the squadron now. All the others have gone."

Alouette sighed. "I'm not sure the petrol will do me much good if I cannot get my motor-car fixed."

Captain Jeanneros scratched his head. "I can give you one tip, madame. Do not stay long in this district, or soon you may find it impossible to leave at all."

They had passed the first houses in Picquigny on the return journey when Alouette heard the farm woman suck in her breath. Alouette sat straighter in the cart, catching sight of a crowd assembled in the spot where she'd left the car. To her horror, she noted two armed gendarmes approaching.

"Now you've really done it," the farm woman muttered.

The gendarmes paused near the back of the cart. "Hand over your papers," the shorter one commanded.

Alouette did as she was bid, her heart racing. She garnered that her presence in the back of the farm cart, combined with her Parisian attire, not to mention her presence in the war zone, must have looked suspicious to the rural population of Picquigny.

The short gendarme folded Alouette's papers and tucked them into the pocket of his uniform.

"Sir," the farm woman spoke up. She hesitated for a brief second before resignedly pointing a gnarled finger to the cans of fuel in the rear of the cart.

Alouette's heart sank at her escort's sudden betrayal.

"Where did you get that petrol?" the other officer demanded. "Why are you harboring fuel when the Allies are in desperate need of it?"

"Monsieur—" Alouette attempted an explanation, but the short gendarme cut her off. "You must come with us." He gave a sharp whistle and the farm woman set the horse in motion, both officers keeping pace on either side of the cart.

"Death to the spy!" an old man shouted as the crowd of villagers also started moving forward.

Alouette felt terror rise in her chest. The mob swirled around the cart like an ocean tide. The villagers had already deemed her a traitor and any attempt she made to contradict them would be futile.

She was under arrest.

The mob of villagers followed the gendarme-escorted farm cart to the police station.

One of the gendarmes pulled Alouette out of the cart. "Lynch the spy!" someone shouted as a spray of gravel landed at her feet. She looked up to meet the angry glare of a white-haired man. The tears that gathered in her eyes did not soften him—if anything, they seemed to be an admission of guilt—and he drew back his arm to launch the next cluster of rocks. "Die, double-crosser!" This time a sharp stone connected with Alouette's jaw and the tears coursed their way down her face.

Although the villagers were not permitted into the police station, the window in the room where Alouette was taken for questioning stood open and the crowd gathered outside of it.

The evidence of Alouette's supposed damnation was spread out on the table. Her revolver was placed prominently in the center, surrounded by the cans of petrol and the documentation she had presented to the gendarme.

An older officer sat himself at the table across from the still-standing Alouette. "Name?" he demanded.

"Alouette Richer," she replied, a hint of pride in her voice. She briefly crossed her fingers behind her back, hoping he would recognize her name from the newspapers.

The village gendarme gave no sign of appreciation as he copied it down. "Sit."

She fell into a chair with a sigh. She had recently flown from Crotoy to Zürich, to great fanfare, and the Parisian papers followed her triumphs, publishing several articles and photographs of her in aviator gear standing beside her plane. But now that war had come, a curtain had dropped over everything that had occurred before its outbreak.

"You have no right to a revolver," the officer commented, a growl in his voice. "How did you come by it?"

"My husband, Henri Richer, gave it to me. He knew I'd be traveling alone and wanted to ensure my safety."

Once again, the gendarme showed no recognition of the name. "Let me see your handbag."

Reluctantly, she passed it across the table.

He dug out her wallet and pulled out a wad of bills. "Who gave you all this money?"

Alouette bit back another sigh. She supposed the 300 francs in her wallet was a small fortune to the country inspector, who probably earned less than half that in a month.

"I am not a spy," she insisted. "My husband is a wealthy man…"

"I know, I know," the gendarme held up his hand. "He must have given you all that money to ensure your safety." He rose heavily to his feet. "What he didn't understand was how incriminating carrying that amount of cash would be in a warzone. I have no choice but to detain you."

"But monsieur—"

"Pending further inquiries, of course," the inspector remarked as he shut the door behind him.

Alouette was left in the room for over half an hour. She used that time to compose herself. The last thing she wanted was to show fear to the men at the station. Indeed, when a younger officer at last unlocked the door, she kept the expression on her face neutral. He escorted her to an empty cell.

Alouette patted the pillow and then spread her skirts prettily before she sat on the bed.

The young gendarme watched, an amused expression on his face. "This is not the first time you've spent the night in jail," he stated.

"Oh, it is monsieur," Alouette said, taking her hat off and running a hand through her golden hair. "But it's better than sleeping in my broken-down motor-car by the side of the road."

"Indeed, it probably is." He returned shortly with a packet of biscuits and stale coffee. Alouette could sense that she'd at least made a friend of one of the aloof gendarmes.

That same young man came in early the next morning to announce that Alouette had been released. He waved a telegram with the word PARIS stamped on the front. "It seems you have friends in high places."

Alouette picked her hat off of the chipped nightstand and tucked her hair beneath it. "It would seem so, wouldn't it?"

"Where will you go now?"

She pursed her lips. "My petrol?"

He shook his head. "Seized for the army."

"Then I shall walk to Amiens."

The young man's face spread into a smile. "Good luck, Madame Richer."

"And to you, monsieur."

Alouette passed many villagers going the opposite way as she. They were obviously refugees, judging from their weary, and in some cases, panic-stricken expressions. The pronounced silence was only broken by the occasional droning of an airplane. As soon as one became audible, the bewildered townspeople would duck their heads, as if heeding an unheard call, the call of terror that an enemy warcraft was about to drop a bomb upon them.

Alouette found Amiens in utter chaos. Every door stood open as the townspeople rushed to and from their houses, packing up all of their belongings. Children, dogs, and a few roosters ran wildly through the streets. All roads that led to the town seemed to be filled with refugees repeating the same desperate phrases: "The Germans are coming. What shall we do?"

She headed through the hordes of anxious people gathered outside the railway station. She found a man in a conductor's uniform to ask about the next train to Paris.

"Trains?" he asked in an incredulous voice. "My lady, this station is closed, and the rest of the staff has been cleared out. Gone to war," he continued proudly, but Alouette was only half-listening.

For a moment, she thought she would give in to the same useless panic that had overcome the people surrounding her. She allowed herself a few seconds of despair before returning to reality. She needed to find some other way to get to Paris if she desired to not be in a region that was about to be infested with the enemy.

She spotted an open garage across the street and walked over to it. A young woman in a tattered dress sat on the steps leading toward the door. She glanced up as Alouette approached. "They say that the Germans murder any children they see." She sniffed. "And I have two little boys." She buried her head in her handkerchief.

Alouette climbed up the steps and put a tentative hand on the woman's shoulder. "Nobody can be so cruel as to hurt young innocents," she stated. "Not even the Germans."

She handed the woman a soiled but dry handkerchief. The woman blew into it noisily before stating, "If you are looking for a vehicle, I have nothing left."

"Not even a cart?" Alouette asked, the hopelessness threatening to surface again.

The young woman looked doubtfully at Alouette's dress. "I do have a man's bicycle. Do you know how to ride?"

Alouette took a deep breath. Her brother had had one when they were growing up, but she was never allowed to ride since it couldn't be ridden sidesaddle. "Not exactly, but if I can fly planes, surely I can ride a bicycle." She dug into her purse to find the gendarme had left her a few francs, which she extended to the young woman. The woman pulled herself up, using the banister to steady herself, and led Alouette into the garage.

Alouette walked the bicycle along the road until she was well out of the way of the crowds. The threat of falling on her face paled in comparison to the possibility of being taken as a German prisoner if she stayed here. Mounting the bicycle proved a difficult feat given her dress and handbag. As she pushed down on a pedal, the bicycle wobbled sideways instead of going forward and she hopped off, the bicycle plunging into the dust of the roadway.

She heard a low noise and turned her head with her eyes closed, hoping that it was not the stomping of German boots. A young soldier in a blue coat and bright red trousers was sitting on a nearby bench, laughing.

Alouette put her hands on her hips. "Well, don't just sit there. Give me a lesson, would you?"

He pointed at the bandage covering one of his eyes. "Even I can see that is a man's bicycle."

"Oh, do you have a woman's available?"

The soldier shook his head.

"Then do you know of another reason why I should not ride this bike straight to Paris?"

"Yes," he said, recovering from his earlier mirth. "The road to Paris has been captured by the Germans."

Alouette wiped her sweaty palms on her skirts and gazed at the dust blowing across the road. A German invasion in the carefree French capital seemed as far-flung a threat as someone predicting a thunderstorm on a sunny day. "My husband is in Paris."

"Oh?" The soldier's voice dropped an octave. Alouette smiled to herself. There was something so naively amusing about young men thinking that every woman was ready to fawn over them.

"At least I think so," Alouette replied. "He enlisted as an ambulance driver, but hasn't gotten orders yet. I had to detour to Crotoy to check on our plane."

The young man raised his eyebrows.

"Confiscated," Alouette said in answer to his unasked question.

"Yes, the military will do that. When I was at Charleroi—"

"You were in the Battle of the Sambre?"

"Yes, why?"

Alouette looked down. "No reason." They said that war had a way of turning boys into men, but the young man's affable manner hadn't struck her as though he'd seen many hard battles. Even despite that bandaged eye.

"Anyway, both sides are using airplanes for reconnaissance now." He shrugged his shoulders. "What war innovations will they think of next?"

Alouette was lost for a second, dreaming of being in the sky, finding the enemy among the trees. When she returned to reality, all she could focus on were the man's bright red pants. "Those uniforms... are they new?"

"They are, but the style dates back to Napoleon."

"Perhaps General Joffre might want to reconsider the color of your trousers. A line of soldiers all wearing those would be quite easy to spot from the air."

"Perhaps," he agreed with a smile. "I think that trains are still running to Paris from Abbeville."

Alouette picked up the bicycle. "Well, what are you waiting for, then?"

The soldier taught her how to keep her balance. In only half an hour's time, Alouette was able to ride steadily, although she was only able to mount the bicycle from the curb and could not stop except by jumping off. "I think I'll be able to manage myself, now. Thank you for your kindness."

The young soldier tipped his hat toward her, revealing a bruised and bloody forehead. "Good luck, mademoiselle."

Alouette had no idea riding a bicycle could be such taxing work. She passed numerous refugees on her way to Abbeville. So preoccupied were they in their own misery that they did not pay much heed to the girl wobbling along, trying both to balance and keep her dress out of the bicycle's chain at the same time. She kept her berth wide, lest she fell again, and called out to a man pushing a wheelbarrow, who heeded her by moving closer toward the side of the road. As Alouette overtook them, she realized the wheelbarrow was not filled with food or worldly possessions, but an invalid woman.

Alouette saw she was approaching a hill and leapt off the bicycle. She tossed her hat into a ditch before picking the two-wheeler back up and walking up the summit. She could feel her stamina fading fast, but would not allow herself to rest, fearful that if she sat down, she might not be able to get back up again.

Catching a train proved just as difficult in Abbeville as Amiens. The watchman there told Alouette that there was no way to know when the next train to Paris would leave.

Alouette was about to turn around in anguish when the man told her there was a branch line in Sergueux. Knowing that was her last chance, Alouette managed to get her aching limbs mounted once again on the bicycle and pedaled off.

She was relieved to see a train sitting in the station, although it seemed to consist mostly of open cattle wagons. "Will that be leaving shortly?" Alouette inquired of an official standing near a car.

The man shrugged. "We are waiting for information on the movement of the troops."

Still, Alouette bought a ticket and boarded a cattle wagon.

Enjoyed the preview? Purchase *L'Agent Double: Spies and Martyrs in WWI!* Thank you for your support!

Books in the Women Spies Series:
    355: The Women of Washington's Spy Ring
    Underground: Traitors and Spies in Lincoln's War
    L'Agent Double: Spies and Martyrs in the Great War

Now available: Books 1-3 in one ebook bundle !

Sign up for my mailing list at kitsergeant.com to be the first to learn of new releases!

ACKNOWLEDGMENTS

Thank you to my critique partners: Ute Carbone, Theresa Munroe, and Karen Cino for their comments and suggestions. Also thank you to my Advanced Review team, especially Jackie Cavalla for her eagle eyes, as well as Matthew Baylis for his excellent editing skills and Hannah Linder for the wonderful cover.

And to Mike Sergeant, Sr., for helping me sound more authentic on things I have no clue about, such as head injuries and the difference between a pistol and a revolver.

And as always, thanks to my loving family, especially Tommy, Belle, and Thompson, for their unconditional love and support.

Printed in Great Britain
by Amazon